NINETEENTH PRECINCT

The beat is New York's posh Upper East Side—a playground for the prosperous, a hunting ground for the larcenous . . . and a killing ground for the murderous.

NINETEENTH PRECINCT

Now it's the beat of Detective Joe Dante, the tough renegade cop who earned his bars, and his scars, the hard way in *Sixth Precinct*.

NINETEENTH PRECINCT

It's the electrifying new novel of cops against crime by red-hot author

CHRISTOPHER NEWMAN

D1021103

Also by Christopher Newman
Published by Fawcett Books:

MIDTOWN NORTH
MIDTOWN SOUTH
MAÑANA MAN
KNOCK-OFF
SIXTH PRECINCT
BACKFIRE

NINETEENTH PRECINCT

Christopher Newman

FAWCETT GOLD MEDAL • NEW YORK

A Fawcett Gold Medal Book
Published by Ballantine Books
Copyright © 1992 by Christopher Newman

Library of Congress Catalog Card Number: 91-93152

ISBN 0-449-14732-0

Printed in Canada

First Edition: April 1992

This one is for Knox and Kitty

Suddenly my eye comprehended one shadow which was blacker than the others which were at the foot of the cliff and the evil smell now assailed me in such a manner as to upset my stomach. I halted there to collect my wits and to grasp my courage. Before I had the opportunity, nevertheless, to do either of these two things, the black object moved from where it was. Despite the great terror which captured me at that moment, my eyes observed every detail clearly before them.

FLANN O'BRIEN
The Poor Mouth
Chapter 5

ONE

The silent alarm system was a new one, part of a recent upgrade in services offered here at the Overton House on Madison Avenue. Most of the problems with it were basic, but the house detective, Chester Garfield, wanted to strangle the man who'd chosen it. False triggerings were driving him nuts. Each night at one or two in the morning one of the tenants or their guests would set shoes or a tray outside the doors of their suite. Too often they wouldn't deactivate the security unit first. Each time the alarm buzzer and room indicator light went off on the ground-floor security office console it was Chet's responsibility to rush upstairs and check it out. The three-week shakedown period since the system's installation had been a nightmare.

As a moonlighting cop who put in a regular eight hours in a detective squad on Manhattan's Upper East Side, Garfield liked this midnight-to-eight-A.M. detail best when it was quiet. He wanted to walk the occasional rounds and spend the rest of his shift in the security office catching some shut-eye. When everything went smoothly, this was a sweet gig. The Overton was a residence hotel. The tenants, most of them corporate heavyweights, were easy enough to please. They were interested in a no-hassles night in town when a day at the office or board meeting ran late. Many enjoyed an occasional infidelity, and Chet liked the extra cash the regular cheaters slipped him to watch for suspicious spouses or

1

nosy private dicks. If his experience here had taught him anything, it was that a man in a compromising situation hates a late-night knock on his door.

Tonight's tripped alarm was up in 1103: the Magnetronics suite. Ralph Kane, the company's CEO, had exclusive use of it. He had a steady girlfriend who arrived here every Thursday, a real looker who dressed well and seemed intelligent when she spoke. The boys at the front desk thought she flew in from out of town somewhere: Cleveland or Chicago. Once she and Kane hooked up for their weekend rendezvous they rarely stayed out late and never made noise. Half the time they had room service bring food up rather than eat out.

Chet tried to stifle a yawn as he rode up in the elevator to the eleventh floor. He'd worked a four-to-midnight all this past week, and if his caseload was any indicator, the whole city was going to hell in a hot pink handbasket. After Labor Day the summer-type crime generally slacked off; tourist muggings, rapes on the street. Not this year. The tourists were staying longer, and the freaks were out extending the season right alongside them. Day after tomorrow it would be October. September rapes in the 19th Precinct were up, not down. Muggings were holding steady. The B & E rate was through the roof.

On reaching the eleventh floor Garfield started to yawn again and shook his head. He went left from the elevator; a big, solid man who moved with a kind of fluid grace. Nearly bald, Chet was already going gray at the temples. He looked older than his thirty-four years but still stayed in decent shape.

It was barely discernible, but sure enough, the door to 1103 was just a hair ajar. A room service trolley piled with dirty dishes stood outside, complete with ice bucket and upended champagne bottle. It looked like Kane and his friend were a bit tight tonight. As he stood examining the evidence, Chet couldn't help envying Kane. Envying him his money, his beautiful woman, and their private little world here. He was soft-spoken, often seeming preoccupied. And while he wasn't exactly a geek, he wasn't Cary Grant either. Kane didn't have the smooth moves you'd associate with a man who ran empires and had beautiful women flying into town to bed him. Chet heard it from the desk staff that Ralph Kane could buy most anyone else in residence here, lock and stock.

One ear to the door, Garfield didn't hear any sound coming from inside the suite. It was nearly three; late for one of these alarm events. Chet figured the occupants to be asleep when he realized the alarm had only been tripped—what? Five minutes ago? Procedure dictated that occupants of these security-breached suites be advised of the incident and sign Garfield's logbook, no matter the hour. He reached to rap lightly on the door panel.

"Mr. Kane?" He cushioned the words, keeping his tone low and respectful. "House security, sir."

No answer. With the impact of Chet's knuckles the door clicked off the striker plate in the jamb, swinging inward a foot. The light from a wall sconce behind him spilled into the suite from over the detective's shoulder. The swath of illuminated carpet was no more than a few feet wide, stretching from the threshold to the fireplace hearth across the room. It was close along the edge of that illuminated strip, still partly hidden from view behind the door, where Chet saw the woman's hand.

The question of whether or not he should enter the suite no longer occupied Garfield's mind. He shoved the door wide and saw the woman's naked body lying sprawled behind the sofa, blood soaking the carpet beneath her head and shoulders. It sent a jolt through him that made his molars ache. And then he spotted Kane around the end of that chintz-upholstered sofa. Kane was down on the carpet, too, sprawled in a similar graceless pose. In that light Garfield couldn't see Kane as well, but the cop in him was already assuming the worst. He abandoned all caution, hurrying forward to see if either occupant was still alive.

Movement. Garfield sensed it as he dropped to one knee and pulled hair back from the woman's neck to feel for a pulse. His head came up just as a black-clad figure pulled up short across the room. He heard a quick, involuntary intake of breath. And then a muttered expletive as the gleam of a pistol became part of the shadow figure's right hand. The neat, dark hole of the muzzle aimed at Garfield looked a lot like the hole he'd just seen behind the dead woman's left ear. Chet stared at it, open-mouthed, for what seemed like an eternity. Then the lights went out.

TWO

Detective Lieutenant Joe Dante was growing accustomed to being called out of bed at all hours. Since assuming command of NYPD's Major Case squad less than a year ago these predawn calls to action were becoming a regular part of his routine. Today's came at five-thirty. The Manhattan North Homicide Task Force had responded earlier to the scene of a double homicide at the Overton House. The case also involved the shooting of an off-duty detective. A Chester Garfield, currently assigned to the squad at the 19th Precinct, was hit once in the head and still alive. He'd been transported to University Hospital, where he was undergoing neurosurgery. As soon as the task force people determined the identities of all three victims they'd had the Operations Desk roust Chief of Detectives Gus Lieberman. Once the C of D had his command post established he called in Major Case.

Dante was the only member of his team who lived in Manhattan. He was the first of them to arrive. The one cup of coffee he'd conned out of the attendant at his parking garage wasn't quite enough to get his cerebral engine firing on all cylinders. By the time he reached the eleventh floor of the Overton House and stepped off the elevator he figured he was hitting on no more than half of them, tops. Fortunately he didn't have to waste any energy seeking out the chief. Lieberman was huddled up right there in the hallway, his head bent in conversation with two plainclothes detectives. As Joe approached, all three looked up.

"You made good time, Joey," the chief greeted him. "I know you know Chip, but how about Wesley here?"

Chip was Chip Donnelly, the lanky, rawboned commander of the Crime Scene Unit. The other guy, built wiry and compact like a runner, had to be Lieutenant Wes Sherwood, the new whip of the Manhattan North Homicide squad. Sherwood was just recently assigned here from Bronx Borough Command, the news of his promotion posted with last week's orders. Dante reached to shake the task force man's hand.

"Welcome to lifestyles of the rich and famous, Lou. What's the story here?"

Sherwood deferred to the chief, who lifted his chin toward the door to suite 1103. Two uniforms stood at either side of it, monitoring traffic. The low conversations of detectives and technicians could be heard coming from inside. Dante observed the occasional flash of a photographer's strobe.

"Nasty one, Joey," Lieberman told him. "There're two down in there who ain't gettin' back up. Both naked as newborns; one male, one female. Each of 'em took one in the back'a the head."

"Do we know who they are?" Dante asked.

"You've heard'a Ralph Kane?"

Joe frowned, waiting for those last couple of cylinders to finally kick in. "Why's that name ring a bell, Gus? Corporate giant of some sort, isn't he?"

"Major league," Lieberman confirmed. "Kane was a pioneer in something called magnetic resonance imaging. That's the latest X-ray–type technology; cutting edge diagnostic stuff. My wife Lydia and his wife Amanda were in the same class at Smith. You *have* heard of Amanda Gregory?"

Dante had indeed heard of Amanda Gregory. The Gregory family played an even bigger role in New York financial circles than Lydia Lieberman's had. While the chief's wife was the granddaughter of William B. Cox, founder of a Wall

Street speciality brokerage, Amanda's father and uncles were sixth-generation members of the New York Exchange. It was difficult to open an issue of *Vanity Fair*, *New York*, and even the occasional *Spy* without seeing a photograph of Amanda at some gala benefit, art premiere, or celebrity birthday bash. Just last month she'd appeared on the cover of *Mirabella*. Joe guessed the woman to be in her early fifties, but she still looked better than most women twenty years her junior. He glanced toward suite 1103 again.

"Can I assume that the naked lady in there isn't the wife?"

Gus gave the question the grunt it deserved and started patting his pockets for his cigarettes. "Tell him what we've got so far, Wesley."

The homicide cop lifted his chin toward the elevators. "All we've got on her is what we've been able to learn from the staff downstairs—that and what we found in her pocketbook. Name's Veronica Tierney; last name spelled the same as the old movie star. Driver's license is State of Illinois. Address in Deerfield, a suburb north of Chicago. Age twenty-eight. All major credit cards, all of them gold. She's got a lot of the better department stores, too. Bergdorf here in the city. Marshall Field. Neiman-Marcus. That sort of shit. The guys working the concierge desk downstairs don't think she's a hooker; at least not local. If she is, it's at the high end of the trade. She's showed up here every Thursday evening for the past year and a half and always left on Sunday afternoon. Usually arrived carrying a garment bag and a briefcase. Beautiful broad, even dead."

Dante glanced to the Crime Scene Unit whip. "What about your guys, Chip? Find anything interesting?"

Donnelly took a cigarette from the pack the chief offered and paused before answering while Lieberman lit it. "I doubt she needed even a small suitcase. The master bedroom and bath have everything she'd need to set up permanent housekeeping. Those two weren't having your garden variety, wham-bam–type affair. That suite's provisioned for serious

7

nesting. Somebody was even doing work there. Serious work. The second bedroom is set up as an office.''

Dante's curiosity was piqued by this last revelation. ''An office?''

''Yep. Schematics unrolled across a big drawing table. A half-full cup of coffee weighting a big pile of penciled notes. Apple Mac computer. Two four-drawer file cabinets crammed with files.''

''What about the overall condition of the place?'' Joe wondered. ''Any indication that the perp was after something?''

The Crime Scene boss shook his head. ''Negative. I suppose it'd make your job a whole lot easier if there was, but my guys didn't even find the cap off the toothpaste. If his motive was robbery, then he knew just what he was looking for and right where to find it.''

Dante took a deep breath, glancing at Lieberman. ''I guess it's time to take a look, huh?'' He turned toward the suite's front door with the chief, Donnelly, and Sherwood trailing.

Twenty-three years on the job didn't make confronting a homicide scene any easier to stomach. Dante still had to steel himself. He paused just inside the door to decompress, his eyes taking in the surroundings. The walls of the large living room that stretched before him were painted in a pearl gray. The cabinets, bookshelves, heavy Victorian moldings, and mantel of the fireplace at the far end were done in white. The several pieces of art hung around the room were set off in heavy Italianate gilt frames. The carpet, bound at the edges to reveal a foot or so of the parquet beneath, was a deep, dusty rose. There was nothing overstated about any of it. A handful of Crime Scene technicians were busy packing equipment near the fireplace. Closer to the door four plainclothes cops loitered in subdued conversation. Everyone put a discreet distance between himself and the dead. All four detectives smoked cigarettes, tapping ashes into cupped palms. The cloying odor of death had insinuated itself into the atmosphere, climate control notwithstanding. Tobacco smoke helped cover it. Some homicide cops lit cigarettes; others preferred cigars.

A bath towel was draped over the murdered woman's nakedness. As Dante stepped forward, his eyes fell to her face. Framed in masses of wavy chestnut hair, her features were frozen in pained terror: a wide, well-accented jaw, sculpted cheekbones, and high forehead. The eyes were open but without the luster of life. Hazel eyes, the whites now visible all the way around the irises. As he squatted onto his heels for a closer look, Joe knew that whenever he would think back, trying to picture this victim in his mind's eye, it would be those eyes that he would remember.

Donnelly pointed. "She took one behind the left ear there."

Around the room the idle conversation of the other detectives and Donnelly's technicians had ceased. One by one they drifted over to watch Dante as he lifted hair with the end of his pen. There were blackened powder burns surrounding the entry wound, indicating that the shot came from extremely close range. Joe pointed at them and nodded toward the second body on the floor at the far end of the sofa.

"The same story with him?"

"Exactly," Donnelly replied. "Same side of the head, same point-blank range."

Dante began a routine examination of the woman's wrists and ankles, searching for any evidence of restraint. There were no discolorations of the skin in either place. He pushed up off the carpet, rising to face his boss.

"Nice hidey-hole like this must cost a fucking fortune, Gus. Any idea whose name is on the lease?"

"Magnetronics," the chief replied. "Kane's corporation. Most'a these leases are corporate. A place for an executive to stay if he's gotta work late or the company needs to put up a guest. Wesley's people talked to the night manager. He says Kane maintained this place exclusively for his own use."

Dante eased his hands deep into his pockets. He wandered the length of the sofa to stand peering down at Ralph Kane's corpse. A bath towel had been deployed here, too, draped over the dead man's loins.

"Give me a rundown on the wounded cop, Gus. How'd he wind up here and how bad off is he?"

"According to the night manager, Garfield's been working the midnight-to-eight house dick shift for a little more'n two years now. Steady. Dependable. Three weeks ago the management started offerin' this new security system on a subscription basis. They'd had some trouble with burglaries of unoccupied apartments; shit like that. Problem with this setup is that once it's activated, you can't open the hall door or any of the windows without *de*activating it. Garfield's been having quite a bit of trouble with tenants forgetting and tripping their alarms."

"They trip it and what happens then?" Joe asked.

"Silent feed runs downstairs to the security office. They ain't got any alarm bells or anything up here on the individual floors. Too much trouble with other tenants trying to sleep."

"Okay, so this one was tripped and the silent feed alerts Garfield in the security office. When was that?"

"Night manager thinks it happened 'tween two forty-five and two-fifty this morning. It's the sixth time that somebody'd tripped one'a these things this week."

"So Garfield responds and walks in on the intruder," Dante concluded.

Lieberman opened his hands, fingers spread, and closed them again, his eyes squinting through the smoke of a butt clenched in his teeth. He was a big bear of a man, and his were huge, thick-fingered hands. "That's about how Wesley and his people got it figured."

"How about the M.O.?" Dante touched behind his ear. "Same?"

"Nope. Hit in the cheek on the right side. No powder burns this time. Same light-caliber bullet. Garfield was lucky it hit bone on the way in. Took a lotta the steam outta it."

"How bad was he when they took him out of here?" Dante asked. "We gonna be able to get his side of it?"

Gus handed this one to homicide cop Wes Sherwood. "You were here, Lou. He was actually conscious, wasn't he?"

The task force whip nodded. "Believe it or not. He was

sort of slipping in and out, but he looked a long way from going over the big edge. I think he's gonna make it.''

Joe turned away from Kane's corpse to approach the hall-way leading back past the powder room. The first bedroom he encountered was the smaller of the two, the one Donnelly had described as an office. The beds had been removed, and the only concession to comfort was an expensive-looking leather sofa installed along one wall. Dominating nearly half the room was a large drafting table complete with four-legged stool, swing-arm work light, automatic pencil sharpener, and other amenities of serious work. The surface of the table was covered with rolls of schematic design blueprints, many piled with rubber bands around them and others flattened, presum-ably for examination. The pile of scribbled notes weighted by the half-filled coffee cup was prodigious. Somebody had been busy here. The Apple Macintosh computer was set up at what appeared to be a sort of secondary workstation. The desk sur-face surrounding it was so neatly ordered that it was difficult for Dante to imagine that the same person who worked at the drafting table was responsible for the condition of both areas. The residue powder of the Crime Scene Unit's fingerprinting activity made it difficult to be certain, but Joe got the feeling that two people had been working together in here.

"Okay if I open a few drawers?" he asked.

"Go wild," Donnelly told him. "We're through in here."

Dante stepped up to the desk to paw quickly through its contents. When he found nothing unusual he made a mental note to have one of his squad give it a more thorough going-over later and moved on.

Unlike that first bedroom, the master bedroom looked to be precisely that. The king-size bed was a maelstrom of twisted blankets and sheets. A slinky peignoir lay in a heap on the bedside carpet. There were empty champagne flutes on the end tables, magazines heaped with yesterday's *Times* on one of the chairs, and an open overnight bag set atop an-other. A pair of women's aerobic shoes was tucked beneath the dresser, and one of those gym outfits with all the startling colors was draped over the dressing-table chair. After a quick and uninformative examination of the dressing table and dresser drawers, Joe moved on to the bath. Judging from the array of cosmetics and other beauty tools discovered in the various bathroom cabinets, he thought Lieutenant Chip Donnelly's "love nest" analysis justified. As Dante surveyed that array of expensive cosmetics, Gus drifted in to stand alongside.

"Looks like she went first-class all the way," the chief murmured. "You see the labels on her clothes?"

"You bet," Joe agreed. "I think we should contact the job out in Deerfield, Illinois; see if we can't get a better read on this girl: who she is, where she comes from, how Ralph Kane met her. The works."

Gus had picked up a bottle of perfume and squirted some on the back of his hand to sniff it. "Imagine what the media'll do with a homicide like this."

Dante sighed, shaking his head. "It's got everything they love. You kill a man of Ralph Kane's stature and leave a widow as highly visible as Amanda Gregory, you've got the media doing back-flips for weeks."

Gus paused to butt the most recent of his smokes in the bathroom sink and wash the ashes down the drain. "I'm trying to figure a motive here, Joey. It don't feel like robbery. The only thing that looks like it was tossed is the fuckin' *bed*. I hope for their sakes that the last one was the best."

"A shooter who hits executioner-style," Dante mused. "Light-caliber weapon, probably noise suppressed. Nobody heard a thing, right?"

Gus nodded.

"Okay. So who hires a shooter like that? Anybody with the right connections and the money. As unlikely as it seems, I don't think we can afford to ignore the jealous spouse angle."

Gus grunted. "Amanda? I s'pose she's got the money, all right, but the whole fuckin' world's Amanda Gregory's oyster, Joey. Besides, rich people been screwing around and looking the other way for hundreds of years. They hate making a scene over infidelity. It just ain't considered civilized. You've got a problem, you don't hire a hit man, you hire a lawyer.''

"Same thing," Joe growled. "Somebody's gonna have to break the news to Mrs. Kane, Gus. When the media gets wind of this they'll trample each other trying to reach her for comment. Nobody should have to hear it that way.''

Lieberman glanced at his watch to discover that it was now nearly seven. "I was thinking maybe I should call Lydia; see if she'll meet me over there. The two of them were never close, but it's better to get that kinda news from a familiar face than some total stranger.''

"I'll want to ask her some questions, Gus. Civilized or not, she's a suspect. I'll wait here until my people and the M.E. show up. We need to put our heads together with Chip and Wes; see what ground we haven't covered here. That should give you the time you need.''

It was obvious that the chief wasn't looking forward to this visit. He merely nodded and turned to leave the room.

Billy Mannion wondered why the sex was always so good when he had fresh blood on his hands. It was like these crazy bitches actually smelled it on him. And maybe they *could*. He did always find the same sort of woman at times like these; the sort who got frenzied with the muskiness of the kill filling their nostrils. The one writhing beneath him now was no exception. She dug her nails into his back and sank her teeth into his shoulder, every inch of her straining to suck him into her vortex.

He'd come here straight from the job, and they'd been at it for nearly three hours. Same as always, he'd started her out slowly, letting the smell of the kill seep into her brain, triggering all the predatory little synapses that turn the docile, domesticated animal into a devouring beast. Once the fire was kindled he fanned the flame, allowing her to drift to the edge a score of times, and each time jerking her back. Now, as dawn broke over the world outside, its light glistened along the length of her sweat-soaked body. She'd reached a tight-strung juncture where every vibrating sinew screamed for total immersion.

Billy supposed the time had come to get it done. He had other work to do. Seamus would be pacing the floor, eager to have a look at the goods. These last three hours had been complete self-indulgence. It was time to go.

"The alarm system, love. Your forgetting to mention it. Just an oversight?"

He timed his final thrusts to hit her just as she went slack to grab a breath. The force of it saw her gasp in pain.

"*Alarm* system? *What* alarm system?"

Billy pinned her hands to either side of her head, those savage thrusts of his lean hips and powerful thighs aimed at sustaining the level of pain. With them he was driving a stake into the heart of any communion. Billy was interested only in the fire he'd built and how it could burn.

"The one in the fuckin' suite, love. The one you forgot to mention and the girlfriend tripped when she opened the door to me."

When her lips twisted slowly to match the leering, sadistic smile on his face, Billy's thrusts became more violent and his breathing heavy.

"You got what you were after, didn't you?"

She was declaring herself impervious to the pain. Her tone and smile boasted she could handle anything he could dish out . . . and more. Her eyes gleamed in direct, stubborn challenge, that twisted grin of pleasure never changing.

"You'd better pray I did," he growled. His breathing became labored. "A man from house security put in an appearance. I don't take kindly to being surprised like that."

She grunted, the grin unwavering. "Oh yes? I'll bet you had less trouble pulling the trigger then than you're having right now."

By the time he exploded within her and collapsed atop her in sweat-drenched exhaustion it was all he could do to keep himself from wringing her neck. Three fucking hours at it. Three hours spent dancing on the edge of hell, and the unrepentant bitch had destroyed the entire thrill of it for him.

14

THREE

Gus Lieberman hated this part of the job. His thirty-two years of service had taught him how to handle bureaucratic bullshit, how to hit a political curveball, and how to read and lead the men and women of New York's Finest. The one thing those years hadn't taught him was how to turn off emotionally when delivering terrible news. Lieberman's wife Lydia knew how this part of the job affected Gus. When he'd asked for her help this morning she agreed to meet him in the lobby of Amanda Kane's exclusive co-op apartment building on the corner of 67th Street and Fifth Avenue. On arrival Gus was surprised to learn from the doorman that there were *two* Kane residences on the premises. Ralph and Amanda's daughter, Elizabeth, also maintained an apartment here, on the third floor. When Lydia arrived they rode upstairs together to the elder Kane's lavish duplex penthouse on the seventeenth floor.

"It's hard for me to believe this," Lydia murmured en route. "I saw the two of them together at that Save the Children dinner last Wednesday. You're sure this other woman was his *mistress*?"

The door of the elevator slid back to reveal an elegant mahogany-and-hunter-green vestibule outside the Kane apartment. Gus stood aside, nodding thanks to the operator and allowing his diminutive but tough wife to pass. He kept his voice low as they approached the front doors.

"There was only one bed slept in. And neither of 'em was

15

wearing a stitch. We found a shitload'a cosmetics in the bath. She had an entire wardrobe hanging in the closets. I don't think there's much doubt what they were up to.''

The doorman had called ahead from downstairs to advise Mrs. Kane that the New York Chief of Detectives and his wife were on their way up. As Gus reached to depress the bell button the left-hand panel swung inward. They were greeted by a uniformed maid: middle-aged, pale, and pinched. She seemed harried.

''I'm sorry sir, ma'am. Mrs. Kane only just got up. She isn't dressed and would like to know what this is about.''

Gus slipped his shield case from his inside jacket pocket to show her his chief's tin. ''I'm afraid it's an official visit, miss. We'd appreciate it if you'd tell Mrs. Kane it's a matter of some urgency.''

The maid barely gave the credentials a passing glance before asking them in and leading the way to a vast, window-lined living room overlooking Central Park. Before leaving them she asked if they'd care for coffee. Both thought they would.

''I'd heard they had a nice place.'' Lydia was still on her feet as the maid departed, and Gus sat. She was glancing around and assessing with an appreciative eye.

Her husband snorted. ''Nice? Ten or twelve thousand square feet on Central Park? Two floors? I'll say it's nice.'' He pointed to one of the paintings hung on the opposite wall. ''Who's that painter, Liddy? Looks awful goddamn familiar.''

''Renoir. It's been in Amanda's family since the 1920s. I'd hate to imagine what the Japanese might pay for it today.''

Gus spotted an ashtray on the table beside him and reached to pull it toward him. Lydia scowled like she always did as he shook another nail from his pack and lit it.

''Did you know they have a daughter?'' he asked. ''One old enough to have her own apartment?''

Lydia nodded. ''Elizabeth. Beautiful girl. God, how old is she by now? Twenty-five? At least that; maybe even a few

16

years older. Amanda and Ralph were children when she was born.''

"Children."

Another nod. "Mandy was just out of Smith and doing graduate work at Berkeley. She couldn't have been any older than twenty-three."

Lieberman sat playing with that one for a moment. He was chief of detectives in a city where only God knew how many children were born to mothers not old enough to vote. In Lydia's parallel world, a twenty-three-year-old woman bearing children was still a baby.

"Must be nice to have your own Fifth Avenue apartment before you're thirty," he ventured. Movement across the hall caught his eye. He turned that way as the maid entered, pushing a tea cart. Amanda Gregory-Kane followed in her wake, a robe pulled on over silk pajamas. Her honey-colored hair was brushed back and held in place with a black velvet band. To Gus's eye it was difficult to believe that this woman and his wife were the same age. Lydia took good care of herself, watching her weight and getting exercise through tennis and aerobics, and she looked good for a woman of fifty-one years. Amanda Kane looked good for a woman of forty.

"Lydia. Gus. What's this about? Mildred tells me it's urgent."

Lydia glanced to her husband, her eyes saying she'd take it from here. "Maybe you'd better sit down, Mandy. I'm sorry about the indecency of the hour, but this *is* urgent, I'm afraid."

"Maybe I'd better *sit down*?" The woman's face had clouded with concern. "Why, Lydia? What is it? What's happened?"

"It's Ralph, dear. I don't know how else to tell you this. He's been murdered. Gus has just come from the scene. We're both so sorry."

Amanda Kane's jaw went slack, her brow furrowing in an expression caught between horror and disbelief. "Th-that

17

can't *be*!'' Her head began to move slowly from side to side. "It's not possible. Why, just . . . No!"

Lieberman stepped forward now. "Amanda, do you know where Ralph was last night? Or at least where he said he would be?"

She'd buried her face in her hands. "The Overton House. Working." And then her eyes emerged, her fingers steepled between them. Wide with fear and trepidation, they asked the same question she could barely voice. "Why?" she croaked. "Where'd they find him?"

Gus saw Lydia watching him and realized his hands were opening at his sides in gestures of nervousness. He folded them in front of him. "We found him in the living room of the Magnetronics suite at the Overton House. An intruder tripped the silent alarm. An off-duty policeman working as the house security officer responded and was also shot."

The reality of it seemed to hit home for the first time now. "Oh my God!" The words escaped her lips as a strangled, sob-muffled cry. "Why? Why would anyone . . . ?"

Lydia hurried to the sobbing woman's side. She dug a handkerchief from her pocketbook, pressed it into Amanda's hands, and slipped an arm around her shoulders.

"The why is exactly what we're trying to figure," Gus told the stricken woman. "When I asked you where he was, you said he was supposed to be working. What did you mean by that?"

Instead of answering Amanda shook her head and broke down, her body wracked by a series of great, choking sobs. "He was *obsessed*!"

Gus waited. The maid, recognizing her employer's distress, had hurried from the room and returned now with a box of tissues. Amanda grabbed a fistful, blew her nose, and eventually started to regain control. When she finally looked up, making an obvious effort to keep it together, Lieberman tried again.

"Obsessed with his work? Is that what you're saying? And that he did it at the Overton House?"

Her voice no longer quavered as something else got in the way of her grief. She seemed suddenly angry. "Every weekend for the past year and a half. He kept saying he was onto a big breakthrough; going to make it any minute." Her eyes left Lieberman's to lock with Lydia's. There was a lost, bewildered quality to her gaze. "Magnets. Can you *believe* it? God damned magnets. His whole *life* was magnets."

"Where's Liz, dear?" Lydia asked softly. "I think you should try to reach her. This isn't going to be easy for either of you. She should be here."

"Easy? It will probably kill her." Amanda's tone was surprisingly bitter. "Her whole life is that company, too."

Gus could see he wasn't going to get much further in this direction. Kane had apparently used the Overton House suite as some sort of weekend getaway, a place where he could seclude himself to work . . . and play? That led him to the indelicate subject of Veronica Tierney.

"Amanda, I know you've just had an awful shock and probably aren't thinking too straight, but I'm gonna need to ask you about one other thing. You've gotta understand that it's important. The first thirty-six hours after a homicide are the most crucial to us. Some of these other matters can wait a few hours, but later this morning a Lieutenant Dante'll be paying you a visit. He's probably the best detective I've got. I want you to be frank with him." He stopped, trying to formulate his next question. He quickly discovered there was no easy way. "I'm sorry I've gotta ask this now, but the media's gonna sensationalize a homicide like this. If they think it's to their advantage, they'll get nasty. You need to prepare yourself for it. I need to know what you know about a woman named Veronica Tierney."

Amanda seemed perplexed. "Veronica? She and my daughter shared an apartment in Northampton during college." Her tone was total bewilderment.

"During college. How long ago was that?"

More bewilderment. "I don't know. What? Eight years?

19

Elizabeth was in her senior year at Smith, and Veronica was some sort of computer whiz at U. Mass.''

"Have you heard anything of her since that time?" Gus pressed.

Amanda glanced once again to Lydia and nodded. "Surely." She said it slowly, trying to figure out where this was headed. "Ralph hired her right out of school. She worked for Magnetronics for a while in Princeton, and then they sent her off to a Ph.D. program somewhere. MIT, I think it was. After that she moved out to Chicago to head up some sort of design team for Ralph. Why are you asking all this, Gus?"

Lieberman swallowed hard, and just as he was about to take the plunge, Lydia rode to the rescue once again.

"This is difficult, Mandy. The girl was found with Ralph. Killed the same way."

Amanda foundered, her lower lip quivering again. "I—I don't understand. I'm sure there's an explanation. I know Ralph was very hard at work on this project of his. Maybe she was helping him. I've heard him crow about how brilliant she was; a whiz at . . . programs." She paused, frowning. "*Creating* programs. That's it."

As Amanda spoke, Gus watched her twist Lydia's handkerchief fiercely between two clenched fists.

"You don't understand, dear," Lydia soothed.

From the nervousness that had Lydia buzzing like a high-tension wire, Gus suspected Amanda understood all too well.

"It's the *way* they were found," Lydia explained. "They'd been sleeping together. There's not much doubt of it, and that's what Gus means by the newspapers trying to sensationalize this."

"I guess that's the question I've been trying to ask, Amanda," Gus interrupted. "You don't know anything about an affair?"

Amanda's eyes were squeezed shut again, and this time she was biting hard into the back of her right index finger. As Lieberman's question hit home her whole body shuddered with its impact.

Nineteenth Precinct

* * *

Joe Dante was thankful to have five of his own handpicked people in his Major Case squad. Once they all assembled at the crime scene he was able to delegate crucial responsibilities. Detectives Don Grover and Rusty Heckman, recognized as the team's best detail men, would make follow-up visits to the labs and medical examiner's office to collect ballistics, latent print, autopsy, and other forensic evidence reports. Meanwhile Melissa Busby and Guy Napier would conduct interrogations of the Overton House staff and residents who were on hand at the time of the incident. Sergeant Beasley "Jumbo" Richardson, Dante's regular investigative partner, would contact the Deerfield, Illinois, department in an attempt to get a line on Ralph Kane's beautiful young girlfriend. If Jumbo came up empty in Illinois, he was prepared to put in some time with NYPD's own Public Morals Division files. Leads would soon develop, but for the moment the entire team was feeling its way in the dark. As a rule Dante covered as many gaps as he could see and watched for where the coverage sprang leaks.

The Kane address on 67th and Fifth was so close to the Overton House on Madison that Dante decided to leave his car parked and walk the seven short blocks. This last day of September was shaping up crisp and clear, with a light breeze fanning Manhattan from the northwest. Foot traffic was light along the Fifth Avenue sidewalk while rush hour congestion in the street alongside was murderous. Joe was glad he'd decided to walk. A rugged, athletically built martial arts devotee, he was in superb shape for a man of forty-two years. He maintained that trim by staying off his butt as much as he could and with workouts at his Greenwich Village karate dojo.

The building on Fifth where Ralph Kane had lived was no more or less impressive to the casual observer than any other lining this avenue of the mega-rich. Like the other Fifth Avenue buildings between Grand Army Plaza and 101st Street, it had its own petty but unique internal politics, its small army of uniformed door personnel, and an awning stretching from door to curb. As Dante approached he spotted building staff dressed in maintenance coveralls rolling garbage dumpsters from the service entrance on 67th Street.

Dante's mind returned to the current homicide investigation as he moved past the row of dumpsters now lined up along the 67th Street curb. He wondered how Mrs. Kane was taking the news of her husband's death and the circumstances. He was *not* wondering who or what might be lurking inside one of those dumpsters. When a lid beside him suddenly moved it gave him a fair-size jolt. He'd barely caught it out of the corner of his eye and stopped to convince himself he wasn't seeing things. The sidewalk in his wake was temporarily empty. If he'd continued on by, the coast would have been clear for the black nylon knapsack emerging from beneath the dumpster lid to fall unnoticed to the sidewalk. It was followed almost immediately by a slender but muscular white man dressed in black: jeans, sneakers, and a long-sleeve turtleneck shirt. When the man realized he was being observed he paused, stopped to retrieve the knapsack, and flashed Dante an unabashed grin.

The face was matinee-idol handsome. Below a dark mass of curly black hair glowed a pair of piercing blue eyes. Almost as remarkable as those eyes was the sculpted quality of the face: strong jaw, a pair of deep laugh lines on either side of the mouth, chiseled cheekbones. This was a near-perfect composite of masculine features. It was also so familiar that Joe wondered for an instant if it wasn't indeed some media star he'd caught sneaking out his back door to avoid the paparazzi. And then he knew. He knew *exactly* where he'd seen that face before. Not in person. A photograph. Recently. A detective from the job's Intelligence Division and an FBI special agent showed him that photograph just last Tuesday. It was a briefing on an IRA attack in Europe. A British officers' club at NATO Command in Brussels was bombed last April. Interpol suspected the ringleader in the attack was now being protected by the Irish community in either Boston or New York. William "Billy" Mannion.

That grin turned to a scowl as Dante took a first step forward. The dumpster dweller had straightened and was slipping his arms through the straps of the knapsack.

"What the fuck're you staring at, mate?"

Dante was sure now. The voice fairly reeked of the old sod. He knew he had to be careful here, avoid showing his hand too soon.

"Take it easy, friend. You scared the hell out of me, pulling a stunt like that." As Joe spoke he took a sidestep, attempting to box Mannion in between the dumpster and the building.

The black-clad fugitive's eyes went wary as they saw the only route of escape being cut off. "I suggest you mind your own fucking business." He eased back a step and seemed to set himself, darting a glance past Dante's right shoulder and across Fifth Avenue beyond. In the next instant, as Dante prepared to launch and pin the man to the building wall, Mannion was off like a spooked jackrabbit.

Joe hadn't quite eased himself into range, and the Irishman managed to twist past his outstretched hands. A driver approaching the light at the corner of 67th and Fifth hit his brakes and swerved to avoid hitting the fugitive as Billy leapt from the curb and sprinted south. The car ended up with one wheel on the sidewalk, effectively blocking Dante's pursuit while the quarry gained the opposite side of the street and was making his escape down Fifth Avenue. Joe hurdled the hood of the car and took up the chase. Before he had up a full head of steam, Mannion was already a good twenty yards downfield. The quarry was in sneakers and better equipped for a footrace. He also looked to be in decent shape and was probably five years Dante's junior. The only advantage Joe had was pure animal speed.

They'd covered three short blocks down the Fifth Avenue sidewalk and were just crossing the intersection with 64th Street when Mannion must have realized he wasn't going to outrun the pursuit. He twisted to slip free of the knapsack as he ran, and Dante was ready to see him fling it aside when Billy went for the zippered closure instead. A warning klaxon went off in the back of Dante's head. Interpol described this man as a mad dog, a cold-blooded killing machine who gave no quarter and expected none. That bag had a weapon in it. Billy was reaching for it right now.

Instinct took the controls. Joe snatched at his own weapon in his waistband holster and dove for the cover of a parked car. Ahead, Mannion drew abreast of a building awning, stopped, and started to turn, a noise-suppressed automatic pistol now brandished in one hand. Three teenage girls emerged from the building lobby and out onto the sidewalk before Dante could get himself set and line up a shot. Joe cursed under his breath as Billy recognized the provident nature of the girls' appearance. When they walked directly in front of him, oblivious to the drama unfolding, he grabbed the one most convenient to his free hand and jerked her to his chest as a shield.

For Dante a fluke collar was fast becoming a nightmare. Ahead of him the two girls who'd escaped Mannion's lunge ran screaming back toward the building. In the confusion of the instant they'd spotted Dante crouched behind the car, his pistol trained in their direction. Mannion was meanwhile dragging their helpless friend toward Fifth Avenue. The friend was too petrified even to struggle.

Joe had no choice but to remain down on his haunches. There was no cover anywhere out there on the sidewalk. He was helpless to aid the girl without completely exposing himself. His heart thundered in his chest as he searched desperately for any viable option. Around him all peripheral noise had gone white, isolating the hysterical screaming of the hostage's friends. A few seconds' time became an eternity as Mannion suddenly flung his captive into the street in front of an oncoming car. The scream of rubber joined those human screams of high-pitched hysteria.

A shocked commuter skidded to a stop just ten feet from where the girl fell while a cabbie, oblivious to the unfolding drama, gunned it into the gap. Dante watched in horror as the sickening thud of flesh on metal reached his ears. Another cabbie swerved to avoid the one who'd hit the girl, setting off a chain reaction of fender benders that snarled traffic all the way across the avenue. Drivers were suddenly swarming from their cars and shouting. Pedestrians stood frozen in their progress, gaping in startled confusion.

Dante emerged from cover to sprint down the sidewalk. As he neared the gap between cars where Mannion had pushed the girl into the street he could see Billy darting into the crowd on the opposite sidewalk. Mannion vaulted the low stone wall fronting Central Park just as the chauffeur of a parked limousine opened his door into Dante's path.

Joe caught the movement of the door out of the corner of his eye and barely had time to register it before it caught him full in the chest and stomach. The impact, amplified by the speed at which he'd been moving, all but knocked him out. With the wind driven from his lungs, Dante was helpless as the doorman from the building opposite raced over to latch onto his gun wrist with both hands. The third time that Dante's hand was slammed hard against the concrete his grip gave.

"Fight with me and I break your motherfocking neck!"

The huge Eastern European doorman was just as jacked up on adrenaline as Joe was. Dante, on the other hand, was in no shape to be fighting anyone. He was paralyzed, all his attention focused on one, singular purpose: to draw breath. When the doorman sensed his captive's surrender he pushed away to retrieve the gun. Joe squeezed his eyes shut and sucked against his frozen diaphragm. This wasn't the first time he'd had the air knocked out of him, but he couldn't remember it ever being more agonizing. After another eternity it finally came back. While drawing it deep, time and again, he just lay there tasting its simple sweetness. Then, with his eyes still closed, he did a quick assessment of the damage. His right hand was starting to throb, the skin on the back of it burning like hell. His ribcage where he'd impacted with the car door ached, but he didn't think anything was broken. When he opened his eyes he found the muzzle of his own weapon trained inches from his nose. The doorman's hands were shaking, his eyes gone wide.

"Inside jacket pocket. On your right." Joe tried to keep his voice soft, controlled.

His captor was suspicious. "What are you saying, mister? You do any stupid focking thing and I blow your brain out. Understand?"

"Police officer."

Doubt crept into the other's eyes. He scowled, trying to mask it. "You expect me to believe this? Bullshit." But doubt persisted, and one hand slowly left the gun to reach into Joe's jacket. Their eyes never broke contact, and the gun muzzle never drifted more than a quarter inch from either side of Dante's nose. The doubt Joe saw deepened as the man's fingers made contact with and then withdrew a shield case. The doorman flipped it open and flicked a glance at it. Joe moved cautiously toward higher ground.

"It's real, friend. You mind getting the gun outta my face?"

It had been an hour now since Billy Mannion gave that copper the slip, and his heart was still pumping at an accelerated level. As he pushed open the front door of the apartment a mask of fury veiled the fear he still felt. He'd spent the past hour trying to convince himself that if the cops had *known* he would be there, they would have sent an army to stake out the building. It made no sense to send just one man to apprehend someone of his notoriety. That meant he'd been both too careless in his movements and too arrogant in his assumptions. In disgust with himself he threw the knapsack across the living room and onto the sofa beside Seamus Cowan. The weight of it, with the pistol inside, sent a billow of dust rising on impact. Cowan, immersed in a back issue of *Byte* magazine, looked up in surprise. Across the room at the chrome-and-laminate dinette, ex-welterweight Paul Murphy also looked up.

"What's *your* fucking problem?" Cowan wondered. "And what took you so long, Billy?"

"What's my problem?!" Mannion fairly exploded with it. "They know I'm here, which means they know *we're* here. My problem's your problem, too, mate."

Seamus, a slender-shouldered, pale man of medium stature had the deep furrowed brow of an intellectual and the steel-rimmed spectacles of a Marxist radical. He prided himself on his ability to forgo an impassioned response in favor of reasoned logic. He turned that inner calm on Billy now. "They. Who are they and what do *they* know, William?"

Mannion stood stripping out of his turtleneck. Once he tugged it free of his head he wadded it into a ball and threw it through his open bedroom door. "*They* are the fucking cops. Which cops, I've no idea. Spotted me on the corner of 67th Street and chased me three blocks down Fifth Avenue." He related how he'd managed to shake his pursuit by threading his way through rush-hour traffic and make his escape through the undergrowth of Central Park. In the telling he conveniently left out the part played by the teenage girl.

"Hold on," Seamus stopped him. "This copper. You say he spoke to you?"

Mannion nodded.

"What sort of accent?"

"Yank. Definitely Yank. Big sod; tall as me and thicker through the chest. Didn't look as fast as he was, but Jesus and Mary could he fly."

Behind Mannion, Paul Murphy abandoned his game of solitaire to stand and pace. "On Fifth Avenue you say, Billy? What're the chances it was the cunt spilled the beans?"

Tall for his welterweight class at just over six foot, the slender, sinewy ex-fighter still worked out daily and liked to brag that he'd never let himself go an ounce over ten stone seven, or 147 pounds. At thirty-four he was younger than Billy by three years.

Mannion dismissed the suggestion out of hand. "*No

chance, Paulie. This copper was all alone. He looked just as surprised to see me there as I was to see him.''

"It could be that he *was*," Seamus reasoned. "Y've seen the newspapers. The hunt's on for us worldwide. We'd be fools to think they aren't looking for us here. Now that we *know*, we'll just have to be more careful. The important thing's that you're home safe, William.'' He reached to retrieve the knapsack from the cushion beside him and unzipped it to peer inside. "The operation itself went well, I take it? You're sure this is all of them?''

Mannion shrugged. "Those are all I found. There were none loose on the desk, and I took the one that was still in the machine, just like you said. There was an alarm. She swears it wasn't there the last time she was. I tripped it going in. A house copper showed up. I had to get out of there fast.''

Cowan's eyes went wary. "What sort of problem was he?''

"No problem at all, cousin.'' Billy loosened his belt and popped his fly button as he wandered toward the bedroom doorway. "So where's the bitch?''

"Doing the marketing,'' Murphy replied. "You know, Billy, you need to start going a bit easier on her. She's a bundle of nerves, that one. It don't help the atmosphere 'round here none to have you riding her like you do.''

Mannion's face went red with rage. "That's none of your bleeding *business*, Paulie Murphy! You're here to do a job and part of that job is taking orders from me. You'll recall that Siobhan McDonough *volunteered*, just like the rest of us.''

"But . . .''

Billy held up a hand to stop him. "No buts, Paulie. We spent a lot of money to send the bitch over here, to get her set up. She's here, what? Three years now? Not a worry in the world. We get her a job so's she can send money home. We get her this apartment and don't ask nothing in return save she be here should we need her. The minute we *do* need her she thinks she's had a change of heart. Like bloody hell. This is a *war* we're fighting, mate.''

FOUR

Isolated from the clamoring media hoard, Joe Dante sat in the back of an Operations Division van facing Gus Lieberman and Police Commissioner Anton Mintoff. Dante was despondent. He felt directly responsible for the death of the girl Billy Mannion had shoved into Fifth Avenue traffic. The commissioner was taking a less personal and more practical view of the situation. The dead girl proved to be the daughter of shipping magnate Hubert T. Poole, New York's honorary vice-mayor of culture. In contrast to the subdued Dante, Big Tony Mintoff was agitated.

"We're talking political *shit storm* here, Lieutenant. Courtney Poole was the only child Hubie Poole *had*. And let's not forget just who Hubie Poole *is* in this city. He chaired the mayor's fund-raising effort in the last election. Hizzoner owes Hubie Poole *big*. The least the mayor can do for his good buddy is have the D.A. crawl up your ass and *my* ass!"

It was obvious that Dante's sympathies weren't with the mayor. "I repeat," he countered. "The man I chased was Billy Mannion. He had a gun. You'll pardon me, but I don't give a flying *fuck* what anyone else says he saw or didn't see. Those two other girls were hysterical. And yeah, the doorman *is* a better witness, but he admits openly he never even focused on the other guy. What the girls were screaming about was *me*. Nobody saw Mannion's gun? Fine. I saw it. Nobody else can positively identify Mannion's face? I can.

29

I've been at this twenty-three years. You know my record. You also know you can take my word to the fucking bank.'' He paused to turn and stare out the window of the van at the throng on the sidewalk. ''And if you don't want to take my word, you can have my tin. Right here, right now.''

Chief Lieberman moved in now before the P.C. went haywire. ''Whoa, I don't think the commissioner's saying he don't believe you, Joey. What he's saying is that it might not matter. We've got half-a-dozen witnesses saw you chasing *somebody* down Fifth Avenue. They all agree that the man you were chasing grabbed the girl and threw her inta the street. What we gotta be able to defend is *why* you were chasing him.''

''And you *can't*.'' Dante threw up his hands as he said it. ''Why? Because nobody else can *identify* the fucker. For all anybody but me knows I was chasing some mutt stealing car radios. I used excessive force, and when the shit hit the fan, I made up some crock about IRA terrorists. Hell, the Intelligence Division briefing on Mannion and his crowd is a matter of departmental record. The D.A.'ll contend that I grabbed the handiest alibi I could conjure.''

At barely five foot eight Tony Mintoff was small for an old-school cop. Often likened to a weasel, he had the dark, darting eyes and quick, furtive movements of the animal as well as many of its predatory instincts. He hated a corner, and right now he saw himself being backed into one. It evoked an anger he was barely able to control. Dante and Chief Lieberman knew the signs. Mintoff adjusted his perfectly adjusted tie and shirt cuffs. He picked an invisible speck of lint from one trouser leg.

''There's no doubt in my mind that this is going to get nasty, Lieutenant. This department is prepared to stand behind you as far as it can. . . .''

''But don't count on us being able to work miracles.'' Dante had to exert the toughest control over himself to avoid mimicking the P.C.'s tough-guy Spanish Harlem speech.

Mintoff scowled. ''I beg your pardon?''

"This isn't the first time I've been in hot water, *sir*. I've heard the company line before. It's a hand job. Let's face it: without Mannion, I'm fucked. Hubert Poole's gonna want my shield, and the mayor's gonna get it for him. Meanwhile my hands will be tied, because you'll have me on modified assignment. I know who I saw. I'm the one who watched what he did. I'm the one who stood helplessly by while he grabbed that kid and threw her into the street. I *want* that son of a bitch, *sir*."

Some of the starch went out of Mintoff's shirt. Still scowling, he spread his hands. "There's no way I'll be able to avoid chaining you to a desk, Lieutenant. That's the least the mayor will accept until this blows over."

Dante shook his head. "I'm formally requesting a leave of absence, starting now. I've got at least four weeks of personal time stockpiled and another two months' vacation."

Mintoff glanced helplessly at his chief of detectives. "Talk to him, Gus."

Lieberman pinched the bridge of his nose, closed his eyes, and slowly shook his head. "What good's the best investigative mind I got do me chained to a desk, Tony? I got a major homicide just starting to take shape. And now I've got Mannion. There ain't a doubt in my mind that Mannion is who Joey saw. That puts him here in New York, so now the Feds'll be underfoot. I need the lieutenant on this Kane mess, not running around the city hunting Mannion like the Lone fucking Ranger."

Mintoff continued to scowl. "My hands are going to be tied there, Gus. The mayor tells me to put the lieutenant on modified assignment, I've got no choice."

"But I *do*," Dante countered. "You put me on modified, I don't show up for work, and leave of absence or not I start burning personal days."

"Is that some sort of threat, Lieutenant?"

Before replying Dante reached into his jacket and extracted his shield case. "I'm gonna find Mannion, sir. You want my tin? Here. Take it. There's a sixteen-year-old girl in

31

a rubber bag on the way to the morgue. I didn't shove her in front of that car, but I might as well have. I know damn well who *did* shove her, and whether I've got to hunt him as a cop or a civilian, his ass is mine.''

The P.C. stared at the proffered shield case with a mixture of disbelief and distaste. ''I'm not as stupid as you seem to think I am, Lieutenant. If I accept your shield case, I'm telling the whole town I think you're at fault. You think I'm just another prick with scrambled eggs on his hat brim and a hard-on for the rank and file. Well, you're wrong. I know you're a good cop, and I *don't* believe you're feeding me a line of shit.''

''Wait a sec,'' Lieberman interrupted. ''That might not be such a bad idea. You take his tin and Hubert Poole ain't the only one who's gonna be mollified. It'll cool the Feds, and it just might put Mannion off his guard, too. Meanwhile we can hook Joey here up with Pete Shore over at Intelligence Division. Let him chase Mannion from deep cover.''

Mintoff stared at Lieberman in surprise. ''You're serious.''

''What the hell good is he gonna be to me chained to a desk?''

''Jesus Christ.'' Mintoff was at it again, straightening his tie and adjusting his cuffs. ''I can't believe I'm listening to this.''

Lieberman grinned. ''Or worse. Buying it.''

Ten minutes later Dante sat facing Gus in the backseat of the chief's car. As Lieberman's driver started into traffic to give Joe a lift to where he'd left his own car parked, Gus got on the cellular phone to contact Jumbo Richardson. Once the Op Desk was able to connect them he asked Richardson to meet him in the lobby of Amanda Kane's building. On replacing the handset Gus twisted in his seat to regard Dante's profile.

''I'm sure you already got some plan of action brewing, Joey. Fine, but do me a favor and talk to Pete Shore. I know how much you hate the snoops, but Pete's good people. And stay in touch. I'll need to know how to find you."

They'd rolled south five blocks on Fifth and were looping around to catch Madison going back uptown. Dante was staring out the window at pedestrian traffic on the 59th Street sidewalk. A handful of casually dressed people stood clustered before the ground floor showroom windows of the GM building, ogling the latest Chevys, Oldsmobiles, Pontiacs, and Buicks. Joe judged them to be tourists, European from the cut of their clothing.

"Today? I guess I'll take your advice. Spend some time with Pete Shore at Intelligence Division. Pick his brain. If I catch a sniff of something, I might check it out."

"You got your beeper?"

"In my car."

"Don't turn this into a vendetta, Joey."

Dante turned from the view outside. Not only was Gus his direct superior, he was also one of his oldest and closest friends on the job. Gus was the first squad commander Joe worked for after getting his gold shield. That was at the Sixth, downtown on West 10th Street and another of those tiny eternities ago. In the job's vernacular, Gus Lieberman was Dante's rabbi: a mentor, confessor, and guardian angel all rolled into one. For years now they'd spoken freely to one another, each saying what was on his mind.

"I watched a man murder a girl today, Gus. I saw him use her and throw her out with no more regard than I'd give a paper cup." He paused and slowly shook his head. "A vendetta? Naw, Gus. Us guineas know a vendetta can be mediated. Harmonized. Billy Mannion and me? We're never gonna be harmonized."

Beasley "Jumbo" Richardson already had a lot on his mind when he was called out of bed that morning. Tomorrow he and Bernice would drive their daughter Michelle to Washington to begin a one-year internship in waste control management with the EPA. Missy was understandably nervous about the move. It was a long way from home, and for the first time in her life she'd be living by herself. On the one hand Jumbo thought something like this would be good for the kid. On the other, this was his baby girl, twenty-two years old or not. It hadn't helped to start the day off looking at somebody else's baby girl lying naked on a living room floor with a guy twice her age and a bullet in her head. He'd just learned from the Deerfield, Illinois, police that Veronica Tierney wasn't exactly the good-time girl everyone was assuming her to be. No, this baby girl had graduated from MIT with a Ph.D. in electrical engineering. Second in her class, no less. She was not only sleeping with Ralph Kane, she also ran a Magnetronics think tank in Chicago. According to the woman Richardson subsequently spoke to at Magnetronics headquarters in New York, the dead woman had recently been promoted to vice-president.

Jumbo was thusly preoccupied as he entered Ralph Kane's apartment building. One glance around, taking in the bank-lobby atmosphere of the marble, the plush carpeting, and the cut-crystal chandeliers, gave him the distinct feeling that most black visitors didn't use the front door here. Surely there were brothers like Cosby and Bryant Gumbel who could well afford the going rate, but this was a world where price wasn't the object. This was the world of the mega-rich, and the mega-rich tended to be clannish. He knew, for instance, that up and down this block there were buildings filled only with rich WASPs, or rich Jews, or rich Catholics. The exclusionary nature of a building's politics was rarely acknowledged openly. Just the same, it might as well have been carved in its cornerstone.

Jumbo had no more time to contemplate that separate reality. Chief Lieberman entered the lobby moving at a hurried clip. He looked harried. The big black detective crossed to intercept, his own concern evident in the worried knit of his brow.

"What the hell happened, Gus? How's Joey? Dudes on the Op Desk couldn't tell me shit."

Lieberman looked Jumbo straight in the eye and shook his head. "You ain't going to like it any more than I do, Beasley. Joey gave Big Tony his shield. Hubie Poole's gonna demand his balls on a platter, and he figured he'd save the mayor the trouble. I don't think I've seen him this down since Sam Scruggs got it."

A shocked Richardson stood searching for words. Scruggs, Dante's former partner, was killed in the line of duty. Jumbo hadn't known Dante then.

"Jesus. Just like that? No investigation? No nothing? How bad did he fuck up?"

Gus grunted. "Does it matter? He thinks he saw something he can't prove. A civilian was killed because of an action he took. Unless he can find this guy Mannion and prove he's the perp, there ain't no way that little girl's father is gonna buy his story."

"He's gonna go after him then, ain't he?"

Gus nodded. "Oh, yeah. He wants this Mannion's ass. Wants it bad."

"So what's going on upstairs?"

The chief glanced toward the ceiling. "I had Lydia help break the news to Mrs. Kane. She took it pretty hard. That sorta shock's a funny thing. One part of the reality sinks right in. The other takes more time." Gus went on to describe how he'd discovered the Kanes had a daughter who also lived here and how the daughter knew the Tierney woman while at college. "Amanda don't seem to be aware of Ralph's involvement with this broad. I'd like to know how much the daughter was aware of, Elizabeth. From what I gather, she works for the company, too."

Jumbo reported on what he'd learned from the Deerfield, Illinois, police and the woman at Magnetronics headquarters. Gus digested this new information.

"Okay. Seems to jibe. There's a good chance the daughter and the Tierney broad kept in touch. Mrs. Kane is gonna try to reach her; get her home."

"What about the office we found at the Overton? You got any idea what he was working on there?"

"She said he was on the verge of some kinda breakthrough. Something to do with magnets. That ain't a whole lot to go on, considering that everything he did had something to do with magnets. Either way, he used it as his excuse to hole up there every weekend for the past year."

"Magnets," Jumbo mused. "And a good-looking dead girl who also just happened to be an electrical engineer. You s'pose they had a *legitimate* reason for being there together, all hanky-panky aside?"

"That was Mrs. Kane's contention before we told her about the evidence of romance. She figured the girl flew in to help Kane with some phase of the project."

Jumbo jerked a thumb toward the elevators. "You gonna sit in on this?"

"Negative. There's no way Tony Mintoff's gonna ride this other shit storm out alone. I've gotta get my fanny over to Gracie Mansion; give hizzoner a chance to kick it up and down the front lawn."

The maid who answered the front door of the Kane apartment seemed surprised to find a well-dressed but very large black man on the other side of it. Unlike his more gracefully assembled partner, Jumbo was cast from the same mold as the chief. At an even six feet he was a couple of inches shorter than Joey and had Lieberman's bull neck and massive torso. Several years ago, before undergoing a medically supervised diet, Richardson was a fat man, weighing in at over three hundred pounds. Hence the nickname. Today he carried two-twenty and kept himself trim with regular exercise. The nickname still stuck.

"Sergeant Richardson," he told the maid.

She frowned at his shield and identification. "I was told to expect a *Lieutenant* . . . uh . . . Dante?"

"Something came up. I'm the lieutenant's partner. Mrs. Kane, please."

36

Nineteenth Precinct

The maid led him into the entry gallery of the largest New York apartment he'd yet seen. An ornate, sweeping staircase ran up to another level dead ahead. Off to the right of it he could see a huge formal dining room with its gleaming parquet floor, mahogany refectory table and at least a dozen chairs. Another maid was setting out a large vase of cut flowers in there.

"Wait here please, officer. I'll inform Mrs. Kane that you're here."

Jumbo was allowed enough time to observe a small army of uniformed help drifting soundlessly to and fro. As well as being grand in scale, the place gleamed, every surface spotless. In the course of investigations Richardson had visited townhouses and apartments all over the Upper East Side from Fifth Avenue to Turtle Bay Gardens and Sutton Place. This was as fine a residence as he'd ever seen.

"Sergeant Richardson?"

Jumbo turned to find himself approached by a woman of perhaps thirty. Tall, at close to his own height, she wasn't at all heavy but had the kind of bone structure that made her appear a bit on the stout side. The boxy, conservatively cut gray business suit she wore did little to flatter. To accentuate the severity of the sharp lines of her face, she wore her straight black hair pulled tight into a twist and held it in place with a simple tortoise-shell clip. She was pale, almost ivory, and the makeup job was best described as basic. A little something around her eyes and little else. A single strand of pearls worn outside the collar of an emerald silk blouse was the only jewelry he saw. No rings, no earrings. Jumbo thought that dressed more softly and with a smile on her face she might be attractive. As it was everything about her demeanor chilled the temperature of the gallery as she entered it. He waited until she reached him and then shook her outstretched hand. The grip was firm, almost manly.

"I'm Elizabeth Kane, Sergeant. Mr. Kane's daughter."

Richardson was puzzled. Where was the grief? "Ah. Then your mother reached you."

"In Princeton. We do all our manufacturing and most of our design work there. What the hell happened, Sergeant?"

"Someone murdered your father, Miss Kane. Your father and his girlfriend."

"I *know* that." She snapped it, taking the interrogator's tone. "What *else* happened?"

"Else? How do you mean, what else?"

She made no attempt to hide her impatience. "Was the place ransacked? Did either or both of them appear to have been tortured? Did anyone *see* anybody?"

Jumbo held up a hand, pushing at the air between them. "Slow down, Miss Kane. Ransacked? Tortured? What'd lead you to suspect that?"

She snorted contemptuously. "Five billion dollars, Sergeant. The amount of money the United States Department of Energy will pay to whomever is awarded the magnets contract for the new supercollider." She paused, scrutinizing the expression she saw on his face. "You don't *know* about this?"

"Is that what your dad had on his drawing board in there? *That's* this breakthrough he was getting so close to?"

She got immediately suspicious. "Who said anything about any breakthrough? Where did you hear that, Sergeant?"

"The chief of detectives got that much when he talked to your mother earlier. I believe that's about *all* he got. Maybe you can expand on it for me."

His last words were spoken to her back as she spun on her heels and charged down the same hall from which she'd emerged. She was halfway along it when he heard her mutter. "I don't believe this" under her breath.

By the time Richardson could follow this strident young woman's progress and emerge into a stadium-size living room overlooking Central Park and all of mid-Manhattan, Elizabeth Kane was already on the attack. Seated on one of the several sofas was the woman Jumbo and the rest of New York knew to be Amanda Gregory-Kane. Looming above her, arms akimbo and face reddened with rage, stood her daughter. At first glance it was difficult for Richardson to believe they were even related. The contrasts between them were that marked. Mrs. Kane was diminutive at no more than five foot two or three. She was blond, stylishly dressed, and looked no older than forty. She and her daughter shared none of the same features.

". . . for Cris*sake*, mother! He never told you anything about that project that wasn't in absolute confidence. I demand to know who *else* you told."

Jumbo lingered in the doorway instead of jumping between them.

"You *demand* to know, Elizabeth dear? I'm your mother. Did I even once question him when he went off every weekend to lock himself away with his precious work? Every weekend for nearly a year and a half? No, dear. I took him at his word. He told me he was on the verge of a breakthrough that would have the Department of Energy *begging* Magnetronics to take their contract. I guess I thought I knew him better than I did. He'd been running off at all hours to work on his pet projects ever since you were born. Why should I have suspected he'd suddenly became interested in *sex*?"

"Ahem!"

Startled, both women looked up. Jumbo pushed off the doorjamb and ambled into the room.

"I beg your pardon, Sergeant," Elizabeth protested. "I don't recall inviting you down here."

Richardson forced a precise little smile. "We were right in the middle of a conversation concerning a police matter, Miss Kane. I don't recall your excusing yourself." Without waiting for a reply he turned to her mother and extended a hand. "Mrs. Kane, I'm Detective Sergeant Richardson. I know this is a tough time for you, but we've got some questions we hope you'll be able to answer. I'm sorry 'bout the intrusion on your conversation with your daughter here, but I've got a double homicide on my hands. I'm a busy man." He straightened to turn as Elizabeth started to leave the room.

"No reason you can't be here, too, miss. You might have something useful to add."

The younger woman stopped but stood her ground, moving no further back into the room. "You've already managed to coerce a breach of Magnetronics security from my mother, Sergeant. What can I add to that, other than that much of what we do is classified secret by the federal government."

"*Coerce*, Miss Kane? Your mother shared that information with this city's chief of detectives in the course of a homicide investigation. We're trying to establish motive here. If you've got anything material to that interest, we'd like to hear it."

"A *motive*, Sergeant? Five billion dollars isn't enough motive for you? In a city where a crack-crazed freak will kill you for a neck chain?"

Richardson had his notebook out and was uncapping his pen. "I understand you left this building for work this morning around eight. You were home all night?"

Elizabeth Kane became openly angered again. "What is this?" she demanded. "My father's dead, and you're asking me where *I* was?"

"It's routine, miss. A large percentage of homicides are perpetrated by family or friends of the deceased. I find it interesting how broke up you are about this one. You were home last night?"

There was pain in her eyes now. Jumbo thought it was probably real and didn't understand why she was working so hard to keep the emotional side of it in check. "I had dinner with the account executive from our advertising agency. She dropped me here around ten."

Richardson turned to Amanda. "How 'bout you, ma'am?"

"I was in all night . . . doing work on a party I'm supposed to hostess next weekend. It's a fund-raiser for the Hamptons Shoreline Preservation Fund."

Jumbo waved his pen back and forth, indicating his surroundings. "Your people. How many of 'em live in?"

Amanda shook her head. "None, Sergeant. The building

40

is very secure, and I like my privacy in the evenings . . . even with Ralph away, working on his projects.'' She stopped, her lower lip starting to quiver as she reached for a tissue. It was evident from the redness of her eyes and the general puffiness of her face that the woman had been doing quite a lot of crying.

Jumbo turned back to Elizabeth. "How 'bout you, Miss Kane? Any staff, roommates, *anyone* with you from ten last night to eight this morning?"

"No."

Richardson tapped his notepad against the tip of his nose, and feigning deep thought walked to the window overlooking Fifth Avenue. When he turned back both women were now together in his field of view. "I'd like you to search your memories for anyone who might hold a grudge against Mr. Kane. And you, Miss Kane: I know you think the motive is clear, but try to understand that we need to investigate from every possible angle. I know that you and Veronica Tierney were friends once, or at least roommates. Did you keep in touch? Is there a jealous boyfriend or jilted lover? Somebody who'd be angry 'bout this affair she was having with your father?"

"Veronica and I did have contact from time to time, Sergeant. We were both vice-presidents of the same corporation. But no." Elizabeth shook her head. "If there was another man in her life, I'm unaware of him."

"Another man. You say that like you knew 'bout her and your dad."

The daughter shot a quick, furtive glance at her mother. She found Amanda sitting up more stiffly now, her return gaze unwavering. "I'd rather not speak to that here, Sergeant."

Amanda abandoned that expectant posture on the sofa to come to her feet. "You'd rather not speak to that *here*?" She was not as tall as her daughter by nearly half a foot but was every bit her equal now, her presence seeming to grow with her outrage. "Your *slut* of an ex-lover was having an affair with your father, and you *knew* about it? I can't believe this is my *daughter* talking.''

"She was *not* my lover, mother! We were nothing more than friends!''

"Oh? Who do you think you're kidding, Elizabeth? You move out of the residence hall at Smith because you don't like the *atmosphere* and move clear across Northampton to live with some girl from another college? Veronica Tierney was a goddamn dyke! How do I know that? She made a *pass* at me!''

FIVE

Intelligence Division had its headquarters at 325 Hudson Street, in the little limbo between Greenwich Village and SoHo. The building, like most buildings housing the job's less-visible speciality units, was unremarkable. Most of the job personnel working within it appeared unremarkable, too. That was pretty much the idea. Intelligence Division was the closest NYPD got to having a clandestine arm.

Joe Dante had grown up within the job learning a certain rank-and-file disdain for Inspectional Services Bureau. The hated shooflies of Internal Affairs were run out of ISB, as were Intelligence Division's snoops. It was commonly held that anyone who worked in either function had stuck his nose up some Palace Guard's ass to get the assignment. They worked the kind of regular hours that none of the rank and file enjoyed; eight-hour days and weekends off.

As far as Dante was concerned, Deputy Inspector Peter Shore was a rare animal at ISB. He wasn't an asshole. Pete Shore and Gus Lieberman had graduated in the same Academy class. Shore ran Intelligence Division's Special Service Unit, but unlike many administrators who worked at his level, Pete was recently from the street. He'd run the Seventh Division up at Detective Borough Bronx for six years before coming downtown. He was also the man who'd shown Dante the picture of Billy Mannion last Tuesday afternoon.

Shore, another one of Intel Division's average-looking

guys, lounged in a squeaky desk chair behind a green metal desk. Nearly bald and gone jowly, he wore suits cut for comfort and not style. Today's was a charcoal gray job, and Dante knew that yesterday's probably was, too. The clothes were slightly rumpled, the cordovan wingtips scuffed. He had one leg up across the edge of his desk and had a cigar going; something disgustingly cheap by the smell of it. Dante figured that if this weren't 325 Hudson and Pete didn't have the butt of that little snub S&W .38 peeking out from inside his jacket, this man could have been anything from an aging mechanical contractor to a garment district notions purveyor.

"Don't get me wrong, Dante. What I want to know is not *if* it was him crawling outta that dumpster, but *why*." Pete's voice was gravelly. He talked like Satchmo used to sing. "Dressed like a fuckin' cat burglar, no less. What the fuck was he up to?"

Dante sat across from him in one of the office's several oak chairs. They, like every other piece of furniture in here, had to be at least forty years old.

"That gun wasn't the only thing he had in his knapsack, Pete."

"You're sure he came from *inside* that building?"

"Pretty much. I watched the maintenance staff push that dumpster out the service-entrance door."

"But nobody admits seeing him go in, right?"

"So they claim. The doorman's got no record of him entering out front. The super says the service door was locked all night."

Shore fingered the file on Mannion lying open on his blotter.

"According to this, Mannion made his rep early on as a specialist at getting in and outta high-security setups. What I'd like to know is, why there? What the fuck was he up to? I unnerstand sympathetic donations from the American Irish are way down since they started killing innocents and spouting Maoist crap. Maybe he's hurting for cash and has turned cat burglar."

It wasn't a possibility Joe could reject out of hand, but he'd checked with the 19th Precinct and learned that no burglaries were reported at that address. With help from the building's super he'd inspected the doors of all apartments where the tenants were currently out of town. None revealed signs of forced entry.

"I really doubt it, Pete. Not unless he's got someone on the staff in cahoots with him. Someone with access to keys."

Shore jotted something on the yellow pad at his elbow. "We'll wanna have a background check run on everybody draws a paycheck there. It's my bet the Feds'll wanna handle that." He smirked. "If I know them assholes, they'll wanna handle everything."

Dante came forward in his seat, a new fire of intensity in his eyes. "Fuck them and what they'll want to handle, Pete. I want this guy. Me, personally. He was in that building for a reason. Right now trying to figure that reason is the only angle I've got to work. That is, unless you've got some *other* bright idea."

Shore smiled, his leg coming back down off the desk as he swiveled around to face Dante straight across the desk. "Me? I'd probably concentrate on the Irish community. They've got their ghettoes, same as every other immigrant population in this beautiful mosaic. If it was me, I'd concentrate my efforts there."

Hubert T. Poole had never felt so absolutely impotent in all his fifty-seven years. Originally Hubert Pulijal, the son of a Ceylonese tea merchant and a British Army nurse, he'd moved mountains in his lifetime. Disowned by his father in the wake of his parents' bitter divorce, he'd traveled to Brazil as a teenager, gone to work for a Brazilian shipper, and in ten years owned the company. From there he'd leapfrogged up the South American coast to Caracas and began leasing tankers to carry contract oil. Today he owned a fleet of ships, had real estate holdings worldwide, and even owned his dead father's tea company. A small man at barely five and a half feet, he was dark complexioned but distinctly Anglo in his features. A tiny, clipped mustache and full head of curly silver hair conjured an image best described as dapper. While he had built and today ruled an empire, this morning a crown jewel in it had been smashed to dust at his feet. If only they'd gone upstate to the farm last night. If only that other kid hadn't left her riding britches at home up the block. Jim Simpson's brat, that pompous ass. Why couldn't that maniac have grabbed her? Or Donahue's kid? Poole's helplessness in the face of events left him feeling foolishly exposed; naked and angry.

"Fairy tales!" he ranted. "Who does this man of yours think he's trying to fool, Commissioner? My little girl is *dead* because of him." Poole turned from Anton Mintoff to the mayor. "You know me too well, David. You know I will not sit still for this. My wife and my daughter are the two most important things in my life. Because of this cop, this *hotshot*, a man whose *word is as good as anyone's on the force*"—his eyes shifted to glare at Mintoff—"half of my precious family has been taken from me. Look at my wife, for God's sake!"

Beside him Myra Poole was sobbing hysterically. A former Tampa Bay Buccaneer cheerleader and a woman twelve years Hubert Poole's junior, she'd fallen apart amid wads of tear-dampened tissues. Even in her grief she was a handsome woman, in that long-legged, sweater-girl way. Years of excessive sun had left her face more deeply creased than any plastic surgery could erase, while the rest of her appeared young and tight. Her surgeon down in Rio was a wizard at glorifying an aging body. A breast bob here, a tummy or thigh tuck there. After sixteen years of marriage she remained the apple of her Hubie's ever-hungry eye.

The mayor was in a spot, caught between the rock of political expedience and a law-enforcement hard place. "You've got my very deepest sympathy, Hubert; this *city's* deepest sympathy. You *know* how much I personally treasure your support and advice. You have my word that there will be the fullest investigation I'm empowered to underwrite."

As Poole slowly shook his head he raised his right hand, its index finger moving back and forth like the pendulum of a metronome.

"If it weren't for this man, this hotshot cop, my Courtney would still be alive. He is going to pay. I want his *head*."

The mayor glanced nervously at Mintoff. Poole watched their wordless exchange like a snake watches mice. When the mayor spoke his tone was almost apologetic.

"I'm going to speak to the district attorney, Tony. It's justifiable in this situation. An inquiry is put into neutral territory that way; the responsibility for drawing a conclusion from it would be out of our hands."

Mintoff wasn't about to argue. The mayor had absolute control over his job. Fighting his boss would be committing political suicide. Police Commissioner of the City of New York was the plum he'd worked his entire career to pick. He thanked his C of D silently for already helping him get this ball rolling.

"Lieutenant Dante surrendered his shield to me two hours ago, Mr. Mayor. Until this matter is investigated and resolved he's been put on suspension."

With eleven years of electrical engineering study under his belt, first at Britain's Durham University and then at MIT in Boston, Seamus Cowan was well acquainted with the problems of the task now at hand. A man couldn't dive right into a job like this and expect to pluck a prize from depths of the purest crystalline logic immediately. No, these depths were sure to be murky.

Seamus had an Apple Macintosh II FX computer set up on the table before him. He'd whispered a silent prayer of thanks on opening the box of disks to discover them all labeled and in alphabetical order. Four hours ago he'd started with the one marked "A," inserting it into the drive to study the menu and get some sort of overview. Every programmer had his or her own signature technique. Seamus had spent most of the morning and early afternoon attempting to familiarize himself with this one. The program was extremely complex, based on mathematics as pure as any he'd ever encountered. He felt exhilarated to be peeking, like a voyeur through a window, into Ralph Kane's world. It was a pity such a mind had to be destroyed, no matter how just the cause. Kane's reputation for genius in the fields of electromagnetics and accelerated particle theory was never more clearly demonstrated. Cowan stood in awe.

The bedroom door behind him opened. Billy, just risen from his nap, emerged as Seamus switched off the monitor screen and screwed the heels of his hands into his eye sockets. Mannion squinted, focusing on the sheets of yellow legal pad strewn liberally over the tabletop. They were covered with the penciled scribblings of mathematical frenzy. The sight of them made Billy grin like a contented cat.

"Good sleep," he announced, stifling a yawn. "God, I needed that. So how does it go?"

Seamus craned his neck to regard his team leader. "Best I can say for now? Promising. And that's the best I'll be able to say for a while yet. This material is *dense*. I'm only just into it, but it makes sense so far."

Billy sniffed the air, having caught the odor of cooking food emanating from the kitchen. "Oh my, that smells good. She in there?"

Seamus nodded and began to shuffle that sheaf of papers into order. "Go easy on her, please William? She's nervous as hell about t'night. I can tell."

And as Cowan spoke those words of advice a woman of truly stunning beauty appeared in the kitchen doorway. Of medium stature, she had the slender, fluid grace of a dancer. A ratty apron and the wooden spoon clutched in one hand did little to detract from her surprisingly full figure. But it wasn't her body that held the appreciative gaze for long. There was a fierce Celtic challenge in cool, slate blue eyes. A full, pouting mouth accentuated it, supporting that challenge and giving it voice. Her skin stretched smooth and flawless over sharp cheeks, a strong jaw, and a long, graceful neck. Right now it was flushed with the barest blush of anger. This woman embodied the same physical credits to her gender that Billy Mannion did to his.

"I'm not going through wit it, Billy Mannion. I'm not a whore." Heavy with the brogue of her County Armagh upbringing, Siobhan McDonough's tones strove toward shrillness and failed. "You're a pig to ask it of me. Find some tramp to help you wit your dirty work. There are surely enough of *them* in this city."

"But not a one so beautiful. So captivating." There was amusement in Billy's voice. "I think it's interesting, Siobhan. You've been gone from home for how long now? You've had your head so turned by all your Actors Studio friends that you've forgotten your three nieces and nephews? And not to mention all we've done for you here? This place, rent free. The job at McNulty's. It must be nice, being able to afford all your acting lessons and still send money home. To listen to you, a body'd think we made a bad choice; that the one girl we sent to live in the lap of American luxury has turned selfish. She's saying she no longer believes in a free Ireland wit her whole soul and body."

"I can't do it, Billy." She was pleading now.

"Of course you can. What was it I used to say to you when I had you in my class? You have more talent than any ten acting students I'd ever taught. Combined."

"This is different. It's disgusting. I *won't* do it."

Mannion lifted his hands in a gesture of indifference. "Fine then. But think about it this way, Siobhan. Once your sister Deirdre's children are dead, how can you ever go home again?"

Detective Melissa Busby was dead on her feet. The first game of the American League Championship Series had gone into extra innings last night, and like a fool she'd stayed up to watch it all. Everyone else in the Major Case squad was tired, too, but none seemed as tired as she and her partner, Guy Napier. It didn't much matter to her that the Yankees hadn't made the play-offs this year. Both Melissa and Napier were avid baseball fans. They'd spent a rare work night together at his place, finally turning out the lights around one-fifteen. When the Op Desk woke them at half past five, they'd dragged their weary asses out of bed, driven from Flatbush into Manhattan, and had been on the go ever since.

At four o'clock that afternoon the team assembled in the Major Case squad at One Police Plaza to plot directions. For Busby it felt odd to be at that table without Dante occupying his accustomed seat at the head. Beasley Richardson, now temporarily in charge of the Overton House homicide investigation, sensed the awkwardness. He was leaving the floor open to anyone who wanted to take the ball and run with it. Don Grover and Rusty Heckman had spent the day at the morgue and forensics labs, and Grover had the ball right now. Melissa listened as her team's analysis expert reconstructed that morning's events.

"The way the crime scene guys figure it, the perp must have popped the girl right inside the front door," Don was telling them. A thin man with a hollow-leg appetite, he spoke in a deep, reassuring bass. "Kane hears something, and he gets out of bed. There's that little short wall right here at the end of the hall." He pointed to a floor plan on the easel beside him. "The angle's right for the perp to have been waiting behind it. Say it took a minimum of a minute for Kane to respond to the noise—and that's actually a lot of time—that would mean both occupants were already dead within eighty, ninety seconds of the alarm reaching Garfield downstairs. Garfield takes another three minutes minimum to reach the scene. That's more than enough time for the perp to get the hell out of there if all he was after was the two occupants." Grover paused to search the faces around the table. Every eye was on him. "But he *didn't* get the hell out of there. He was still there when Garfield arrived. That's maybe as many as five or six minutes after the perp first entered. Rusty and me? We think he had to be after something.''

''That's what Kane's daughter thinks, too,'' Jumbo reported. He then described Elizabeth Kane's capacity with Magnetronics and her theory that the perpetrator was after a new technology Ralph Kane was developing. Melissa lost him at the mention of superconducting magnets and a new supercollider.

''Whoa, Sarge. You're starting to speak Greek here. What the hell's a supercollider?''

When Richardson looked helplessly around the table, Grover rushed to his aid. ''Big rig the Department of Energy wants to build down in Texas. Somewhere near Dallas, I think. It's a monster cyclotron is the best way I can think to describe it. A machine designed to accelerate particles up near the speed of light and smash them. Physics-types figure it'll help them unlock the secrets of subatomic structure, how the universe was formed. Shit like that.''

The expression on Melissa's face told them she was really no better informed than before asking her question. Richardson attempted to pick up where he'd left off.

''We may be speaking Greek, but the bottom line here is five billion bucks. That's right; five *billion*. That's what Elizabeth Kane claims the government's magnetics contract on this project will be worth. You can buy a whole lotta motive for that kinda cash.''

''How do we know if it was stolen or not?'' Melissa pressed. ''All those drawings on the table looked undisturbed. The office sure as hell wasn't ransacked by anyone racing a clock. The coffee in the cup would have been dumped. Paper would be everywhere.''

''Not if he knew just what he was looking for,'' Rusty Heckman reminded her. ''And where to find it.'' Of all of them assembled here, Heckman looked least likely in his role. His height and weight had been barely adequate to get him into the Academy fifteen years ago. Today all those meals shared with his perpetually hungry partner were starting to tell on him. He'd grown a soft doughnut of fat around his middle. That, combined with his unruly shock of red hair, made him look less like a detective and more like Bozo the Clown. But looks deceived. He was the squad's master at spotting the tiniest bubble of entropy on a sea of order. That made him invaluable.

"You're talking inside tip?" Napier guessed.

Rusty nodded. "He knew the Overton House well enough to slip in undetected. He knew where the suite was and that somebody was gonna be home."

"Hang on," Jumbo stopped him. "How'd he know that?"

"He didn't try to force entry," Rusty explained. "There's no evidence of it. It looks like he just knocked on the door and waited for someone to answer it."

"You're saying he *wanted* to kill them," Jumbo concluded.

"Yep. That's what I'm saying. Why? Sole proprietorship. You just told us what Kane was working on is potentially worth five billion. I don't suppose it'd make much sense to steal it and leave its creator alive. A creator can also *re*create."

The squad sat in silence a moment, digesting Rusty's theory. From the looks she could read on the faces assembled around the table, Melissa knew they liked it.

"Okay," she ventured. "I can see how a lot of it fits an inside tip scenario, but what about the alarm system? Why wasn't the perp aware of it?"

"Brand-new installation," Grover explained. "It's less than three weeks old."

"So we're talking about someone close enough to Kane to know the details of his setup there but maybe not close enough to know recent changes."

Beside her Napier brought his six-foot-six-inch frame up out of his thinker's slouch. "Or close enough to Veronica Tierney." Nicknamed Boy Wonder, Busby's lover was the youngest member of the squad by six years and a gifted athlete. As males go, she also acknowledged him to be quite intuitive. "It could be someone from *her* circle," Guy continued. "All we know about her is that she ran a subsidiary outside Chicago. Okay, so maybé she told someone out there what she and Kane had cooking. Maybe that someone had the hots for either her or her job, was pissed off that she was screwing the boss. It would be tempting with information like that in hand to cash in."

"Damn," Jumbo complained. "We're talking about what here? A couple dozen suspects under an umbrella like that. Maybe more?"

"In New York, Chicago, and *Princeton*," Grover reminded him. "If we prioritize this industrial theft angle, it gets huge fast. But I like it. All the indicators point to our perp being a pro. Light-caliber weapon, most probably noise-suppressed. Quick in and out. No forensic-evidence trail to speak of other than the slugs he left in his three victims. And when Garfield showed up on the scene the perp kept his cool; dealt with the problem and moved on."

"What about Garfield?" Jumbo asked. "What's the update on him?"

"I called the hospital again just before we sat down," Melissa reported. "He was in surgery eight hours, and they'd just rolled him into recovery. I'll stop by once they get him into ICU. Should be sometime around seven."

"How'd he make out?" Richardson pressed. "You able to learn anything there?"

"Yeah. I talked to the surgeon." Melissa paused to refer to her notes, flipping a page and finding her place. "He said the bullet entered through the right cheekbone, severed the facial nerve, went clean through something called the parotid gland and the jaw mandible. It lodged in the ear canal and that's where the surgery got tricky. The bottom line? He's going to have a permanent paralysis similar to Bell's palsy, and he'll be deaf in one ear. Other than that he should come out of it with all his faculties."

"Could be we'll get lucky there," Jumbo supposed. "Maybe he saw something."

"I wouldn't count on it," Heckman growled. "Meanwhile we've got our work cut out for us. How do you wanna divide up the pie?"

"I'm open to suggestions. Who wants what?"

Rusty tapped his pen against his notepad, his eyes regarding his partner. "I'd like to follow up on this supercollider business; see who else is in the running for this big money contract and who'd *like* to be in the running. How about it, Donnie? That sound good to you?"

Grover said it suited him fine.

Napier spoke next. "It might make sense for you to stick with the family angle, Sarge. You've already met the players and have the insight there. Let Mel and me run with Kane and Tierney; see who else they worked with; who might've known what they were up to; who might've held a grudge."

"Manpower," Richardson lamented. "I can see it already. 'Fore long we're gonna need a lot more manpower."

Like everyone else working on the Overton House homicides, Gus Lieberman had been in action since well before dawn. With the Courtney Poole homicide now piggybacked atop the others, the chief's energy levels were drained bonedry. Deaths involving New York families perched on the highest rung of the economic ladder, and a political backlash resulting in the suspension of the best street cop Gus had . . . It got him thinking long and hard about retirement. He had as much time in as he needed to draw the best pension package available. Another few years' service might see his salary increase and boost his pension accordingly, but what did a few more bucks matter at this point in his life? His wife was drawing an income from a six-million-dollar trust. No, Gus stayed on because he loved the work. Without it he'd have no idea what to do with himself. Except on days like this. On days like this he thought it might be nice to take up gardening.

Lydia had something on with the City Opera this evening, and yesterday Gus had invited Dante to join him for an early dinner at their favorite Vietnamese dive in Chinatown. Circumstances had changed since the invitation was extended, but Joey hadn't called to cancel. Lieberman was at work on his second beer and thinking about ordering food when Dante finally appeared on the stairs descending into the place. He spotted the chief at a table in the back corner and crossed to pull up a chair. At that hour the restaurant was only half full. As usual the rest of the clientele was exclusively Oriental.

"You're twenty-five minutes late," Gus observed.

"I got hung up at Intelligence Division. You should have started without me."

"You look like you could use a drink."

"You mean I probably *will* . . . once you tell me what went on this afternoon."

"You heard? Fuckin' news travels fast on that goddamn grapevine, don't it?"

The waiter appeared to take Dante's drink order. When he'd gone away again, Joey picked up his chopsticks and toyed with them, eyes on Gus. "Yeah, boss. I heard. I just dropped my wheels in the garage and got it from Beasley. A *grand jury* investigation? Jesus, Gus. That's for cases where they're looking to hand down a *criminal* indictment."

Gus opened his hands in a gesture of helplessness. "There's no way they'll get one, Joey. You know this is bullshit. Tony Mintoff knows it's bullshit. Even the mayor knows it's bullshit. Poole and all the money he dumped inta the last campaign have hizzoner by the balls. Hubert wants the city to cut yours off. Once the mayor passes the buck t' the D.A., it's outta his hands."

"We *work* for these lunatics?"

Gus shook his head, his red-rimmed eyes sad. "Negative. We take orders from 'em. They come and they go. Who we work for never changes, Joey."

"Pete Shore wants workups on all that Fifth Avenue building's personnel, Gus. But before he gets them he knows the Bureau is gonna glom on and try to shut him out. Fine. I want those workups. Pete's already shown me his copy of

Mannion's Interpol file. He's also turned me onto Captain Ray Costello in their Organized Crime Monitoring Unit. Ray's working on putting me in touch with the Free Ireland mob through the back door.''

"You been busy,'' Lieberman mused. "Ray Costello's a good man. Organized Crime's an interesting avenue. Which back door?''

"The Westies.''

The Westies were the old Irish mob that once ruled the Hudson River waterfront. A shift in emphasis to containerization moved New York shipping from the west side of Manhattan to places like Brooklyn and Bayonne, New Jersey. Most of the old Hell's Kitchen neighborhood fronting the waterfront was either repopulated by later immigrant waves or gentrified. Still, the hard core of the old Westie organization survived to play an active role in the control of various construction trade unions and other nearly invisible muscle enterprises.

"Costello tells me there's a Westie move afoot to insinuate themselves into a control position with the Painters, Union. A couple years back we broke the hold the families had on District Council Nine, and that left a vacuum. Ray says the Westies have been sanctioned to make a move on it. They've already got a stranglehold on Local 19 in the Bronx. They're close to having a lock on Manhattan Local 18. As much as they can, they load the memberships up with Irish nationals. They help them get residency visas, green cards, the whole shot. As long as they're hard workers, and most of them seem to be, nobody complains.''

"With all the ass-dragging that goes on in this town?'' Gus growled. "Why should they? I still don't understand how you plan to get close. You don't look no more Irish than you do Italian.''

Fact was, Dante *didn't* look Italian. His family hailed from the Northern Italian city of Bolzano, in the foothills of the Italian Alps, and looked more Aryan than Mediterranean. Dante's sandy blond hair and blue eyes were not at all uncharacteristic for the Bolzano region, but they weren't the look people generally associated with the heritage.

"Ray's gonna put me in touch with one of his informers, a man working inside the District Council. He was placed there by the union administration in Washington. The way Ray tells it, the people on the national level are just as upset about the control problems up here as we are. They're working with us, hand in hand."

"Be careful there, Joey. The Westies got a reputation for playing rough."

"For keeps," Dante agreed. "Just like Billy Mannion."

Lieberman drained off the last of his beer and shook out a smoke. As he lit it he squinted down at his menu. "I heard from Chief Liljedahl just before I turned out the lights t'night, Joey."

Jerry Liljedahl was Lieberman's opposite at Inspectional Services.

"He says the agent in charge'a the New York Bureau office is having wet dreams over this Mannion sighting. Thinks it's gonna be his ticket to a deputy directorship in D.C."

"Don't tell me," Dante countered. "The message: Joe Dante better not even *think* about fucking it up for him. Right?"

"That's pretty much the size of it."

"And Liljedahl wants you to make sure that I don't get some wild hair; queer his nice butt-buddy relationship with the Bureau."

Lieberman glanced up from his menu. "Consider yourself counseled, hotshot. Frankly I don't give a shit *who* brings this asshole down, just so's somebody does."

Dante sat tracing idle patterns in the dew coating his beer bottle. He hadn't yet looked at his menu and probably wouldn't. He wasn't hungry. Gus could do the ordering. "Strikes me as being a touch ironic," he murmured. "The mayor is more than glad to see me suspended because his pal Poole won't believe it was Mannion I was chasing. At the same time, the FBI's siccing Jerry Liljedahl on you to make sure I don't steal their thunder. Maybe hizzoner and this agent-in-charge oughtta get together."

Lieberman snorted. "Sure thing, Joey. Just like every Christmas should be white."

Dante got serious now. He hunched forward over the edge of the table, his gaze intent. "This guy's mine, Gus. I know tomorrow's Saturday, but I need you to do me a favor. I got my own list of everyone employed in that Fifth Avenue building from the super. If I want the jump on this Bureau bozo, I'll need background checks as soon as you can run them." He reached into his jacket to retrieve a folded piece of paper and hand it across. "I found no evidence of forced entry to any of the unoccupied apartments there, so if Mannion wasn't inside to pull a robbery, what *was* he doing? I'm looking to make a connection."

Gus glanced over the list of names and addresses before refolding the sheet and pocketing it. "It may take a day or so, but consider it done."

"Thanks, boss. So what's going on with the Overton House investigation? Any breaks?"

"Nothing earthshaking, but maybe we've got a direction. You know anything about this ten-billion-dollar piece'a shit the Department of Energy wants to build down in Dallas?"

Dante nodded. "The supercollider."

"You're kidding. You've heard of it?"

Joe chuckled. "You keep forgetting I'm one of the few people in your command who can *read*, Gus."

SIX

These Friday nights were what Phillip Wright looked forward to all week. On Friday nights Phillip and his mates from the rugby club had a standing date with the South Street Seaport and several gallons of beer. They'd leave the wives stranded at home with the kids in the burbs, fuel up on a few pints of something cold and play grab-ass with all the other Young Turks populating Manhattan's Financial District. If the mood suited him, Phillip might even put the move on some dewy-eyed little morsel. The British accent worked wonders. These secretaries with their contrived hairstyles, tight skirts, and empty, impressionable minds were easy prey. Once he got warmed up he'd explain—in all modesty, mind—that he worked for Lloyd's and with his master's in finance from the London School of Economics he was one of the insurance giant's anointed. Indeed, his assignment as a risk assessment manager in the Lloyd's New York operation was a fast track to an underwriter's post. Few women he met had any idea what all this meant, but it impressed them. And it was the truth, after all. More or less. He *was* the fair-haired boy over here. At thirty-three he was the youngest department manager in the history of Lloyd's stateside World Trade Center operation.

Phillip had gotten hung up this evening working on some specs faxed this morning from Hong Kong. A Seattle firm was purchasing a grain carrier and seeking Lloyd's indemnification of their first cargo. Last week Wright had sent an engineer over to take a look at the vessel. By Monday he was expected to have a proposal ready. He would have had it ready now if it weren't for the pollen count and the effect it was having on his blasted sinuses. A midmorning appointment with his allergist took a big bite out of his day. The antihistamine prescribed for his problem was leaving him feeling tired and sluggish. By six o'clock he'd decided to hang it up and return to the city tomorrow morning from his home in Larchmont to finish up. Tonight he was going to party.

At quarter past six Phil Wright shrugged into his jacket, ran a comb through his hair, and headed for the elevators. Because he was coming back tomorrow he left his briefcase and rode downstairs unencumbered. It wasn't until he reached the lobby that he remembered to remove his wedding band and clip it to his key ring. The late September weather was holding nicely, pollen and all, and he didn't need his overcoat for the short walk across lower Manhattan via Fulton Street. When he arrived he found the Seaport mobbed as usual with the getaway-day crowd.

Downshift to casual: hands in pockets, coat draped over left forearm. His was a good suit, purchased last autumn on London's Bond Street. At six foot four and in good trim he wore such garments well. He knew his strawberry blond hair, strong jaw, and flashing blue eyes reinforced the image he cut. Wherever he went in life he'd always attracted attention. He saw it tonight as he watched the birds out of the corners of his eyes. There was that same familiar reaction; most of them trying to be coy about it, pretending they weren't really looking. Phillip knew differently. He knew they were impressed. But this was not yet the moment for conquests. Not here, not now. Gianni's was just up the way. The Brooklyn lager was flowing. His mates were no doubt deep in their drink. He had some catching up to do.

No sooner did Phillip enter the appointed watering hole than Craig Palmer exploded from his chair like a lava cap from an erupting volcano. "Oh ho! We'd about given you up for dead, Phil-boy!"

Palmer was a huge, happy-go-lucky bond trader who'd come to Wall Street via the cornfields of Nebraska. A true rugby enthusiast, he'd traveled to all corners of the crumbled British Empire playing the game. He fancied himself an Anglophile. Phillip had joined Palmer's Westchester Rugby Club shortly after arriving in the States six months ago.

Wright pulled up a chair, shook hands with rugger buddies all around the table, and sat to have three brimming pints of Brooklyn lined up on the table before him. Phil loosened his tie with great drama and extended his arms forward, fingers interlocked, to pop his knuckles. "How many of these am I behind?" he asked.

"All three," Hugo Mendez told him. The mad Argentine securities analyst had the pie-eyed look that he always got with a load on.

"Bloody hell! In half an hour?"

"We're just getting warmed up, Phil-boy! Down the hatch."

Wright lifted the first pint to his lips, threw his head back, and didn't come up for air until he'd drained it. Gasping, he slammed the mug to the table, wiped his mouth on the back of his jacket sleeve, and belched. By the time he'd drained the second in similar fashion, he'd drawn the undivided attention of every eye around the table. As he raised the third pint to his lips a steady chant of "Go! Go! Go!" started to his right and was quickly taken up by the whole group.

Bloated to painful capacity, Phillip watched Palmer refill one of those three mugs and slam the empty pitcher on the table.

"Next round's yours, Phil-boy. Drink up."

Wright noticed that everyone had a nearly full mug and that two more pitchers on the table still had plenty of beer in them. He relaxed a bit and lifted his glass. He sipped slowly this time, listening to a conversation develop around the game they were scheduled to play against a club from Greenwich come Sunday. Twenty minutes and a fourth beer later he scraped back his chair and rose to head for the gents.

"Take these empty pitchers with you, Phil-boy," Palmer suggested. "Save you having to tip a waitress."

Wright rolled his eyes and tapped one of the help on the shoulder in passing. "Three more pitchers of Brooklyn for that table there when you get a chance, right love?" She nodded brusquely and continued on her way while he moved past the crowded bar area to the restroom alcove. He'd all but forgotten about the antihistamine he took earlier that day, and right now it was mixing unfavorably with the two quarts of beer sloshing around in his guts. He usually held his liquor pretty well, but over the past twenty minutes he'd felt himself starting to get drunk with alarming speed. Once he gained the men's room he locked himself in one of the stalls and induced the vomiting of most if not all of the beer he'd consumed. The booze was really starting to buzz his brain now, the edges going a bit soft and rubbery. As he exited the stall and washed his face at one of the basins he cursed the effect that American air had on his respiratory system. He'd had allergies as a child but they were mostly to molds and had never been as bad as they were since moving across the Atlantic.

Phillip was so busy trying to maintain an air of nonchalance during the trip back to his table that he failed to see the woman approaching on a collision course. She was paying as little attention to where she was going as he was, and the impact was jarring. Wright's reflexes were still just good enough to enable his catching her before she took a tumble onto her backside. She'd been carrying a full glass of white wine. As he steadied her they both looked down to find her drink now soaking the front of her dress.

"I'm so sorry," he apologized. "How bloody stupid of me. Are you all right?"

He was having a bit of trouble tearing his eyes from the way the slinky fabric of that dress had gone translucent and plastered itself to her breasts. No doubt he would have had

62

trouble tearing his eyes from any woman's breasts, but these were special. For starters, she was wearing no brassiere. Even without support they seemed to defy gravity. Perched high and proud, their slightly upswept nipples had gone erect with the chill of the wine.

"Do you *mind*?" a cross yet melodic voice demanded.

Wright forced his eyes upward with effort only to be stunned all over again by the beauty of her face. He was truly torn. Even while annoyed she had a radiance that filled the space around her, occupying it. Her eyes held him poleaxed. As she leaned forward to unplaster her dress and shake some of the wetness from it, he found it impossible to follow the movement of her hands. Her gaze held him spellbound.

"It was my fault," he murmured. "Completely."

"Malarkey." More annoyance. "I wasn't watching where I was going neither."

"Wait a minute." The light of revelation dawned. "You're Irish!"

"And you're a clever one, aren't you? I'll bet you're just as good wit the Chinese, right?"

"Phil-boy! Your round! Who's that you're molesting over there?"

Wright ignored Palmer to continue staring into her eyes. She had a quick, sharp tongue to go with her good looks. God, he thought, maybe he'd died and gone to heaven.

"Listen. You *must* let me make this up to you."

"I must?" Eyebrows arched in *amused* annoyance now. "Why is that?"

"Because I've just run headlong into the most beautiful woman I've ever seen in my life. I think it's an event of divine providence."

The annoyance vanished to be replaced by a soft, faraway smile.

"That's sweet. But I don't think I'd better let you make anything up to me . . . uh . . . ?"

"Phillip. Phillip Wright. Why *shouldn't* you let me?"

The look got evasive. "I might be meeting someone soon.

I don't think it would look too good for me to be having a drink wit you.''

"You *might* be meeting someone?"

"It's complicated."

He snorted. "*Too* complicated. No man in his right mind would make a maybe-date with a woman like you."

She smiled again. "You've got no idea what I am, do you, Phillip?"

Confused, Wright frowned, his eyes leaving her face now to travel clear down the length of her, to the floor and back up again. That dress front wasn't quite as plastered to her breasts anymore, but it was still clinging a bit. The slinky fabric of it nipped in at the waist before riding back out again, stretching tight over slender but womanly hips. It ceased to exist about a foot above her knees. Her legs, encased in dark stockings, were well-turned and muscular, like a ballerina's.

"What you *are*?"

She leaned close, her breath warm in his ear. "I'm a *prostitute*, Phillip. For a thousand dollars a night I make men's dreams come true." That said, she backed away again batting her lashes. "But you don't go to hookers, do you Phillip? You're a big, strapping lad who gets birds easily enough wit'out having to pay such a preposterous sum. A thousand dollars, you're thinking. Imagine."

Again Wright was dumbstruck. He knew women like this existed, but all his experience contradicted everything he was seeing. Back home there were plenty of tough, hard-bitten tarts who strutted the pavements of London's Soho. In business he'd encountered the cool, detached women who worked the lounges of the nicer hotels, turned out in suits or elegant dresses. But this woman was something else altogether. Her sexuality, like everything else about her, was forthright. Direct. There even seemed to be warmth in her.

He chuckled, slowly shaking his head. "Come off it. You're pulling my leg."

Those eyes probed deep into his again. God, he'd bet she *could* make a man's dreams come true. A challenge flashed in that look now, burning like the blue heart of flame. "Believe what you want to believe. Me? I've got to run and change."

Wright glanced at his watch. "Wait. When was this someone supposed to be here?"

"He's flying in from Japan. The party who made the arrangements didn't know how tired he would be."

"And if he doesn't show up, you're out a thousand dollars?"

She laughed a gay, musical little laugh. "You *are* naive. If I wasn't paid already, I wouldn't be here. I'm booked for the weekend."

"But tonight," Phillip persisted. "If he doesn't show up tonight. That would mean you're free, right?"

"Free? Oh no, Phillip. I'm never free."

Wright surprised himself by removing his billfold from his inside jacket pocket, opening it, and digging into a tiny inner pocket. He watched the woman's eyes as he extracted a small packet of folded cash, flattened it, and fanned five crisp hundreds.

"I'll pay. This five now and the other as soon as we can get to my automated teller."

"You're serious."

He was drunk was what he was. A little voice screaming in the back of his head told him he was crazy. He was barely able to stand on his feet. His wife Julia's face flashed before his mind's eye. She hated these Friday night piss-ups as it was. He was going to have his work cut out for him, calling and trying to convince her that he was stuck at the office and staying in town tonight. Especially in his current condition. Maybe a bit later, once he could get his head straight. Maybe. Oh, what the hell, he would cross that bridge later.

"How much longer must you wait for this someone?" he asked. "I work for Lloyd's. My bank's got a machine downstairs from our offices in the World Trade Center. That's six downtown blocks from here."

"How convenient. I'm booked into a room at the Vista."

The Vista Hotel was situated directly between the two towers of the World Trade complex, just across the West Side Highway from the Hudson River and Battery Park City. She checked the time and shrugged.

"Be a pity to waste it, I s'pose. He was to be here by half six. I usually wait an hour, and it's quarter past seven now."

"I'll *wait* the fifteen minutes," he pressed.

"Phil-boy! What's the hang-up over there? Let's see your green. We're thirsty over here!"

She tipped her head toward that table of drunken rowdies across the room. "What about your mates, Phillip?"

He extracted another fifty from his billfold. After awkwardly fashioning it into a paper airplane he took aim and lofted it in Craig Palmer's direction. Palmer watched it with a quizzical expression and made a clumsy lunge when it arrived. "What's this?" he bellowed.

"The next round," Wright called back. "And the one after that."

"What the hell, Phil-boy? You've got perfectly good beer sitting here."

Wright slipped a hand along his newfound treasure's waist and applied gentle pressure, starting her toward the door. "You drink it, Craigie. I just met the girl of my dreams."

When they reached the promenade outside Gianni's, the beautiful woman peered at her watch and smiled. "I think I've waited long enough for my date, Phillip. He won't be coming tonight. I've been at this long enough to know."

Wright grinned happily and gestured toward the west. "It's a beautiful evening. Would you prefer to walk or take a cab?"

"Walk," she replied. "You look to've had a fair amount to drink. Maybe some air will help you get your wits straight."

He leered down at her. "My *wits* straight? It's not my wits you should be worried about, beautiful. And you shouldn't be worried there either. You've got me as hot as a stud ram in rut."

"A stud ram finishes his business in an awful hurry, Phillip. Try to let your imagination go. We've got all night."

Wright peered once again into those fathomless blue eyes and any gnawing misgivings took flight. This was a chance of a bloody lifetime. In the parlance of Wall Street, a thousand dollars was chump change for a night spent with a woman this hot.

"I don't even know your name."

"Call me Deirdre."

"*Call* you that? It isn't your name?"

That wan smile again. He thought he detected a sadness in it now.

"This is a fantasy, Phillip. Your wildest dream come true." The smile widened, that brief sadness vanishing. "In it I'm Deirdre. Deirdre O'Dreams."

SEVEN

Melissa Busby hated hospitals. They always got her thinking about her mother and brother. Both had entered a hospital through its front doors and been carried out via the basement. Ted was the first, dead of a rare blood disorder at age fifteen. Melissa was eleven. Then came her mother, who'd lingered and finally died of head injuries inflicted by a hit-and-run driver. Melissa was a junior in high school at the time. Today, eighteen years after her mother's death, Melissa couldn't enter a hospital without being overwhelmed by the memories.

University Hospital had a special power to evoke dread. Her mother was Christmas shopping in midtown when she was hit, and it was here that she was taken in the wake of her accident. While statistics suggested that University might be the best hospital in the entire country, Melissa's feelings were not tempered as she entered its lobby. When she called ahead half an hour ago Garfield's surgeon agreed to meet with her for an update. He'd sounded exhausted. Now, as she loitered before the lobby elevators, she noticed that they hadn't changed any since her last visit. She might well have spent an entire day of her life standing in this same spot, waiting for these infamously slow cars to arrive.

When she reached her floor, the act of stepping onto the Neurological ICU was sickeningly familiar. Garfield's doctor was waiting for her at the nurse's station. Dark-eyed, slender, with fine features, he extended a hand while introducing himself.

"Paul Brandeis, Detective."

Melissa shook, forcing herself to be upbeat. "Any relation to the Supreme Court justice?"

He grinned. "Maybe. He was Jewish. So am I."

She liked a guy who could keep his sense of humor, even under duress. This one had performed an eight-hour surgical procedure today. "Touché, Doc. How's our man?"

"In a word? Lucky. He's breathing on his own. There's a full range of responses to stimuli. Excepting the deafness in his right ear and a partial facial paralysis, we're hopeful of a full recovery."

"Can I talk to him?"

"You can *talk* to a wall, Detective. The question is whether Garfield can absorb any of what you say. Right now he's probably still pretty groggy from the anesthetic. Maybe for another twelve hours."

"I'd like to try."

Brandeis didn't see any reason why not and led her down the hall to the same unit where her mother had died. The doctor must have seen the look on her face as she paused, gathering herself, at the door.

"Something wrong?"

She shook it off. "No." And then closed her eyes, nodding. "My mother died in there."

"I see."

She opened her eyes, ready to tell him that no, he didn't see at all. The face she confronted was full of obvious compassion.

"In my business I lose as many as I win," he told her. "I've got two in there right now who won't make it, short of an act of God." His tone was low, almost reverent. "I see a lot of the same anger as you're feeling right now, every day."

It was like he'd read her mind. "How did you know what I'm feeling?"

"Just a good guess. When I say I lose as many as I win,

I'm not talking baseball or profit and loss in business, officer. I'm talking about human lives.''

Brandeis led the way inside and to the foot of Detective Chester Garfield's bed. Swathed in bandages, the entire right side of the wounded man's head was hidden. Monitoring equipment measuring his vital signs loomed alongside, blinking soundlessly in the subdued light. He seemed to be breathing regularly, his left eye closed as though in sleep.

"Chet." The neurosurgeon's voice was gentle, soothing. Melissa watched as the doctor reached to place a reassuring hand on the wounded cop's chest. She noticed how delicate that hand was: carefully manicured, the nails cut short and their edges polished smooth. Surgeon's hands.

Garfield's left lid fluttered, and the eye slowly opened. There wasn't a lot of focus in the way he looked at Brandeis.

"Someone here to see you, Chet."

Busby stepped forward, her shield case held open so Garfield could see her tin. The eye blinked, and his mouth moved as he swallowed.

"I'm Detective Busby, Chet. Major Case squad. You walked into a real hornet's nest today, didn't you."

The eye sustained a steady but blank regard. Half the face then frowned. "W-what happened to me?" It was almost a whisper. "Head feels like mush."

Melissa forced a reassuring smile. "*You* tell *me* what happened, Chet."

Another frown. "Shot."

She nodded. "What can you tell me about it, Chet? Who shot you?"

He started to shake his head and winced for his trouble. "Ongh! Hurts! Ah fuck, it hurts!"

"Who did you see, Chet?"

Garfield's focus remained vague. "Dead. Naked."

"Yes, Chet. Ralph Kane and his girlfriend."

"On the floor."

"Did you see who killed them, Chet? Who shot you?"

The eye closed. "Tired."

70

The surgeon's hand touched Melissa lightly on the shoulder.

"Let's not push him tonight. He needs rest. He should be a great deal more lucid in the morning."

Melissa gave it up and followed Brandeis back out into the hall.

"Is that unusual, Doctor? That he seemed to be able to recall bits and pieces, even in that state? God, he's zonked."

The surgeon's head, with its thinning hair and bemused eyes, moved slowly from side to side. "He's had a terribly traumatic experience, Detective. After this sort of injury *everything* the human brain retains or blanks out about the experience seems a little unusual. His memory of events might be quite good. The emergency room staff says he experienced periods of lucidity down there. He's a big, healthy guy with a lot of reserve strength to draw on."

"What time can I see him in the morning?"

He shrugged. "Anytime, I suppose. He won't be anywhere near this docile, so come prepared. He'll be in a good deal of pain. That could make him irritable. Your next interview might be less cordial."

Melissa grinned. "No problem there, Doc. I can handle less cordial." As Melissa extended a hand and Brandeis shook it, she saw how deep his exhaustion ran. "I appreciate your sticking around to meet with me, Doc. I know you must be whipped."

"Not a problem," he replied. "I get pretty wrapped up in a case after that kind of surgery. It usually takes me a few hours to unwind."

As Deirdre inserted the key into the knob of her hotel room door, Phillip Wright leaned close to inhale the scent of her. Ten minutes ago he'd handed her the other half of her thousand-dollar fee. Now she was his. His to have and to use in any way he desired. He loved the way her backside felt as he ran the palm of his hand over it. Fabulous; as hard and taut to the touch as a gazelle's flank. He loved the strength he could feel as she got the door open and started into the room.

"You've never seen dreams like my dreams," he whispered into her ear. "Not like the dream I've got of us right now."

She stopped inside the door, letting him come full up against her for the first time and press himself into her. "Is that right, Phillip? You're feeling good right now?"

He chuckled; it came from deep in his throat. "Good? I'm feeling something considerably better than good."

She took each of his hands in hers, lifted and eased out of his embrace. With an exaggerated, seductive swaying of her hips she stepped into the middle of the room and kicked off her shoes. One hand swept her hair forward and held it there as the other reached to find the zipper at the nape of her neck.

"I'd love it if you'd help me wit this, Phillip."

"Only if you'll return the favor, beautiful."

He was sure he saw her mouth crease in a smile as he stepped up to tug the zipper clear down the length of her marvellous back. Gently he peeled the slinky fabric right and left, pushing it forward across her shoulders and exposing her milk white flesh. There were no tan lines here. Her muscles were tight and well defined. Again; like a dancer's. As he leaned to drag his tongue up along her spine his hands gripped her hips. In a series of quick, urgent thrusts he drove his pelvis hard against her backside.

"Will you bloody *look* at that," Paul Murphy marveled. "The fucking Brit wants to *bugger* her. Shit. That's disgusting."

Murphy, with Billy Mannion sitting alongside, sat staring at a dim but graphic picture on the video monitor screen before them. Their own room was a mirror image of the room they watched next door; king-size bed, love seat, armchair, writing desk, dresser, television, and bath beyond. The modern miracles of fiber optics, hypersensitive microphones, and low-light video recording technology were bringing the room on the other side of the wall right into this one. The scene they watched was simultaneously being recorded on the cassette in the Handycam at their feet. The two watched eagerly as the Lloyd's risk assessment manager rushed headlong into his liaison, indulging in the frenzied pawing at, slobbering over, and dry humping of their beautiful bait.

Siobhan's orders were simple enough. Lure the Brit here and get him to compromise himself as graphically as possible. She seemed to have had little problem luring him, and right now he was so intent on compromise that he might not have time to disrobe. Very little participation was being required on Siobhan's part.

Then, just as suddenly as he'd thrown himself into it, the big Brit backed off, his breath coming hard enough for the microphone to pick it up. Siobhan straightened and spoke, her voice low and throaty, like the purr of a cat.

"I thought you were headed for the finish line right out of the gate, Phillip."

He laughed, his fingers working the knot of his tie before stripping it from his collar. "Got a bit carried away there, didn't I?"

"Carried away? Ah no, Phillip. That's what a fantasy's all about."

Next to him, Paul Murphy noticed Mannion fidgeting. Billy had those worry beads he'd carried home from Tripoli and was working them fiercely between the thumb and forefinger of his right hand. On the screen Siobhan was wriggling out of her dress. The Brit's efforts had already hiked it up over her hips, and the garment still hung from her upper arms. Getting out of it was a simple matter of grabbing hold and tugging it over her head. As Wright watched, his own urgent attempts to disrobe became a confused, awkward fumble of fingers.

"Here," Siobhan offered. "Let me help you."

"Jesus 'n' Mary," Murphy hissed. "He's crocked. Right up to his bleeding eyeballs."

"Just so's he's capable," Billy growled.

There was venom in it, and Murphy turned, puzzled. "You're not having any second thoughts, are you, Billy? I know she was your girlfriend once, but that's been over for years. You said so yourself."

"Sod off," Billy snarled.

Murphy nodded back toward the screen. "There go any doubts concerning his capability."

The Brit was now rid of his jacket, shirt, and tie. Siobhan was squatted before him with his trousers down around his ankles. Lifting one foot at a time, she freed him of them and started to rise, her thumbs hooking into the waistband of her hose.

Tension gripped the two observers as the Brit planted the palm of a hand atop her head to stop her progress. Slowly he pushed her back to her knees.

"That's not my fantasy right now, beautiful. This is."

Both of those big hands cupped her head, pulling her toward him.

Angry and exhausted but still determined, Joe Dante returned home from his dinner with Gus Lieberman. His determination ran the gamut from the avenging of a sixteen-year-old girl's senseless death to rubbing a chickenshit mayor's face in proof of his own gutlessness. The vehicle toward both ends was going to be Billy Mannion. Joe would find him and bring him down even if it meant defying an FBI hands-off order. Vivid pictures of the terror on that sixteen-year-old's face kept flashing before his mind's eye. Alternating with them were images of Mannion's face; that look of absolute indifference.

There were work lights ablaze all through Dante's half-finished 27th Street loft as he stepped off the freight elevator. Back in the area of his new kitchen the song of a gravel-voiced female singer and a hard-driving rock band filled the air. Harmonizing alongside the recording was the live voice of a woman sounding remarkably similar.

"Diana?"

The harmonizing stopped, and the volume of the recorded music dropped. As Dante paused to remove his jacket and hang it in the makeshift closet a woman appeared in his kitchen doorway.

"Hi, Joe." Her speaking voice sounded nothing at all like her singing. She inclined her head back toward the kitchen and waved a paintbrush at it. "I had a few minutes this afternoon. Guess I got carried away. What time is it?"

Dante unclipped his weapon from his belt and set it atop the television in passing. "Just after eight. I thought you were in the studio until midnight."

The woman who stepped from the doorway into his living room was wearing a pair of paint-dabbed bib overalls, a sleeveless T-shirt, and beat-up canvas skippies. The legs of her overalls were rolled to the knee, and she had nearly as much paint on her bare calves as she'd gotten on Joe's kitchen woodwork. Pleasant-featured, she had the bright eyes, peaches-and-cream complexion, and wide, goofy grin of a fun-loving girl next door. She was actually the girl from upstairs, and her current appearance was a bit deceiving. Diana Webster was better known to rock audiences of the world as the glamorous lead singer of Queen of Beasts, a band whose last album sold in excess of three million copies. Dump the baggy overalls, pour the body hidden beneath into a skin-tight, sequined jumpsuit, and watch out. This girl next door could melt hearts.

"Danny's been fighting a flu bug for the past two days. He showed up this morning looking green. We took pity."

Danny Phipps was the Queen of Beasts' bass player.

"You hear anything from our boy?" Dante asked. Diana's husband and Joe's combination best friend/landlord was currently in Tokyo installing a work commissioned by the Nissan Corporation. A sculptor, Brian Brennan was an acknowledged star in his own right.

"Just this morning. He's close to being finished with the actual work, but they're wining and dining him to distraction. He isn't sure *when* he's getting back."

Dante'd reached the kitchen doorway, pecked her on the cheek, and now peeked inside. For all the paint she'd managed to get on herself she was actually meticulous with a brush. Brennan and Dante had built the kitchen cabinetry themselves in Brian's upstairs shop. They'd hung it all three weeks ago. The countertops and tile backsplash were in place, and Diana was helping with the finishing touches. Joe was on his way in for a closer look when his neighbor noticed his bandaged right hand.

"Oh Christ, Joe. What now?" In the six years she'd known him, Diana had seen Dante slashed, shot, and in various other ways mauled in the line of duty. Now she saw his eyes cloud as he shook his head.

"I take it you didn't watch the news."

"Sorry. I've been obsessed with trying to figure a better harmony for one of our new tunes."

Joe glanced over at her portable cassette player perched on the table of his breakfast nook. The start, stop, and rewind buttons were smeared with paint.

"What happened, Joe?" Diana pressed.

Dante opened the cabinet housing his meager wine collection and pulled a bottle of red at random. "An action I took this morning got an innocent bystander killed, Di. A sixteen-year-old girl."

He placed the bottle on the counter and pulled the cork while relating the details of the incident and his suspension.

"I've been over and over it a hundred times in my head. I was confronted by a butcher with the blood of God knows how many people on his hands. A guy who trained with Abu Nidal and the PLO in one of Qaddafi's camps, for Crissake. And there I was standing toe-to-toe with him. What the fuck was I supposed to do? Tell him to have a nice day?"

Diana left her brush in a jar of thinner and approached to

run a calming hand up and down her friend's back. "You did what you thought you had to do, Joe."

"That doesn't make Courtney Poole any less dead, does it?"

Diana dropped her hand to her side. "No, I don't suppose it does." She stood a moment contemplating the hurt in his face. "This smoke-screen suspension. What does that mean? Are they saying you can't go after this guy?"

"Would I give a fuck, even if they did?"

"I've met Hubie Poole, Joe. It was at one of those Bowling with the Stars benefits the Second Stage does. Not to speak ill of a man who's just lost a child, but that guy's an asshole. A very *powerful* asshole. Be careful. He can make big trouble for you."

"I didn't kill his daughter, Di. Billy Mannion killed her, whether Hubie Poole wants to believe it or not. What *I* did was fuck up. I knew the man was dangerous and *still* underestimated him."

"You're human, Joe." Diana pointed to the bottle he'd set on the counter. "And tonight you're going to try to dull it a bit, right?"

Dante scowled. "I've got to get some sleep somehow. The longer I let this maggot Mannion crawl loose, the deeper he digs his hole." He opened an overhead cabinet containing stemware. "You gonna join me?"

Diana sighed and wrapped her arms around his waist to hug him close, the strength of her loyalty fierce. "I think maybe I'd better."

EIGHT

At ten o'clock on Saturday morning Amanda Gregory-Kane and her daughter Elizabeth met in the Helmsley Building offices of Quinn, Oliver, and Sellers for the reading of Ralph Kane's last will and testament. It had rankled Amanda's father that Ralph insisted on using a college pal when he embarked on the Magnetronics venture. For nearly two hundred years only one law firm had handled all Gregory family business. Benton Gregory viewed Joshua Sellers and his partners as upstarts. In time they became prosperous enough, but in the mind of the old patriarch they lacked a most valuable asset. They lacked history.

While Ben Gregory found Josh Sellers to be the least polished and presentable kind of attorney, Ralph knew Sellers to possess a brilliant legal mind. Back in 1965 when Ralph incorporated Magnetronics he'd consulted with Ben Gregory's firm first and felt ill-treated by them. It was his contention that the Gregory lawyers viewed his enterprise as no more than an amusing distraction. After refusing to deal further with them he'd taken it to the young and struggling Josh Sellers. Because Ralph was a friend, Josh was willing to break one of the legal profession's cardinal rules. He did the Magnetronics legal work in exchange for a 10 percent interest in the company. When Magnetronics went public in 1971, Ralph retained 51 percent control of the company, Sellers retained his 10 percent, and common shares were issued for the other 39. Today Josh Sellers was a very rich man.

Amanda also held some of her proud father's disdain for Josh Sellers, but she didn't actually dislike him. Right now, seated across from her in his big leather chair, Josh seemed uncomfortable with the business before him. He fidgeted. Some years ago he'd started dragging lank strands of hair across the crown of his head the way self-conscious bald men do. Amanda could see sweat glistening in the bare spots. The attorney's chair also swiveled herky-jerky from side to side.

"Ahem. I want to thank you for coming here today. Amanda. Elizabeth. I know this is a terrible time for you, and I want you to know I also share your sense of loss. Ralph was a good friend for nearly forty years. You have my sympathies and this *firm's* sympathies. I understand the service has been arranged for Monday?"

"At Trinity," Amanda replied. "Eleven o'clock. He's being cremated, and his ashes will be placed in my family's crypt."

"Anything I or this firm can do," he assured her.

Amanda thanked him, and Sellers moved to address her daughter.

"I don't know how much you know about the legal history of your parents' marriage, Elizabeth. Your mother's family asked your father to waive all right of election as part of a prenuptial agreement. Through it he renounced all claim on assets and income your mother inherited from the Gregory trust."

Amanda glanced briefly at her daughter's impassive face. They still hadn't spoken since yesterday's blowup in front of that detective. Elizabeth sat, as cool as ever, not a hint of emotion betrayed.

"At that time we insisted on one stipulation," Sellers continued. "We deemed it only fair that your mother's access to his assets and income also be limited. In the end that's how the prenuptial document was written. Your mother waived right of election to your father's property. He was free to dispose of his own assets as he saw fit.''

"You might also mention that I was the one who later pushed him into writing a will,'' Amanda interrupted. She wished he would dispense with the background and get on with it. "Not at first, because he *had* no assets. But when Magnetronics went public, Ralph was suddenly worth a lot of money. You were only nine years old, and I was trying to protect your interest. I thought it unwise to risk your father's dying intestate. It would have eaten up half the estate just trying to untangle the mess in probate.''

Elizabeth averted her face, her eyes on the attorney. "My mother's a Gregory. It's likely that she saw a good thing getting out of her control. A Gregory would hate that.''

Amanda saw red. "We were husband and wife, for God's sake!'' She turned to Sellers. "My lawyers provided you with a copy of my will at the time, did they not?''

Sellers nodded. "They did.''

"And did it not leave everything to Ralph?'' Amanda demanded.

"Everything in your control. Yes.''

"And what does *that* mean?'' Elizabeth countered. "The men in the Gregory family have always controlled everything.''

"Your mother's investment assets were substantial,'' Sellers explained. "There is no tax on an estate passing between husband and wife. Her attorneys provided your father with a full disclosure of what your mother was bequeathing him despite his having waived all rights to it.'' He picked up a manila envelope, unwound the string clasp, and removed the contents. "Shall we proceed?''

Amanda only half listened as the lawyer dispensed with the usual "of sound mind and body'' preamble before getting into the meat of the document.

". . . the cash sum of three million dollars each to my undergraduate alma mater, Princeton University, and my graduate studies alma mater, the University of California at Berkeley.''

"Excuse me," Amanda stopped him. "There was a codicil added? Ralph didn't *have* six million dollars when he wrote his will. Not in cash."

Sellers shook his head. "Not a codicil, Amanda. Since the execution of that first will, Ralph had me rewrite it completely on two occasions. May I continue?"

A sense of foreboding gripped Amanda. She nodded, the color drained from her face.

"My remaining cash and securities assets exclusive of my interest in Magnetronics Corporation are hereby bequeathed to my daughter, Elizabeth." Sellers paused and looked to Elizabeth. "There is a life insurance trust in place which is designed to cover any inheritance taxes on these monies. You are the sole beneficiary."

Amanda didn't like it but knew Ralph was more approving of their daughter than she was. Elizabeth had joined her father's company straight out of business school to work in marketing. Ralph always hated the commerce end of the business and seemed to appreciate Elizabeth's enthusiasm for it. This was something he would do.

Alongside Amanda, Elizabeth seemed to sit up straighter.

"Lastly, I bequeath my twenty percent interest in the Magnetronics Corporation to my wife, Amanda. . . ."

"*Twenty* percent?!" Amanda fairly gasped it. "Where's the other thirty-one?"

Sellers looked up from the document. "Twenty percent is all he ever owned; at least outright. When he decided to take the company public he was worried about control of the company in the event of his death. Thirty-one percent was put in trust, in Elizabeth's name. Ralph was one trustee, and I am the other. Two years ago it was amended to revert to Elizabeth's control should Ralph predecease her." The attorney made this declaration matter-of-factly, his eyes clouded with a faraway look. "Ralph was very happy to see the interest

Elizabeth showed in his creation, Amanda. He felt you were never terribly supportive of it.''

The room did funhouse gyrations before Amanda's eyes. "But . . . that's *outrageous!*"

"He didn't seem to think so. You are a woman of independent means. Twenty percent of Magnetronics is still worth a great deal. In my recent discussions with him, Ralph seemed to feel that Elizabeth is quite capable of guiding the company in the direction he envisioned for it.''

Amanda was unable to control an involuntary shaking of her limbs and gripped the arms of her chair so hard her knuckles went white. "I'll sue, Josh. She and her lesbian girlfriend did this. They alienated my husband's affections.'' She turned abruptly to her daughter. "My own flesh and blood. I never approved of your sexual perversion, so you stuck this knife in my back!''

"You're ranting, Mother. I was nine years old in 1971.''

"*Ranting?* I wouldn't put it past you and your jealousy to kill him and that dyke slut yourself!''

Elizabeth heaved herself to her feet, her bearing erect and her face wooden. "Time for one of your pills, Mother. Maybe two or three. I'll be in touch with you, Josh. Thanks for your time. I've got a busy schedule.''

Amanda hadn't finished. "You think you can just walk out of here? You won't get away with this. I *will* litigate, Elizabeth. My lawyers will tie you in so many knots, you won't be able to move for a millennium.''

Elizabeth's regard for her mother was still cool, controlled. "Move, Mother? Where would I want to move? I control thirty-one percent of a company worth in excess of five hundred million dollars. I have a job with it that pays me two hundred and twenty thousand dollars a year. I like where I am just fine.''

As always the morning after put a different slant on Phillip Wright's infidelity than the lure of it had the night before. He realized, once the woman who called herself Deirdre showered, dressed, and left at eight o'clock this morning, that he never asked how to reach her again. The moment she passed beyond that door she disappeared from his life.

Not that Phillip considered her departure necessarily a bad thing. Surely, she'd plucked more than a few of his strings, and yes, she looked magnificent with her clothes off. But he was so primed by the time she took him into her mouth that he'd been unable to restrain himself. Release came instantaneously. Chagrined, he'd insisted on mounting her immediately, but even that was short-lived. The four pints of beer he'd consumed conspired to lay him low. Phillip had fallen off to sleep within half an hour of entering the hotel. He had a dim recollection of trying to have another go at her at some time during the night. The room started to spin before he got very far. Soon thereafter he was hugging the commode. Somewhere in the wee hours he awakened on the bathroom floor and dragged himself back to bed. In the final analysis Phillip had paid a whore a thousand dollars for a blowjob. Deirdre was cordial on her departure, but not nearly as captivating as she'd been in seducing his wallet.

He breakfasted downstairs in the hotel, going light on the toast and eggs and heavy on the Bloody Marys. The booze did a little something for a pounding headache and nothing for the guilt gnawing at the pit of his stomach. He was seated at his desk now. The report on that grain carrier was spread before him. For the moment he was totally unable to focus on it. Instead he confronted the knowledge that he'd never called Julia last night. No matter how he examined it, the consequences of that oversight looked grim.

"Morning, Phillip."

Saturdays were generally dead around there. Occasionally the cleaning crew might happen onto the floor to catch up on their windows or carpet shampooing, but they always made plenty of noise on arrival and had never yet greeted him by his Christian name. The sudden appearance of a stranger in his doorway gave him quite a start.

"Do I know you?" he asked. Irritation was clear in his tone.

"Ah. Got a bit of a hangie, do we?"

"I beg your pardon?" Wright was confused now. This tall, angular fellow confronting him was far too striking for Phillip to have forgotten meeting him. No, he was sure he hadn't.

"There's no need to beg, Phillip. All will be revealed, I assure you." The accent was Irish. That was confusing, too. Wright watched the man enter and saw he was carrying a nylon equipment bag.

Phillip came out of his chair to confront this interloper face-to-face. "What's the meaning of this? Who *are* you? And what do you think you're doing? This is my *private* office."

The visitor stopped on the other side of the desk to set the case between them and unzip it. "Who *am* I, Phillip?" He shrugged. "A friend of a friend, I suppose. Give me a minute, and I'll show you what I mean." While he spoke the stranger removed a Sony Watchman from his case, propped it on the desk where Phillip could see the screen, and clipped on the input lead from a compact video camera. "Here we go then."

When the screen of the tiny television lit and an image appeared, Phillip got a nasty knot in the pit of his stomach. The scene was all too familiar. He was watching the empty interior of the hotel room in which he'd spent the night. And as he watched the door opened. Deirdre appeared first with him following, his hands all over her.

"Stop it!" he demanded.

"But why, Phillip? We ha'ent even gotten to the good parts yet. The parts your wife is *really* going to enjoy."

Phillip launched himself and was in midair, outstretched over the top of his desk, when he discovered how nimble the stranger was. The man sidestepped his lunge with the quickness of a matador, and Phillip landed hard, the front edge of his desk catching him in the ribs beneath his right armpit.

He lay there, wincing with the pain of it and trying to recover himself as the precise, definite click of metal on metal reached his ears. A split second later the coolness of a gun muzzle touched him just beneath the chin.

"You think I'm stupid enough to let fucking scum like you get the drop on me, Phillip? Ah no, laddie. I cut my eyeteeth on pricks the likes of you."

The words were spoken just inches from Wright's left ear, the breath they rode on as hot as the hatred behind them.

"What do you want?" Wright gasped.

"That's better, Phillip. No more of these macho displays. Agreed? If you'll just sit back in your chair like a good fellow, I'll explain."

When Wright started to push himself upright, a hand temporarily restrained him.

"One other thing, Phillip. Your wife's name is Julia. Not much up top but nice legs. You have a three-year-old daughter named Carolyn. You and your family currently reside on Mayhew Street in Larchmont. I'll tell you right here at the outset that should I not receive your full cooperation, not only your wife but also your direct superiors here and in London will receive copies of last night's escapade. Are we clear on that?"

Wright nodded.

"Fine then. Sit back and listen. My friends and I need your assistance in obtaining certain, ah, materials."

Melissa Busby and Guy Napier spent the first four hours of their Saturday tour interviewing Overton House staff. Recollections of events often changed with time. An interview subject was less tempted to try too hard or tell too much once the bright lights faded. And even when stories remained the same, an alert detective could often pick something out between the words; something that was missed in the earlier telling. This morning they'd found most of yesterday's information substantiated. Veronica Tierney's schedule of appearances here was as precise as clockwork. For a year she'd arrived at the Overton House every Thursday evening; always by cab, usually by eight, and rarely later than nine. She would leave on Sunday evenings with much the same regularity. She and Kane went out occasionally for a brief meal or shopping trip. When they did, it was generally on foot. For the most part they dressed casually.

Once Busby and Napier finished their interviews, they toured the crime scene again. They were loitering in the living room after that inspection when Napier broke an extended silence.

"Something strikes me as odd."

"About what?"

"This whole setup. Jumbo says Mrs. Kane knew about this apartment. She knew that Ralph locked himself away here every weekend, supposedly to work. What she didn't know about, or so she claims, was the affair her husband was having."

Melissa wasn't following his direction yet. "Okay. So?"

"What kind of shops line the street outside this place? Who patronizes them?"

Madison Avenue outside the Overton House was arguably the most exclusive stretch of shopping east of Rodeo Drive.

"You mean those boutiques with only ten or twelve dresses in them, each going for twice what I make in a month?"

"Right," Guy replied. "And all those filthy rich babes who have nothing better to do with their time than wander up one side of Madison and down the other, spending money. If they feel energetic, they might work west a block and poke into Bergdorf's. Veronica Tierney had a Bergdorf's card in her pocketbook. These people here say Kane was usually with her when she went out. Just walking out the front door he was on the one sidewalk where his wife or one of her friends was most likely to see her."

"What you're saying is that Ralph wasn't trying too hard to keep his affair a secret."

"You got it."

"Okay, but *everyone* seemed to know that Ralph and Veronica were working together. Wouldn't they go out to lunch occasionally? Maybe stop into a store on the way back?''

Napier made a wry face and shook his head. ''You saw her, Mel. How many friends is he gonna meet on the street and get to swallow a business lunch story? Take my word; when she walked down the street she made people's eyes pop. . . . And I don't care *what* sorta whiz she was with a fucking computer.''

As Napier spoke Melissa couldn't resist prowling some more. She'd started back down the hall and threw her response over her shoulder. ''What you're saying is Amanda Kane *had* to know. So answer this: What's her motive for lying about it?''

''Good question.'' Napier followed now and together they entered the master bedroom. ''I'd be interested to know what her friends thought was going on. If they were good friends, they'd tell her. If they weren't, it'd be all over the rich-bitch grapevine.''

''We've got to work on some of this gender-specific trash coming out of your mouth, big guy.'' As she said it, Melissa stood idly pawing through the beautiful clothes hanging in the bedroom closet. Here and there she paused to finger fabric or examine a label. These were all top-quality designer garments. The shoes in the rack were beautiful Italian creations, many with matching handbags. Veronica Tierney had lived well.

Napier's attention was drawn not to the clothing and accessories but to a handsome oxblood leather briefcase wedged between the shoe rack and the end wall of the closet. He remembered seeing one of the Crime Scene Unit techs examining its contents and dusting it for prints yesterday morning; remembered being surprised to see it crammed with computer printout. Curious as to why it was left here instead of in the makeshift office across the hall, he stooped to draw it out and lay it on the bed.

''What's up?'' Melissa asked.

Napier shook his head while digging through the thick

wad of printout. Nothing he read there made any sense to him. "What do you suppose all this means?" he wondered.

Melissa crossed to his side, pondered the cryptic calculations a moment, and shrugged. "More Greek."

"That's strange." Napier withdrew a pair of three-and-a-half-inch floppy disks from one of the lid's back pockets and stood tapping them against the palm of his other hand.

"*What* is?"

"It should have occurred to me before. They've got a computer set up in that office over there. State-of-the-art Macintosh FX. There's huge hard-drive capacity with a machine like that, but they'd want to back a lot of their data up on floppies like these. I don't remember seeing a single one. Look." He pointed to a designation code hand-lettered in ink on a self-sticking label. It read:

SupCon Prod "N"

The other disk had a similar code, with the letter "O" following the designation.

"N and O," Melissa speculated.

"Yep. Makes you wonder where A through M went, doesn't it?"

NINE

Joshua Sellers had intended to drive up to his country place in Columbia County that Saturday afternoon, see if he could salvage some of the weekend. Instead he received a call from a Sergeant Richardson, asking to see him at one o'clock. The sergeant explained that because Sellers not only acted as Magnetronics's chief corporate counsel but also as Ralph Kane's personal attorney, Josh might be able to offer the Kane homicide investigation unique insight.

It was a bit more than an hour since Amanda and Elizabeth Kane departed the Quinn, Oliver, and Sellers offices. Josh had used some of the time to draft letters to the presidents of Princeton and Berkeley. At noon he faxed a lunch order to the Carnegie Deli. Hot pastrami and Gruyère on rye. The attorney was in the middle of eating his sandwich when one of the weekend word-processing staff showed Sergeant Richardson to his office door. Richardson entered as Sellers hastily grabbed a napkin, wiped his fingers, and rose to shake hands.

"Please come in, Sergeant. Have a seat."

"Looks like I've interrupted lunch. Sorry. I guess I'm a few minutes early."

"No problem. If you'd care to join me, I can send out and get you something."

Richardson thanked him and declined. "Afraid I'm one'a those guys who's gotta watch his weight."

Christopher Newman

Maybe, Sellers thought, but the big black detective was by no means fat. *Competent* sprang to the attorney's mind; as in hard and tough. The detective took a chair.

"From our phone conversation it sounds like you've got quite a few questions, Sergeant. Before you get started I've got just one of my own. Have you people made any headway?"

"Pretty simple to answer that one, I'm afraid," the detective replied. "Nobody's come forward and confessed. We're working all the available angles."

"I appreciate your frankness. Okay, your turn."

Richardson gave him an easy smile. "I'm wondering what you can tell us about the deceased, Mr. Sellers. How well you knew him. How long. Things like that. It's interesting that you're both his corporate and his personal counsel. Is that unusual?"

"Not really. Not when one considers our history." Sellers paused, looking back over thirty years. "Ralph Kane and I met in a physics class at Princeton in 1957. I was taking it mostly because I thought it would look good on the transcript. Ralph studied physics because he loved it. When we became friends he helped me see that world through eyes I never knew I had." He smiled sadly, the memory fond. "Ralph was a man of tremendous imagination, you see. I'm afraid I wasn't."

"1957. That's thirty-five years. It sounds like Kane was sort of a mentor."

"I guess he was. In many regards." Sellers stared off again into an unseen distance. "Those were heady times. Kerouac published *On the Road* that year. The villain Joe McCarthy dropped dead. Congress passed the first-ever civil rights bill. I was living in the same world my parents lived in; isolated from what came to be called the counterculture. Ralph helped open the doors to that world."

"And you *stayed* friends."

"Yes, we did. We lost touch for a while when Ralph went West to work on his Ph.D. and I stayed here in the East to

90

study law. Ralph was out there from sixty to early sixty-five. He met Amanda, and they had Elizabeth. Never did get his doctorate. Not the program's fault; Ralph was just moving too fast for them. He'd been doing a lot of work with accelerated particles and magnetic field theory. He'd married an heiress. In sixty-five he came back here to New York looking for financing to produce some of his revolutionary new technologies.''

''Did Mrs. Kane help him with that?'' Richardson asked. ''To find the financing, that is?''

Sellers took a moment to think it over, wondering how much he was prepared to divulge. Amanda and Liz Kane now held huge interests in the company he represented. Still, there was certain ground the police had a responsibility to cover.

''Let me put it this way, Sergeant. There are certain circumstances peculiar to Mrs. Kane's situation. Yes, she is an heiress to the Gregory fortune, but that fortune is largely controlled by her brother Jonathan. Her maintenance is provided for, but she has no control over the assets. When she and Ralph came East with their baby girl, all Amanda could do was intercede with her father on Ralph's behalf. Old Benton Gregory indulged her by having his attorneys go through the motions, but Ralph wasn't satisfied with how they handled him. He got back in touch with me. I looked over what he was proposing and encouraged him to try and make a go of it *without* major financing. Within a year of incorporation he obtained his first patent. The technology behind it revolutionized medical radiology. Ralph got rich.''

Richardson smiled again. ''I understand you did, too. Was that just a simple case'a being in the right place at the right time?''

Sellers wasn't at all surprised to learn how deeply his association with Magnetronics had been researched. The police would treat a homicide like this with the very highest priority.

''More or less. Ralph couldn't pay me up front. He offered

me a ten percent interest in the venture instead. I had a lot
of faith in Ralph Kane's imagination. I saw the way he held
people spellbound with his ideas—other people in his field.
Once he got cranked up it was hard *not* to believe him.''

"But Amanda Kane's father chose not to.''

This comment evoked a chuckle. "Much to his chagrin,
Sergeant. The Gregory family was heavily invested in domestic oil exploration at the time of the post–Arab embargo
glut. The strain of it is what probably killed old Ben. Today
I don't imagine his son Jon is scraping the bottom of too
many barrels, but that one giant hit they took really staggered
them. I'm sure old Ben Gregory went to his grave kicking
himself for failing to see his son-in-law's potential.''

Richardson took a moment to jot a few notes before asking
his next question. "What do you know about this latest project Mr. Kane was working on? Seven days a week, no less.
Sounds like he'd caught the scent of something.''

"He was directly responsible for a lot of the theory behind
the Department of Energy's proposed supercollider, Sergeant. As such he was committed to seeing Magnetronics
get the project's superconductor contract.''

"How many people knew what he was working on?''

Sellers frowned. "That's a tough one. Ralph had it under
tight wraps. Veronica and her theory team in Chicago. Some
other people on the engineering end at the plant in Princeton.
He and Liz were also close. She knew.''

"What about Mrs. Kane?''

"Perhaps. She was famous for taking little or no interest
in Ralph's work.''

"And you?''

"Yes. Ralph and I were working out the legal end of going
into a production partnership. Magnetronics doesn't have the
capacity here in the States. We were exploring some less
costly foreign options. Overseas looked and *still* looks like
the most cost-effective alternative to building our own bigger
facility.''

"You say Miss Tierney and her theory team knew. What was their function?"

"It was their responsibility to check all of Ralph's theoretical models. He produced the mathematics, and Veronica took it home to her team to see if it stood up. When she brought the end results back, she and Ralph would work out the bugs."

"Were you close enough to Kane to know he was also having an affair with her?"

Point-blank. Josh eased back in his chair and regarded the detective with appreciation. Richardson knew how to walk his shots in toward a target before dropping one into the heart of the matter.

"I did. Yes. Ralph was head over heels about that gal. Claimed she made him feel like a young boy again."

"Don't they all?"

Sellers chuckled. "Maybe. But Ralph said one thing that I tend to believe. He told me he and Amanda were never really in love. They were both idealistic in that way so many college kids used to be. Ralph claimed that, while they thought they were in love with each other, what they were really in love with was all the same ideas."

"How far was he prepared to go with Veronica Tierney?"

Sellers took some time considering how he would answer. His sandwich was all but gone now, and after taking a bite of his pickle he crumpled the wax deli paper to toss it into the trash.

"I believe he would have eventually divorced Amanda."

Richardson seemed surprised by the attorney's frankness. "You got any idea how long eventually might be?"

"Sorry, Sergeant. I'm not prepared to speculate on that."

"Okay. I don't see no other way to ask this next question so I'll just shoot. When we talked this morning on the phone you mentioned you were getting set to read Kane's will. Did anything in that document reflect this, ah, *alienation*'a his wife's affections?"

Again Sellers took a moment to formulate a reply. He

busied himself sweeping crumbs off his blotter with the side of his hand. "This will soon be a matter of public record, so I don't see why I shouldn't tell you. Ralph made his daughter Elizabeth a thirty-one-percent shareholder when he went public in 1971, long before he ever met Veronica. He wanted Elizabeth and not Amanda and her family to control his company's future."

"A nine-year-old kid?"

"She's always been her daddy's girl, Sergeant. The apple of his eye. Besides, the stock is in a trust that he and I controlled as trustees."

"Did Mrs. Kane have any knowledge of this arrangement?"

"Not until this morning. No."

Richardson paused to reflect on that. "Must'a been quite a shock to *both* of them. How did they react?"

Sellers shook his head. "I can be frank with you up to a point, Sergeant. I'm afraid my client's reactions are privileged information. You're free to ask either of the two parties, of course."

"Okay; fine. So let's look at it from another angle," Richardson pressed. "From a corporate counsel point of view, how do *you* feel about it?"

Sellers smiled. "This is strictly my opinion."

The detective nodded. "Understood."

"Liz Kane is a marketing genius, Sergeant. Her father was a technological visionary, not a businessman. Before Liz came aboard, Magnetronics had let its market share start to slip. Ralph just didn't care enough about that end of the business. When Liz started shaking things up, there was a lot of grumbling about daddy's little girl running roughshod. You told me on the phone that you met Liz yesterday. You've no doubt gotten a glimpse of how she operates."

"But she did manage to get the job done, right?"

"And then some. Sales are up fifty-six percent . . . in just six years. Two years ago, on her twenty-eighth birthday, she was promoted into the top spot in the sales and marketing division.''

''I couldn't help observing that mother and daughter aren't on the best of terms. What're Mrs. Kane's options now? Twenty percent's still a lot of stock, isn't it?''

Sellers eased back in his chair and crossed one ankle over a knee. Interlocking his fingers, he placed his hands atop his head and exhaled. ''In my opinion, Sergeant? Amanda will poll the board; see what sort of support she can gather in her corner.''

''And asking you to speculate again, just what sort'a support *could* she gather?''

Sellers only partially succeeded in suppressing a smile. ''Let me put it to you this way, Sergeant. You're a major stockholder. In recent years you've watched your sales figures climb from a stagnant annual level of around three hundred million to one now approaching five. Your stock's value has increased commensurately with that sales growth. Who are you going to align yourself with? The disgruntled widow of the former controlling shareholder? Or the force behind the new vitality in the company? You are keeping in mind, of course, that difficult personality aside, the force behind that new vitality also controls the single largest block of stock.''

''Sounds like you'd be shooting yourself in the foot to line up behind Mrs. Kane.''

''You might draw that conclusion.''

Melissa Busby and Guy Napier emerged from the elevator into University Hospital's Neurological Intensive Care Unit. An earlier call to Chester Garfield's surgeon confirmed last night's prognosis. Garfield slept through the night without incident. Today his condition was improved. Melissa also noticed that her own condition was improved. Something fundamental had happened as a result of her visit here last night. She'd made her peace with this place.

En route to Garfield's bedside the partners stopped at the

nursing station. The plump, middle-aged nurse greeting them was upbeat.

"The doctor last examined him at eleven-forty. All his vitals were normal. Considering the shape he was in when he arrived yesterday, I'd say that's one lucky man. In another day or two I'm sure we'll be shipping him upstairs so all the others can get some rest."

"What's he doing, making a lot of noise?" Melissa wondered.

"Not really. He hates it that his jaw is wired and we're feeding him a liquid diet, but it looks like his main problem is finding the time to see all his visitors."

"He's had a lot of them, has he?" Napier asked.

The nurse chuckled. "A bit of an understatement, officer. First his parents. Eight-thirty this morning. Then his partner and some of the men from his precinct. A sister and her husband after that and now the woman who's in there."

They thanked the nurse and started back along the hall toward the unit door. Melissa hoped all this visitor traffic hadn't exhausted their subject. They needed him alert.

Chet Garfield's female visitor was a tall, rawboned woman dressed conservatively in a gray suit, her dark hair pulled straight back in a no-nonsense twist. Melissa thought the overall look a bit severe, especially for a woman so young. As the two cops approached, Garfield squinted with his one available eye.

"Hi, Chet," Melissa greeted him. "Remember me?"

Garfield scrutinized her and frowned before his right hand came off the bed. His index finger tapped air. "Yeah. Last night. You're the detective come in here with Doc Brandeis. Wow. I just *barely* remember. How out of it was I?"

Melissa noticed Garfield's visitor react when he said the word "detective." Her mouth tightened, and her eyes darted back and forth between the two cops.

"You were pretty out of it," she admitted. "The desk nurse tells us you're feeling a lot better today."

"Better? I feel like hell. They tell me I've lost my hearing

96

in one ear; that I'll be paralyzed on one side of my face unless they can get a nerve graft to take. If it don't, I'm gonna wind up lookin' like the Phantom of the Opera. Other than that? I'm just peachy.''

"We're sorry, Chet. It's a tough break. We're also sorry that we've got to ask your friend to leave us alone with you for a few minutes. You weren't in any shape to answer questions last night. It's something we've got to do.''

Garfield looked toward the tall woman. "Maybe she should sit in. How about it, Miss Kane? This is your lucky break. You can get it right from the horse's mouth.''

"Whoa there," Guy commanded. "Let's back up a sec.'' He turned to address the dark-haired woman directly. "I'm Detective Napier, ma'am. This is my partner, Detective Busby. You're Elizabeth Kane?''

"That's right.''

"I don't understand why you're here, Miss Kane.''

Elizabeth Kane had barely glanced at Napier up to that point and she took a moment now to give him a thorough once-over. She was accustomed to looking most men directly in the eye. Now she was forced to incline her face slightly to engage the much taller detective.

"I'm trying to find out what exactly happened yesterday morning, officer. I spoke to your Sergeant Richardson, and he either couldn't or wouldn't give me any details surrounding my father's death. I feel I've got the right to know.''

"I see. And you thought Detective Garfield could help you.''

Her dark eyes flashed anger. "He was there, wasn't he? The same man who shot my father shot him. I thought he might have seen something.''

"Like what? Specifically. What do you think he might have seen?''

From Melissa's vantage the woman seemed to get taller, her nostrils flaring and face coloring slightly.

"What the hell is *that* supposed to mean? What are you implying?''

97

Guy stayed cool. "I'm not implying anything, Miss Kane. I'm *conducting* a homicide investigation. Detective Garfield is a material witness to that homicide. Your presence here constitutes interference with that investigation."

Elizabeth Kane stood her ground. "Interference? My *father* was killed!"

"We appreciate that, ma'am. But what you're doing right now potentially compromises . . ."

"Will you excuse us a moment?" Melissa interrupted. She turned and led Elizabeth Kane out of the line of fire. "You've got to forgive my partner," she murmured. "I realize you've had a tremendous shock, but I'm afraid Detective Napier is right on the one count. You shouldn't be here right now." She kept her tone measured.

"Nobody will tell me anything." The agitated woman's dark eyes returned from Napier's lofty height to engage the shorter Melissa in a more relaxed manner.

Face to face, Melissa was fascinated by the contrasts between herself and this other. Aside from the difference in sheer size, Liz Kane's presence exuded a strength that Melissa envied. The lady cop thought her own look too soft for the job; a mixture of strawberry blond curls, a soft-edged, heart-shape face, and freckles dotting the bridge of her nose. Her build, in contrast to the Kane woman's, was compact and tended toward the slightly plump if she didn't kill herself for at least an hour a day at her gym.

"When you spoke with Sergeant Richardson yesterday he didn't tell you anything because he didn't know very much. None of us did, and we still don't. We're trying to piece this together, one bit at a time. It's very early on yet."

Elizabeth had control of her anger now. "I'm sorry. It's just that . . ." She shook her head. "Never mind. I'm not used to feeling so helpless."

"I understand," Melissa sympathized. "What did you and Detective Garfield discuss? Was he of any help to you?"

"Not very much, really. The killer surprised him. He was bent over Veronica, trying to determine whether she was still alive. He heard movement, looked up, saw a shadow coming at him from the hall, and then everything went black. The next thing he remembers is waking up here with half his face under bandages.''

Melissa thanked her and dug out a business card. ''That's my office number downtown. If you've got any questions, I'll be more than happy to try and answer them.''

It was a dismissal. Elizabeth Kane took a moment to tuck the card into her purse and then headed for the door. Melissa watched the tight, controlled way she walked. When the woman disappeared into the hallway, the lady cop returned to Garfield's bedside. As she arrived, Napier flashed her a questioning look.

''How'd you do?'' he asked.

''She said she and Chet talked about what he saw.'' Melissa turned to address Garfield. ''It doesn't sound like you remember much, huh Chet?''

''Not much,'' he agreed. ''I remember finding the door open a crack and then finding the two of them down on the rug. The woman was closest so I went to her first. Then I remember hearing this guy's voice mutter something. It came from the general direction of where the other body was, so I'm thinking maybe *he's* still alive. I look up to see this shadow coming out the mouth of the hall. That's about *all* I remember. The lights just went *out*. After that I . . .''

''Hold on,'' Melissa stopped him. ''You heard a man's voice *mutter* something? The shooter's ?''

''Must'a been. Yeah.''

''You told Elizabeth Kane that?''

The visible half of Garfield's face betrayed confusion. ''Sure.''

Melissa shook her head. ''She just told me you heard *movement* and looked up.''

''More than that. The bastard muttered under his breath; like he was pissed off. Pissed off that I'd shown up. Got in his way.''

''Muttered *what*?'' Napier pressed.

"That's the odd part. What he said was 'fucking hell.' I can still hear him saying it. *Fucking hell.* Seems odd, don't it?"

"Fucking hell," Napier echoed. "You're sure. Not 'What the fuck' or 'Ah, fuck'?"

"Nope. Fucking hell. That's what hit me when he said it. People don't talk like that."

Melissa looked to her partner and then back at Garfield. "You're half-right, Chet. Some people talk like that, but Americans sure as hell don't."

"Fucking hell!"

Seamus Cowan had been working with Billy's pirated program for more than twenty-four hours. He'd gotten close to no sleep. Now he threw his pencil to the table, switched off the monitor, and scraped back his chair. Working like a madman he'd managed to churn through the entire package. Every one of the sequentially filed disks had been examined, starting with "A" all the way through "M." Much of the data was redundant; different approaches to the same ends. Checks and balances. While Seamus loathed the tedium of it, he had to admire Ralph Kane's thoroughness. He'd left no stone unturned.

"Something wrong?" Paul Murphy asked. The ex-fighter, after napping the morning away in the back room, had emerged for lunch and then started in on his daily exercise regimen. For the moment he lay stretched on his back, grunting his way through a series of weighted leg lifts.

"Wrong? I'll say there's something wrong. We've been cheated, Paulie. The damnable thing isn't all here."

Murphy dropped his legs in the middle of a lift and sat upright.

"But Kane said he'd finished it. I'n't that what the bitch told Billy?"

Cowan grabbed up a fistful of scrap paper and crumpled it in frustration. "I don't give a fuck what she told him, Paulie. I've just finished running everything he brought me.

It all makes perfect sense, surely, but I get to the end and it's like the road just drops away. Into oblivion, for Jaysus' sake. It i'n't all here.''

The front door opened, and Mannion entered, a wide, triumphant smile on his face. There was a cocky buoyancy in his step as he crossed the living room to deposit his equipment bag on the sofa and shrug out of his jacket. "Good news, lads. We've scared the piss out've Phillip Wright. The Brit scum turned to putty once he got a look at our tape.''

"Maybe not such good news, Billy," Murphy countered. He jerked a thumb toward the computer while still seated on the floor. "Seamus says your girlfriend might've played you for a fool.''

"No might've about it, William," Cowan concurred. "I've been through this package upwards and down, backwards and forth. It's a brilliant piece of work, but the payoff's missing.''

Mannion got wary. "What're you saying, Seamus? What *exactly* are you saying?''

"I'm saying it i'n't finished, William. Not in this form.''

"She swears he said it was.''

"I don't care what she swears, William. We've got trouble. The Korean's due here Thursday. He's taking a certain amount of risk, meeting with us. It's my suggestion you start thinking seriously about contacting him and canceling till I can get this sorted out.''

Billy's face went hard. "I'm not canceling nothing, Seamus. I'll stall him; say something's come up. At most I can probably get us another week. Surely that gives you the time you'd need. You said yourself that it's a brilliant piece of work. With what you've got, a fortnight should be enough time to finish it, no?''

"You've finally gotten it, William. No. With *no* time restrictions I might be able to do something with this, but surely not in a few more days. Kane and Veronica had a tremendous advantage o'er me. They had all the material and cost analysis figures. The nuts and bolts of it. I'm a theoretician,

101

William, not a fucking production engineer. I can do confirmations, yes. What I *can't* do is create a production scheme out of whole cloth. I don't have access to enough information."

The bedroom door behind Seamus opened. A sullen Siobhan emerged from her bedroom with her pocketbook in hand and a light jacket over her arm. The conversation died as she made her way toward the front door.

"Don't mind me, you bloody bastards. I'm off to work now."

"What about our tea?" Mannion demanded.

She stopped and turned to him, smiling sarcastically. "Your *tea*? You can fix it your fucking self from now on, Billy Mannion. You got your pound of flesh from me last night. It's the *last* you'll get, too. We're even now. You harm so much as a hair on any of my family's heads, and you'd better kill me first. I'll cut your rotten heart out and feed it to pigs."

Mannion laughed with wicked delight. "Listen to this, will you? She'll cut my heart out. Oh my, Siobhan. You ask me, you were a lot more impressive as a knob-sucking whore than you'll ever be as a tough. Each of us to his calling, yes?"

She came at him in a rush, arms flailing, knees pumping, and screaming like a banshee. Before Mannion could cover up she managed to sink a nail into his neck below his right ear and draw a nasty scratch forward onto his jaw. Billy bellowed in fury, backhanding her across the face. The force of the blow knocked her to the floor.

Panting, a rush of adrenaline coursing through his veins, Mannion loomed above her with one boot drawn back. "Get away from here afore I kick your teeth down your fucking throat."

Siobhan scrambled crabwise toward the door and used the knob to haul herself to her feet. "Take a good look in a mirror, Billy. Then tell me who's the fucking whore. Nobody threatened you wit anything to get you to crawl inta bed with your latest mongrel bitch. It was *you* that wanted something, Billy. What's that make you?''

She had the door open and was halfway through into the hallway when Mannion came at her. He made a diving grab and came away empty-handed as she slammed the door in his face.

TEN

The plan seemed simple enough on the surface: Gain access to the Irish community in New York by going to work for one of the trade union locals recently stocked by the Westies with Irish nationals. Dante's cover was being built on the fact that he'd long ago worked summers as a laborer on various Brooklyn construction projects. He'd since forgotten a lot of what he once knew, and in an effort to refresh his memory, the business agent for the Painters and Allied Trades, District Council Nine, was brought on board. It was Greg Payne's job to turn Dante into a materials expediter for a drywall contractor. Just recently Payne was installed in his position through a power play engineered by his union's Washington headquarters. Mob influence in the New York locals threatened to undermine Washington's control totally. Part of Payne's job was to work closely with NYPD's Organized Crime Control Task Force.

In seven short hours Payne had given Dante quite an education. Drywall stock dimensions, screw gauges, screw guns, screw gun tip sizes, joint compound (mud), waterproof drywall (green rock), joint tape, corner bead, mud knives, utility knives, sanding poles, et cetera, et cetera, until an exhausted Dante's head began to swim. What staggered him even more than mastering the great variety of tools and material items employed by his new trade was the sheer volume necessary for the job his prospective employer was about to undertake. Payne explained that a thirty-six-story apartment tower could consume tens of thousands of sheets of "rock," a ton or two of screws, and enough joint compound to fill the Central Park Reservoir. The logistics involved in getting these materials delivered to the site were intimidating. There were boom trucks to book, suppliers to contact, the soliciting and acceptance of bids, a whole host of availability queries to be made. The responsibility for all these tasks did not rest entirely on the shoulders of a single materials expediter, but it *was* his responsibility to orchestrate everything on the job site, constantly ride the front office for purchase orders, gauge progress, and monitor stock levels, anticipating demand.

To avoid his being observed by anyone who could make trouble for Dante later, Payne had taken Joe thirty miles west into New Jersey, to a big new corporate park project in Morristown. The job site was dead as a ghost town that Saturday. Because Payne had a good relationship with the general contractor, he and Dante had the run of the place. It was four o'clock before they got out of there and another forty minutes before Joe pulled into his slot in the One Police Plaza parking garage.

It felt strange, easing the low-slung Turbo Z between that familiar pair of painted lines. The gleaming black sports car was an indulgence Dante had allowed himself after his buddy Brennan, through his current connection with the Nissan Corporation, arranged to get it at cost. It rarely left its midtown garage, save for an occasional pleasure trip upstate or out to Brian and Diana's beach place on the Connecticut shore. Today he no longer had the luxury of driving his beatup job sedan. For the first time in two years he was without company wheels. In another half hour he would also be without a desk. Last night Gus had advised him that Commissioner Mintoff wanted a temporary replacement installed as whip of Major Case.

Joe wasn't surprised to find the entire Major Case team gathered upstairs when he entered the squad. That morning the Overton House case had shared headlines with the Poole girl's death in all the tabloid dailies. The information being held back in the Poole matter left that story a bare-bones affair, while circumstances surrounding the Kane/Tierney homicides were laid open to all manner of juicy speculation. The first seventy-two hours of an investigation of this magnitude always found the team run ragged trying to get it organized.

The presence of Captain Robert "Bud" Costanza surprised Dante. Up there at the head of the table where the whip customarily sat, Costanza appeared to be running the show. He'd just asked a question of Rusty Heckman, and Heckman was starting to respond when Dante's appearance brought all conversation to a halt.

"Evening, Cap," Joe greeted the new whip. "Don't mind me. This is the first opportunity I've had to grab some things from my desk."

"Glad you found the time," Costanza returned. "I been having a little trouble figuring where to hang my hat around here. I took the liberty'a having Support Services send up some file cartons. It don't look like you've got all that much personal shit, huh?"

Dante ignored the question and met the sympathetic gazes of his team before turning for his office door. They all knew the bum's rush when they saw it. They also all knew they had a bona fide turkey installed up there at the head of the table. There was no way that Bud was Gus's first choice for this assignment. He'd most likely been forced on the chief by the commissioner. Bud Costanza and Tony Mintoff both graduated from the same Academy class. At fifty-six years of age Costanza already had thirty-eight years in. In another two years he could retire at the maximum pension level, but pensions were taxed, and Costanza was playing a different game. With Mintoff's help Bud had recently landed a succession of gravy short-term assignments like this one. In between them he would go out sick with job-related back problems. Those alleged problems stemmed from a fender bender on Costanza's record dating back twenty years. Everyone familiar with this scam and Costanza's recent record knew that Bud was lining up to retire with a line-of-duty disability. That would pay him three quarters of his last year's salary tax free. When he went out he'd be pulling down close to sixty thousand no-strings dollars a year.

Behind Dante, out in the squad, Costanza turned back to Rusty.

"As you was saying, Sarge."

"Okay. Our man from the Physics Department up at Columbia believes that the Japs are probably the front-runners right now in landing the government's magnetics contract. The way he describes the logistics here is enough to boggle the mind. The rig they're building down on the Texas range is fifty-five miles in circumference, a tunnel ten feet in diameter. They intend to fill that tunnel with ten thousand superconducting magnets, each about fifty-seven feet long and weighing eighteen thousand pounds. Somebody's got to build those magnets, and right now we've got nobody in the U.S. with that capacity. The price tag being tossed around is purely speculative. Five billion dollars could end up being as much a pipe dream as a hundred-billion-dollar S & L bailout was."

"You say the Japs are out front. Who else is in this race?"

"The French, believe it or not. They've got a fairly state-of-the-art design for a passenger train powered at high speeds by superconducting magnets. They're making a strong bid. There are also some rumblings about the South Koreans taking advantage of their more favorable labor market. They may be gearing up to mount a campaign, too. And then there's Magnetronics. They may have access to the best technology of the lot, but they don't have the production capacity. That's where this Korean rumor came from. Some people believe that Ralph Kane was maneuvering to cut a deal somewhere in the Far East; his technological and managerial expertise for their construction-cost advantages and probably a large capital investment up front."

Dante had trouble ignoring the conversation outside his office door as he began emptying his personal effects from the drawers of his desk. Ever since he'd first heard about it almost a decade ago, Joe thought the supercollider sounded like a pork-barreling politician's wet dream. At the same time as the Department of Energy was encouraging Americans to search out ways to conserve fossil fuels, they were actively seeking to build a subatomic particle smasher that operated at a whopping twenty trillion electron volts. Dante distinctly remembered reading that this nineteen-thousand-acre, ten-billion-dollar installation would be obsolete in twenty years; too radioactive to be safe after that. Meanwhile New York City's bridges, roads, and entire aqueduct system were threatening to collapse from neglect.

"What about Kane's family situation?" Costanza asked. "Tell me how you read it, Richardson. First you say there's some sorta split 'tween the mother and daughter. And now Kane drives the wedge deeper by giving his daughter the bigger share'a his controlling interest. I don't need to remind any'a you that close to eighty-five percent'a all homicides are crimes'a passion."

From his desk chair Dante had a good vantage of the squad through the glass office partition. He watched Jumbo formulating his reply and could only imagine what was going through his partner's head. Costanza hadn't asked him what he thought; he was *telling* him what to think.

"Amanda Kane claims to've known nothing about her husband's affair," Jumbo replied. "I don't know if that's true, but when she learned of the thirty-one/twenty split during the reading of the will, she was flabbergasted."

"Who told you that? Her?"

Richardson nodded. "I talked to her about two hours ago and then reached Sellers to confirm. He wouldn't reveal either party's reaction during our interview earlier this afternoon, but he didn't have any trouble backing up what Mrs. Kane told me. He says she wasn't only blindsided by it, she was outraged. *She* told me she's considering litigation."

Don Grover jumped into it here. "I'm not saying it couldn't

all be an act, but if it is, it sounds like a good one. And if it *isn't*, then we've got a problem with the Mrs. Kane angle.''

"How so?" Costanza sounded irritated.

"She got the smaller slice of the pie. If she wasn't even *aware* she'd been given short shrift, then any revenge-type motive postdates her husband's death.''

Melissa Busby spoke up now. "Here's something else interesting—about the daughter. The Boy Wonder and I found her with Chester Garfield when we went to visit him in ICU today." She quickly brought them up to date on what she and Napier had learned from the wounded cop and what Elizabeth Kane had neatly omitted in recounting her own conversation with him.

"Fucking hell?" Heckman asked. "Don't *English* people say that?"

"That's what I thought, too," Melissa told him. "And one other thing." She related how Napier had reexamined a briefcase found crammed with computer printouts and discovered two computer disks that seemed to be part of an alphabetical series. "It should have occurred to us before. The one thing we didn't find in that bedroom office was a disk file for that computer. Guy and I wonder if that isn't what the shooter was after.''

For the moment Dante had forgotten about cleaning out his desk. He watched as Costanza surveyed the faces of his troops.

"You all seem pretty stuck on this industrial espionage angle," the captain observed. "And yeah, I'll admit that five billion or whatever is a lotta cash. But we ain't got any *evidence* that our victims even had the goods in there. Right now it's all conjecture. Computer disks. Pie-in-the-sky breakthroughs. That's *all* hearsay. For all we know the shooter was down the hall 'cause he hadda take a leak. Did Garfield see him with anything other than a gun in his hands? No. And whose word do we have that Kane was *on* the verge'a any breakthrough? The daughter's; the same broad who's ex-girlfriend is diddling her daddy.''

"That's raw," Melissa objected. "Elizabeth Kane's been pretty up front on that count. She admits being aware of the affair. If she was jealous, why would she have *both* of them killed?"

"Maybe she just learned about it recently and reacted outta pure spite," Costanza countered. "Did she *say* how long she knew? We gotta put ourselves in her shoes; wonder how we'd feel if Daddy tells us he's getting set to divorce Mom and take the walk down the aisle with our ex-lesbo lover. If he did intend to do that it would put the daughter and her old girlfriend in direct competition for his affections. What did Richardson here say the lawyer called her? The apple of his eye? I think we need to focus down here. You ask me, this five-billion-dollar motive could just as easily be a balloon full'a hot air floated by the daughter to get suspicion aimed elsewhere."

"We can't ignore it altogether," Grover argued.

"I'm not asking you to. But I'll be damned if I'm gonna let this entire squad chase the first bait dangled by some clever little rich girl. Grover: you and Heckman can run with it a couple'a more days, but the rest'a us is gonna dig inta this family situation. Let's see what kinda worms we can turn. Eighty-five percent is good odds. They ain't the kinda odds this old cop ignores. You give me them, I'll take 'em to the track and come back a rich man."

More discussion, mostly of schedules and a possible manpower increase, ensued. Dante returned to emptying his desk and then removing the few personal effects from his office walls. It was his nature now to keep such mementoes to a minimum. Early last summer he'd lost everything but the shirt on his back when a fire gutted his old Greenwich Village apartment. He'd since resolved to simplify his life. Here the walls were virtually bare. He'd recently assembled enough night school credits to finally earn his master's degree in criminal psychology from John Jay. That sheepskin hung on the wall behind his desk. Hanging alongside it was a framed pencil sketch of him and Diana in beach chairs up on the

Sound, done by Brennan one afternoon this past August. The members of Dante's squad had asked why he didn't hang a few of his commendations in there. He invariably replied that only pinheads and politicians framed commendations. He didn't need to. He *knew* how cool he was.

A knock came at the doorframe behind him. "Permission to come aboard?"

Joe turned to find Bud Costanza standing half-in and half-out of the office. The captain's appearance was gung ho clear down to spit-shined shoes. Steel gray crew cut. Pronounced jug-handle ears. A lean, sinewy body complete with faded forearm tattoo; "Semper Fi" the tattoo read, the words wrapped around a globe skewered on an anchor.

"It's your ship now, Cap."

"Yeah. I guess it is. Been a long day, and I'm getting set to check out. Just wanna let you know that your team's in good hands . . . that and to wish you luck with this grand jury investigation."

Dante hoisted the single carton he'd filled and started around his replacement. "Luck is for crapshooters, Cap. And it's you who's in good hands. You give that squad their heads and they'll make you look like a genius." He stopped at the door, standing eye-to-eye with the new whip. "Don't insult the intelligence of these people, Bud. I handpicked each of them because they're gifted detectives. I like to think they might have learned a thing or two from me, but I'm also proud to say I've learned a lot from every one of them. You don't hitch a racehorse to a plow."

Costanza stood quietly and watched Dante cross the squad to the hall door.

Joe passed Jumbo, Melissa, and Napier en route. "You three got a minute?"

Jumbo was the first to follow into the eleventh-floor corridor. As the door closed behind them he threw up his hands in a gesture of hopelessness. "What was that, Joey? Dante's first lesson in how to win friends and influence people?"

"He's got his head up his ass," Dante growled.

"Thanks for pointing that out."

"No problem. You didn't go to Washington this morning. Does that mean you're free for dinner?"

Jumbo sniffed suspiciously. "What kinda dinner? Chinese again?"

"Barbecue, Beasley. Tonight's your lucky night." Joe turned to Melissa and Napier as they emerged from the squad. "How about you two lovebirds. You got plans?"

"Your place?" Guy asked. There was suspicion in his demeanor, too.

"That's right. I'll pick up some chicken and beer on the way home. There's something I just overheard in there that I want to kick around a little."

"Bullshit, boss. You've got something heavy you need us to help you either hang or haul."

Richardson chuckled. "He's got your number, Joey. You've put a hammer in his hand one too many times."

"Free food. Free beer," Dante pressed.

Napier was still scowling. "No strings?"

"Only one," Dante promised. "This shooter of yours. I dropped an ear on that story Mel told during your round table in there. It gave me a funny feeling."

"Didn't give our new fearless leader any funny feelings," Jumbo grumbled. "He's already so sure it was one of those two Kane women had it done that he's taking his bet to the window."

"Eighty-five percent odds," Melissa reminded him, "are hard to beat."

If the truth were ever known, and it wasn't likely to be, Melissa Busby still entertained the occasional fantasy about her suspended boss. Eleven months ago, when Dante first asked Melissa to come aboard at Major Case, she'd developed a full-blown crush on the man. Those feelings had since been diluted, partly by time and partly by Guy "Boy Wonder" Napier. The Boy Wonder was a bright, tender man who had a lot of Dante's physical presence, a terrific sense of humor, and the good sense to fall in love with her. She was happy with him. Nonetheless there were still those occasional moments when Dante lit one of those delicious, private little fires in her. He was ruggedly handsome and yet seemed unaware of it. He appeared to live a glamorous life complete with rock star, artist, and fashion model friends, but she'd seen inside his private world and found it reserved, tranquil, and by no means contrived. The man was *real*. He was absolutely confident of the space he occupied. That left plenty of room for others to occupy spaces of their own.

Dante's neighbor Brian Brennan was still out of town, and Brennan's wife Diana was working in the recording studio tonight. Joe and his guests had the building's roof garden to themselves. They were gathered around the grill eating chips and drinking beer. Guy helped Joe split chunks of hardwood while Melissa and Jumbo leaned on the fence, staring out at the view. She loved it up here, with all of midtown spread before her like that. Behind her, to the west, the Hudson sparkled with the reflected lights of Hoboken, while downtown at the foot of the island the World Trade Center shimmered among the lesser towers of the Financial District.

"How you doing this bird tonight?" Jumbo asked their host. "I'd be more'n glad to mix up some of Richardson's famous finishing sauce."

Dante was a city boy, born and bred in the Canarsie section of Brooklyn. Since becoming friends with Brian Brennan he'd also caught the sculptor's infectious passion for barbecue. Not gas grilling, mind, but the real thing. Hot coals, log burning, with plenty of hickory, apple, mesquite, and oak kept stockpiled near the pit. While Brennan went in for a constant parade of experimental sauces and tended to favor them as Jumbo did, Dante liked the simpler grilling traditions of his Northern Italian heritage. They'd argued the finer points of each approach all summer long.

"Not tonight," Joe replied. "Tonight we're going with salt, pepper, olive oil, and a few herbs. Same thing on the vegetables. You're gonna love it."

113

Melissa knew from prior experience that they probably would. The resulting fare would be nothing like the food her father had burned religiously in his Queens backyard every Fourth of July.

"I hate to change so deep and important a subject," Napier interjected. "But I'm curious about this funny feeling you were talking about, boss." He'd set aside the hand axe to pull up a lounge chair and tucked Dante's cat Toby into his lap. "Mel and I hit Criminal Records right after we got back from the hospital this afternoon. Had them run every known hitter-for-hire born in the British Commonwealth. They came up with twenty names; half of them either from the Islands or the Far East. Garfield didn't say anything about the shooter sounding Jamaican or Chinese. We pushed him pretty hard, trying to narrow down the inflections. It sounded like the man was maybe British or Australian. Nobody on the Records list we came up with is known to be within three thousand miles of New York. Who'd we miss?"

Dante shook his head. "I wasn't thinking along those lines. Not along the usual hired gun line at all, actually. In fact, I'm wondering if you and I aren't after the same man."

Jumbo turned away from viewing the skyline to give his old partner a puzzled look. "Billy Mannion?"

"I don't like coincidences, Beasley. Now I've got two. An Irishman's just as likely to say 'fucking hell' as an Englishman. You suspect your shooter went in there to do more than just kill Ralph Kane and Veronica Tierney. You think he was there to pirate something. Mel thinks it was something small, like a computer disk file. Yesterday morning I went to Ralph Kane's Fifth Avenue building to question his wife, and who do I see sneaking out the back way? An Irishman dressed like a cat burglar who had an automatic pistol with a noise suppressor screwed onto its muzzle. I saw that little black knapsack he was carrying and assumed he'd been pulling some sort of job inside that building. Now I've got other ideas."

Melissa had no trouble adding up Dante's coincidences

and seeing where he was headed. "That's a nasty picture you're painting, boss. If it's true, it means that one of the Kane women is involved."

"Not necessarily," Dante cautioned. "It's a good bet, but let's look at *all* the possibilities. We've got no idea who else lives in that building. The tenants in a setup like that tend to be thick as thieves. There could be another Magnetronics bigwig living there, or even another member of the Gregory family."

"*Two* Gregorys," Jumbo interjected. "I already checked."

"Okay," Melissa allowed. "We need to pursue that. But meanwhile let's look at it *another* way. For all we know this whole bickering feud between mother and daughter is an act. It's just as likely, considering Ralph Kane's relationship with his whiz kid helpmate, that *both* Kane women are involved."

"That'd make our fearless new leader half right," Jumbo mused. "The motive'd be a lot more complex than simple passion, but the immediate family part of Costanza's equation'd stand up strong."

"Slow down," Dante cautioned them. "There's one thing his Homicide 1-A equation *can't* explain. Why would anyone who'd killed a man and inherited controlling interest in his company want to simultaneously pick the eyes out of it? I can see Mannion's motive. Terrorist campaigns don't fund themselves. They're expensive. He'd want the money he could make from selling technology like that. But why would either Elizabeth or Amanda Kane kill a goose about to lay a golden egg?"

"Maybe it isn't about to," Guy argued. "Maybe all this breakthrough talk is just so much bullshit; Elizabeth Kane blowing smoke up our asses. Magnetronics is still worth a lot of money. This whole technology theft angle could be a ruse to throw us off. Right now I can't imagine how a guy like Mannion and women like the Kanes could ever make that initial connection."

"So it's farfetched." Melissa wasn't about to give up on

this avenue until they'd run it out to the end. "It still might well be worth Mannion's while to knock Ralph Kane off for hire. What would someone be likely to pay if they really wanted to have it done? Fifty grand? A hundred?"

"Neither number's outta the question," Jumbo agreed. "But *listen* to us. In the past ten minutes we've jacked the scope of this investigation open wider than Bud Costanza's asshole."

"So let's try to narrow it down," Dante pressed him. "Conversations like this are the only way you're gonna get anywhere. You're sure as hell not gonna get any useful guidance from your new whip. He's already got one foot out the door. So why not design and take control of this investigation yourselves?" He extended a closed fist and raised a thumb. "Number one, there's the question of whether Magnetronics really *was* on the verge of a breakthrough. Somebody's got to look into that. The possible alliance with a Korean manufacturer is interesting. Maybe it's for real, but somebody's gotta find that out." His index finger sprang up beside the thumb. "Second, there's the question of what sort of financial shape these ladies are in. What are their possible motivations here, *other* than passion or spite? Has either of them liquidated any holdings recently?" Up came another finger. "Three. The Boy Wonder's basic problem with all this: How does someone like Amanda or Elizabeth Kane get hold of a Billy Mannion or any other hired gun?"

Busby jumped in here. "Four. Who would have the strongest motive for stripping the company if Kane *was* on the verge of nailing down something that size? Is there something hidden that we're not seeing yet?"

Jumbo held up his empty bottle. "And five is who wants another brew. I think I'm gonna need several."

For all her stuck-up breeding, Billy Mannion knew the bitch loved the danger of these trips to the North Bronx. The squalor of his digs seemed to thrill her: the mattress on the floor, the cockroaches, and the rust-colored water flowing from the tap in the bath. Writhing naked in the throes of passion with a notorious fugitive was a denial of everything she'd been raised to believe and hold dear. Recklessness affected her like chemical stimulants affected other people. She got higher than a kite on it.

Seamus and Paulie had left over an hour ago for McNulty's Bar, their announced intention being to have a few pints and get something to eat. Billy suspected they would also try to make peace with Siobhan. Both hated watching him fight with her, but neither had tried to live with her for three years only to have her leave one night and later beg the movement to cut her free. They hadn't seen the flame of Maoist zeal in her gutter and die. She'd softened, and Billy had no stomach for anyone who lacked the most basic ideological discipline.

When Billy's rich bitch arrived he made no mention of the problem Seamus was having with the program. There was a right way to lead into it: appeal to her vanity and let her think she was appealing to his; turn her to putty by bringing her off and get his own end away in the process. She wasn't easy, this one. Like so many women, she wanted to be worshipped and not actively participate, but this one also seemed to enjoy observing his exertions; seeing herself fawned over and stimulated by a man who was just as emotionally detached from the act as she was.

Lying on his back now he panted hard, a mixture of his sweat and hers coating his naked torso, loins, and thighs. He hadn't wasted any time toying with her at the edge this time. Instead he'd driven her hard directly to the top of the mountain and pushed her off. She was trying to catch her breath, and he knew she wanted to savor this moment without distraction.

"How long did you expect me to sit still once I learned you'd sold me a bill of goods?" he growled. Instead of moving to make eye contact as he asked it his eyes remained glued to the ceiling.

She moved. She came up on one elbow. "What the hell is *that* supposed to mean?"

117

He frowned, feigning deep thought. "I dunno, love. I guess I'm wondering what it is I'm s'posed to be able to sell. My buyer's expecting a completed superconducting magnetics proposal. Technology. Production cost breakdowns. Everything he'd need to win that government contract free and clear. But you didn't deliver, so nor can I."

She was up on one hip now, straight-arming the mattress and glaring hard at eyes that still refused to meet hers. "We had a deal, you two-timing bastard! What are you pulling here? You agreed to my terms, and I delivered."

Billy clucked his tongue off the roof of his mouth, his head moving slowly from side to side. "No, love. *I* delivered. You wanted a funeral to attend; I got you that funeral. In exchange I've got a worthless box of computer disks. I don't think that's equitable."

"Worthless?! Delivered into the right hands, those disks are worth billions! You're the one with the connections, mister. You knew going in just how much you could expect to get for them."

Billy's eyes drifted over to make contact for the first time. "I'm not fool enough to sell anything without first authenticating its value, love. My man's been examining what I took out of that suite, and he says they're worthless; a thing of beauty so far as they go, but they don't go far enough."

"That's impossible. He told me he'd finished, that Veronica was having her people do a final polish to update the material cost figures. She was bringing it all back with her Thursday night."

"Right, love. And then Magnetronics would be all set to complete negotiations with the Koreans and formalize their bid; submit it to the Department of Energy perhaps as early as mid-October. I've *heard* all this, love. I've heard it, and you know what I think? I think you're either a lying cunt or he pulled the wool o'er your eyes."

Billy saw the anger reach the flash point and anticipated her reaction. He caught her in mid-lunge, wrapped his arms around her waist, and bore her backward onto the mattress.

One thigh fended off a knee aimed at his groin. Her nails raked his back, and she bit him in the shoulder as he and his superior strength fought her to submission. He was breathing hard again by the time he gained the upper hand.

"I expect to be compensated, but I'm not an unreasonable man, love. You've got twelve days." He'd pinned the right side of her head with his left forearm and held her in check by pulling tight on a fistful of hair. The words were snarled directly into her ear. "If the fucking thing *is* finished, I suggest you use every means at your disposal to get your hands on the rest of it. And even if you don't, I expect the two million I planned to sell it for anyway. I think our mutual friend'll understand, so don't underestimate my determination, love. You try to cheat me, I'll make *sure* you pay. You won't like that alternative one bit, love. I know every dirty trick in the book."

ELEVEN

Before this Mannion mess surfaced, Gus and Dante were scheduled to head out to the Meadowlands Sunday for a one P.M. kickoff. Instead, Joe was busy trying to learn an entire building-trade job in two days. Gus was meanwhile stuck cross-referencing a list of Fifth Avenue building personnel with the National Crime Information hookup, Customs and Immigration, Interpol, and the job's own Criminal Records Section. It wasn't the sort of favor the chief of detectives would do for just any cop.

It was nearly four o'clock before Lieberman's driver pulled to the curb outside Dante's loft. Gus had listened to the final minutes of the game he'd missed on the car radio. While the Giants had lost to San Francisco by three points, the postgame wrap-up suggested that anyone just tuning in had missed an exciting, seesaw battle. This fact did not improve the chief's disposition. The Giants played only eight games a season at home. At least three of the remaining games would be played in frigid conditions and another would likely be played in the rain. From Gus's office window on the thirteenth floor he'd been able to see the way the sun streamed down onto the East River and over the outer boroughs beyond. Perfect football weather. Just the sort of day he should have savored from seats on the fifty-yard line.

Because Dante's building was a warehouse and Brian Brennan still leased to commercial tenants, the elevators carried freight as well as people. For security reasons each tenant controlled access from upstairs. Gus knew the drill well and buzzed Joey on entering the lobby. He then waited until Dante freed the elevator with his key. Four floors up the winch motor kicked in and cables started to rattle as the ancient car made its descent. Gus hadn't been here in a couple of weeks, and as he started up he wondered how Dante's kitchen had turned out.

When the elevator finally wheezed to a stop at his destination, Gus found Dante in the middle of his half-finished living room, surrounded by piles of tools and building materials.

"C'mon in, boss. You see any of that game?"

Lieberman tugged the gate back. "Don't even start with me," he growled. "So where's your teacher?"

"Just left. I think he figured he'd crammed about as much into me as was gonna stick."

"You still think you can pull this off?"

Dante glanced down, eyes surveying the material strewn at his feet. "Beats me. I'd like to think so, but maybe I'm just too thick to see the writing on the wall."

"You know what all that shit is?"

"Pretty much. I've been talking nothing but trade lingo for two days." As he spoke, Dante slipped on a pair of safety glasses and fitted a battered yellow hard hat onto his head. They combined well with a dusty, well-broken-in pair of work boots, faded Levi's, and a gray long-sleeve work shirt. "So what do you think? Would *you* buy this?"

"Maybe. How long were you in Saudi Arabia, Mr. Expediter?"

"Eight and a half years."

"No shit? Where? I've got a cousin works on a drill rig in . . . Riyadh."

Joe grinned. "No oil in Riyadh, boss."

"Bumfuck. Wherever."

"I worked pretty much all over the gulf. Two years on an office tower in Riyadh, almost three on a refinery expansion in Ras Tanura, more than three on an oil workers' residential compound outside Dhahran. Before that I worked a couple years in Oman and three in the Emirates. Who's your cousin?''

Gus was impressed. "Pretty thorough on such short notice. Who built it?''

"Some of Pete's people over at Intelligence. He even brought in a retired Exxon engineer. I spent an hour this morning looking at his slides.''

"You might just pull it off.'' Gus was carrying a file folder and now handed it across. "Here's the shit you wanted on that building's personnel. Pretty slim pickings. Most'a the people working outta the basement are immigrants, but not the right nationality. Yugoslavs, not Irish.''

"You see anything that got your pulse up?''

"Not much, deep as I dug. The elevator operators and lobby people are all citizens, born here. Three of them are retired from the job. The concierge and one of the doormen worked for twenty years at the Plaza.''

"I'm wondering if we're looking in the wrong haystack there, Gus.''

"How so?''

"Something else's come up.'' Dante proceeded to recount the Saturday night revelations of Melissa Busby and Guy Napier. "I think we should start exploring connections between the *residents* of that building,'' he concluded. "When I saw Mannion climbing out of that dumpster I assumed he'd been inside ripping somebody off. Now I wonder.''

Lieberman was scrambling. "Slow down a sec. You think *Mannion* killed Kane?''

Dante removed the safety glasses and hat. "Think about it, Gus. The timing's right, and he was there in the area. He had a gun with a noise suppressor screwed onto it. I saw him emerge from the building where one of his victims lived and that victim's wife and daughter *still* live. The wounded guy, Garfield, heard the shooter say something that's distinctly either British or Irish. From where I stand there are too many coincidences to ignore.'' Joe tossed the glasses into the hat and set them aside. "On top of all that, Mel and Guy have their computer disk file theory. The knapsack I saw Mannion carrying could easily hold something like that.''

"Or the cash he was paid for stealing it,'' Lieberman mused. He dug out his smokes and tapped the pack against the palm of his hand. "If that technology's real, if it's worth what they're saying it is, somebody in a position to broker it'd pay a pretty penny to get his hands on it, right?''

Dante slipped away from his mounds of equipment and sat to unlace his boots. "I want financial workups on everyone who lives in that building, Gus. Starting with the Kane women and working right through the lot. Club memberships, business affiliations, corporate boards they sit on, the works.''

Lieberman shook out a cigarette and lit it, pulling deep. As he formalized his response he pushed the smoke in his lungs back out in an impatient whoosh. "You realize, of course, just how wild a shot this is? Some of it makes sense, maybe, but it's still a huge fuckin' reach.''

Joe removed his boots and slipped into a pair of flip-flops before standing to pace the room. "My replacement at Major Case thinks it's a crime of passion he's investigating, Gus. I do, too, but where Bud Costanza and I part ways is over the *nature* of that passion. The only kind of passion a guy like him can imagine is the old-fashioned lover's jealousy kind. Me? I'm looking at other possibilities. Religious zeal is a passion. Politics can be a passion. So can fast cars, golf, or coin collecting. But when I see that Fifth Avenue address and think about all the different people who live there, I've got to presume they've all got one particular passion in common. You're an imaginative guy, Gus. What would you think that passion might be?''

All the crankiness and foul humor that had hung over Gus Lieberman's Sunday like a storm cloud vanished. Over the years he'd watched his wife Lydia's brothers play the game Joey was referring to. Bart and Larry Cox had been raised with it. They knew only one set of rules. When you stepped into the arena with the big boys you either played with a passion for winning or you got killed.

"Money," he murmured.

Dante nodded. "It's the grease that makes all the wheels spin, Gus. Terrorists need it, and rich guys always seem to need more."

As far as Jumbo Richardson was concerned, any deal the City of New York had to cut to get Captain Bud Costanza off the job's active-duty roster would be well worth the money spent. Many years ago the captain had committed the tenets of police work—as set forth in the *Patrol Guide*—to memory. Since then he'd lived by those words as literally as a creationist interprets Genesis. Everything Jumbo admired about a good cop was absent here. Costanza was rigid rather than creative, a bully rather than compassionate, self-involved rather than team-oriented.

First thing that Sunday morning the captain told Jumbo they were going to pay Elizabeth Kane "a little surprise visit." Richardson suggested they call ahead to make sure the woman was home, and Costanza scoffed. His way of doing things was to catch them with their pants down. It was a Sunday, so where could she be? Church? Bud doubted it. No, he'd catch her with her head still half-full of sleep. Grill her about her visit to Detective Chester Garfield's bedside. Hit her with a barrage of questions about this technology breakthrough she was so eager to foist off as the motive in her father's homicide.

When it turned out that Elizabeth Kane wasn't home and hadn't been since sometime around three the previous afternoon, Costanza hit the roof. He had plans for that afternoon; a family dinner at his son's place out on the Island. If they had to wait long for this "dyke bitch" to return from her night of "muff diving," he'd be lucky to get table scraps.

Six hours, a trip back downtown, and an undigestible lunch later, Richardson found himself back on the sidewalk outside

Elizabeth Kane's building. A quarter-to-four phone call had finally found her at home. She'd promised to remain there while the detectives traveled back uptown to interview her.

"All right, Sergeant. Here's the game plan." They stood together under the awning, Costanza pulling Jumbo close to prevent the doorman from overhearing. "You've already had your shot at this one. Now it's my turn. If there's a raw nerve there, I'm gonna needle her till I hit it. You're the good guy, but let's not play it too good, huh? Just act like you're here to make sure I don't break nothing."

"It's your show," Beasley replied.

"Good. I'm glad you see it the same way I do, Sergeant. I want you to know I intend to break this fucker wide open. When I do there's gonna be plenty of glory to go around. We do it my way, and we're gonna get results. Guaranteed. Yesterday in that squad room I noticed a lack of focus. That's what I'm gonna bring to this investigation. You've got to focus down. They didn't invent the thumbscrew to crack nuts, for Crissake. They invented it to screw *thumbs*."

Beasley realized that he'd just bitten his tongue hard enough to draw blood. While his mouth filled with the taste of it he blinked back tears and sat hard on an urge to accidentally trip this guy and stumble on his head. He turned away and headed for the front door.

Elizabeth Kane's apartment was one of two on the third floor. When the elevator door opened, Richardson and Costanza stepped out into an anteroom a dozen feet square, with one apartment's entrance door at either end. The setting wasn't quite as dramatic as the penthouse level, but the decor was every bit as rich. The walls, covered in a pleated, water-stained raw silk, were trimmed in walnut. The panels of the hip-high wainscoting were walnut burl. The floor was a white-veined green marble.

"Nice, huh?" Costanza grunted. He'd stepped up to ring Elizabeth Kane's bell and now stood surveying his surroundings. "You imagine wallpaper like this in *your* house?"

Richardson didn't bother to reply and was relieved when

Elizabeth Kane answered her door. Instead of finding her dressed in the conservative business attire of Friday morning, Jumbo observed a casual and distinctly softer look. She was clad in moccasins, loose-fitting tan chinos, and a navy pullover sweater. Again she wore no jewelry, but today she'd abandoned the severity of Friday's makeup and tightly pulled back hair. This was the Ivory girl look; just a hint of eyeliner and her hair done in a loose French braid. Wisps of it hung free on either side of her face.

They were invited in and led to the living room. Down here on the third floor she had a closer and more intimate view of the park than her mother had upstairs.

"Have seats, gentlemen. Would either of you like coffee?"

"I'm afraid this ain't a social call, Miss Kane." Bud Costanza was jumping right in. "I'm the new commander of the unit that caught the investigation into your father's homicide, and frankly I've got some things that trouble me about it."

Jumbo watched the woman closely. She didn't bristle or stiffen at Costanza's tone; not as he'd expected the woman he met Friday morning might. In fact she seemed decidedly relaxed today; a posture that became her. Friday morning she was all business, cut-and-dried. Today, in this more softened Sunday afternoon persona, she was giving him a look at something besides her anger. She was big, yes, but by no means heavy. The fanny filling out the backside of those pants was hung on slim hips, the muscles tight. Those angles in her face no longer seemed so severe. Today they were almost striking.

"What sort of things would those be?" she asked. "I've tried to be as up-front as possible. Both with Detective Richardson and with the two detectives I met at the hospital yesterday afternoon."

Costanza scowled, trying to boost the power of his hardass approach. "I'm glad you mentioned the hospital, miss. It's one'a the problems I was having. In particular I'm still trying to figure what you were doing there. Maybe you can explain it.''

"What I was *doing* there? I was trying to find out what the hell had happened, Captain. Nobody was telling me anything, and when I heard that the house detective who was shot had survived, I wondered if he had seen anything.''

"Seen something like what, miss?''

She frowned. "Like who killed my father. A physical description. Something I could match up with . . . I don't know . . . something else I might know.''

"What else might you know?'' Costanza bore in. "You just got done telling me you've been real forthright with us already.''

"Nothing specific,'' she replied. "Perhaps something that could give me a clue to who is behind this. I know most of the people who were in a position to know about what my father and Veronica were working on. Not all the people in Chicago, but everybody out here. I was hoping Detective Garfield would have a description; something to help me make a connection.''

"And he didn't.'' It wasn't a question.

The young woman had taken a seat in a deep chair directly across from them. The Sunday *Times* was piled on the floor at her feet, and she had a cup of coffee on the little lamp table beside her. She lifted the cup now to sip and shook her head. "No, Captain. I wasn't that lucky.''

"But he did tell you something the perpetrator said. Just before he pulled the trigger.''

"Nothing terribly revealing,'' she replied. "He cursed. Like he was frustrated . . . or just pissed off.''

Richardson continued to be surprised. The angry exchange he'd witnessed Friday morning was subtly restrained, both the mother and daughter trading nasty but controlled verbal blows. Now, for the first time, Elizabeth Kane was not playing the daughter. This was her home, and she was in control here.

Costanza came forward in his seat, his demeanor increasingly aggressive. "I'm interested to know why you didn't mention this, ah, cursing when you talked to Detective Busby. Or the fact that the perp talked with a British accent. It was Garfield had to tell her that."

She frowned, seeming to examine the question from all sides before answering it. "I didn't mention it because I hadn't had time to analyze it yet, Captain."

Costanza rose to his feet, his hands going deep into the pockets of his sans-a-belt slacks. "Analyze it?" Total disbelief. "You were withholding information, Miss Kane. This is a *homicide* investigation. You may feel you're better qualified to conduct one than we are, but your city and state governments *don't*."

The young woman's body tightened visibly. Her voice was also tight in her throat now. "While you and your legions are out stumbling over each other looking for who pulled the trigger, I'm trying to determine who *ordered* this attack, Captain. As I attempted to explain to Sergeant Richardson on Friday, there are billions of dollars at stake. My company has French, Japanese, and Korean interests competing with it to land a very lucrative D of E contract. We weren't aware of any *British* interest even in the running. When Detective Garfield told me that the man who shot him had a British accent, I knew there were people I had to talk to. People who have a better grasp of the competition and where they stand."

The disbelief never left Costanza's face as he strutted stifflegged before her. "Don't tell me. Let me guess. That's why you didn't come home last night. You were with the troops in the trenches, trying to assess the damage."

The young woman bristled and pointed to an end table. "There's the phone, Captain. Call Ken Amasuka. He's the Magnetronics chief production engineer. We were up half the god damn night."

Costanza shrugged. "Maybe you were, miss. Amasuka?" He had his notebook out and was jotting the name into it. "Believe me, we'll check your story out. Is that where you stayed the night? His place?"

She closed her eyes. "I stayed at *my* place, Captain. I have a condo in Princeton. I drove down there in the late afternoon, spent most of the evening at the plant, went *back* to the plant early this morning, and spent most of today there. Not that it's any of your business . . . unless you're trying to say that *I'm* a suspect in your investigation."

Costanza squared up before her and beamed a smug little smile. "A suspect, Miss Kane? Let me explain how I've gotta look at it. I've got a man and his apparent mistress dead. In the course of my investigation I discover that this dead mistress has a strong connection to the dead man's daughter."

"*Strong* connection?" Elizabeth interrupted. "We work for the same company. Nine years ago we were college roommates."

Costanza smiled. "At *Smith* College, right Miss Kane?"

She bristled all over again. "What are you implying, Captain?"

Bud went all innocent. "Nothing at all, Miss Kane. I collect information and draw certain conclusions. I've got a daughter who may or may not have known that her old college roommate was having an affair with her father. If she *did* know, I've gotta wonder how she *felt* about that."

Elizabeth snorted. "I certainly didn't feel like *murdering* them."

Now Costanza chuckled. "And you think I'd expect you to tell me if you did? No, Miss Kane. My responsibility is to look at the preponderance of evidence. I've got a daughter who's been indulged by her father since the day she was born. A daughter who he gave the controlling interest in his company. Then along comes a rival for that affection who can use the one tool on him that this daughter *can't*. Jealousy's *the* prime motive for murder, little lady."

Jumbo could see Elizabeth Kane's chest start to heave as Costanza spoke. Now she was breathing hard, her whole body quivering like a plucked bowstring.

"Get the hell out of my house, Captain." Low and throaty. "Now."

"I *thought* maybe I hit a nerve."

The young woman came quickly to her feet and stood almost eye-to-eye with the object of her ire. "I said get out, Captain. The next time we speak my attorney will be present. This interview is over."

Bud stood his ground. He wasn't playing it *smarmy* nasty anymore. Now he was a cold, calculating hardass. "Fine, Miss Kane. I think I *will* be talking to you again. Make sure your lawyer's a good one. You might need the best money can buy."

Phillip Wright's entire world was threatening to come apart. Friday morning Julia had dropped him at the train with a quick kiss and her usual proclamation of undying love. When he returned home Saturday afternoon, he found all her things moved into the baby's room. She told him for the first time that she'd hated her life ever since they moved to America, that she'd only been willing to tolerate it because it was an important step for Phillip up the corporate ladder. Now she wasn't sure why she should care. Over the course of a Friday night and Saturday morning spent alone in this house she'd realized that it wasn't Larchmont and the States she hated, but the change she saw in Phillip. While she was left isolated here, her husband ran off drinking with his mates and whoring half the week. At first she'd seen it as some sort of aberration; him trying to find his way in a strange land. Now she no longer cared. She wouldn't tolerate it any longer. If he didn't change his tune soon, she would take their daughter and head back to England. Meanwhile, until such a time as she was convinced that the profuse apologies heaped on her were heartfelt, she intended to keep her distance.

That Saturday night, spent tossing and turning alone in the master suite's king-size bed, yielded no obvious solution to the most troubling dilemma Phillip now faced. Should he refuse to cooperate with his Irish tormentors that video footage would surely be his undoing. His handlers in London weren't likely to view any such threat made to Lloyd's security favorably. A thing like this could well kill his career . . . to say nothing about his marriage.

Sunday morning Phillip attempted to speak with his wife, hoping that the light of a new day had softened her resolve. He'd been treated with polite coolness. It was teatime now, and Phillip was still far removed from any reconciliation. Julia was feeding the baby in the dining room. She'd earlier announced she had planned to eat dinner out with several of her new friends. Half an hour ago he'd called out for a pizza that hadn't yet arrived. Banished to the library, he stared blankly at the final round of a golf tournament on the television and drank beer. He'd just opened his fifth Budweiser of the afternoon when the phone rang.

"Hello?"

"Phillip, lad."

An audible click told Wright that his wife had also picked up.

"It's for me, Julia." The open extension line went dead. "Why are you calling me here?" Wright hissed.

"Why, Phillip? To *chat*, lad. To make sure you're not having any second thoughts. Or thinking about calling the coppers in. This is a friendly call, Phillip. Just to make sure you've kept your wits about you and to find out what sort of progress you've made."

"Didn't I say you'd get your lists?"

Another chuckle. "That you did, Phillip. But you didn't really say *when*. Any thoughts on that?"

"The early part of the week is out of the question. We'll have auditors in from the home office until Wednesday at least. I can't promise anything before the weekend."

The caller clucked his tongue. "I'm on a schedule, Phillip. You wouldn't be stalling me, would you lad?"

"Call me at my office Friday," Wright growled. "You'll get your fucking lists." Before the Irishman could respond Phillip hung up the phone.

131

TWELVE

The first impression was the most important one. Greg Payne tried to emphasize the importance of this tenet over and over during Dante's crash course in materials expedition, and Joe had taken it to heart. Monday at seven A.M. sharp he arrived at the job site on West 95th Street driving his turbocharged Nissan 300-ZX. Right now it was parked on the street alongside his new employer's trailer office. From where he sat across the desk from Tim O'Brien, Dante had a good vantage of the car through a streetside window. A steady stream of workers were arriving on the site now. Many were stopping to peer into the Turbo Z's cockpit and to admire its sleek, low-slung lines.

"I don't know what you've heard about the history of this job, fella, but this fucker's been a nightmare from day one."

O'Brien spoke with the faint brogue of a man who'd left the old sod as a teenager. Dante guessed the sawed-off, barrel-chested man to be about fifty-five now. He was no doubt prosperous but took pains to leave most trappings of that prosperity at home. His office was a bare-bones desk, drawing table, and files setup. His hands were thick-fingered workingman's hands. There were creases in his work chinos and in the sleeves of his matching gray shirt, but the boots were as scuffed as the hard hat on the desk at his elbow. Greg Payne had described O'Brien as a "hands-on" type.

"I know the first drywall contractor was just thrown off

the job," Dante replied. "That he's being investigated by a federal grand jury for bid rigging. I know the high steel was six weeks late coming in and the curtain wall contractor is at least a month behind right now."

O'Brien nodded, pointing to the ceiling. "Twenty-eight through thirty-six are still wide open up there. The plumbers've only just pushed the rough up to twenty-three. Interior studding's completed to nineteen, but the electrical's only roughed as far as twelve. Today I'll be running crews onto six and seven, trying to pick up where the other man left off. The minute he got the boot he pulled every last piece of rock and bucket of mud outta there. My crew chiefs've done most of their own expediting in the past, and let me tell you, they think you've got your work cut out for you. Shipments of materials'll be arriving seven hours a day for the next two weeks. A crew of seven is all I can spare you right now, but they're good, strong lads, every one of them."

"Okay if I leave my car parked there?" Joe asked.

O'Brien shrugged. "Probably be as safe there as anywhere. Nice set of wheels, that. I guess they paid well, them ragheads."

"Well enough."

"So why'd you come back? You don't look like the type to be intimidated by a little unrest."

Dante smiled, playing it confident and relaxed. "I've got two daughters I hadn't seen in fifteen years. One started college this year. My ex-wife is remarried and moved to Colorado. I guess I just got homesick."

O'Brien grunted and planted his hands to push himself to his feet. "I guess you can't blame a man for missing his home. I try to get back over every few years myself. Then again, I don't imagine Ireland's much like Saudi fucking Arabia."

"Not hardly," Joe replied. "I understand a man can get a drink in Ireland."

O'Brien smiled. "That he can. Surely. So what do you say, Mr. Expediter? You ready to head upstairs?"

Dante grabbed his lunch pail off the scuffed linoleum and stood. "You bet. If we've covered everything here."

"Just one other thing. You watch your backside up there. My predecessor, Mr. Joe Tarantino, didn't much like how he got the boot. Word has it his whole family's mad as hell. His uncle Marty's got the interior wall building contract, and Marty Octavio's mean as a snake. He's also connected, and if he tells his people to make trouble for us, they'll make trouble."

"Why you?" Dante asked. "You aren't the one he's got a gripe with."

"I got the job. Octavio believes in getting even from the bottom on up. He'll hate me for earning his nephew Joey's bread and hate the accountants in the GC's front office for fingering Joey's crooked game. This job's already two months late, and the longer it takes to complete, the deeper delays eat into profits. It in't all that hard to fuck up a production schedule. Out and out vandalism's one way, and accidents are another. Like I said; you watch your ass up there."

Rusty Heckman thought Princeton, New Jersey, looked exactly like an Ivy League university town ought to look. He was a State University of New York man himself, but the ivy-covered walls and hallowed halls of schools like Princeton still evoked strong archetypal images. The kids wandering the streets here looked pretty much like college kids anywhere, but the streets themselves set this place apart. Stately stone buildings with crenellated battlements and windows of leaded glass. Huge mature trees lined the sidewalks with manicured lawns and lovingly tended gardens beyond. Rusty dreamed of one day retiring from the job and teaching. He'd attended night classes whenever his schedule allowed, and one day soon, when he finished a thesis on Civil War battles fought above the Mason-Dixon line, NYU would award him a master's degree in history. He could see no reason to stop there, and Princeton looked like just the sort of place an ex-cop could be happy earning his Ph.D.

Nineteenth Precinct

Before heading out to the Magnetronics plant south of town on Route 583, Don and Rusty had eaten a late breakfast in a coffee shop near the Princeton campus. Out of habit Heckman had already grabbed a bowl of cereal before leaving the house that morning. He could have skipped this second morning feed, but his partner had an appetite that demanded nourishment half-a-dozen times a day. Rusty had no idea how Grover managed it, but while his own waistline had grown four inches since the two of them started working together, Don maintained the exact same one hundred sixty-eight pounds on his six-foot one-inch frame.

When the partners arrived at their destination both noticed how carefully the complex was designed to integrate with the lush terrain surrounding it. A small security office at the main gate was the only part of the plant visible from the road. They followed the access road deep into oak and maple-studded woods and finally found the Magnetronics facility nestled down along the shore of a small private lake.

"Nice place to work," Heckman commented.

Grover agreed. "I wonder if the security guards get fishing privileges. If they do, I might be tempted to make an application."

As a young woman from Public Relations escorted them to their meeting with the chief production engineer, they passed through several areas where production was in evidence. Heckman remarked that it didn't look at all like any factory floor he'd ever seen. Their escort explained that most Magnetronics medical equipment was assembled in a dust-free environment. Hence entire teams of workers dressed in white paper overgarments, head coverings, and latex gloves. She further explained that these paper garments were disposable and that each technician donned a new set each shift.

"Expensive," Grover commented.

"So are these machines," she replied. "When a hospital spends three million dollars for magnetic resonance equipment and depends on it to save lives, it expects that equipment to be functional whenever they need it. It's our job to make sure it will be.''

When they reached a large, naturally lit office with windows opening out on the waters of the nearby lake, Rusty was surprised at how young the production engineer proved to be. Ken Amasuka was no more than thirty-two or -three; a slight man of medium height with short-cropped jet hair, rimless spectacles, and a quick smile. He was seated before a computer terminal as they entered and kicked away from it to rise in greeting.

''Gentlemen. Welcome to Magnetronics.''

The detectives introduced themselves, and Amasuka indicated chairs. Once they were settled the engineer opened his hands in the classic gesture of availability.

''You're probably wondering why I'm not at Ralph's funeral. Well, the last thing he'd want his death to do is set back his dream of seeing Magnetronics win the electromagnetics contract for the D of E supercollider. Right now that looks like exactly what it's done.''

''How so?'' Rusty asked. ''Our information is that he was on the verge of a breakthrough.''

''On the verge, Sergeant? He was a whole lot closer than that. He'd nailed it.''

''So how has his death set you back?'' Heckman pressed.

Amasuka flashed that quick smile. ''We never got all the final data. Not here at the plant. Ralph was getting more than a little paranoid in his old age. He would keep every phase of research and production separated out until it came time to put them all together. I don't know what you've heard about our unit in Chicago, but that was one end of it. My people here would feed him his production cost analysis figures, material costs, all the nuts-and-bolts stuff. Ralph did most of the theoretical work himself, with backup from Veronica and her pool of eggheads out in Illinois. They did verifications of his numbers and plugged our production data into them.'' He pointed to Heckman's chair. ''Last Monday Ralph sat where you are now, Sergeant. He came here to tell me he'd finally broken through. Some of the production values he was working with were more than a year old, and he wanted me to update them. I faxed the latest figures to Chicago last Monday, and we were supposed to get the completed project this morning. Instead Ralph and Veronica are dead, and I'm scrambling to reconstruct the final phases based on the data already delivered.''

Grover and Heckman glanced at each other, and Don asked the next question. ''Just what would this delivery have looked like?''

Amasuka snorted, his frustration obvious. ''One or two lousy computer disks. Ralph had duplicates of everything else he'd done to date locked in his office safe. He'd already shown me most everything, but without those missing disks we're still groping in the dark. I got off the phone with one of the guys in Chicago just before you got here. He says Veronica got on the plane with them Thursday afternoon.''

''They don't have duplicates in Chicago?'' Rusty asked.

Now the engineer laughed outright. ''Duplicates? Oh, sure. But you had to know Veronica to understand what that means. Double Ralph's paranoia and toss her own deviousness into the pot. She has a least two thousand disks in her personal files out there, each of them camouflaged with a labeling code she kept up here.'' He tapped his forehead. ''They're sorting through them, one at a time.''

Grover and his slightly hyper metabolism found themselves too antsy to sit any longer. He pushed himself to his feet and wandered to the window overlooking the lake. ''Who else had access to what you were doing, Mr. Amasuka? Here on the East Coast?''

''Nobody else.''

Grover turned. ''Why was that?''

Again the open hands gesture, this time accompanied by a shrug. ''I've been Ralph Kane's protégé for twelve years, Sergeant. He and one of my professors at Stanford worked at Berkeley together. Ralph hired me out of the second-year electrical engineering class. I like to think I'm good at what

I do, but there are a lot of people here who are good. I'm where I am in the hierarchy because Ralph trusted me. There aren't many people he trusted.''

Don returned to gazing out over the water. A pair of geese had landed, and one of the resident swans was hurrying to run them off. "Who else would he have trusted with what he was doing? Not with the specifics like you and the Tierney woman were, but with a more general overview of his directions.''

Amasuka needed no time to reflect on this one. "His daughter Liz, definitely. Maybe Josh Sellers. He and Ralph go all the way back to the beginning together. Everyone else worked on a strictly need-to-know basis.''

"The daughter told two detectives interviewing her yesterday that she was here working with you on damage control most of Saturday night," Rusty mentioned. "She's that close to it, huh?''

"Liz? You bet. She was here a lot of Sunday morning, too. She and Ralph weren't only close, but he knew she had one hell of a sell job ahead of her once he got the bugs worked out. He was depending on her to help him format the contract bid.''

"Any rivalry between her and the Tierney woman?" Rusty asked.

"Liz and Veronica? Not that I heard. Veronica and the Kanes go way back, too. She and Liz knew each other in college.''

"How about Mrs. Kane?" Grover wondered. Out on the lake the swan had driven that pair of geese back into the air and had returned to looking regal and subdued. Don started to pace. "How involved was she in company affairs?''

Amasuka gave it a quick, negative shake of the head. "Involved? Not at all. So far as I know she has very little interest." The engineer paused, seeming to consider the direction of their conversation. His eyes moved back and forth between the two cops, the sparkle of curiosity in them. "You think somebody stole the project when they killed Ralph and Veronica.''

Grover's face remained impassive as he replied. "We don't think anything just yet, Mr. Amasuka. It's too early for that. But yes, it is one of the possibilities we're exploring.''

"I guess the money motive would be hard to ignore, huh?''

"We're hearing figures like five billion dollars,'' Don replied. "Even a penny on the dollar for a prize that size would be one hell of a temptation, right?''

"I said I think Amasuka..."

Mel snorted. "C'mon, Shea's Grover's for God's sake."

While Jumbo and Bud Costanza attended the Kane funeral at Trinity Church in downtown Manhattan, Guy Napier and Melissa Busby had the squad to themselves. Their assignment this morning was to collect the financial workups on Kane family members requested from Records Division and give them a thorough examination. It never ceased to amaze them how quickly something could be done when the right people wanted it. Costanza had made his request for this material on Saturday afternoon and by ten A.M. Monday some rather exhaustive files had been compiled and delivered. Much of the data was protected and could only be accessed via subpoena. The fact that it was all here now, spread before them on the squad room table, meant that somebody with a lot of clout wanted a quick resolution in this case. Wanted it badly.

They'd been at it since the files arrived. It was lunchtime now, and instead of breaking they'd called out for sandwiches. Melissa sat across from Guy, half a BLT in one hand and a pencil in the other. As she chewed she scanned a page of the Elizabeth Kane report, the point of her pencil sweeping down it in serpentine fashion. When she reached the bottom she flipped the page aside and started at the top of the next. Napier was working through Amanda Kane's profile in a similar manner.

Across the table, Napier stirred. After three hours spent scrutinizing tax returns, bank statements, brokerage summaries, and other bits and pieces of financial information, he thought he was seeing a trend emerge.

"This is wild," he murmured.

"What's that?" Melissa didn't look up, her tone distracted.

"I think she's going broke."

Melissa glanced up now, a frown creasing her brow. "Say what?"

"I said I think Amanda Kane's going broke."

Mel snorted. "C'mon. She's a Gregory, for God's sake. How *could* she be?"

Certain people in American society simply had too much money to ever be faced with insolvency.

"By spending more than she takes in. And that wouldn't be hard, according to what I've been reading. I didn't believe it either. Not at first. But I've been over it twice now."

Melissa was on her feet and coming around the end of the table. "You're *sure*? You're not reading something wrong?"

"I don't think so." Guy spread a dozen sheets of the file like a solitaire hand on the surface before him. "Let's do it this way. Here." He pointed to the first page on the upper left. "Her banking summary from two years ago. It gives a good idea of what her month-to-month expenses are. Household, with the maid, chauffeur, all that crap. Travel. Entertainment. Purchases. Payments to the credit card companies. It adds up to seven hundred eighty-six thousand bucks. That's an average monthly nut of sixty-five grand." As he spoke Napier reached for the sheet on the upper right. "Now skip over all this other shit and look here." He handed the sheet to Mel. "Her income that year was five hundred twenty-five thousand, tax free, and another couple hundred thousand in income from investment holdings. That first figure's her annual allowance from the Gregory trust. The last money's all taxable, and she comes out the other side with what? A hundred and a quarter?"

Melissa scanned the page before her, found the figure, and

nodded. Napier resumed his analysis by handing her his own scratch pad.

"It isn't hard to figure the bottom line. This woman spends three quarters of a mil a year and takes in at least a hundred thirty thousand less than that. When you're talking about one person spending that much it all sounds like funny money. The shortfall alone is equal to what you and I make in a year. Combined."

The pair of them sat in silence a moment, looking first at the figures before them and then at each other.

"How long do you think this has been going on?" Melissa asked.

Guy shrugged. "At least the three years we've got here. It starts adding up, doesn't it? More than a million bucks every ten years. Take a look at her assets. I don't know what they once were, but last year they were just under two million. She liquidated close to two hundred thousand just to make ends meet. At that rate she'll be zeroed out by the end of the decade."

Melissa was still scanning as she nodded. "I don't get it. If *she* was spending this much money, what was her husband spending?"

"Good question. There must be a whopping huge maintenance on that penthouse of theirs. I can't find it listed anywhere here. She paid the help and her driver, but we already know he had his own wheels, paid for by the corporation. Here's something else interesting. She files her returns separately."

Melissa didn't seem to think it that unusual. "Wealthy people file separately all the time. Especially if they go into a marriage with significant assets. I wonder if Jumbo covered any of that in his talk with Kane's lawyer."

"I guess it stands to reason they had some kind of arrangement," Napier agreed. "Look at the will. Kane had total control of Magnetronics back when he incorporated." He dropped his pencil and sat back. "If I had the sort of cash drain Amanda Kane's experiencing, I'd be a little uneasy about the future. Look at her overhead.''

"Granted," Mel argued. "But what's twenty percent of a company like Magnetronics worth? Maybe a hundred million?''

Napier rubbed his face with his hands and yawned. "At least. She might not be happy about getting the short end of the control stick, but she's still sitting pretty.''

"Look at these numbers." Melissa held up the banking statements for 1991. "One month she writes a forty-seven-thousand-dollar check to American Express. Another twelve to Visa. I'm sure you're as curious as I am what she's spending that kind of money on.''

"Let's request copies of her card receipts.''

"Couldn't hurt," Mel agreed. "I'll bet she spends a quarter million on clothes alone.''

Guy lifted his chin toward the pile of papers over which Melissa had been pouring. "We *know* what kind of shape the daughter's in now, but how was she doing before she got the good news?''

"Judging from what we've got here? She was already rich. She made a quarter million in salary last year, paid a healthy chunk of that in taxes, and has an eighteen-hundred-a-month maintenance on her co-op apartment. Other than that all her business expenses, her car, a condo in Princeton, and travel were paid for by the company. Out of pocket it looks like she lived pretty frugally. She just turned thirty this year, and even without control of Magnetronics she's worth well over five million. Her mother's assets are dwindling to the tune of two hundred thousand a year, while hers were growing more than twice that fast.''

What a day. If Joe Dante harbored any doubts about his ability to do this job, this day had provided little evidence to dispel them. Tim O'Brien made every effort to ensure that his crews were adequately supplied when they arrived for their first day of work, but Dante soon discovered that many of these stopgap materials were still on the ground floor. Before the rock hangers could begin skinning the five thousand feet of open stud wall on the sixth and seventh floors more than a thousand sheets of 5/8th-inch drywall and fifty kegs of screws had to be delivered upstairs. An expediter is meant to organize the movement of materials. The current situation demanded Dante do more than just supervise. He needed every available hand at his disposal, including his own two. By ten A.M. he was stripped to an undershirt soaked through with sweat. By the noon lunch break he and his seven-man crew had gotten far enough ahead to catch their breaths. The tapers were already at work finishing the rock hung earlier that morning. That meant more deliveries: joint compound now and seam tape.

They'd been back at work for an hour after lunch when Tim O'Brien located Dante on the ground-floor loading dock.

"I've been talking to the lads upstairs, Mr. Expediter. It looks like you're making good progress." His tone was approving, even impressed.

Dante paused after steering the tines of a pallet jack beneath a load of mud buckets. Straightening, he wiped his brow with the back of his forearm. "Starting to get it in hand," he agreed.

"You're satisfied with your crew?"

To best utilize his manpower Joe had divided his crew of seven men into teams of three and kept the odd man out to assist him. That odd man was a slender but surprisingly tough kid named Tom McCarty. From his conversation with McCarty at lunch, Dante learned he was a recent arrival in the States. He and three other friends lived in a North Bronx apartment. His roommates were immigrants as well, all working construction. Joe glanced to McCarty now.

"You kidding? They're working their asses off. Every one of them."

O'Brien again seemed pleased. "They're good lads, them. You look like you've burned a few calories yourself."

"It's good for me," Joe told him. "Beats hell out of running on a treadmill."

O'Brien eyed his expediter's glistening arms and shoulders. There was a nasty scar up high on the left side, the faint whiteness of it trailing down to his back from his jawline. His build was impressive for any man, let alone for a man in his early forties. A powerful upper body tapered to a waist that hadn't thickened much with age. The hands were hidden by gloves now, but the contractor had noticed them earlier. Knuckles thick with scar tissue. Palms heavy with callus. There was little doubt in Tim O'Brien's mind that this character had done some brawling in his day and could probably still hold his own in a bar fight.

"Looks like you're starting to get a little ahead."

Dante glanced around, assessing the dent made in the stacks of material. "A little. I'm not gonna be satisfied until we're at least a floor ahead of demand. We keep moving like we've done today, we'll be there by the end of the week."

"Well, now. The business agent assured me you were a get-the-job-done sort, but I'll admit I had my doubts. It looks like I was a bit hasty with them."

O'Brien went over some inventory figures and left Dante to head upstairs with his load of mud. When the elevator reached the seventh floor the operator heaved the steel-mesh gate aside, and Joe gunned the battery-powered pallet jack ahead onto the landing. Seconds later McCarty arrived with his own load in the car opposite. As the elevators departed, Dante started his stack of plastic joint-compound buckets forward. He'd gone only a few feet when he frowned and backed off the handlebar throttle. McCarty noticed the look on his face.

"Something wrong?"

"Listen."

The youngster's head turned, face hardening in concentration.

"I don't get it," Joe murmured. "It can't be a power cut; the elevators are still running."

All morning this floor and the one below had been engulfed in the din of screw guns in action; a sharp, high-pitched *z-i-i-i-p* lasting approximately a second. There was a crew of a dozen men hanging rock up here, half of them equipped with these power tools. It didn't make sense that all of them would be out of action at the same time.

From far off at the opposite end of the floor a resounding crash reached them followed by muffled but definitely angry shouts. Another crash. And another. Dante left the load of mud right where it was and started forward at a trot. As he approached the source of the shouting around long stretches of newly skinned wall, the words came clear.

"Fuckin' mick bastards! Go the fuck back where you fuckin' came from and stop stealing American jobs! Who the fuck you fuckin' people think you are?"

There were more thuds and crashes as Joe rounded the last wall separating him from the scene of the altercation. Behind it he found the members of O'Brien's crew confronted by three burly men in hard hats and work clothes. And while those odds weren't particularly intimidating, the three-foot lengths of black iron pipe carried by these interlopers were. Two of them loomed in threatening poses out front while the apparent ringleader stood behind them, swinging his length of pipe at a fresh stretch of wall. Ragged holes had already been torn down the length of it and the ringleader was now turning his attentions on an intersecting wall.

"Some sorta *problem* here?" Joe shouted.

All heads turned. The ringleader scowled at this new arrival, not recognizing him.

"Butt outta this, pal. This ain't got nothing to do with you."

Dante stepped forward, his eyes holding this other's one-on-one. "Says who? You?"

"That's right. Me. And my business is with this job-stealing scum here. How 'bout you take a hike!"

"I don't think so." Joe took another step toward the man, his progress bringing him dangerously close to one of the

145

bully's henchmen and his length of black pipe. "I *work* with these guys. That wall you just wrecked is wall I busted my ass hauling up here. I don't know what your problem is, friend, but your attitude pisses me off."

Joe saw confusion mix with the irritation in this other's eyes.

"You don't *sound* like one'a these mick fucks, but you listen to me anyway, pal. The way Tim O'Brien got this fuckin' job ain't the way it was s'posed to happen. He ain't part'a the agreement."

"Oh? I'm not sure I know about any agreement. I doubt he does either."

The kingpin's eyes narrowed. Not a tall man at maybe five foot six, his build emphasized girth. A belly carefully cultivated into his middle years hung heavy over his belt. The cocky way he held himself suggested a man accustomed to getting his way. Thick, short-fingered hands made little agitated gestures as he spoke.

"I don't give a *fuck* what you're sure of, pal. What *I'm* sure of is that you're in my fuckin' face. You either get out of it, now, or I have my boys here rip youse a new fuckin' asshole."

Dante recalled his earlier conversation with O'Brien. Marty Octavio was the name of the bid rigger's uncle, the guy who'd lost the project's first drywall contract.

"I don't think so, Marty. That's your name, isn't it? I'm giving you and your boys ten seconds to clear this floor." Joe paused to glance at his watch. "One." A beat. "Two."

Octavio looked to the larger of his two henchmen. "Who *is* this fuckin' guy? You ever seen him?"

The henchman shook his head, shrugging heavy shoulders and taking a step in Dante's direction. As he moved he lifted his length of pipe and tapped the palm of his other hand with it. Joe found himself wondering how much actual construction work the man did. The boots were too new, and the nose had been broken more times than the Yankees have won the World Series.

"Three."

Octavio scowled. "Just keep counting, fuck face. At the count'a nine, Rocco here's gonna take your fuckin' head off. Right, Rocco?"

The big guy with the bent nose nodded.

"Four," Dante counted. "I'm afraid Rocco's way out of his league today, Marty. Five."

Octavio's face flushed with sudden anger. "Enough'a this bullshit! Teach this mick fuck a lesson he won't forget, Rock. Now!"

Rocco reacted like an attack dog on command. He had a little Darryl Strawberry hitch in his swing; he tucked his lead shoulder, cocked that length of pipe, and started it around with vicious force.

His target suddenly vanished. Dante dropped like a rock, landing almost flat, his palms catching him to absorb impact. In the blink of an eye he was on his feet again, now standing on the back side of his attacker's swing. One hand flashed out, caught Rocco by the wrist of his follow arm and jerked it backward hard against a raised knee. The thug screamed in pain as his elbow joint exploded. Joe caught the length of pipe in midair as Rocco dropped it and sagged to his knees. From behind Dante, Octavio's second man rushed in, swinging. Again Dante vanished from the path of the blow. He tumbled forward in a shoulder roll and recovered to stand facing his attacker in a crouch. With the weapon now in his own hands he easily parried a second wild swing aimed at his head.

"*Get* his ass, Anthony!" Octavio snarled.

"Anthony?" Dante asked. He stood facing his attacker head-on. "Quit now and you won't get hurt, Anthony."

"I'm gonna kick your ass," his opponent seethed.

Dante shook his head. "You push this any further and you'll find *your* ass in the nearest hospital." Joe took a circling step to his left and tossed the length of pipe toward his group of coworkers. Barehanded now, he continued to circle. "Take your best shot, Anthony."

"I said *get* him!" Octavio screamed.

The thug came at Dante in another mad rush. This time he swung the pipe in short, chopping strokes aimed at his target's legs. Dante feinted twice, toying with him and watching fury cloud his judgment. On the third feint Anthony gave up swinging, lowered his weapon like a battering ram, and came straight ahead. Dante caught the front end of it and kept it moving past with a quick jerk. Anthony stumbled. Joe glided to one side and aimed a nasty snap kick at his opponent's nearest knee. The pain of it was everything the thug knew. He couldn't cover up as Joe threw an instep into his midsection and clubbed him across the back of the neck with both fists. The air went out of him, and Anthony crumpled to the floor face-first.

Ten feet away Marty Octavio was down on one knee lifting his pant leg. Before he could clear the little .25-caliber Beretta holstered on his ankle, a forearm to the throat sent him sprawling. His gun clattered to the floor.

Joe pounced on the loose weapon and tackled the choking Octavio as he tried to make a break through a nearby doorway. The two of them went down, Dante hooking an arm beneath the heavier man's right thigh and jerking up hard to pin Octavio's shoulders to the concrete floor. With his free hand he shoved the muzzle of the little gun hard into the underside of the wall-building contractor's jaw.

"I'm not a mick fuck, Marty. I'm a guinea fuck, just like you." Joe broke eye contact to find O'Brien's foreman, Henry Roark. "Get their wallets, Henry. How much damage would you say they did here? Two, three thousand bucks worth?" He peered back down into Octavio's face. "You and your boys are still alive, Marty. You start pulling guns around me, you're lucky I let you walk away. This one I'm keeping as a little souvenir. I ever see your fat ass anywhere near an O'Brien crew, you're gonna wish to God I'd pulled the trigger on this little piece of shit right here and now." Once Tom McCarty had collected Octavio's wallet, Joe stood. As he backed off, McCarty handed it to him. There looked to be close to a thousand dollars in big bills in there. Joe extracted them and threw the wallet at Octavio's feet. "Now get the fuck outta here, Marty . . . and take your garbage with you."

THIRTEEN

The minute Bud Costanza got a whiff of Amanda Kane's money problems he locked on the scent like a buck deer in rut. Monday morning he and Jumbo Richardson saw little to excite them at victim Ralph Kane's funeral. Bud was hungry for a break, and Mrs. Kane's situation looked to be just the opening he sought. As with so many such directions, this one demanded the investigation procure a plethora of substantiating documentation. Subpoena requests took most of Tuesday to obtain, and the squad didn't have Amanda Kane's brokerage, credit card, and other specific transaction records in hand until late Wednesday. Costanza was undeterred by these delays. For his money Amanda Kane fit perfectly. No matter how far he had to go to prove it, he knew he had his perp.

It wasn't until after lunch Wednesday that Costanza thought of requesting Mrs. Kane's FBI file. She was a woman of some social standing after all. What could the Bureau possibly have on her? How many socialites had criminal pasts? Just as they were preparing to swing out that evening at the end of their shifts, Richardson returned from Records with the file. The minute Costanza opened it he knew he'd *really* hit pay dirt.

"Look at this!" the captain crowed. "God damn it, I *knew* it!"

Jumbo didn't have to look. He'd scanned the report on his

way back upstairs and seen what he knew would attract Costanza's immediate attention. "I ain't sure what having a radical experience or two in college has to do with who the woman is today," he countered. "That was almost thirty years ago."

Costanza snorted. "A radical experience or *two*? Amanda Gregory was a fucking *Communist*, Sergeant. The SDS was a goddamn commie terrorist organization."

"What I read said she was suspected of sympathizing with them, Cap. Or maybe helping 'em raise money. It don't say a word about them ever proving none of that. She lived in Berkeley, for Crissake. Back in them days everybody at Berkeley was a red, at least so far as J. Edgar Hoover was concerned." Beasley had the cheeks of his rear end wedged over the edge of the credenza in Joey's old office while Costanza sat watching him from the other side of Dante's desk. Busby and Napier were the only other members of the squad present. They sat listening outside the open office door. "Even if she did help raise money for the antiwar movement in the sixties, what's that got to do with her husband bein' killed now?"

"We're looking for motive here, Sergeant. First Napier discovers the wife is teetering on the edge'a bankruptcy. Now we learn she's got a commie past in her closet."

"I'd hardly call a woman with an allowance of half a million a year and two million more in the stock market bankrupt, Cap. Living a little beyond her means, yeah. But not broke. Not by a long shot."

Costanza rolled his eyes in frustration. "She's clearly up against it, Sergeant. Desperate people do desperate things. Her husband's screwing some bimbo half her age. She's got that high-profile image she's trying to maintain and is looking at the possibility'a it being cut off. You yourself told us 'bout the arrangement she and the victim had. His money was his and hers was hers, to do whatever the fuck they wanted to do with it. If she claims she didn't know how her old man was pouring it to his assistant, she's giving you a hand job.

I seen pictures'a that dead broad. You don't let your husband run off and lock himself inta the company suite three days a week with a broad like that; not without your eyes wide open you don't. They're gonna play footsie, guaranteed. It's the nature'a the fucking beast.''

Richardson had trouble arguing with the man there. Then again, if what he'd witnessed from Amanda Kane on the morning of her husband's murder was an act, it was a good one. So good that he still believed it. If that was a hand job Amanda Kane had given him, then she'd missed her calling.

"You're saying you want us to concentrate on the wife from here on, right?"

"Fuckin' A right I do. I can smell the stink of it on her, Sergeant." Costanza leaned back in his chair, eyes on the ceiling and a satisfied smile stretching his lips. "It's classic, the assumption she made. Who's gonna suspect some rich broad? The world just assumes she's already got as much money as her old man. Without the dwindling funds angle, there's no tie-in.''

Napier had risen from his chair and stepped to the open door. He wedged one shoulder against the jamb, wearing a look of puzzlement. "One thing doesn't fit with pinning it on the wife, Cap. The whole industrial espionage and technology hijacking angle. That five-billion-dollar contract is too much motive to just ignore.''

Costanza rolled his eyes once more, his chin dropping to his chest as he took a deep breath and exhaled. "You disappoint me, son. Everything I've heard tells me you're one'a the best, but you're wrong here. This ain't no puzzle; it's simplicity itself. There *wasn't* no technology theft. You yourself found them two disks overlooked in that briefcase, correct? Them and five miles'a printout. So what's missing?" He held up a cautioning hand. "I know. All the other disks in the sequence before them, but that's a purely theoretical assumption. Did anyone ever see them? Has it been *established* they're missing? No. And why? Because this shooter-for-hire who busted in there and killed them two was hired to do no more than just that. End of story. Now all we've gotta do is find the evidence we need to pin it on the wife. That shooter's out there somewhere with a big wad'a cash burning a hole in his pocket. We're gonna find him and squeeze him till he sings.''

"Joe."

The four o'clock whistle had just blown. Dante was wedging his empty lunch bucket beneath his arm for the trip downstairs when he heard his name called and turned. The man approaching him was the foreman of the drywall crew accosted by Marty Octavio and his goons Monday afternoon. Not much older than most of the men working under him, Henry Roark had already begun developing little laugh crinkles at the corners of his eyes. Irish skin in its mid-thirties started to do that.

"Yeah, Henry. What's on your mind?"

Roark fell in alongside as Dante started down one of the new seventh-floor corridors toward the elevators. "I know the lads 'n' me have perhaps seemed the slightest bit standoffish; you being the new fella and all. We don't want you to think we're ungrateful for what you did the other day. I could see you know how to handle yourself, but still it took balls. It wasn't even your beef.''

"Sure it was, Henry. O'Brien's got a legitimate contract, and I work for him same as you do.''

Roark shrugged, his head bobbing to one side and then the other. "Maybe so and no matter. I'm wondering if you'd let me stand you to a pint somewheres. We all live way up north in the Bronx, but if you've got an idea about some place close by, the first one is on me.''

In a way, Dante thought, maybe he was being felt out. He *was* the new guy, and if he'd learned anything these past three days, it was that the Irish all seemed to stick together. Strangers in a strange land. Many of them carpooled down here from the Woodlawn, Kingsbridge, and Norwood sections of the North Bronx, seven or eight to a van. At night they journeyed home again in precisely the same manner, while he straggled off to an entirely different world. Right now Henry Roark was attempting to learn whether their worlds were at all compatible.

McAleer's Pub on Eighty-first and Amsterdam seemed like just the ticket. Blue collar down to its duckboards, it had stout on tap and just the right atmosphere of sour beer and stale smoke. Twenty minutes after Roark's approach upstairs on the job site, Joe and Henry sat shoulder-to-shoulder atop a couple of stools, the bar around them filling quickly with an after-work crowd.

"Tim tells me he's never been more pleased with the job a man has done for him," Roark commented. "There've been no supply complaints from the lads either. Your bosses in the Gulf must've hated to lose you."

The cold beer felt good in Dante's parched throat. Breathing drywall dust all day had left him with a powerful thirst.

"I got so I just couldn't look at another grain of sand, or another woman in a veil, or a drink mixed with bathtub gin, or a cop caning some poor pissant in the street. Every year I'd come back home for Christmas, and this year I decided to come home early and not go back."

Roark sighed. "An expatriate's lot. No matter how long you stay, it's never home." He paused to sip his beer and then glanced back over. "I suppose you're thinking a discussion of how you've done your job can't be why I asked you for a drink. No, it's an assessment of just what this Marty Octavio threat represents. The lads and I haven't got much experience with the sort of violence he looked ready to commit before you stopped him. Plenty of us have scrapped some in bars, but this is different. The lads are afraid that guns might be next."

As Dante listened he tried to examine Roark's fears from as many sides as he could. He couldn't very well tell him not to worry. The Octavio threat was real. On the other hand he could see where this might lead. The temptation to fight fire with fire was just too great in disputes like this.

"You're asking me, as a guy who seems to have a little experience with matters such as these, whether I think it's time Tim O'Brien put on a little protection of his own. Am I right?"

Roark nodded.

"You don't want a war with these people, Henry. You can't win one. You're outmanned and outgunned. It's my guess that Octavio is pretty small time and trying to look bigger than he really is. He tried throwing his weight around and got more than what he gave. It's been quiet as a church the past few days. Maybe he's discovered he just doesn't have the stomach for the game he was trying to play."

Roark stared straight ahead into the back-bar mirror. "I've talked to Tim about it, and he feels the same way you do, but for different reasons. You're mistaken about one thing, Joe. We'd be neither outmanned nor outgunned were Timmy to exercise one option. We Irish have become a force to be reckoned with once again in this city, but Tim O'Brien will have nothing to do with the men behind that force. He won't become beholden to them."

"He's a wise man, Henry." Joe drained off the rest of his beer and signaled the barkeep. "How about it? Will you have another?"

Roark peered at his watch and shook his head. "I'd better not, but thanks, Joe." He finished his drink and planted his feet to stand. "I'll admit I had some second thoughts when I heard the union was plantin' an unknown on us. You get so you like to know the men your work depends on. I've got no second thoughts anymore, Joe. And I'm glad we had this chance to hoist one together." He pushed one of his big mitts in Dante's direction, and Joe grabbed hold to shake.

"Pleasure's mine, Henry."

Dante watched Roark's progress in the mirror as he approached the door and passed out into the gathering gloom. For the past three days he'd wondered if he might ever penetrate the shell isolating him from his coworkers. Tonight he'd finally broken through.

* * *

After returning late from a week of extradition hearings in Utah, James Patrick Quinn called the office Thursday morning and told his secretary he wouldn't be in until after lunch. As overseer of the small but profitable criminal defense interests at Quinn, Oliver, and Sellers he had no pressing court appearances on his calendar today. The few meetings scheduled could be moved. Right now he had his hands full here at home. As Amanda Kane emerged from his bathroom he absorbed the seductive roll of her hips and licked his chops. Her feet and legs were bare. His silk robe was tied loosely at her waist, the front of the garment left to hang open.

Where women were concerned Jim Quinn didn't care if they were fifteen or fifty so long as they were enthusiastic and kept themselves in decent shape. Amanda Kane dovetailed nicely with his criteria. There was no mistaking her ardor. He had no idea how she was with other men, but when she came to his bed she always came to play. Two centuries of powerful Gregory men bedding creatures of great beauty had produced some handsome stock indeed. Sound stock, too. At fifty-two Amanda had the skin and muscle tone of a woman half her years. Anything her genes couldn't support plastic surgery had. Hers were a young girl's breasts and ass; a thirty-five-year-old's face.

Quinn drank all this in as she stood haughty and proud before him, the robe dropping away to the floor. Beneath it she wore lace lingerie, the panties cut high on her hips and the bra pushing her breasts forward like fruit tumbling from an overfilled cornucopia. She was an artist, as adept at making him want her as he was at discerning her motivations. She needed him; not for sex but for her very survival. Jim enjoyed that knowledge.

"What's this I hear about a problem?" he asked.

She came toward him where he lay reclined on his bedroom sofa, easing herself to her knees alongside him. "Problem?" One of those elegant, long-fingered hands slid across

156

his pajama-clad thigh, her nails raking across his crotch ever so gently. "You mean the one Billy claims to be having with the program?"

Her fingers found their way inside his fly and pulled him free. He felt the heat of her breath and the delicious sensation of her tongue being dragged the length of him. If she intended to distract him, she was doing a credible job. As much as he hated to, Quinn caught her chin between thumb and forefinger, lifting her head. He locked gazes and smiled.

"First things first, babe. *You* called *me*, remember?"

Amanda sighed and sat back, planting one hand on the carpet.

"Billy is claiming it isn't all there, Jimmy. That the end of it is missing."

The attorney frowned. "And you don't believe him."

Amanda leaned close, her face all earnestness. "I don't see how it can be. We planned this for how long? I watched that bastard Ralph leave every Thursday to shack up with his dyke bitch and never said a word. You think I didn't want to stop it sooner? But you told me to be patient, so I was patient."

"I know that, Mandy. But that isn't what . . ."

"Wait a minute," she cut him off. "You think maybe I'm *wrong*? How, Jimmy? That I didn't hear him right, or that I couldn't take it anymore and jumped the gun? Not on your life, mister. I *stroked* that son of a bitch; played the loving, understanding wifey. The weekend after he finally tied it all together he could barely contain himself. As soon as Veronica cleaned up the numbers they were taking it to bid. This past weekend was the only window we *had*."

Quinn remained impassive. "So what's going on? You think Mannion's playing games?"

"He's claiming it isn't all there, Jim. How can we argue with him? He says he's got some sort of expert. Saturday he told me I either pay him what he would have sold it for or he hurts me."

"I don't think Billy'd do that. There's too much he's got

157

to lose if he gets found out. Big Bill Doyle'd have his balls cut off."

"He doesn't seem terribly frightened, Jimmy. For all I know he's playing us *all* for fools. Selling it *and* demanding money from me."

Quinn tucked his flagging enthusiasm back into his pants and sat upright, shaking his head. "I know you two had to meet for logistical reasons, but I was never in love with the idea. You just couldn't resist fucking him, could you?"

Amanda snorted, rolling her eyes. "Don't be ridiculous."

"What was he doing at your place Friday morning, babe? That was just plain stupid."

She scowled. "At *my* place?"

"Nice try, Mandy. You forget who I am? I've got sources inside the police department that the D.A. doesn't have. They're saying it was Billy who threw Hubie Poole's daughter in front of the car. The cop who was suspended claims he spotted Billy coming out of your building." He paused, shrugging. "I don't really give a damn whether you fucked him or not, but your timing really stinks."

"Who are you kidding, you don't *care*?"

"I never had an exclusive, babe."

"Oh? Didn't you ask me to marry you? Or am I confusing you with someone else?"

He grinned. "I did, didn't I."

"You're goddamn right you did. And I'm thinking about holding you to it."

"Might be handy," he admitted. "A wife can't testify against her husband."

She smirked. "Or vice versa. I can't imagine you'd mind being married to a Gregory anyway. It couldn't *hurt* your image."

"Could even help it," he agreed. "But I'd do it just to see the look on Josh Sellers's face."

She laughed as she came up off the floor, undoing the clasp at the front of her brassiere. Her breasts fell free but didn't fall far. "That's all somewhere down the road, and this is where we are now, Jimmy. You want to know what I think you need to do in the meanwhile? I think you'd better speak to your friend Mr. Doyle. That handsome weasel he found us is engineering a double cross.''

Quinn rose from the sofa and swept his pajama top over his head. "No problem, babe. But like you said, that's all somewhere down the road." He tossed the shirt aside and started on the pants. "*This* is where we are now."

Phillip Wright was just returning to his office from the coffeemaker Thursday afternoon when his secretary buzzed him. A Mr. Derry Green from Belfast was on the line. When Wright picked up he was greeted by his Irish tormentor's acid cheeriness.

"Phillip, lad! Why don't you step downstairs to the concourse and answer the third pay phone on the left when it rings?''

Ten minutes later Wright stood hunched over one of the pay instruments in the bustling World Trade Center lobby. The Irishman was cutting right to the meat of it.

"Tomorrow is Friday, Phillip lad. I expect a man in your position with the firm should be able to slip away a few hours early.''

"Early?'' Wright complained. "I told you last weekend I would have auditors crawling all over the office. They only left this morning and there are mountains of work piled up. I *can't* get away early. I simply can't.''

"Tsk, tsk, Phillip. Can't? Either you can, or I can make a trip to Larchmont. Julia will no doubt be most interested in what I'll have to show her.''

Defeated, Wright continued to listen without further protest.

"So here's the plan, Phillip lad. You'll not take your regular train to Larchmont. You'll take the Harlem line to Brewster instead. When you walk out of the train station there you'll see a white Ford Escort parked at a meter across the way. The key and a map'll be under the passenger seat. Follow the map.''

"Brewster? How the hell am I to get home again? That's a bloody long way.''

The Irishman chuckled. "You'll drive the *car*, Phillip. After all, it's rented in your name. If you don't turn it back in the good folk at Hertz are liable to think you've stolen it.''

"In *my* name? You'd need a charge card and my driver's license to do that.''

"That we would, Phillip. A Visa card in this instance. It's quite obvious you've had no call to use yours this week. Have a look in your wallet . . . and don't panic. Your card and license will be under the passenger seat.''

Wright reached around to his hip pocket and was still removing his billfold when the line went dead.

While further harassment on the job site had failed to materialize, the flood of new material shipments had continued to mount throughout the week. Friday promised to be no different. With one of the windows on the sixth floor removed to provide access, Dante and Tom McCarty were at work unloading drywall from the cradle of a boom truck's crane. Both were sweating profusely, and each trip to the cradle exposed them to the chill of a stiff autumn breeze. Late Wednesday night and again last night Joe had spoken to Gus and learned nothing new about Billy Mannion's connections to the Irish community. He'd also spoken on several occasions to Jumbo, Melissa Busby, and Guy Napier. Bud Costanza had them chasing their tails in an effort to pin the Kane/Tierney homicides on Mrs. Kane, and they'd made no further progress in their search for the shooter. It was frustrating, being forced to take a backseat in that regard, but Dante was still convinced he was on the right trail here. Since Wednesday night the rest of Tim O'Brien's crew had loosened up around him in perceptible ways; little things, like offering to grab him a coffee from the lunch truck.

Joe and McCarty had just emptied the cradle and were

catching their breaths when an unfamiliar figure stepped into the sixth-floor supply area.

"I hear there's a mick-loving wop down here thinks he's tough. I bet some friends'a mine upstairs I could kick his ass."

From twenty feet away Dante surveyed the man confronting him. This one wasn't huge like the two goons Marty Octavio had with him Monday; maybe six foot and a hundred-eighty pounds. Joe had him by a couple of inches and at least twenty pounds. He also saw enough in the way the man carried himself to know any size difference didn't much matter. Those others were run-of-the-mill leg breakers. This one was a fighter.

Dante spoke quietly, modulating his voice. "There's nobody here got any beef with you, friend." Inside he was dropping into himself, finding his center. He willed his respiration to a level of calm, denying the tiny drop of adrenaline already at work in his bloodstream.

"Wanna fuckin' bet? *You* got a beef with me, shithead. You wrecked my cousin Rocco's elbow. Wrecked it good. Time I get done with your ass, your whole fuckin' *body*'s gonna be wrecked."

As Dante's challenger spoke, Tom McCarty drifted up alongside his boss, a sixteen-ounce clawhammer gripped in one hand. "Say the word, Joe," he murmured. "Just tell me what you'll have me do."

Dante lowered a cautioning hand to the hammer. "You don't want any part of this guy, Tommy," he whispered. "You get anywhere near him with that thing, he'll kill you with it."

McCarty's eyes widened. "Him?" he hissed. "He's no bigger'n me."

Dante shook his head, eyes still glued to his adversary. "Forget everything you know about barroom brawls, Tommy. Get as far away from him as you can. Go on."

The other man was in sneakers while Joe was in work boots. Dante knew he'd stand a much better chance fighting

161

barefoot or even in stocking feet. He also knew he'd never get that chance. One advantage he did have was the morning's exertions. He was loose, as warmed up as he was going to get. And maybe he was a little smarter. This guy was about thirty at the outside. He exuded too much confidence, probably backed up by a black belt in one of the popular styles. Joe hoped he hadn't yet developed the ability to read between the lines. Right now the man was eyeing him the way a cat eyes a bird with a broken wing. Easy meat.

Fact was that Dante had fought in Jae Doo Roh's Sixth Avenue dojo for twenty years. When he trained there he still wore the white belt of the novice and remained unranked because he wouldn't compete. It was unlikely that Jae Roh was unknown to this man. Roh was a legend in New York karate circles; a seventh-degree Tae Kwon Do master. What Dante's challenger couldn't know was that Joe first bested his teacher in a one-on-one training session seven years ago.

"Where do you fight?" he asked.

The other laughed. "What the fuck's it to you?"

"Just curious. Most disciplines teach respect. I can see that yours doesn't." As he said it Dante removed his work gloves and tossed them aside.

Those eyes darted to Dante's hands, and for the first time they registered doubt. Doubt and anger. "C'mon, you fuckin' puke. Enough'a this bullshit. You wanna take your best shot or am I just gonna roll up on you? It's your choice."

Dante shook his head. "Like I told you, friend. The beef's not mine." Out of the corner of his eye he saw they now had an audience. Marty Octavio and several others he didn't recognize had appeared in the doorway.

"What's this?" Joe taunted. "You thought you'd need backup?"

That was the button. His opponent forgot any doubt and attacked. As he came ahead, Joe was impressed with his speed. Arrogant or not, that first series of punches and kicks was thrown with good power and a fluid grace. Instead of countering with an attack of his own, Dante assumed a defensive posture enabling him to assess the other's skill. His best assessment of it was the sweep kick that caught him in the shin. The pain of it shot the length of his right leg, blinding in its intensity. In the one split-second attention lapse that followed, a solid knuckle punch caught him in the forehead above his right eye. It staggered him.

As Dante stumbled back a step, fighting from within to recapture his focus, Octavio's man backed out to gloat.

"Your ass is *mine*, old man!"

The words were barely out when Dante attacked. He came straight ahead in a rush, broke it off abruptly with a feint to his left before going airborne. He was in midair, left foot coming around in the clockwise arc of a roundhouse kick, when he reversed field in mid-execution. The lead leg hit the floor, flexed and propelled him upward in a counter motion; the right foot whipped hard around the back side of the surprised man's defenses. The instep of Dante's work boot connected flush with his opponent's jaw. Joe knew he'd delivered it with knockout force even before the younger man's knees buckled. In his sparring sessions with Jae he always pulled that shot at the last instant. This time he didn't. He felt bone give.

"Jesus!" someone gasped.

The defeated fighter's face went gray as he collapsed. It turned a nasty shade of green-white once he hit the floor. None of the onlookers gathered at the door came to his aid as sweat broke out on his forehead and he began to writhe, moaning. Dante started forward, searching for Octavio. When he realized the wall-building contractor had disappeared he ignored the stragglers and turned to McCarty.

"Call for an ambulance, Tommy."

McCarty pointed to the knot developing on Dante's forehead. "Are you okay, Joe?"

"Just fine."

McCarty started for the floor phone near the elevators. "Fucking *hell*, you're fast! Where'd you learn to fight like that?"

Dante found his denim jacket and dropped to one knee, covering his fallen opponent's torso with it. "Practice," he muttered, mostly to himself. "Thousands of hours of it, Tommy. Starting when I was about your age."

FOURTEEN

Billy Mannion had places he had to be, and he didn't like being called on the carpet. He'd received Bill Doyle's call a few minutes before noon and agreed to meet the man out here in the wilds of Van Cortlandt Park. For all the help the man and his organization regularly gave the movement, he owed him the courtesy. But now the self-righteous Westie kingpin was sitting here on this bench, his silly little dog on his lap, calling Billy's sense of honor into question. Billy was loading up to give this fatass clown a piece of his mind.

"Just you hold your tongue a moment, Mr. Doyle!" As he snarled it, Mannion leaned close enough to make Doyle's bodyguards nervous. They were loitering ten yards away and shifting anxiously from foot to foot. "She's accusing *me*? Of double-crossing *her*?"

Doyle nodded, the jowls of a once-hard face jiggling slightly. "She swears her husband said the goods'd be there, Billy."

"I don't give a fuck *what* she swears. I held up my end of our deal and've got nothing to show for it."

"She says you threatened her."

Mannion straightened briefly and then leaned close again. "I haven't even started threatening yet, Mr. Doyle. I had a meeting set for yesterday with a man who's agreed to pay me two million dollars for that technology I was to steal. When I discovered I didn't have the goods I managed to put him off a week. Next Thursday morning, if I don't have what he wants, he walks away."

"And you're sure this man Cowan knows what he's talking about."

Mannion was still up close, his glare boring directly in on Doyle. It turned instantly to a maniacal grin. "Oh yes, Mr. Doyle. I'm sure. Seamus Cowan did the same course at MIT as did Veronica Tierney. That's why we were interested in your friend's proposal in the first place. She graduated second in her class. Him? First. He's as well equipped as any in the business."

Doyle nodded and raised his open hands. "It's not good, Billy. None of this is. My guy is well connected in this town. He tells me certain cops've made you a priority. Says they want you for that Poole kid's death."

Billy laughed. "Me? Why?"

"That one bull they suspended? He claims it was you he was chasing; you who threw the kid inta the street."

"To be sure, Mr. Doyle. And you believe him?"

"The cop claims he spotted you coming outta the back door of Amanda Kane's building. You deny you were there?"

Billy rose from his seat, exasperated. "What am I? A fool? It was her insisted on meeting me, Mr. Doyle. Some crock of shit about making sure I got the details of that suite exactly right. You ask me, she's a fucking thrill-seeker; likes the danger of getting up close. But she came to me and not the other way round."

"So what do I bring back to them, Billy? I'm sure Mrs. Kane can be convinced to accept some sorta compromise. What are your terms?"

Mannion snorted. "Terms, Mr. Doyle? My entire operation's dead in the water wit'out fundin'. I accepted the task of hitting her husband and his whore because I could raise two million dollars out of what I carried away from it. Two million's still my price. Your friends've got till four o'clock the afternoon of Wednesday next. You tell them I don't take kindly to being stiffed. They try to double-cross me, and it's the last clever thing they ever do.''

When two cops arrived with the EMS ambulance at the construction site they ran into a wall of silence as cool and solid as stone. Fortunately for Dante neither of them recognized him. His story was the same as McCarty's: The man with the crushed face fell off a ladder. Dante'd seen it starting to happen and rushed to help, only to be hit in the head by the falling ladder for his trouble. The older of the two uniforms wasn't swallowing it, but without any other witnesses he had little choice. The I.D. on the fallen man identified him as Albert Longobardi, residence in Bath Beach, Brooklyn. He carried a card from Carpenter's Local 5, the usual credit cards, and a driver's license. Dante doubted that the union was getting any construction work out of him. No, Al Longobardi was a craftsman of another sort.

Before the EMS paramedics packed it up and departed with the moaning Longobardi strapped to a rolling stretcher, one of them pointed to the knot on Dante's forehead. ''Your eyes looked fine to me, and your pressure's stable. Still, I think you should have yourself checked out, buddy. Anytime you sustain a blow to the head like that it's a good idea. If I were you, I'd get my ass to an emergency room.''

Dante thanked him for his concern. He pulled his gloves on and was ready to get back to work unloading sheetrock when Tim O'Brien stopped him.

''The man had a point, Joe. Something happens to you and my liability premiums go through the roof. I want you to see a doctor.''

''Fine,'' Joe agreed. ''But what're you gonna do about Octavio, Tim? If I thought you were ready to go to the cops with this, I wouldn't have told them the story I just did. Was I wrong?''

O'Brien frowned. ''What're you saying?''

''I'm saying that everybody knows what's going on here; that there's a war on for control of the unions. The cops ran the Italian mob out of the Painters a couple years back, and the Westies moved right in. Now the Italians want it back.''

The drywall contractor looked troubled. "And you assume I've thrown in with the Westie lot, right?"

"I *assume* you're walking a fine line, just like most everybody else. That guy Payne at the local told me you're one of the few straight shooters around, Tim. That's why I wanted to work for you.''

O'Brien dug a cigar out of his breast pocket, bit off the tip, and started to pace. "If you understand that fine line then maybe you understand why I won't go to the Westies and ask 'em to help me out of this. Hell, they'd be more'n happy to send one of their lads around. Catch Octavio stepping out for the morning paper and shoot him in both knees. If I did that they'd own me, lock and stock, inside of six months.''

"Then maybe the cops *are* your answer.''

O'Brien lit the cigar and sucked nervously on it. As he exhaled he gave Dante's suggestion a quick shake of the head. "Problem there, too, Joe. Half my lads are working on a cousin or uncle's green card. The original owner is long gone back to the old country, enough coin in his pocket to buy a pub maybe, or a bed 'n' breakfast. They pass their documentation along to the next one in the family. The IRS don't care so long as somebody's paying the tax. The cops don't care so long as nobody makes trouble. And I don't care because they're the best workers my money can buy.''

"Sounds like you've got a problem, Tim.''

O'Brien scowled at his smoke and pitched it away in disgust. It was the first one Dante'd seen him actually light. "That I do, Joe. And you're standing square in the path of it. You've already hurt three of the thugs Marty's thrown at me. Hurt 'em bad. I'm sure that's made him mad, and I'm fearful of what it might mean for you.''

"Don't worry about me, Tim. I can take care of myself.''

"No doubt, Joe. But right now I'd like to see things cool

off some. After you see the doctor why don't you take the rest of the day off. I'll call you this evening, and we can talk. I need some time to think this out."

Dante felt genuine sympathy for this man and his predicament. He ran a tight, efficient operation, and his people *did* work hard. Tim O'Brien was an immigrant himself, and he would find it difficult to begrudge a countryman the same grab at the brass ring that he'd had.

"I've got a better idea than your calling me," Joe offered. "How about you buying me a drink?"

O'Brien smiled. "Surely. You name the . . ." He stopped, a pained look crossing his face. "Damn. There's something on for your fella Tom McCarty's birthday. I'm sorry, Joe. I forgot all about it." He paused again, and this time the frown completely vanished. "Unless, of course, you'd like to join us. Kingsbridge in the North Bronx is an awful long way to come, but Guinness drawn with a hand pump is worth the drive."

Dante shrugged, spreading his hands. "I'm too newly back in town to have developed much of a social life yet. Believe it or not, I've got nothing else scheduled."

"So you'll come?"

"I think I'd like to. What are you getting Tommy?"

O'Brien shook his head. "You let us worry about that. You're our guest."

"How do I find this bar?"

"The Major Deegan to Two Hundred Thirty-second. Drive north on Broadway a few blocks, and you'll see it on the right. McNulty's. You can't miss it."

Phillip Wright knew that if he had any guts at all he would go to the police. But Phillip had no guts; not with his wife already threatening to leave him and his very career in the balance. When Wright departed the office early that afternoon complaining of nausea he had the documents demanded by the extortionist secreted in his briefcase. The 2:55 train out of Grand Central deposited him in the village of Brewster at half past four. The white Ford Escort described by his blackmailer was parked just where he said it would be. Phillip climbed behind the wheel to find the rental agreement, his driver's license, his Visa card, and an ignition key beneath the seat beside him. He unfolded a photocopied map and typewritten instructions in his lap and then sat gripping the wheel, staring blankly ahead. His conscience was engaged in a furious tug-of-war.

If his superiors at Lloyd's knew of the security breach and what Phillip was carrying in his briefcase right now, they would not hesitate to have him arrested. If he chose to burn those documents and force the Irish madman's hand, he had no doubt that his tormentor would use that videotape against him. Lloyd's might not fire him in that case. Indeed, they might even pat him on the back for refusing to buckle to an extortionist's demands. But in the long run they wouldn't be able to erase the memory of that sexual compromise from their minds. The story of it would forever be whispered behind carefully manicured hands. Frowns would crease brows and heads would shake. Phillip Wright's meteoric rise within the company would be over. If he did the right thing here, his future in that world was doomed.

The instructions told him to drive north from Brewster on New York Route 22. His destination was a turnout in the road about four miles above the village of Pawling. As Phillip fitted the key into the ignition and started the car he spotted a Putnam County Sheriff's car passing in his rearview mirror. One last chance to change his mind. He waited until the way was clear, slipped the console lever into reverse, and backed out into the street. He'd be damned if he'd let one episode of drunken indiscretion destroy his life. Lloyd's was resilient; a heavyweight in any arena. Phillip wasn't. He'd been targeted because he worked for them and not the other way around. Sod them. Because of this attack he risked losing everything.

* * *

In the week since Billy hit her, Siobhan McDonough had avoided him by shutting herself in her room while at home and leaving for work as soon as Connor McNulty opened for business. Her face was still tender, and the bruise that developed across the plane of her left cheek was yellowing now. Even artfully applied makeup couldn't hide her injury, and she'd purposely missed her classes at the Actors Studio this week. She didn't want to answer questions about her face; fabricate some lie. She was afraid she might not be able to contain her anger and thought it better to stay close to home until she had a better handle on it.

Twenty minutes ago McNulty had fetched the cake out of the walk-in and carried it upstairs to the bar. One of the lads who worked for Tim O'Brien was having his twenty-first birthday party tonight, and Siobhan had spent the hours since lunch helping with decorations and setting up a cold buffet in the back room. It wouldn't be long before the construction crew descended like a swarm of locusts. Four-thirty was their usual arrival time, and many stayed late. They were a noisy, fun-loving, and often rowdy bunch, but Siobhan didn't much mind. They made good money and were free with it. They tipped well. A number of them were taken with her and behaved like altar boys when approaching the bar. McNulty, a huge, totally bald bear of a man, made sure there was no trouble in his joint. No one had ever really bothered Siobhan here.

Henry Roark and the birthday boy were two of the first to arrive, followed shortly by more members of Tim O'Brien's crew. As the bar filled Siobhan got busy filling pints of stout and letting the half-full glasses stand the way Guinness must. As she worked her way back down the line of them, adding the next quarter measure, she thought this crowd seemed unusually subdued tonight. A knot of them had gathered around Roark's table over in the far corner. At times the tone of their conversation seemed heated. When one of the regulars in that crowd approached the bar to buy a round, Siobhan lifted her chin toward the corner convocation.

"What goes on there, Michael?"

171

The man, his clothes dusty and his mop of curly red hair pulled back from his face in a ponytail, glanced back over his shoulder before answering. "That? More big doings on the job site, Siobhan. We're on this new project barely a week, and already they've tried twice to run Timmy O'Brien off."

Siobhan lined up the six pints he wanted and took his cash to the register on the back bar. "Who's they?"

"Another contractor. They say he's Italian mob connected. His brother or cousin or some such had the drywall contract afore Tim did."

She returned with his change, laying it atop the bar. "You expecting more trouble?"

That got her a grin and a wink. "Maybe not after what happened today." He went on to describe the incident earlier in the week where the contractor and two of his thugs broke up a lot of wall and O'Brien's new materials expediter ran them off. "I never seen him afore this week. They say he's just back from Saudi Arabia; working over there. Big man. Been working right alongside his crew, not afraid to get his hands dirty. Today this fella Octavio sent one of the mob's hired heavies after him. No weapons or nothing; just feet and fists like one of those Chinamen you see on Saturday telly. Our new expediter broke his jaw."

Siobhan paled slightly. "And did he himself get hurt?"

"Some bruises and not much more. It must have been something to see. I watched him working against those leg breakers earlier in the week, and he moved as quick as a jungle cat. This isn't a fella you'd want to meet up with in a bar brawl, I'm telling you."

This was a better story than most Siobhan heard here. She thought this new fella of Tim O'Brien's sounded just a bit bigger than life. "You say none of you have ever seen this man before?"

Michael shook his head. "Never. And you know what's the oddest thing? He's not even one of us. He's Italian, just

172

like Octavio." Something caught the man's attention, and he looked up toward the front door. "Speak of the devil."

Siobhan followed the direction of his gaze to see the familiar face of Tim O'Brien just entering the bar. The man who entered alongside him was tall and sandy-haired.

"Who?" she asked.

"That's the fella I was just telling you about. Tim's new expediter."

As Michael collected four of his six pints and moved off into the barroom with them, Siobhan studied this stranger. On the surface he was nearly as handsome as Billy Mannion. A better build, with bigger shoulders and hips every bit as lean as her ex-lover's. The face wasn't quite so delicately pretty though. This one was more rugged; weathered and with a stronger jaw. He had the nose, eyes, and high forehead of a Brando gone lean with age instead of fat. Below the surface there was something about the way this man carried himself that further intrigued her. As an actress she loved to watch others; to observe a demeanor and play little mental games trying to guess the motivations behind it. Working the bar in McNulty's afforded her plenty of opportunity to indulge in these exercises. This "expediter," as Michael had referred to him, was a cool one but also easygoing. She watched the way he shook hands with his coworkers, took an offered chair, and settled right in. Still, he watched in much the same manner as she watched him. He was an observer, not content to just sit, drink, and laugh it up. His eyes darted here and there around the room, assessing his surroundings, cataloguing them.

Connor McNulty lifted the flap at the end of the bar and approached down the duckboards. "I think we'll open the back room to them now. You think you'll be all right up here by yourself?"

Siobhan waved away his concern. "Once you tell them the food's on their boss? It'll be quiet as a tomb up front here."

McNulty reached around to ring the back-bar bell and get the room's attention. He announced that Mr. Timothy

O'Brien was providing a cold buffet in the dining room tonight in honor of Tom McCarty's twenty-first birthday. O'Brien's foreman, Henry Roark, then stood with his glass raised. Young McCarty was pushed ahead of the crowd surging toward the dining room doorway.

Siobhan was so distracted by the assembled company's rush toward the free food that she hadn't seen Tim O'Brien and the object of her earlier scrutiny approach the bar.

"I think we'll wait till the hoards've eaten their fill 'fore we risks our necks in there, Siobhan." As O'Brien said it he pulled up a stool and sat. "Meet my new expediter, Joe Dante."

Siobhan turned to meet a pair of blue eyes unsettling in their familiarity. They were the same slate blue color as her own, and for one disorienting instant she was looking at herself in a mirror.

"Siobhan?" This Dante's outstretched hand came across the bar. "The pleasure's mine."

She was surprised by the gentleness of his grip. That hand didn't look at all gentle, with scar tissue covering the knuckles and hands rough with callus. "Pleased to meet you," she told him. She turned back to O'Brien. "What'll it be, Tim?"

The contractor deferred to his guest. "Joe?" He slapped a twenty onto the mahogany.

Dante glanced over the bottles arranged along the back bar. "It's been a long day. How about a shot of Black Bush?"

O'Brien shot him a surprised look. "I'm impressed. It would appear you know your Irish whiskies."

The expediter nodded toward the bottle now in Siobhan's hand. "That one's been a longtime favorite. I didn't get a lot of it in the Arabian desert, and it's been a pleasure getting reacquainted."

The contractor pointed to the glass Siobhan was filling. "I think I'll join him, love. That's a nasty bruise you're sporting there."

Siobhan's fingers flew to her face, touching her cheek lightly in an involuntary gesture of self-consciousness.

"Looks pretty bad, does it? My neighbor's fool child left a tennis ball on the stairs. I was carrying groceries and didn't see it. Took a nasty fall, I did." She grabbed a second shot glass from beneath the bar and set it up. "So what's this I hear about trouble today? And so soon after the last?"

O'Brien clapped his new man on the shoulder. "Just a little misunderstanding, right Joe?"

Dante raised his glass. "I hope so, boss. You can stomp a snake like Marty Octavio, but if you want him to stay dead, you've got to cut his head off. We're not outta the woods there yet."

As the two men clicked glasses and drank, Siobhan turned to replace the bottle on the back-bar shelf. She considered how Dante delivered his warning. There was no fear in it but plenty of caution. It told her that this was a man who'd seen a jam or two in his time, respected danger for what it was, and knew that cockiness was of no use when facing it.

Many McNulty patrons left for their homes and families once the candles of the cake were lit and they sang Tom McCarty a rousing rendition of "Happy Birthday." Now, with the clock just a few ticks from eleven, a dozen regulars sat watching television at the bar, and a handful of Dante's new construction pals still occupied a barroom table. Dante sat with a near-empty pint of stout before him and one boot up on the edge of his neighbor's chair seat. He hadn't really known what to expect, coming up here to the North Bronx. It was a step he knew he had to take if he wanted to find Mannion, but he hadn't expected to enjoy it quite so much. Most of the construction guys he remembered from his high school and college days in Brooklyn were a coarse, angry bunch. This crowd was different. There was a strong sense of camaraderie here. And humor. Not once had anyone edged him into a corner to confide how many times he'd screwed his wife last night or how much he was getting on the side. These people seemed content with who they were. As an outsider Joe was surprised at how comfortable they'd made him feel.

"This next one's gonna be my last," he announced. He drained the remaining drink from his glass and heaved himself to his feet. "Who else is ready?"

"You're not buying, Joe," Henry Roark reminded him.

"I think it's my turn," Dante replied. "I want this round, okay?"

Roark shrugged. He watched Dante reach to collect some of the nearly dozen empty glasses cluttering the tabletop and frowned, making a "leave them" gesture with his hand. "Don't worry about those. Siobhan'll get them."

Dante continued to collect mugs until he had five in each fist. He turned away for the bar and plunked them down, getting just as surprised a look from the beautiful barkeep.

"Thank you, Mr. Dante. You didn't need to do that. It's my job."

Dante winked at her. "My father was Mr. Dante, Siobhan. I'm Joe . . . and I never miss an opportunity to ingratiate myself to a beautiful woman." For the second time that night Dante watched her blush. "How about another round for me and the fellas there?"

She got busy in a hurry, trying to mask the obviousness of her pleasure. Joe extracted two twenties from his wallet, laid them atop the bar, and waited patiently as she filled six pint mugs to the halfway point and set them to settle out. Another time Joe might have minded the time it took to pour Guinness correctly. Right now he found himself wishing it took even longer. This was the best-looking woman he'd seen in months, and New York was a city full of beautiful women. It made him wonder why she was working in a North Bronx tavern. She had a face like Maureen O'Hara and a body like a young Grace Kelly.

"So where do you live, Joe? Here in the Bronx?"

Dante had been listening to Irish accents all week, and this one had a different quality. There was something musical about it. He shook his head. "Manhattan."

"Really? Where?"

"Way west. In midtown. I just moved back from the Middle East, and a buddy helped me find a warehouse loft. I'm still converting it."

Her eyebrows went up as she worked the stick on the Guinness pump. "A *big* loft?"

He smiled, nodding. "Big enough. Enormous, in fact."

"Ah, you'd be the envy of my teachers at the Actors Studio with a space like that. It was once they were cheap, they say. No more. Now they're something an acting teacher would kill for."

The Actors Studio, no less. Dante was glad to know she wasn't letting all that beauty languish up here in Kingsbridge.

"If you're serious about an acting career, you'd better stop tripping over tennis balls," he advised. "A face like yours is one in ten million. You play your cards right and keep the tools intact, the world can be your oyster."

She was starting to make blushing a habit. "Not with my accent, it won't be. I don't think anyone'll be doing a remake of *The Quiet Man* anytime soon."

"But you're working on losing it, right?"

"It i'n't as easy as it sounds. I've been at it two years now."

"You're making it harder on yourself, living up here where everyone else sounds just like you."

She shrugged. "No green card, Joe. I need to eat."

Dante lifted the first three glasses she pushed at him. "I guess it's never easy, right? You don't sound like you've given up hope and that's half the battle. Hang in." He turned for his table.

Henry Roark had a frown on his face when Joe arrived. As Dante set a drink before him he beckoned Joe close. "Careful there, laddie. That one's off-limits."

Dante's return gaze was puzzled. "I'm afraid you're gonna have to explain that one, Henry." He murmured it in the same hushed tone Roark had used.

"I'm saying she's connected, Joe. To some very nasty people. Let's just leave it at that, eh? A word to the wise."

Joe straightened. A jolt of fresh excitement edged his respiration up a notch. He had no idea he might get this lucky this fast. As he headed back to the bar he found himself regarding Siobhan in a whole new light. Henry's "nasty people" had to fall into one of two categories. The first was the Westies. The other was the Free Ireland crowd. Either way, he knew he was in luck. The former might not be directly connected to Billy Mannion, but there was no way he and his people could operate undercover in the Irish-American community without the Westies knowing about it. Dante knew he'd done as much as he could tonight without putting his strategy at unnecessary risk. He had to take this one step at a time. When he reached the bar he collected his remaining beers and turned to leave.

"You forgot your change." Siobhan threw it back over her shoulder as she reached to adjust the volume on the television. It was eleven now, and the network had just cut to the local news.

Dante glanced back at the ten-spot and silver still on the bar. Anyone looking for a tip would have broken the Hamilton and left a small heap of Georges, hoping he'd grab some and leave a few others. "Keep it," he told her.

Back in his chair he started on that last pint of stout. Tomorrow might be Saturday and a break in his exhausting new regimen, but he was beat and still had a thirty-minute drive home. Once he got on the road he wanted to give Gus a buzz; ask him to run Connor McNulty's name through Records tomorrow. Around the table now, most of the others had turned their attention to the late news. Up there on the screen, one of Channel Seven's stringers was standing somewhere in the dark with flashing lights behind her. She described how a Lloyd's insurance company division manager had left work early that afternoon in lower Manhattan, complaining of stomach pain. Four hours later his body was discovered in a Dutchess County gravel pit. He was still dressed in the business attire he'd worn to his office. Cause of death was a single bullet behind one ear. As Dante listened he was struck by the coincidence of method in this new homicide.

In the next moment that connection was pushed from the fore. As Dante listened to the broadcast he had only one eye on the screen. He was also watching Siobhan behind the bar. Once she'd adjusted the volume of the television she returned to washing glasses and straightening up in the aftermath of Tom McCarty's party. When that last item came onscreen she continued with her chores until mention was made of the victim's name and where he worked. She stopped abruptly then to turn and watch. Before the program could move to the next item she threw her towel onto the bar and disappeared into the kitchen.

When Dante stood several minutes later and started for the door, Tim O'Brien rose from his chair across the table to drift alongside. Together they emerged from McNulty's onto the sidewalk. Overhead the elevated tracks of the IRT were washed in the amber glow of streetlights. Joe turned up the collar of his denim jacket against the chill October night.

"You had a good time tonight?" O'Brien asked.

Dante glanced back at the door to the bar. "Yeah, Tim, I did. I'd stay longer but I'm bushed. It's been a long week."

"That welt on your forehead doesn't look as bad as it did this afternoon. What did the doctor say?"

"Not a lot. He took my blood pressure, made me sit around for half an hour, and then took it again. They gave me an ice pack for the swelling, and by the time I left the hospital it was all but gone."

O'Brien nodded and looked off into the distance down Broadway. "I've been thinking more about what we discussed earlier. I'm not ready to go to the police just yet, but perhaps by Monday I'll have changed my mind. I'm happy to have the two days of the weekend to consider my other options."

"Just promise me you won't do anything rash or stupid,

Tim. If people are gonna start shooting at each other, I want time to run and hide. I really hate guns.''

Tim grimaced and shook his head. ''You've been invaluable to me in dealing with the problem so far. What I'll promise is that I won't do anything without talking to you about it first. Fair enough? You liked your evening here so much, perhaps we can get together here for another drink early in the week.''

O'Brien offered his hand, and Dante gripped it to shake. ''Fair enough, boss. Have a nice weekend.''

FIFTEEN

Before turning in Friday night Dante contacted Gus Lieberman to report Siobhan McDonough's reaction to news of that Lloyd's executive's death. He asked Gus to find out who Phillip Wright was and explore any connection between that homicide in Dutchess County and the two last Friday in New York City. He also wanted Lieberman to check the beautiful bartender out for connections to the New York Irish underworld. While he was at it he threw in Connor McNulty. Henry Roark had warned that the bartender was off-limits, and Connor McNulty was the man who employed her. Gus promised to send copies of the Kane/Tierney homicide ballistics reports to the state police first thing Saturday morning. He would send Siobhan and McNulty's names along to Pete Shore. Before saying goodnight they made a date for a late lunch the following day.

Midmorning Saturday Gus called to suggest Joe meet him at a Chinese restaurant on Hudson Street. To Joe it meant Pete Shore wanted to join them, and sure enough when he arrived at two o'clock he found both Lieberman and Shore occupying a sun-drenched table and drinking beers. The chair they'd left for Joe afforded him a view of the sidewalk through the plate glass out front. A chill autumn breeze still swept the streets outside, but the day was a dazzler. When Lieberman asked how Dante's head was feeling, Joe shrugged off the welt on his forehead as nothing. Young Albert Longobardi was feeling a lot worse this afternoon.

Pete Shore shook his head in disgust. "I did a little checking once Gus told me what went down. That character Octavio's a dirtbag. Him and that cousin they bounced outta there are two peas in a pod. Typical ploy, too. First he tries intimidation; see if he can scare O'Brien easy. That don't work, so he sends in a specialist. Now you got him thinking: what's O'Brien got? Muscle of his own? He won't run, Joe. Next time it's gonna be guns."

An attractive brunette in bicycle pants strolled past outside, and Dante watched her progress. "That's what I figure, too." He tore his eyes from the scenery to confront his boss. "You got no objections, I think I'll strap on the iron next week; just to be on the safe side."

As Lieberman grunted in acquiescence, Joe moved on to Shore. "Octavio said something Monday about O'Brien not being part of an agreement. I got the impression that only certain contractors were supposed to bid on that job. It's something the Organized Crime Task Force might be interested in. Sounds like more rigging, doesn't it?"

Shore had one of his bargain-basement cigars out and was peeling the cellophane wrapper. "Sure does. You want, I'll set something up with Ray Costello. You two can talk."

"I've got no time right now, Pete. I think I've got a lead on Mannion. Can't tie myself down."

"We've got something for you there," Gus told him. "That hunch you had about a connection 'tween them two homicides? Bingo, Joey."

Dante experienced a flush of pleasure but maintained his poker face. "Yeah? What've we got?"

"State police came up with a ballistics match. Kane, the Tierney woman, and this new guy, Wright. All of 'em were killed by the same gun."

Dante's imagination kicked into overdrive. "You got any more information on who Wright was?"

"Good question," Lieberman replied. "He managed risk

assessment for the Lloyd's insurance group here in the States. British citizen. London School of Economics. I don't see how he fits.''

''Mannion is how he fits,'' Joe told him. ''Somehow. Some way. I'm not sure what the connection is, but I'm sure there's one out there.''

The chief sighed, disgust contorting his face. ''Bud Costanza had a meeting with me'n' the P.C. this morning. He tells us he's ready to wrap this fucker. Claims he's only half a step away from pinning Kane's old lady for it.''

Their waiter delivered a fried dumpling appetizer. Joe grabbed one with his chopsticks and dipped it in the sauce. ''For all I know he could be right, Gus. But Mannion's still part of the picture. Amanda Kane didn't pull the trigger, and I think Mannion *did*.''

Pete Shore looked puzzled. ''How's somebody like her connected to the IRA? Her ancestors were fuckin' British loyalists in the Revolutionary War, for Crissake.''

Dante bit into his dumpling and chewed. ''Beats me, Pete. But the connection's there.'' He turned to Lieberman. ''How long can you keep that ballistics report under wraps, Gus? We can't risk the media getting hold of it. The minute Mannion hears we've linked the two homicides, it'll spook him. We don't want that. Not yet.''

''You got a plan?'' Gus asked.

Dante snagged another dumpling while assembling his thoughts. ''I want to focus on the bartender I told you about. One of O'Brien's crew warned me she's off-limits; connected somehow. She's also a knockout. I got a chance to watch her a bit, and I think she knows something. I'm supposed to meet O'Brien up there for more drinks on Monday; talk about this trouble with Octavio and how we can protect ourselves. I'm going to wait outside once I leave and follow the bartender; find out where home is.''

Gus turned to Shore. ''What about her, Pete? You able to dig anything up on this girl?''

Shore used a fork instead of chopsticks to shove a

dumpling into his mouth. He spoke around it. "Siobhan McDonough? I got Customs to fax me her file late this morning. Interesting reading. Been in the country two and a half years; entered on a three-month tourist visa. Immigration found out she stayed past her exit date when they caught her in a sweep of small businesses up in the North Bronx. They started taking steps to deport her, and that's when her employer at the bar stepped in. Got her a heavyweight law firm specializing in that sorta thing. They managed to cut her loose. Struck me as kinda odd."

"What's that?" Gus asked.

Shore drew a backward arc through the air with his fork. "I know this guy used to be a federal prosecutor. He works for that same heavyweight firm now, and I gave him a call a couple hours ago. He tells me the standard rate for service like they gave this broad is billed at a hundred seventy-five bucks an hour. A case like hers usually winds up running five or six grand. Seems like a lotta cabbage to lay out for a bartender, don't it? We ain't talking neurosurgery here. Bartenders are a dime a dozen."

A bright smile lit Dante's face. "Not this one, Pete. There are guys who'd spend that kind of money for a *night* with her."

"Looker, eh?"

"World-class."

"You think it's something as simple as McNulty getting his wick waxed?"

Joe chuckled. "Maybe in his dreams. No, I think there's something else going on there. You get any background on McNulty? I doubt he's screwing her, but he fits somehow."

"No problem there," Shore replied. "Connor McNulty's been in the files for years. A Westie foot soldier at fifteen. Lucky for him Vietnam came along before he did something we could nail him for. Did two tours in the Rangers instead. Came back with a chest fulla medals. Big Bill Doyle thought it'd look good for the neighborhood to have a war hero running a bar. It was Doyle who set him up."

"Probably laundering a little cash on the side," Lieberman remarked.

Shore agreed. "No doubt, but we ain't been able to catch 'em at it and neither has the IRS. There's one other thing you might be interested in, Joe. That guy I know at that law firm? He's got home access to their files, and I asked him to bring up Siobhan McDonough's on the Q.T. Guess who referred her to them?"

"No idea, Pete. You tell me."

"The name James Patrick Quinn ring any bells?"

Dante searched his memory. The name was familiar, but he couldn't quite put his finger on it. Then it clicked into place. "Criminal defense attorney, right? Big-time."

Shore nodded. "Oh, yeah. You go to trial with Jimmy Quinn in your corner, it's costing you five grand a day. His record'd tend to indicate you get what you pay for. We've always suspected him of being Westie-connected. Them two-thousand-dollar suits and the Park Avenue address're just a facade. The Feds've tried to put Big Bill Doyle behind bars three times. State of New York's gone to the mat with him twice. Jimmy Quinn argued all five of them cases, and Doyle never did a day's time."

Dante set his chopsticks to rest on the edge of his plate and eased back in his chair. Outside the window a derelict pushed a bottle-laden shopping cart uptown toward a distant Sloan's supermarket. Joe watched his progress. "No matter how Siobhan McDonough winds up being connected, it sounds like she owes some heavyweights in the Irish mob. All this gets me closer, but it still doesn't explain her reaction to the news of Phillip Wright's homicide. There's still something missing. Something basic."

"How do we know both Wright *and* Kane weren't Westie hits?" Gus asked. "Mannion's on the lam. If he's being protected by them, he might owe them a few favors, too—or it could be he did it for the money."

Shore jerked a thumb toward Dante. "If I know your friend here, he's gonna find out." He turned to Joe. "You watch your ass when you follow this broad. Somebody spots you acting suspicious, they'll take a ball bat upside your head. Those people watch their streets like the Italian mobs watch Arthur Avenue. Everybody's got his stronghold up there.''

"Speaking of watching my ass," Dante changed the subject. "What are the chances of Ray Costello's task force putting a couple of people on that job site? They know the players in that game better than I do. With any luck they might spot trouble before it can find a place to park. The minute someone forces my hand and I've gotta shoot somebody, my career as O'Brien's expediter is on the rocks.''

"I'll talk to him," Shore promised.

Their waiter arrived laden with plates of food and asked who ordered the moo shoo pork.

Billy Mannion, Seamus Cowan, and Paul Murphy were gathered around the dining table for a war council. Pages of the lists extorted from Phillip Wright were spread on the table before them.

"I think this is it here," Seamus announced. He held up a sheet of paper with a list of individuals and pound sterling amounts on it. Across the table from him Mannion held another list. His was of ships, their nations of registry, tonnage, and current cargo. Seamus pointed to the name of a tanker on Billy's page.

"The *Southampton Star*. She's a crude carrier working out of the Gulf, correct?''

Mannion peered at the fine print and nodded. "Indian registry. Petroleum carrier. Mostly crude. Under contract to Mitsubishi Heavy Industries.''

"Well, have a look at the indemnity pool she's in." Seamus pushed his lists across the table. "All high-risk routes; every ship in it.''

Billy scanned the names and numbers. A Lloyd's indemnity pool was a fairly straightforward proposition. Instead of the insurance giant exposing itself for the entire value of a property, Lloyd's would sell shares of a particular risk in exchange for very handsome dividend payments. These dividends would be paid from premiums levied on the insured. Dividend shares were sold in indemnity pools administered by Lloyd's for a fee. Lloyd's underwriters set the rates of those premiums after experts like the late Phillip Wright did all the necessary risk assessment. Sometimes special circumstances such as the current instability in the Persian Gulf required that additional premiums be charged above the customary rates. Billy knew from his research that the current rate for cargo worldwide was .0275 percent of value. For ships traveling in the northwest portion of the Gulf, the War Risks Rating Joint Committee of Lloyd's and the Institute of London Underwriters had tacked on an additional premium of .025 percent. That amount was paid for each fortnight a ship spent in the high-risk region. There were investors in that particular pool who'd exposed themselves to losses as high as five million pounds.

"Glory be," Billy gloated. "Will you look at the names here. Lord this. Sir Reginald that. It's like reading the roll in the House of fucking *Lords*."

Seamus leaned forward, his eyes alive. "We hit the *Southampton Star* once she's fully loaded but still in the high-risk zone. Blow a hole in her skin big enough to sink her outright. When she goes down, the bastards on that list'll be out ten million pounds. Before the week's out we hit another target in that same pool. Most of the people on that list can't sustain those kinds of losses. Not in cash, all of a sudden like that. It'll destroy them."

"You tried the computer access codes Wright gave us?" Mannion asked.

"They work, William, but who knows for how long? First ship we hit they'll think it was a mine got her. There's no telling how long it'll be before Lloyd's figures our game. We've got to hit hard and fast while the window's open to us."

"Our hands're tied till our money comes through," Murphy reminded him. "How about it, Billy? Where does Doyle stand? Will he help us there?"

Mannion flashed back over the less-than-cordial encounter he'd had with their Westie benefactor. "This other fella, Doyle's contact with the Kane bitch? He's also Doyle's friend, Paulie. If we can't produce the technology she claims we have, the Korean takes his business elsewhere. Doyle's friend is upset I've threatened their socialite friend. The way Doyle sees it, we're only out a couple of bullets. No more. I doubt he'll take our side in this beyond delivering our message. There's nothing in it for him."

"How about the fight to free Ireland from fucking British scum?" Murphy demanded.

Mannion snorted. "Most of New York's too far removed from Ireland now, Paulie. Bill Doyle's generation's gotten too fat and comfortable to care anymore."

"So what are our options?" Seamus wondered.

When Billy smiled the fire of righteous anger now burned behind his eyes. "Options, Seamus? It's not us who're faced with options. I put it to that fat bastard Doyle as plainly as I'm putting it to you right now. Either the bitch pays us the money or she dies. It's her that's faced with options, not you or me."

Beasley Richardson spent Saturday morning sitting in a parked car out front of Amanda Kane's building on Fifth Avenue. At nine o'clock his surveillance subject emerged to climb into the back seat of her limousine. She traveled two blocks east, left the car, and entered a building at 701 Park Avenue. She remained there for two and a quarter hours, returning home at eleven-fifteen. When Guy Napier relieved Richardson at noon, Jumbo was parked outside the subject's Fifth Avenue building once again. Because of the squad's manpower limitations they worked this surveillance singly, in six-hour shifts. Bud Costanza had decided that rather than ask the P.C. for additional personnel, his team would close out a sure thing alone. The way Bud saw it, their individual slices of the glory pie would be all the bigger this way.

As much as Costanza was eager to nail Amanda Kane, he was also eager to scuttle the squad's technology-theft theory. Today he was accompanying Melissa and Grover to Princeton with the two disks discovered in Veronica Tierney's briefcase. If the materials purported to have been stolen were contained on those disks, Bud would gleefully drive a stake through that theory's heart.

After being relieved Jumbo returned to the squad to spend the afternoon working alongside Rusty Heckman. A more detailed picture of Amanda Kane's holdings and expenditures had been prepared throughout that week. Their task was to comb through it, searching for the money she'd paid her hit man. Before getting started Jumbo grabbed a salad from a nearby deli. The food in his stomach was making him sleepy, and these columns of numbers did little to stimulate him. When the phone rang he was happy for the distraction.

"Major Case. Sergeant Richardson."

"It's Joe, Beasley. You got a sec?"

"You kidding? I got all afternoon. What's up? How's the construction business?"

"Laugh a minute, buddy. Listen: Gus and I've got something for you, but you've got to keep it under your hat."

"Jesus, Joey. Feed me, for Crissake."

Dante told him about his hunch and how the state police had followed it to pay dirt. Some guy killed upstate Friday night was shot with the same gun that killed Ralph Kane and Veronica Tierney.

Richardson was wide awake now. "Mannion?"

"That's the other half of my hunch, the half ballistics can't help me with. I'm not there yet, Beasley. What I need you to do is keep an eye out for a Westie connection. I don't know how, but they're tied in."

"How far along are you?" Jumbo asked. "You got any names?" He dragged a notepad close.

"Just two. One is Big Bill Doyle. If Mannion's behind

those three homicides, there's no way Doyle doesn't know about it. The other guy is a big-time criminal defense lawyer named Quinn. James Patrick Quinn.''

Jumbo stopped writing mid-name. A lightheadedness was washing over him. ''Whoa. Hang on, Joey. You *sure*?''

''About Quinn? He's a name Pete Shore turned. Why?''

After being relieved by Napier an idly curious Richardson had stopped back by 701 Park Avenue and asked the concierge for a look at the tenant list. The name James P. Quinn was on it. He didn't make the connection until now.

''Ralph Kane's attorney's a partner in the firm of Quinn, Oliver, and Sellers, Joey. Joshua Sellers. He's also Magnetronics's chief corporate counsel.''

''Wait a minute. *James* Quinn's his partner?''

''He's got access to all Sellers's files, Joey. For that matter, Sellers himself could be the connection. He ain't just the Magnetronics CCO. He owns a 10 percent interest. Maybe them two are engineering a power play.''

''Wait a minute, Beasley. I don't have Quinn tied within a mile of this. Not yet. All I know is that he helped a saloon-keeper friend of Doyle's get a bartender out of an Immigration jam. You just threw me one hell of a curve.''

''I ain't finished, Joey. Here's the other shoe.'' He described how he'd been working the surveillance setup on Amanda Kane. ''This morning I follow her to a building just a couple'a blocks away on Park. Had her fucking chauffeur *drive* her there. Stayed a couple hours before heading back home. No big deal, right? A social call. Just to cover all the bases I stopped back by 701 Park on my way downtown. There are ten tenants in that building, Joey. Guess who's one of 'em?''

''James Quinn.''

''I'd say that ties him a lot closer'n a mile, wouldn't you?''

The society-page wags were calling tonight's celebrity-studded benefit for the Hamptons Shoreline Preservation Fund a gala event. As co-chair, Amanda Kane thought it her responsibility to be the most expensively dressed belle at the ball. She'd spent seventeen thousand dollars on just the right gown only to leave it hanging in her closet. After all, she'd just buried her murdered husband. Tonight she wore simple, elegant black.

Time and privacy constraints prevented her from speaking to Jim Quinn until after the party. He dined at his law firm's table while she sat at the table designated for the Fund's most generous benefactors. The ballroom of the Sherry Netherland was all but empty before she was able to join Quinn in the backseat of his stretch Mercedes. To ensure privacy, Jim had the partition glass run up. He seemed agitated.

"So what's *happening*?" Amanda pressed him. "You spoke to Doyle. What did he have to say?"

The chauffeur had barely started the engine when Jim had the gin out. He poured himself a generous splash and threw it back. "Yes. I talked with him. You want any of this?"

When Amanda shook her head he poured himself another and slid the liquor-cabinet door shut. "He talked to your boyfriend."

Amanda bristled. "I thought you weren't jealous."

Quinn ignored the barb. He tugged at his tie, the black bow falling out to dangle from his neck. His fingers probed until they'd freed the button of his formal butterfly collar. "We've got trouble, Mandy. Doyle described Mannion as all business. Mannion swears you gave him bum information; that he doesn't have the goods he needs to make his deal. He also contends that he held up his end of the agreement. Billy's demanding to be paid. If he doesn't get his money, he's coming after you. Doyle thinks he can stall him off a few days . . . if you need a little time to get it together."

As Amanda absorbed his message she got a hollow, twisting ache in the pit of her stomach. Her face registered disbelief. "You mean if *we* need a little more time."

Quinn laughed. "Two million bucks? Where would I get my hands on that kind of money in two or three days? Half my equity is tucked away nice and neat offshore, and the rest is tied up long-term. If I scrape, I could get my hands on a hundred thousand. *Maybe*.''

Amanda's fists clenched in tight, white-knuckled balls. The muscles of her neck quivered with rage. ''Two million dollars would clean me out, Jimmy. And what would the police think? They're conducting a homicide investigation. I can't just liquidate everything I own.''

''Not through *regular* channels. That would be suicide. But you just took control of a hundred million bucks worth of Magnetronics stock. Bill Doyle knows people who'd be happy to let you borrow on holdings like those.''

''For what?'' she hissed. ''Ten cents on the dollar? And even if I *was* that desperate, it'll be months before that stock is actually mine.''

Quinn flashed his best patronizing smile. ''That's why you don't get face value, Mandy. And it wouldn't be anywhere near as low as a tenth. Magnetronics preferred is strictly blue-chip. Doyle can probably get you as much as *fifty* cents. He's got no reason to try and fuck you. I'm his attorney, and you and I are partners in this. Any favor he does for you is a favor he's doing for me.''

Amanda was reeling. Quinn was talking losses of at least four million dollars. On the other hand she knew Billy Mannion. The man was dangerous. ''How sure are you that Doyle can convince Billy to give us some time? And if he can't, what will Billy do?''

She didn't like the nervousness she heard in Quinn's laugh.

''He told Big Bill he'd kill you. But I wouldn't worry too much about that. If he knows his money is coming, he'll wait.''

''How much is too much, Jimmy? I want protection.''

Quinn gulped the remainder of his gin and dug back into the liquor cabinet for the bottle. ''I'm a lawyer, Mandy. That kind of protection isn't the sort of service I provide.''

''But Bill Doyle can. I'm serious, Jimmy. Billy scares me. I don't believe for a minute that he didn't get what he was after last week. He's pulling a fast one on us. If he thinks it will strengthen his credibility with Doyle, he'll come after me. That's how his mind works.''

Quinn poured himself more gin and collapsed back into his seat. Outside they'd just pulled back onto Fifth after looping north on Madison to 69th Street. The car slowed as the chauffeur eased to the curb in front of Amanda's building.

"Bill Doyle won't let Mannion kill you, Mandy. That isn't how *his* mind works. You're on board now; a pillar of the god damn community who just hired an international fugitive to murder her husband. He collects people like you; collects them like stamps or old coins. Saves them for rainy days.''

Amanda was trapped and she knew it. The atmosphere in the backseat of Jimmy Quinn's car was suddenly stifling. "You're the one who *sold* me this idea, you bastard.''

Quinn's smile was tired now. "Bastard? That's not a very nice way to talk to your future husband.''

Amanda ignored him. "You're the one who read Josh's files, Jimmy. You set me up.''

"Set you *up*? Where the hell would you be right now if Ralph was alive? I know for a fact that he talked to Joe Oliver; asked him to figure what he had to lose if he filed for divorce. He'd already put the lion's share of everything he owned in little Lizzie's name. If he'd lived to file, you'd wind up with *half* of what you're getting now. Then figure the court costs you'd incur just fighting to get *that* much.''

"You sound like you think you were doing me a favor, Jimmy. What I don't understand is *why*. What was in it for you?''

Calm had returned to the lawyer's face. He sipped at his gin, smug and satisfied. "Besides the elevated social status that comes with marriage to a Gregory, you mean? Well, remember that collection of Bill Doyle's that I talked about? He added me to it a long time ago.''

She frowned. "You? How?''

"Harvard Law was expensive, Mandy, and we weren't Gregorys. You probably don't remember my father. He worked as your uncle Ned's chauffeur until he died of lung cancer in 1952. Strike that. Until six months *before* he died. Ned Gregory fired him when he found out he was sick. My mother worked her ass off and barely made ends meet. She was grateful for Big Bill's checks. Those rainy days? There've been plenty of them, but mostly they rain money now.''

SIXTEEN

With Billy and the others departing early Monday morning to research shipping schedules and whatnot, Siobhan saw no reason to run off to work as soon as Connor opened up the bar. She'd done little more than sleep here this past week, and the place was filthy: kitchen sink piled high with dirty dishes, the front room strewn with newspapers and dirty clothes. She started the day by cleaning the living room first; opening the doors of the men's bedrooms and throwing everything she found lying about into them. Two days after hearing of it the news of Phillip Wright's murder and the anger it provoked continued to burn hot within her. She'd seen little of her flatmates over the weekend and had yet to confront them with it; with how they'd coerced her complicity in an innocent man's murder. As she cleaned, her fury grew. By the time she reached the kitchen she was every bit as angry with herself as she was at Billy; angered at her own lack of courage in the face of his demands. Yes, he'd threatened to kill her sister's family, but that knowledge did little to assuage the pain of self-loathing.

Instead of washing that disgusting pile of dishes she piled them into Hefty bags and lugged them downstairs to the curb. Before returning she purchased paper plates and plastic flatware from the local market. By the time Seamus and Murphy returned midafternoon she had no better control of her anger, but the place looked habitable once again.

Cowan was the first to open a bedroom door. "What's this?!" he exclaimed.

Siobhan had shut herself in her room and was trying to focus on the scene she would do at tomorrow's workshop class. She listened from behind the closed door.

"What's what?" Murphy asked. There was a pause. "Jaysus *Mary*! What the fuck's all this?"

Seconds later Seamus hammered on Siobhan's door. "Siobhan! Bleeding *hell*, woman!"

Siobhan set her script aside and rose, the anger boiling over once again. When she opened the door she found the engineer confronting her.

"What in Christ's name's going on here, woman?"

"What's going *on* here, Seamus? That's something I'd dearly like to know myself. Why'd you have to *kill* the poor bastard?"

Murphy crossed the room behind Seamus, and before the engineer could open his mouth to respond, Paul let out another bellow of outrage. "Jaysus bleeding Christ! She's thrown out all the crockery . . . and the fucking silver, too!"

Siobhan pushed past the tongue-tied Cowan to stand glaring at Murphy outside the kitchen doorway. "You won't wash up after yourselves, you can throw your dishes and tableware in the bloody garbage, mister. I'm not your maid."

As both men stood speechless, a key rattled in the front door. It swung open seconds later, and Billy entered.

"What's all the hollering?"

Murphy nodded toward the kitchen and pointed at Siobhan. "This one cleaned house by throwing everything into our rooms. She threw out the fucking *dishes*, Billy!"

Mannion's eyes scanned the living room, absorbing the transformation. When he opened his mouth to speak, Siobhan beat him to the first word.

"Don't even start, you bloody bastard! You weren't happy degrading me, you had to *kill* that pathetic creature, too. Why, Billy?"

"He was scum. A tool of the British banking machine."

Siobhan's eyes went wild. "He was a pawn, Billy. No more'n that. A bloody *cog*."

"They're *all* cogs," Mannion snarled. "That's how the bleeding machine *runs*."

She laughed in his face. "Is *that* your rationale? You call yourself a Marxist, Billy. A revolutionary. Someone who's gonna change the way the world thinks. Well, you don't fight shame with shameful acts." A heavy sadness gripped her now. "What happened, Billy? You started out on the right path, but all you are now is a spiteful, murdering demagogue."

Mannion looked ready to pop an artery. "Demagogue? How *dare* you! I'm fighting fire with fire and an eye for an eye. The blood of eight hundred years of slavery and butchery is on their hands, not mine!"

Siobhan's voice was calmer now. Reasoning. "No matter who lights it, fire burns like holy hell, Billy. Burns everyone. And blind is blind no matter who plucks out whose eye first. You killed that poor bugger because the only thing that gets you off anymore is the smell of blood and death."

Mannion launched himself at her with no warning. A fist aimed at her midsection caught her hard in the sternum as she tried to dodge from harm's way. It staggered her backward, and she struggled to catch her balance. Another blow caught her in the mouth. She saw stars, her knees turning to rubber and the floor coming up suddenly beneath her. Her left elbow slammed down hard, her hand feeling as though a thousand nails were being driven into it.

Seamus and Murphy were on Mannion before he could land a kick aimed at the fallen woman's head.

"Let me at her!" Billy panted. He struggled like a wildcat in a gunnysack. "Bitch! I'll show you what I get off on!"

Siobhan was on her feet now, hurrying for the front door. When she reached it her left hand refused to grip the knob. She tugged wildly with her right, the door coming suddenly free. With a grunt she sprawled headlong onto the landing.

"Let me *go*, you bastards!" Billy screamed.

Without looking back Siobhan hauled herself to her feet and flew downstairs to the street.

By the time Monday rolled around, Dante had worked most of the kinks of last week's unaccustomed activity from his muscles. Rather than spend Sunday working on his loft he'd let Diana take him shopping for some much-needed kitchen equipment and then coerce him into dinner and a movie. Monday morning he arrived on the job site feeling refreshed and ready to attack the accumulated mountain of materials with renewed purpose. By noon he was once again running sweat and caked with gypsum dust.

The whistle had just blown to signal the end of the lunch hour when Henry Roark appeared on the sixth floor. He approached Dante as Joe was checking a new batch of shipping bills with Tom McCarty. Joe and his crew were finally ahead of immediate demand and were starting to stockpile materials ahead of the crews. For a change the atmosphere in the supply area was no longer frantic with activity.

"Speak with you a minute, Joe?"

Dante nodded, paused to send McCarty on his way with a pallet-load of screws headed for the eighth floor, and then joined Henry to drift toward one of the open windows. The weather had turned balmy again, and the breeze up there felt good. Roark tapped out a cigarette and lit it while formulating his words.

"Tim's decided he's got no choice, Joe. He says the cops are out of the question; thinks he'd risk losing some of his crew if the police start sticking their noses in."

Dante scowled as he shook his head. "What do you mean by decided? Has he talked to anyone?"

"Not yet. He says he promised to discuss it with you over drinks tonight. I'm hoping you can talk him out of it."

"I hope so, too, Henry. He lets some shylock get his teeth into him, he's lost the war before the first shot is fired."

"Especially these bastards," Henry growled. "Bill Doyle and that lot will suck his blood."

Dante feigned only the vaguest familiarity with the name. "Doyle. He's the Westie boss, isn't he?"

"That's right. A real son of a bitch if ever there was one."

"He's got that kind of muscle? The sort it will take to go up against Octavio's handlers? I thought the Westies lost most of their leverage when shipping moved from the West Side to Brooklyn and Bayonne."

"That's true, but they're alive and kicking once again," Roark assured him. "Most of their power is in the labor rackets, in union locals like ours. We Irish stick together and are willing to work harder than most. The man who can harness that commodity wields real power in this city. With the exception of a few stubborn independents like Timmy, Doyle's got Irish labor all but wrapped up."

Dante stared down into the Broadway traffic six floors below and took a deep breath. "If he's already made up his mind, I doubt there's much I can say that will convince him otherwise, Henry. But I said I'd try, and I will. You'll be there?"

Roark nodded. "I hate to see a man lose something he's worked so hard to build. If he won't listen to one of us, perhaps he'll listen to two."

Siobhan's tennis-ball story had worked well enough in the wake of injuries inflicted by Billy a week ago. Today her newly bruised and swollen mouth refused to be so casually dismissed. When she arrived for work Connor had addressed it with his usual bluntness. She told him she didn't want to discuss it, and he'd let it drop. While no one else had mentioned it outright, she guessed that her new injury was one of tonight's prime topics of discussion. Most of the regulars knew she had some sort of republican connection. A handful knew the specifics of why she'd been sent here to America. Most still clung to the spirit of the IRA cause while many had soured to its methods. Terrorists of all stripes had earned themselves a certain ignominy around the globe. Siobhan's mouth was just more evidence of Billy Mannion's brand of ruthlessness. It was her choice and not theirs whether she resigned herself to it. She'd made this bed.

Most of the regulars from the construction trades had been there for over an hour when Siobhan saw Tim O'Brien's new expediter enter and cross to Tim's table. After a brief exchange O'Brien tried to rise. His man placed a restraining hand on his shoulder and turned to approach the bar himself. That welt he'd had on his forehead Friday was barely visible now. The memory of the conversation they'd had made Siobhan acutely conscious of her own bruises.

Dante reached the bar and flashed her that quick, disarming smile of his. "Evening, Siobhan. Two pints of Guinness, please." He extracted his wallet and placed a twenty on the bar.

As she reached for a pair of mugs a twinge of pain shot down her left arm from elbow to wrist. One of the mugs hit the bar and bounced before Dante caught it on its way to the floor. As he placed it on the surface before him he leaned close.

"I don't know who the creep is, but I'd dump him before he kills you." He pulled back, his eyes maintaining direct contact. "Seriously. That's some jig he danced on your face. It's much too pretty to let some guy hammer on it like that."

She swallowed hard and forced a smile. "That's kind of you to say, Joe. But it i'n't as easy as just walking away."

Dante's face hardened. "Why not? Friday night you told me you want to be an actress. Your face is a valuable asset, so what are your alternatives? You either get help or let some asshole destroy your dream."

Before Siobhan could respond, two of O'Brien's crew approached to clap Dante on the back and ask him how he was getting on. She got busy filling glasses. Once she broke the expediter's twenty and made change he picked up his drinks and headed off for Tim's table. Of course he was right, but what options did she have? She couldn't very well go to the police. Tonight she intended to sleep upstairs on Connor's sofa, but sooner or later she would have to go home. All her clothes were there. Everything she owned. She doubted Billy would kill her, but Dante's warning rang more truly than he knew. Billy had changed since their days together at the university in Galway. He'd tasted blood and found he liked it. There was no hope of changing him now.

Countless times over the next hour Siobhan caught glimpses of her bruises in the back-bar mirror. With each glimpse the front gates of the Actors Studio flashed in her mind's eye. She believed she had the talent, the tools, and the guts to make her dream a reality.

At eight-thirty, as Dante rose from his conversation with O'Brien to visit the men's room, Siobhan made up her mind. She *did* have a choice. She wasn't going back to that apartment and her life of subservience to Billy's cause and Billy's wishes. When Dante emerged from the hall to the restrooms Siobhan was waiting for him at that end of the bar.

"Speak wit you, Joe?"

Dante veered in his course to pull up, one work boot finding the footrail. "Sure. Sorry if I upset you. It's really none of my business."

Her eyes darted left and right to ensure they were alone. She shook her head. "Don't be sorry. I want to talk with you about what you said, but this isn't a good place. Could we meet outside somewhere? My break is at ten."

He peered at his watch, and his eyes were gentle as they came back to her face. "Ten? No problem. How about my car? It's parked just around the corner. Low-slung black job. You can't miss it."

She thanked him and turned quickly away as a patron approached, empty glass in hand.

For two and a half hours Dante and Henry Roark tried to convince Tim O'Brien not to put the Marty Octavio problem into Westie hands. Tim talked like whichever way he played it he was already beaten. In defeat he would rather see the Irish mob assume control of his life than the Italians. He relished the idea of a Westie thug holding a knife to Marty

Octavio's balls and explaining the situation in terms he understood. Dante argued as delicately as he could for the police point of view. He contended, once again, that the local cops could care less who had legitimate papers and who didn't on O'Brien's crew. Papers were a federal problem. Potential gunplay on a Manhattan construction site was a different matter, and Joe was convinced that setting the Westies head-to-head with Octavio might lead to that. They went round and round over it, and by the time O'Brien left at nine-thirty, Joe and Henry had still failed to convince him to reverse field. He was desperate, and his worries about the safety of his crew were real. Dante had no choice now but to advise the Organized Crime Task Force of this impending development. It would complicate how Captain Costello and his team played it, but Joe had done what he could. It was out of his hands now. Meanwhile he had the prospect of a meeting with Siobhan McDonough distracting him. He had to be careful; play this one exactly right. He needed a few minutes alone right now—time to think. With half an hour remaining before his rendezvous he drained his beer, bid Henry Roark goodnight, and stood to go.

The night outside the bar had turned crisp enough to force him into his denim work jacket as he started around the corner for his car. Behind him he heard the distant rumble of an IRT train approaching on the elevated tracks. As he fitted his key into the driver's-side door the deafening rumble and clatter of the Broadway train was upon him, shattering the night. He climbed behind the wheel and closed the door, the banshee wail of train brakes instantly hushed. He could think again. His dash clock told him he had another twenty minutes before the bartender emerged on her break. One of the Oscar Peterson tapes Jumbo gave him went into the player. He sat back and closed his eyes, thinking and waiting with waves of sweet piano notes washing over him.

When she appeared, hurrying around the corner and up the block, Siobhan held her head low, her face averted from the street. Joe reached over to pop the passenger-side door as she approached. When she climbed in he lowered the music's volume. Once she was settled he twisted in his seat to face her.

"You wanted to talk."

A quick, nervous bob of the head. "I realize you hardly know me, Joe. And maybe I'm crazy to believe I can trust you, but right now I wonder if I have any choice. Nobody else in there had the courage to even mention my face. They're all afraid."

"Maybe I would be, too, Siobhan. They obviously know something that I don't."

She ignored the implications and plunged on. "I can't go back home, Joe. Don't ask me why, because they'd kill me if I told you. Please just believe me. I can't go to the police either. I wish it were that easy."

Dante frowned. He was a fisherman with an unknown quantity bending his rod, his line taut down to unseen depths. "They'll kill you. No wonder everyone in that bar is afraid. Who are *they*, Siobhan? And what did you do to make them so angry? Angry enough to hurt you like that?" He gestured to her face.

She was suddenly nervous again, her eyes darting up the street to the corner and head turning to check the sidewalk behind. "Can we just drive or something? It isn't safe here."

Dante straightened in his seat and reached for the key. "No problem. You're not expected back in the bar?"

"I'm not going back there neither."

Dante swung away from the curb and turned north at the corner. He had as little idea of where he was going as Siobhan seemed to have. She had no handbag, no overnight case, nothing. He'd unwittingly triggered something tonight, tipped the scales in favor of escape. Now she was plunging ahead, all reservation and caution thrown to the wind.

Broadway fronted the entire western edge of Van Cortlandt Park. When they drew alongside the park's parade ground, Joe pulled to the curb and parked. Once again he twisted in his seat to confront her.

"You left your whole life behind you back there. You sure you're ready to do that? We've met twice, Siobhan. Those people are your friends. From what Tim tells me, your boss is connected to some pretty heavy people. You couldn't ask *him* to protect you?''

Her nostrils flared, eyes suddenly on fire. "*Protect* me? If they knew he was even trying they'd slit his throat and sink him in the Hudson.'' Her anger turned impatient. In her frustration she made a decision. "Oh, what the hell. I'm dead anyway. You've heard of the IRA, yes? That's who *they* are. It's why I can't go to the police for protection, and it's why Connor McNulty and none of the rest of them can do a thing for me. Please, don't ask me any more questions. If you can't see your way clear to help me after what I just told you then drop me somewhere far from here. I'll figure something out.''

The two of them sat in silence. It was difficult for Dante to mask his excitement. Friday night he'd traveled north to take a blind shot at an invisible target. Tonight it hit ground zero. Time to go for broke.

"How about Twenty-seventh Street in Manhattan? Would that be far enough?''

A brief puzzlement passed. "Your place?''

"My cat's place, actually. He lets me live there, too. Like I mentioned Friday, the one thing we've got is lots of room.''

Sculptor Brian Brennan arrived home from Tokyo late Monday afternoon. Diana met him at Kennedy, and the minute she got him home she locked the door, put the phone on service, and hauled him off to bed. That was six hours ago. The weariness of twenty-three hours in the air finally caught up with him, and he dozed. When he woke it was dark outside. Both he and Diana were famished. Foraging in the kitchen, they threw a simple pasta and salad together while bringing each other up to date. The commissioned piece Brennan had created for Nissan was installed in the lobby of their corporate headquarters. Other Japanese firms were impressed, and there was talk of other commissions as well. Meanwhile, here on the home front, their friend Dante was officially suspended; blamed for the death of shipping magnate Hubert Poole's sixteen-year-old daughter. Off the record he was working deep cover to find the man responsible for the killing.

Brennan was concerned enough at hearing this news to get on the phone and dial Dante's number downstairs.

"Damn! His answering machine."

Barefoot and wearing her new kimono, Diana was perched cross-legged on one of the kitchen stools. "I haven't heard the elevator all night. Maybe he's still working."

"This late? On a construction site?"

"He's only using that as a cover to get in tight with the Irish community," she explained. "When we got together yesterday he told me he's gotten his foot in the door already. Some of the guys he works with took him to a bar up in the North Bronx. The way he tells it he was the only guy in the joint who didn't have a brogue."

Brennan digested this and sighed. "So you didn't tell him I was coming home tonight."

She snorted. "When did you tell *me*, Brian? Midnight last night from Honolulu? I haven't *seen* him since then."

"So what kind of progress have you two made downstairs? What's the kitchen look like?"

She hopped down from her stool and grabbed a set of Joe's keys from a hook next to the telephone. "C'mon. I'll show you."

They skipped the elevator and took the back stairs. Brennan was struck by the sheer amount of paint that had been applied in his absence. The master bedroom, guest room, and the first of two baths were nearly finished now. And while the living room and second bath remained unchanged, the kitchen was also nearing completion. He was impressed by the quality of Joe and Diana's finishing touches.

"Beautiful job."

"Thanks. We worked our butts off."

"Hmmm," he growled. "So I see." She had a can of food open and was stooping to dump it into Toby the cat's bowl. As he reached to stroke some of the kimono stretched tight over her posterior, the motor of the elevator across the living room kicked in. Not wanting to start something he couldn't finish, he patted her affectionately and started for the refrigerator. In celebration of his homecoming he helped himself to a couple of Joe's beers and moved into the living room to greet his pal.

Brennan had the two beers held aloft and a big grin on his face as the elevator car appeared behind the open-mesh closure. His smile fell and the beers descended to his sides as the car slowed to a stop and Dante hauled back the gate.

"Hey, Brian. When'd you get back?"

There was nothing effusive in Joe's greeting, and Brennan could see why. He stared in horror at the woman in his friend's company. "Jesus. What the hell happened?"

The woman glanced to Dante in embarrassment, and Joe hurried to put her at ease. "Siobhan McDonough, meet Brian Brennan. Friend, neighbor, landlord. Siobhan's having a little trouble at home. She's going to be staying with me for a few days."

It was obvious just what sort of trouble this lady was having. The yellowing bruise on one side of her face and a fresh, angry welt on the other told Brennan the abuse she suffered was ongoing. Contemplating it made him soul-sick.

"Siobhan?" Brian switched the bottle in his right hand to his left and reached to take hers. "Aye. A pretty Irish name it is." He was surprised by the strength of her grip and the brave front she was able to maintain.

"Thank you, Brian Brennan. Did you know there's a sculptor by your name? Quite famous, he is. There's a beautiful bronze of his at Trinity in Dublin. They say it's of his wife."

Dante chuckled, further breaking the ice. "Careful," he warned. "His head's big enough as it is."

As the young woman's eyes widened, Brennan was distracted enough from her bruises to notice how pretty she was. There were perfect, sharp-cut angles to her bones, and she had a build that rivaled Diana's.

"No. You're not *that* Brian Brennan?"

"Oh, dear." It came from behind Brennan as Diana emerged from the kitchen. "Hi, Siobhan. I'm Di . . ." As his wife drew abreast of him Brennan heard the abrupt intake of breath. "Are you all right?"

"I'm fine. Really I am. There's nothin' broken. Only bruises."

Brennan slipped his free arm around Diana and pulled her close. He raised those two beers in the other and shrugged. "I guess this isn't really a good time, is it," he apologized. "I dragged Diana down here to show me the progress you'd made on the kitchen. We'll get the hell out of your hair."

As Brian released Diana and started for the kitchen to put those bottles back in the refrigerator, Dante stopped him.

"Hang on a sec." He turned to Diana. "Siobhan didn't have time to pack a bag when she left her place this afternoon, and . . ."

"Please," Siobhan interrupted. "I'll be all right until the morning, Joe. I don't want to impose."

Diana moved to take the situation in hand. "Nonsense. I'll bet you and I are about the same size, Siobhan. What are you? A six American?"

"That's right, but please. Don't go to any trouble."

Diana smiled. "No trouble at all. We'll leave these two down here and you come with me." She turned to Dante. "How are you fixed for sheets?"

"I think I'm fine," he replied. "Let me check."

Dante started for his bedroom, and Brennan dug for his pocket knife. He pried the caps off the beers as Dante disappeared and returned a moment later with clean sheets and towels. They all walked together to the elevator, and as Diana stepped into the car, Brian watched Joe press a folded piece of paper into Diana's waiting hand.

* * *

207

Connor McNulty couldn't understand why Siobhan didn't say something to him before she left. She'd taken her break as usual at ten o'clock. It was less usual for her to leave the bar, but every so often she did that, too. He knew she wasn't feeling well, and when she failed to return at ten-fifteen, Connor thought perhaps she'd gone for a walk. When he hadn't heard from her by eleven he voiced his concern.

"I'm worried about Siobhan, Patrick," he told Paddy Griffin. "She weren't her usual self tonight, and her disappearing just isn't like her."

Griffin, a runner for Big Bill Doyle and one of McNulty's regulars, sat hunched over a pint at the end of the bar removed from the television. "You want, I could go round to her place and check on her, Connor. I've delivered a message or two for Doyle and know where it is."

McNulty shook his head, uncertain. "I don't want to make no trouble. Not for the likes of Billy Mannion. I'm worried though. I mean, what if she stepped out for a breath of air and met up with trouble? Niggers or something."

"Or one particular guinea. That big fucker Tim O'Brien brought in here was trying to make time wit her. What's Tim think he's doing, bringing trash like that in here?"

McNulty scowled. O'Brien and his crew were good customers. He had no quarrel with Tim. "They say he's jake, that one. Not just Timmy. All of them. Stood up for 'em against some fella backed by the guinea mob. It got ugly, and he beat the living shit outta the guinea's goons."

Griffin drained his glass and climbed down off his stool. "I don't care what they say. It don't make sense. The wops stick to their kind, and we stick to our'n. I'm gonna drop round, see Mannion. It's likely he dragged the bitch home 'n' forgot to tell you about it. Too busy fucking the b'jaysus out of her. That's what I'd do if I had me a piece looked like that one. Fuck her morning, noon, and night."

"The note," Brennan asked. "What does it say?"
Dante was in action as soon as the elevator took Diana

and Siobhan away upstairs. Brian followed him into the bedroom and watched as Joe jerked open the top drawer of his dresser to remove an automatic pistol in a clip-on holster.

"It says that no matter what, she can't tell Siobhan I'm a cop. Diana knows what my cover is, so she shouldn't have any problem." He looked up from his pawing through the contents of his dresser to jerk his chin at the room. "Give me a hand here. I didn't plan on this particular development."

Brennan headed for the closet. "What am I looking for?"

"Anything that might blow it for me. I'm a construction worker, just back from eight years in the Persian Gulf."

Brennan began looking through Dante's clothes until he hit on Joe's dress uniform. He jerked it from the rod and threw it onto the bed. "Who is she?" he asked. "And who the hell beat her like that? I hardly know her, and I want to kill the fucker."

"Long story. She's connected to the IRA somehow. The guy I'm after right now is wanted for bombing that British officer's club at NATO headquarters last spring. She hasn't told me who hit her. Not yet."

Brian finished with the closet and headed for the door. "What about the guest room?"

"Good question. There's all that stuff in boxes in there."

"Anything in them that you don't want her to find?"

Dante slid the pistol beneath his mattress and box spring, still looking harried. "I'm not sure what all's in them. Most of it's the stuff that came pouring in when people heard my place burned and I'd been wiped out. Let's just haul it all in here."

As Brennan began stacking cartons from the guest room against the back wall of Dante's closet, Joe stuffed his dress uniform into a plastic trash bag and buried it behind them. That task completed, they closed the closet doors and started to make the guest room bed.

"Where's your shield case?" Brennan asked. A slender man of about Dante's height, the sculptor had the build of a runner and the forearms of a blacksmith. His lean, boyish Irish face was wreathed in a head of dark curls that was fast going gray.

"Probably in the commissioner's top desk drawer."

"Oh. Sorry. Your backup gun?"

"Little hidey-hole up under the sink. She'll never find it there."

Brennan finished tucking the top sheet in at the foot of the bed and reached for the blankets. "Tell me more about this job. Diana said something about construction, but it looks like you spent the day demolishing a flour mill."

"Materials expediter for a drywall contractor."

Brennan groaned. "You expect this girl to buy that? All she's got to do is look at the tape joints on these walls and your cover is *blown*."

When Billy Mannion wasn't expecting visitors he took every precaution before opening his door. When the knock sounded he had Seamus hail their caller through the panel while he set up against the wall next to the jamb. Paulie Murphy took up a secondary defensive position behind a living room chair. Once the caller identified himself as Bill Doyle's runner, Mannion gave Seamus the nod. The door swung inward, and as Patrick Griffin entered, Mannion hit him from the blind side. One arm encircled Griffin's neck in a choke hold while Billy jammed the muzzle of his pistol up under Paddy's chin.

"This'd better be good," he hissed. "I hear so much as a footstep out there in that hallway and you'll be the first to join the angels."

"I had no choice but to come here," Griffin defended himself. "You have no phone. It's that girl of yours. She's disappeared, and McNulty's concerned. Have you seen her?"

"Siobhan?" Billy demanded. "What do you mean, disappeared?"

With the muzzle of that gun still wedged beneath his chin, Griffin hurried to explain how Siobhan had gone off on her break and failed to return. "She's never done nothing like that before, and Connor thought either she'd come back here and forgot to tell him or she's run up against trouble. He's afraid it might've been niggers. I say it's that guinea works for Tim O'Brien. He was sweet-talking her at the bar tonight."

"Who's Tim O'Brien?"

"Building contractor. Likes rubbing elbows wit the rank and file. Drinks at McNulty's all the time. Doyle don't trust him. This past week he had the balls to bring this wop around. Drives a fancy sports car and lives somewhere down in Manhattan."

Mannion eased the gun away from Griffin's chin but remained lips-to-ear with him. "Where do I find this O'Brien?"

"I've no idea. Connor might know."

Billy turned to Cowan and Murphy. "Pack everything and get it into the van. Patrick here and I are going to have a talk wit Connor McNulty. I'll meet you on the street downstairs. Half an hour. No more."

It was twelve-thirty before Brennan and Diana retired, leaving Dante and his houseguest to get some sleep. Joe knew he wasn't likely to get more than five or six hours shut-eye, and while Siobhan occupied the bathroom he busied himself in the kitchen, getting it set so he could rush off to work at the last minute. After grinding the morning coffee he slapped a couple of sandwiches together for his lunch. He was tucking those sandwiches and an apple into his lunch pail when Siobhan cleared her throat from the kitchen doorway.

"G'night, Joe."

Dante turned to find his guest dressed in a pink-and-white flower-print flannel nightgown. Diana's mother was forever sending her things like this; a midwestern mother's idea of what decent women wore to bed.

"Night, Siobhan. You having any second thoughts?"

He saw those eyes, the same eyes as his own, watching

211

him. Inspecting and assessing. He leaned against his kitchen counter in a pair of gym shorts, barefoot and shirtless. She shook her head.

"None serious. Not yet."

"Good. You're safe here. Take all the time you need to figure out what you want to do next. There's no rush."

As he spoke the phone rang; not the line dedicated to police business in his bedroom but the line with extensions throughout the house. He grabbed the receiver of the kitchen wall phone.

"Yeah."

"Joe? Tim O'Brien. Did I waken you?"

"It's after midnight, boss. What do you think?"

"I'm sorry, Joe. It's important. I feel kinda awkward calling you like this, but Connor McNulty lost his bartender tonight. You remember Siobhan McDonough? Seems she left for her break at ten and never come back. She i'n't home, and her people are worried. Connor's calling round to see if any of the patrons who were there late might've seen her leave."

"I hit the road right after you did, Tim. Couldn't have been much later than nine-thirty."

"That's what Connor thought, but I had to try, you understand. One of his regulars remembers seeing you talking to her. He thought she might've said something."

"No luck here, boss. It looked like somebody'd smacked her, and I got the impression she was pretty upset. That's *all* I got. She didn't want to talk about it."

"Well, thanks, Joe. Sorry to bother you. See you first thing."

Dante hung up and saw the questions in Siobhan's eyes. "That was Tim O'Brien. Your friend who gave you that fat lip is looking for you. Tim says someone saw you and me talking at the bar."

Siobhan instantly looked worried. "If they think you had anything to do wit me leaving, they'll make trouble for you, Joe. I made a mistake, coming here."

"Nonsense. The address O'Brien has for me is a post office box. You're safe. If anyone wants to make trouble, they can find me at the job site, eight to four."

Toby the cat wandered in from the front room to circle Dante, weaving in and out between his legs and rubbing up against his naked ankles. Joe stooped to pick him up and started for the door. As he switched off the lights Siobhan fell in beside him.

"Those scars you have on your back and side there? You were in some sort of accident? It must've been terrible."

"Chain-hoist collapse. I used to work roughneck on drilling rigs back before I had enough sense to realize I'm not immortal. A load of casing pipe was sixty feet overhead when it busted loose. I thought I was clear but a couple of lengths bounced off a truss beam on the way down. I was laid up in a Kuwaiti hospital for over three months."

A hand touched him lightly on the forearm as he neared his bedroom. He stopped, head coming around to find her looking up into his face.

"You talk like such a tough guy, but you've got a heart soft as sponge cake. I can see it in the way you've treated me; how you treat your friends."

Her body was so close he could feel the warmth of it radiating through all that pink flannel. Less easy to feel, but there just as surely, were all her needs. The need to know she was safe; that there was hope; that she was desirable even in her neediness. He brushed a wisp of hair from her forehead and bent to plant a kiss in its place. "It's late and we're tired, Siobhan. Sleep tight."

SEVENTEEN

James Quinn wasn't surprised. When advised of Amanda's willingness to exchange Magnetronics stock for cash, Bill Doyle hadn't reached any further than into his own deep pockets. Big Bill knew a gold mine when he fell into one. After agreeing on a fifty-cents-on-the-dollar number late last night, Doyle ordered Quinn to draw up the promissory note and get it executed as promptly as possible. Amanda Kane had signed the papers first thing Tuesday morning. Now Quinn sat in Bill Doyle's office at Emerald Consolidated, a freight-forwarding concern located at 43rd Street and Eleventh Avenue in Manhattan's Hell's Kitchen. As they discussed the business before them, Doyle puffed on one of his Macanudo cigars, his head wreathed in smoke.

"There's only one problem I see with any of this, Bill." The attorney indicated the papers spread flat on the front edge of Doyle's desk. "The SEC is going to notice when a stock block that large changes hands. We want to be careful here."

Doyle inspected the lit end of his cigar and grunted with satisfaction. "So route it through one of our accounts on the Isle of Man. Make it look like she's bought into one of our offshore investments."

"Which? The hotels?"

"Sure. Why not? One of the new ventures. Something

speculative. There ain't no crime in making an investment that never pans out, right?''

Quinn smiled. ''She hears we've got hotels in Europe, she'll want me to book us into a few on our honeymoon.''

Doyle sighed, his eyes rolling. ''Still looking t' get your name in the Social Register, eh Jimmy? I'd sleep with one eye open, married to a woman like that. She plays for keeps, that one.''

''How's that different from the way you and I play it, Bill? And by the way, she still believes that Mannion is playing for keeps, too. That he's decided to keep everything.''

''I tell you I talked to the man, Jimmy. Looked him right in the eye. He swore to God that he grabbed everything on the desk that she told him to grab. Claims he came away with a box of computer disks that ain't worth shit.''

Quinn wasn't satisfied. ''I don't care what he claims, Bill. I'm with Amanda on this one. I've got this little voice telling me that Billy's double-crossing us; that he's still off making his Korean deal.''

Doyle waved the wet end of his cigar at the air between them.

''What's your point, Jimmy? What are you saying here?''

''I'm saying it galls me, that sneaking son of a bitch selling what he stole for at least as much as Amanda's paying him. Maybe more.''

Doyle stuffed his smoke back into his mouth and puffed quickly, his impatience obvious. ''You ain't exactly walking away from this empty-handed, Jimmy. You've got that broad *eating* outta your hand; an heir to one of the oldest fortunes in America. Billy Mannion's *my* problem now. I've got ears down inside the movement. Plenty of 'em. If Billy scores big, I'm gonna hear. One word of it and I'll make sure his nuts are cut off. I don't like him any more than you do. He talks to me like I'm some old fart with no stiff left in his pecker. Just let him cross me. He'll find out.''

Quinn nodded and rose to go. ''You know your word is good enough for me, Bill. I've got a busy day at the office.

All this schedule shuffling has me backed up six ways to Sunday.'' He stooped to collect Amanda's copy of the promissory note, folded it and tapped it against his palm. ''So when is it that you're going to square up with him?''

Doyle chuckled. ''Tell your lady friend she's got nothing to worry about. I'm meeting with him this evening. He had a little problem this morning. One of his people's run off; that little girl they sent over to set up a safe house.''

''What does *run off* mean?'' Quinn hoped that his concerns here were Doyle's concerns as well.

''Sounds like some sorta domestic spat to me. Connor tells me Billy slapped her around, bruised her face.''

''Does McNulty know where she is?''

''Not that he's telling. Claims she left in the middle of her shift last night. Flat fuckin' dropped outta sight.''

Quinn had started for the door only to stop a couple of yards short of it and turn all the way back around. ''How much does she know about what we're up to, Bill?''

Doyle dismissed Quinn's fears with another wave of his cigar. ''She's just some broad they sent over from the lower ranks, for Crissake. Mannion ain't survived as long as he has trusting his secrets to the cunts who cook his meals.''

''If she was close enough to Mannion to get slapped around, she was close enough to overhear something.''

The Westie boss heaved himself to his feet and started toward a silver tray cluttered with cut-crystal decanters. He pulled a stopper and poured a glass half-full of whisky. ''There ain't no way that broad'll go anywhere near the cops, Jimmy. She's IRA, and that makes her an accomplice no matter what her involvement's been. She's already been in trouble with Immigration once and has to know she's skating on thin ice there, too. She'll lay low. Trust me.''

''Anyone can cut a deal,'' Quinn reminded him.

Doyle lifted his drink, his cigar now drooping from one side of a lip-twisting smirk. ''C'mon, Jimmy. Where's your faith? She goes to the cops, *you'll* no doubt hear about it before the commissioner. If you do, you tell me. I get word to a couple boys on the inside who owe me and . . ." He snapped his fingers. "Just 'cuz she's in protective custody don't mean she can't be reached. Not in *my* city."

Diana Webster canceled Tuesday's recording session and invited Siobhan upstairs once Joe left for work. When Brian left early to inspect some castings done by a specialty foundry up the Hudson in Fishkill, the two women were left to loiter over breakfast. Diana was no more accustomed to the bruises on Siobhan's face after a night's sleep. She knew that domestic violence was a common problem, but it was rare in her world to encounter it face-to-face. This morning the reddened swelling on one side of Siobhan's mouth and cheek had subsided, giving way to mottled blue and purple. The woman's opposite cheek had turned a greenish yellow.

It was midmorning before they moved to the dressing room in search of some comfortable, casual clothes. The two women were about the same size, and they settled quickly on several shirts and pairs of pants. Diana was looking now for just the right sweater.

"This is the problem with having too many clothes," the singer muttered. "I waste too much time trying to make decisions."

"I've never seen so many beautiful woolens," Siobhan marveled.

Diana removed several sweaters from one of the shelves and shook them out, each getting an appraising once-over. "Right. And look at me. The girl who's most comfortable in jeans and a T-shirt. All this is Brian's doing. He passes a store window and can't resist anything that catches his eye."

"I think that's wonderful," Siobhan whispered. Still dressed in her nightgown, she sat lounging in the dressing-table chair. "Even if you never wear a stitch of it."

Diana turned, her tone turned softer. "I know. And who gives a shit if I never wear it? There's plenty of room here. Besides, I usually do wear each of them around the house a few times."

217

Siobhan lifted her teacup from the saucer on the dressing table and sipped. "Tell me about Joe, Diana. He says he was gone from the country for nearly ten years, and yet you seem like such good friends."

Diana knew Joe's cover was crucial to his investigation, but she hated lying to this woman. It seemed to add insult to the already injured. "He and Brian have known each other forever. And he wasn't away *all* that time. His wife kept moving around to prevent him from seeing his kids, but he kept coming back and trying. He's stayed with us ever since I met Brian; usually for a month around Christmas. Dante's a sucker for New York during the holidays."

"They say he broke a fella's jaw Friday. Some sort of problem at their job. You'd never know it, talking to him last night. It's hard to imagine he could do something like that. He seems so gentle."

Diana paused with one of the sweaters she'd shaken out, eyeing it critically. "Yeah. It's something I noticed about him when we first met. He's got a handle on his anger. He channels it somehow. When he gets upset it's usually about a problem at hand, not a lot of other crap that's built up inside him." She handed the sweater across, Siobhan setting her tea down to take it. "How about this one?"

Siobhan brightened. "It's beautiful. Are you sure it's all right with Brian that I borrow it?"

"All right with *Brian*?"

"You just finished telling me he gave all these to you, Diana."

"That's right. Gave. And now I'm giving it to you."

Siobhan blushed. "Giving? No. I couldn't possibly take it from you."

Diana was bewildered by the force of Siobhan's apprehension. "Why not, Siobhan? I don't need it, and you'll look gorgeous in it."

Siobhan tried to hand it back. "Not a gift from your husband. It wouldn't be right."

Diana was suddenly angry. "Siobhan, listen to me. These

218

are *my* things, not Brian's. I get up in the morning and decide what I'm going to do with *my* day, same as Brian does."

The forcefulness in Diana's tone took Siobhan by surprise. The Irishwoman pulled the sweater back, both hands fidgeting with it nervously. "I'm sorry if I've offended you."

"Don't worry about offending me, Siobhan. Worry about the kind of thinking that made you say what you did. If you don't stop *thinking* like a victim you'll continue to *be* a victim. Guaranteed."

John McGuire was dying to stretch his legs. He'd been parked out here on the corner of 236th and Corlear in Kingsbridge since before dawn. He was also bored. There'd been no observable action upstairs in the two-family house he'd been watching. The shades were still drawn, and the van he was told to look for was still parked half a block up on the left. He was so bored, in fact, that the chirping of the car phone startled him. When he reached to activate the handsfree unit overhead, Big Bill Doyle came on the line sounding a lot more upbeat than John felt.

"Morning, Johnny. Gimme the picture."

McGuire stifled a yawn. "Nothing worth drawing, boss. Not yet."

"Shouldn't be long. He was probably up late. Keep a sharp eye. And that red light you had, Johnny? It just turned green."

"Gotcha, boss man. I know the drill. You want I should pick up after myself or leave the garbage for the city?"

"Leave it for the city. Sanitation's one of the services we buy with our taxes."

Billy Mannion's first priority that Tuesday was to store the explosives and other gear at a more secure location than this. His second priority was to find Siobhan. He couldn't be sure how much she'd overheard of his conversations or how big a threat she represented to the security of his operation. He didn't doubt that she could tie him to Big Bill Doyle, and

Doyle had helped him locate this secondary safe house. A location like this was good only for an emergency, and certainly safe for no more than the one night they'd just used it. With such a busy day ahead and half of it already gone they decided to forgo breakfast and get underway quickly. The morning was yet another dazzler, more balmy calm replacing last week's chill winds. Once they were loaded Paulie climbed behind the wheel and started the van east across Broadway. Their progress took them around the bottom of Van Cortlandt Park and then north on Jerome Avenue to the isolated little Woodlawn section of the North Bronx. Murphy's cousin Monica had a house with a garage here on Martha Avenue. A staunch IRA supporter who'd emigrated from Derry in 1975, Monica Flynn was the team's refuge of last resort. She had worked a late shift as a nurse in the Intensive Care Unit at nearby Montefiore Hospital, and Paulie had to wake her while the others waited in the van. Once the garage door was raised Billy backed the van into the drive and together they unloaded their equipment. Monica appeared wrapped in a robe at the head of the garage stairs as Seamus slammed the van's side door.

"Have you had your tea, lads?" she asked.

Seamus was known to have a soft spot in his heart for this slightly plump but comely lass. He looked eager to accept her invitation and drop up to have a cup, but Billy shook his head.

"Thank you, no, mum. We've got a lot on our schedule this fine day. Perhaps you'll fix us supper."

The sleepy-eyed nurse brightened. "That would be fine, Billy. Surely. I'm off tonight."

They were back in the van and rolling from the drive into the street when Seamus voiced his disappointment. "There's that much of a rush, Billy? We can surely spare the few minutes it would take to eat something."

Mannion turned in the passenger seat to glower aft. "You can play all the footsie you want tonight, Romeo. Right now we're off to have a little chat with that drywall contractor.

Tim O'Brien. This guinea with the fancy sports car knew more than he was willing to tell last night. Perhaps he'll be more cooperative with some friendly persuasion.''

Paulie guided them west to the Major Deegan Expressway and then south to the Henry Hudson Parkway and upper Manhattan. Last night they'd learned from Connor McNulty that O'Brien Construction's current project was a thirty-six-story high-rise located at 95th and Broadway. Murphy exited at 96th and began working his way east. As he got them to their destination and guided the van in tight behind a delivery truck half a block back, Billy and Seamus checked their weapons. Once Paulie switched off the ignition he dug his own noise-suppressed pistol from beneath the seat.

With the warm turn in the weather they'd driven here with the windows down. Now, as Murphy started to roll his up, Billy stopped him.

"Let's leave it unlocked and windows down. You never know how quickly we'll want to be leaving."

They climbed out and approached up the street to where a crew was bending reinforcing bar out in front of the plywood perimeter barricade. One of the men pointed out Tim O'Brien's trailer office, and as they approached it Mannion made a note of the various signs posted along the barrier. One declared it to be restricted to AUTHORIZED PERSONNEL. Of course. Another designated it a HARD HAT AREA. He mounted the wooden steps to O'Brien's office and entered without knocking.

When Captain Ray Costello heard what was brewing between Marty Octavio and Tim O'Brien he decided to take this surveillance himself. Early last month the Feds had nailed Octavio's cousin for bid-rigging and stolen the Organized Crime Task Force's thunder. NYPD did all the legwork only to have the general contractor's accountants hand Joe Tarantino's head to the FBI on a silver platter. Ray didn't trust the Bureau not to steal his thunder again. He wanted an exclusive on Octavio until something broke.

Costello and Sergeant Angel Rivera arrived at the construction site at six o'clock that morning. They'd spent the intervening hours parked thirty yards from the main gate and doing tag-team crossword puzzles. One kept an eye on the street while the other fired "down" and "across" questions, filling in the blanks. They'd polished off the Tuesday *Times* and *Newsday* puzzles and started on the crossword in this week's *New York* magazine.

"Check these three dudes out," Rivera murmured. He had the street and Costello, the pen and magazine.

Ray glanced up. From where the sat they had a good vantage of a row of trailer offices parked along 95th. Tim O'Brien's was the third, parked beyond the electrical and mechanical contractors. Costello watched as three men with their backs to him stopped to confer with a worker on the street and then head down the row.

"Sure don't look like they know where they're going," he commented. "You get a good look at them?"

"Negative. They approached from behind us. The only one I could see real well is that skinny one on the right there. Scraggly blond hair and wire-rimmed glasses. He don't look like no wiseguy enforcer that I've ever seen."

These guys were the fifth bunch they'd taken time to really scrutinize that morning. None of the others turned out to be from the recent annals of the trade union wars, and none seemed suspicious enough to warrant a shakedown.

"Wait a minute," Costello growled. He sat up straighter and plucked his field glasses from his lap. "What've we got here?"

"Where?" Rivera asked.

"At ten o'clock. Tall, skinny, wearing the old Brooklyn Dodgers cap. Him I recognize, but not from the Italian mobs. That's Johnny 'The Iceman' McGuire."

"Who's he?"

"Westie shooter. Damn, they've had the guy under wraps for years."

Costello watched Johnny McGuire saunter casually to the

end of the row of trailers and stop to loiter in the end structure's shadow. There was little doubt that McGuire was watching those other three mount the steps of Tim O'Brien's trailer office.

"I don't know what, but something's going down," he told Rivera. "See if you can get us some backup. I'm gonna work my way closer and try to figure what the fuck's going on. No sirens, okay?" As he said it he had the door open and was already easing his left foot out onto the street.

Tim O'Brien looked up in surprise as the three men entered his office. He had no appointments this morning and recognized none of these guys.

"Can I help you gentlemen?"

"Morning, Mr. O'Brien." It was the tall, handsome one who greeted him while the other two hung back. "You got a man working for you owns that fancy black sports car outside there. Would you mind telling us how we can locate him?"

O'Brien smiled and shook his head. "I'm afraid there's restricted access upstairs, gents. What is it you want with him? Perhaps I can deliver a message."

The spokesman stepped up to lean forward and grip the front edge of O'Brien's desk. "We'd like to ask him a question or two. It's about some property of ours that's missing. I don't believe your delivering a message'll do, Mr. O'Brien. You see, it's urgent."

O'Brien frowned. "A piece of *property*? I'm wondering if y've got the right man. The fella owns that car does work for me, but he i'n't Irish, lad. You sure it i'n't someone else you're looking for?"

The man with the face leaned closer now, his eyes narrowing. "I'm looking for a guinea bastard name of Dante. He *is* the man owns that car. And the property gone missing is a matter I believe Mr. Connor McNulty spoke with you about last night. *Late* last night."

O'Brien suddenly understood, and he knew this other could see it in his eyes. "I spoke to Joe about the

McDonough girl, and he told me what I told McNulty: that he left right after I did. That was close to nine-thirty.''

"I didn't ask what he told you, Mr. O'Brien. I asked you where he is.''

O'Brien pushed himself away from his desk, hands gripping the arms of his chair as he stared more directly now into this other's eyes. If the rumors were true, this man was a fugitive terrorist. Unpredictable. "It sounds like you want to make trouble, and that's exactly what I don't need. We've had nothing *but* trouble here this past week. I won't have any more of it, you understand?''

As the man straightened he turned to his two mates. "Mr. O'Brien here says he don't want trouble, lads. Did I say we wanted to make trouble? No. I said we wanted to *talk* wit the man.''

O'Brien watched the spokesman's right hand go to the small of his back and reappear brandishing a silenced automatic pistol.

"Help yourselves to those hard hats hanging there on the wall,'' he told his mates. "Mr. O'Brien here's going to tell us where we can find this Dante, and then we'll be taking a trip upstairs. We might start some of that trouble our friend here is worried about if we don't observe regulations.'' He took a step forward, the muzzle of his weapon now level with O'Brien's chest. "Now, Mr. O'Brien. To answer my question?''

O'Brien found himself backed up against a wall. There was a gun on him. As soon as they left he could reach Dante by phone; warn him off. "He's my materials expediter,'' O'Brien relented. "You'll probably find him on the seventh floor.''

Ray Costello was on the street, moving inconspicuously into the flow of pedestrian traffic. He'd crossed 95th at the intersection with Broadway when the three men exited the O'Brien Construction trailer. They were wearing hard hats now and looked to be headed onto the site. Ray was confused. What was Johnny McGuire up to? Was he the hired gun brought in to neutralize the next Marty Octavio threat? If so, why hadn't he moved in, made sure those three posed no threat to O'Brien. Instead he'd stayed put, waiting until they emerged to pass within three yards of him. Then he followed them. Costello still hadn't gotten a clear look at the three men, but he knew something was wrong about them. If McGuire was here for protection, he was playing it strangely. For starters, he didn't have a hard hat.

Rather than chase a Westie shooter and three unknown quantities into the confusion of a thirty-story construction project, Costello headed for O'Brien's trailer. He hurried now, not caring who saw him. When an access door cut flush in the plywood barricade swung open he barely avoided colliding with a young worker in dust-covered clothes.

"Sorry." Ray threw it over his shoulder and instead of slowing sprinted up O'Brien's wooden stoop.

The sight of the contractor flopped facedown on his desk made Costello stop short. He stood for several beats before he realized the kid with whom he'd nearly collided had followed him into the trailer.

"Jaysus God!" the man gasped.

Ray spun. "You work for him?" he demanded.

The dust-encrusted workman nodded, his eyes riveted on a tiny rivulet of blood that had escaped from Tim O'Brien's lips. Costello whipped his shield case from his inside jacket pocket and saw the kid's eyes shift to the shiny captain's gold.

"Listen to me. Where are his crews? What floor are they on?" The blank, shocked look he got wasn't encouraging. "There's *trouble* headed upstairs, damn it! Where the hell are those crews?"

The kid snapped out of it, his eyes still wide but focusing now. "Six 'n' seven!" he blurted.

Costello had him by the shoulders now. "Okay, listen to me. My partner's out there on the street. Tall, skinny Hispanic guy in a gray suit. He's got a whole shitload more cops on the way. You tell him what you just told me, all right?"

Ray released the kid before he could reply and started out the door.

The noon whistle was going to blow any minute now, and Joe Dante was huddled up with Henry Roark, the two of them setting up that afternoon's delivery schedule. Roark already had his lunch pail open and was pouring them both coffees from his thermos. The persistent warming trend had them stripped to their undershirts, and Henry's shoulders were flecked with bits of dried joint compound. As Roark screwed the cap back onto his thermos he glanced at his watch in irritation.

"How long ago'd you send Tommy after them inventory sheets? It's been fifteen minutes, ha'n't it?"

Dante dismissed his concern with a shrug. McCarty was nothing if not reliable. "Probably had to wait for an elevator. He'll be here any sec."

As if on cue the top of the right-side elevator cage crept into view. Joe gestured to it and was surprised to see that Tom McCarty wasn't on board. Aside from the operator there were three unfamiliar workers behind the steel-mesh gate. Now Joe was puzzled. Tim had called twenty minutes ago to tell him those sheets were on his desk, ready for pickup. There was no reason it should take this long to retrieve them. If Tommy had trouble catching an elevator, there were always the stairs.

The expanding mesh gate was pushed back. The three passengers stepped off, and Dante watched their progress. In the wake of the recent violence, he and every other member of O'Brien's crew was being extra attentive. Sooner or later Marty Octavio would make a move, and Dante was routinely scrutinizing everyone who came and went on the floor.

A danger signal went off in Joe's mind as his eyes were drawn to their feet. They all wore sneakers. Their dungarees and workshirts fit the scene well enough, but he'd yet to see anyone working on the site in sneakers. The last guy he'd seen up here wearing sneakers had tried to kick his teeth down his throat. Then he noticed their head protection. All three hats matched, the O'Brien Construction logo emblazoned over the bills. Very few of the men on Tim's crew owned one of these company lids. Nobody owned one so clean and distress-free. The last time Dante saw shiny new hard hats like these they were hanging on pegs in Tim's trailer. It was obvious. O'Brien had ignored his advice last night and brought Bill Doyle aboard. Then Joe saw Billy Mannion's face.

Henry Roark gaped in surprise as Dante suddenly dropped to the floor, dove behind a pallet-load of compound buckets, and started crabbing his way across the supply area. He was even more surprised to see Joe crouch out of sight of the door, lift his pant leg, and pull an automatic pistol from an ankle holster. Unable to help himself, Roark turned to watch the three men from the elevator as they spotted him sitting there and turned to approach.

If there weren't at least thirty witnesses on the ground level, John McGuire would have done Billy Mannion and his pals right there on the sidewalk. He was still kicking himself for being surprised when Mannion made that unexpected move across the Bronx to Woodlawn. It might have been another good opportunity, but they were in and out of there before John could figure his angle of approach. Now he figured his chances were better up above the street. He'd been on construction sites like this before where the work was spread out over thirty or forty floors. There were plenty of out-of-the-way nooks and crannies, and John had made his reputation working the seams; drill the target and fade away. He waited as Mannion climbed aboard the right-hand elevator cage and even considered getting in alongside him. Then the left-hand cage made its descent, and McGuire decided to hang back; keep his distance. As Mannion's car started to rise, John began counting floors.

The operator of the left-hand car stopped him as he started

to board. "It ain't that I hate the Dodgers, pal, but that's the wrong hat."

McGuire pointed upstairs, his manner anxious. "It's in my fuckin' tool bag. My buddy Bill took it upstairs while I parked the fuckin' car. Jesus Christ, where the fuck d'ya *park* around here? I'm out there forty-five minutes circling the fuckin' block. First day on the job and I'm already an hour late."

The operator rolled his eyes and jerked the gate shut on them. "What floor?"

"Seven. T'anks, buddy. I owe ya."

When the cage arrived on the seventh level McGuire couldn't believe his luck. The entire area fronting the elevator landing was deserted save for Mannion and his two friends. All three of them were walking away from him and seemed to be in no hurry. As the operator tugged aside the gate so that John could step off, the guy on Mannion's left glanced over his shoulder. McGuire looked away to avoid making eye contact. When he allowed himself a glance out of the corner of his eye, he saw he'd been dismissed as incidental. The shooter grinned to himself. As soon as the elevator cage disappeared back downstairs John reached beneath the loose tails of his shirt and brought his noise-suppressed Colt Python .357 magnum revolver into view. Some shooters didn't like to do a man in the back, but John McGuire couldn't care less. The Python came up with practiced ease. McGuire drew bead.

Ray Costello didn't wait for an elevator. His service weapon out and clutched in one hand, he took the stairs to the seventh floor two at a time. By the time he reached the fifth, he was winded, his heart hammering in his chest. Still he pressed onward, grateful for those twice-a-week racquetball games he played with his brother-in-law.

From the head of the stairs on the seventh level the gasping detective captain had a vantage of the entire area fronting the construction elevators. To his right he spotted Johnny

McGuire aiming a big, heavy-frame revolver with a five-inch silencer screwed onto its barrel. Johnny had the three men who'd shot Tim O'Brien in his sights. Ray made his decision in a split second, threw himself against the wall at the top of the stairwell, and braced his gun arm along it.

"Police, Johnny! Don't do it!"

McGuire whirled and fired at the voice, his bullet taking a chunk out of the wall just inches from Costello's face. Simultaneously Ray squeezed off a shot that caught the lightening-quick McGuire in the hip. His second shot caught Johnny in the chest, dropping him. Costello knew he had no time to admire his handiwork. He turned his attention on the others just as a bullet caught him high on the left shoulder. The impact of it threw him backward. Startled to find himself so suddenly in midair, he lost all orientation and began to tumble head over heels down the last flight of stairs he'd climbed. His head met the concrete of the landing below with the force of a heavyweight's knockout blow.

Joe Dante leapt into action when he saw the man in the Brooklyn Dodgers cap pull a revolver from his waistband. A stunned Henry Roark was perched out there on a compound bucket like a carnival target. Joe threw himself at Henry, his gun clutched at waist level in the two-handed combat grip. He managed to topple Roark by driving a shoulder into the foreman's right hip. Then, before he could right himself again, all hell broke loose. Someone shouted something that sounded like "police." Two loud pistol reports mixed with a series of noise-suppressed shots fired in quick succession. As Joe leveled his own weapon across the top of a screw keg, he saw the guy in the ball cap go down. Billy Mannion was racing for the distant stairwell as his two accomplices scrambled to cover for him.

Dante got the first of the cover men in his sights and squeezed the trigger. His shot caught the lean, intellectual-looking man in the middle of his chest, throwing him backward like a rag doll. Joe watched the more athletically built partner whirl and fire blindly. The shot went fifteen feet wide. This time Joe wasn't so sure of his accuracy. His second shot found the mark but spun the man as it drove him to the floor. As Dante moved on to Mannion he saw the man he'd just hit lurch to his feet and stumble toward the stairs.

Billy realized his friend was in trouble and reached back to jerk him into the stairwell while Dante took his third shot from a distance of at least a hundred feet. It missed wide right as Mannion and his wounded partner disappeared head-long down the stairwell. Dante followed in pursuit, sprinting across the body-littered elevator area. When he reached the head of the stairs, he saw Captain Ray Costello's crumpled body and pulled up. He knew Mannion might use the instinct of one man rushing to another's aid as a trap and proceeded cautiously. It was difficult to tell just how badly Ray was hurt until Joe was almost to the landing. Then he saw the tiny hole behind the task force cop's left ear. Rage gripped him. He threw all caution aside and slammed around the blind corner.

Muffled sounds of angry shouting drifted up the stairwell as Dante reached the fourth floor. The scream of pain that followed couldn't have come from farther away than the floor directly below. Billy was encountering some sort of resistance. Having chased Mannion down Fifth Avenue twelve days ago, Dante knew Billy was quick. Still, with a wounded man in tow there was no way Billy could outrun him. He strained, listening for footsteps as he bounded downstairs, devouring distance with redoubled intensity. All he heard were the moans that followed the scream. When he reached the third level he found a construction worker sprawled at the foot of the stairs, hands clutching his bloodied face. Joe didn't know if Mannion had pistol-whipped or shot the man, but he knew that for all the poor guy's pain he was lucky to still be alive.

Directly below him Dante heard glass shatter. He spun, plate glass rising from knee-wall to ceiling beside him affording him a view of the street below. A garbage truck was pulling out of a loading bay and across the sidewalk. Billy Mannion and his wounded accomplice lay sprawled atop it, the driver apparently oblivious to their presence as he pulled ahead into Broadway traffic. From deep in the bowels of the building the noon lunch whistle blew, drowning the bellow of Dante's frustrated rage.

outline, one of a looking up, and across the sidewalk. Billy
Mogrut and his comrade have stepped up, expecting any of
the dozen approaching individuals to be troublemakers or police
officers, but no one is Nobody to call to or to associate with the
waiting persons, fixed within these boundaries, the police
of these Cathedral area.

EIGHTEEN

Diana was enlisting Siobhan's aid to do paint touch-ups in
Joe's kitchen. The gift sweater was set aside for one of Brennan's work shirts. Siobhan had the sleeves rolled past her
elbows and her hair tied back from her face. Both of them
were on their knees finishing the baseboard and base cap.
Diana had Dante's sound system tuned to her favorite rock
station, the music blasting at high volume. As she worked,
Siobhan felt safer and more at peace with herself than she
had at any time in the six weeks since Billy first arrived in
New York. Detail work like this forced her to concentrate,
taking her mind off the future and immediate past. She liked
Diana and was surprised to find her such a down-to-earth
sort.

The radio programming eased from the latest Robert Cray
single to a one o'clock news segment as Siobhan leaned to
drag the sharp end of her beveled brush close to the intersection of baseboard and floor. The woman newsreader announced a thirty-point midday decline in the Dow Industrial
Average, citing yet another monthly jump in the just-released
Consumer Price Index.

''This just in: A noon shooting at an Upper West Side
construction site has left a policeman and three others dead.
While details remain sketchy, WDRE has learned that Detective Captain Raymond Costello of the police department's
Organized Crime Task Force was killed in a shoot-out with

232

fugitive IRA terrorist William "Billy" Mannion. Mannion is said to have escaped the scene along with a wounded accomplice. Being held for questioning in the incident is Detective Lieutenant Joseph Dante, suspended last week in connection with the death of shipping tycoon Hubert Poole's daughter Courtney. It is not known what Dante was doing . . ."

The rest of the broadcast became a blur as Siobhan's head began to swim. She dropped her paint-loaded brush to the floor and sat hard, the surrounding kitchen swirling in and out of focus.

"Siobhan!" Diana was squatting before her, hands on her shoulders. "Are you okay?"

The Irishwoman took a deep breath. "Tell me it i'n't true, what I just heard."

"I'm afraid I can't. Come on, let's sit down in the living room."

Siobhan felt a fury rise in her. With a violent twisting of her shoulders she shook free of Diana's grasp. "How could I have *been* such a fool? I can understand it from a low-lying copper, but you and your husband?"

Siobhan struggled to her feet, Diana rising with her. If she was sure of anything it was her own stupidity. Remaining here even a minute longer would only compound her mistake. She jerked the elastic tie from her hair and turned to start for the elevator. Diana rushed to block her path.

"You're not going anywhere, Siobhan. Not until you've heard me out."

Siobhan snorted in derision. "You can't stop me, Diana. I'm walking out that door."

The eyes that held Siobhan's had more confidence than challenge in them. "That guy Mannion they were talking about? He's the one who beat you up, isn't he?"

Siobhan averted her gaze. "That's not your business."

"I think it is. Just like Joe thought it was his. Six years ago last August I had a serial killer sitting on my chest and trying to stuff his cock in my mouth. He had a knife at my

233

neck, and he'd already killed five other women who looked a lot like me. Brian was lying on the floor next to me with a bullet in him. That low-lying copper and his partner risked their lives to help us. Joe Dante saved my *life*." Diana paused and watched Siobhan to see if any of her words were sinking in. "Two weeks ago Joe chased Mannion and watched him throw that Poole girl in front of a car. He says it was as cold-blooded an act as he's ever witnessed."

Siobhan didn't know what to believe or who to trust anymore. She stood paralyzed by indecision, hugging herself, one hand pressed to her mouth. "I don't believe I've ever been so thoroughly deceived. I feel so empty."

Diana abandoned her aggressive posture to step over and lower the volume on the radio. "What happened last night wasn't part of Joe's plan, Siobhan. He was working on that job trying to get close to the Irish community because he believes that's where Mannion is hiding. When you asked him for his help last night, you took him completely by surprise. Try to put yourself in his shoes. What was he supposed to do? Tell you no? Sorry? I can't see him doing that."

Siobhan was still torn. She, too, had seen the cold-blooded meanness in Billy's eyes. It was a part of him that she'd tried repeatedly to deny. But when he came at her yesterday afternoon, she could deny it no longer. Her former lover would have killed her and gotten pleasure from it. Setting off a fragmentation bomb in a crowded London department store pleased and excited him. All the lines were erased now. Billy was a mad dog; a warrior-priest made drunk by his thirst for blood.

Diana guessed at Siobhan's thoughts, her tone softening now. "Joe's concern for you is genuine, Siobhan. He knew it would come to something like this sooner or later, and he gave you the help you asked for anyway. I think you owe it to him to listen to his side of it."

Siobhan realized she was hugging herself and slowly relaxed her arms. She wasn't prone to tears, but they came now, uncontrolled.

Nineteenth Precinct

* * *

Jim Quinn was just finished with an arraignment on Centre Street in downtown Manhattan when one of the plainclothes guys from NYPD's Court Division spotted him in the courthouse lobby.

"That's a nasty mess your buddy Doyle's got on his hands, Counsellor. You've got your work cut out, keepin' them from fryin' his ass this time."

Quinn was genuinely puzzled and made no attempt to hide it. "You're one step ahead of me, Frank. What mess is this?"

The cop couldn't believe Quinn hadn't heard. "Where you been, Jim. It's all over the grapevine. That IRA guy they're after? He shows up on a construction site this morning. There's been mob trouble up there, and the Organized Crime Task Force has a surveillance team watchin' the place. They spot Johnny 'The Iceman' McGuire stalkin' this IRA mutt. The way I hear it, McGuire killed one'a the task force guys before our undercover people could drop him. Two of the IRA guys got away." The Court Division cop winked. "It ain't no secret who the Iceman works for, Counsellor. They tie your pal Doyle t' this, he's headed upriver. A cop-killin' rap is murder one."

Quinn was no longer listening. He excused himself abruptly and made for the lobby's bank of pay phones.

The maid who answered on Fifth Avenue explained that the lady of the house was exercising and asked if he could call back in half an hour. Quinn insisted it was an emergency, and within a minute he heard Amanda's breathless "hello" accompanied by the mechanical whirring of gym equipment.

"We've got a problem, Mandy. Pack an overnight bag. I'll be by to pick you up inside the half hour."

The whirring stopping. *"What?"*

"Later. Just pack a bag and meet me out front."

"What the hell is this, Jimmy? I'm in the middle of a workout, and frankly, after being taken over the coals the way I've been, my sense of humor's shot."

"No joke, Mandy. I don't want to say anything else over this phone. I'll explain it to you in the car."

"It's Billy, isn't it? Doyle couldn't stall him off."

"Not on the phone, Mandy."

"Screw the phone, Jimmy. I signed that goddamn note, so what's the problem?"

Quinn sighed. "Just pack the bag, Mandy." And before she could argue further, he hung up.

Police Commissioner Tony Mintoff had his hands full trying to explain Dante's presence on that job site. The mayor was having trouble with the idea that Joe was hired by O'Brien Construction to help with security in the wake of recent violence. On the other hand, O'Brien was dead now and couldn't counter what Mintoff said. The problems the contractor was having were a matter of record at the 24th Precinct. During his interview with the mayor, Mintoff took every opportunity to force the conversation back around to the appearance of Billy Mannion. They mayor was clearly troubled by the implications, and Mintoff pressed the advantage. While Mannion's appearance here didn't prove that he killed the Poole girl, Mintoff used the fact to support Dante's case for reinstatement.

Dante now found himself isolated in the backseat of Chief Lieberman's sedan for the second time in less than a week. He, Gus, and Pete Shore were double-parked on 95th Street, a hundred yards west of the construction site. Down the block the Crime Scene Unit was packing up. Both the mayor and commissioner had just left.

"What about this John McGuire, Pete?" Joe asked. "You manage to run down anything recent on him?"

Pete was extracting a cigar from his breast pocket and peeling it just to have something to chew on. "Negative. The usual crap in a file that's been inactive for more'n two years. Speculation is that he got too hot, and Doyle decided to pull him outta circulation. Nobody's got any idea what the fuck he's been up to since. I been all up and down our list'a contacts. None'a them's heard shit about McGuire for at least a year.''

''Joey thinks he was gunning for Mannion,'' Gus told him. ''That make any sense to you?''

Shore shrugged. ''My first instinct says O'Brien hired McGuire to protect *him*. But that don't make no sense. Ray Costello's partner Rivera says McGuire watched Mannion walk inta O'Brien's trailer and right back out again. He made no move to stop him. That gets me thinking that it *was* Mannion who Johnny was gunning for, right from the get-go.''

Dante spread the fingers of one hand and began counting them off. ''First we tie Mannion to the Kane homicide. Second we tie him to that Lloyd's exec's homicide up in Dutchess County. Jumbo ties Amanda Gregory to James P. Quinn. We tie Quinn to Big Bill Doyle. McGuire we can tie to Doyle and the Westies.'' Joe closed his hand, all the fingers bunched together at their tips. ''There's some thread that ties these pieces together. Not nice and neat, maybe, but together. It's my guess that Big Bill Doyle and Billy Mannion have had some sort of falling out. I'd like to know why.''

Lieberman's cellular unit chirped, and the chief picked up. After a brief exchange he handed the receiver to Dante. ''Op Desk. They've got an urgent call from your friend Diana. It's being patched through.''

Dante lifted the instrument to his ear.

''Joe?''

''Yeah, Di. What's up?''

''It's Siobhan. We were working downstairs in your place with the radio on. She heard the news.''

''Shit!''

''She's pretty upset, Joe. She knows you're a cop. It's been all I can do to keep her here since she found out.''

''But she hasn't left.''

''Not so far. I got her to promise to stay until she hears your side of it.''

''I'm on my way.''

Joe handed the receiver back to Gus and reached for the door release.

"Where the hell you think you're going?" Lieberman demanded.

Dante glanced back as he swung one leg out and planted a foot on the street. "Get me my shield back and then you can talk to me like that all you want. Something's come up. I'll either call you or try to get back by your office before five."

Fifteen minutes later Joe parked his car at the curb out front of his building and hurried upstairs. Once he'd apologized to Diana, he asked Siobhan to accompany him to the roof garden. The weekend's chill breezes had scrubbed the Manhattan skyline clean and now, rising around them like ramparts on three sides, the city fairly sparkled. Joe took a seat in one of the chairs as Siobhan remained on her feet before him, stalking like a caged predator. Beyond his request to join him up here not a word had yet passed between them.

"Siobhan, I think I know how you must feel right now. I . . ."

She ceased her pacing to whirl on him. "I'll bet you think you do! Well, let me tell you something. You've got no *idea* how I feel right now. I *trusted* you."

Dante sat facing her, his work shirt hanging open over the sweat- and dirt-stained undershirt beneath. Too much had happened too quickly, and he hadn't had time to process it all.

"I was faced with limited choices," he replied. "You can either accept that or tell me to stuff it up my ass. Either way, it's a fact. From where I was sitting it looked like your choices were limited, too." He paused, collecting his thoughts. "Let me ask you something. Last night you told me what you were running away from involved the IRA. That's Billy Mannion's handiwork on your face, isn't it?"

She remained where she was, confronting him through narrowed eyes. When she didn't answer, Dante nodded.

"I thought so."

Her look turned accusing. "That's all you wanted me for, i'n't it, Joe? To get to him."

A slow, tired smile crept into the creases around Dante's eyes and mouth. "I was prepared to use anything I had to use, Siobhan. I don't have him yet, so I *still* am. I don't know what your relationship with him is, but let me tell you something about Billy Mannion. He's the kind of moral coward who enjoys murdering defenseless people. This morning he couldn't resist putting a bullet in a wounded cop's head in passing; a man who'd lost his weapon in a fall and presented no danger. Two Fridays ago I watched him grab a sixteen-year-old girl and throw her in front of a car. Earlier that morning he killed two unarmed people in their suite in a Madison Avenue residence hotel. *Executed* them; one bullet to the back of each of their heads. Friday night he executed another man and threw him into a gravel pit in Dutchess County. He's on a fucking *rampage*, Siobhan. There aren't any rules in a game like this. I'll use whatever I can get my hands on to stop him. If that means using you, I'll do that, too."

She seemed to cool off a bit. Turning away, she started to pace again but more slowly now. "I was in love wit him once, can you believe that?"

Joe softened, too. "It isn't easy. From what I've seen of him and you I find it a bit hard to picture. Tell me about it?"

"He was different then." She seemed to be looking off into the past as she said it. "He was a stage actor who lectured on method at my university. We were together two years when he quit teaching to go underground wit the movement. I quit my studies to go wit him. Then he went away to North Africa for nearly a year. When he came back he was changed. We tried to pick up where we left off. When that failed I left to go back to university and finish. I'd not gotten in deep enough to be a threat to the movement. They agreed to let me go."

"But you didn't sever your ties entirely, right?"

She stiffened, suspicious again. "What do you mean by that?"

"You had some trouble with Immigration here in the States a few years back. Some very heavy people in New York Irish circles got you the best immigration lawyer money could buy. They had a reason for wanting to keep you here. And since Mannion came across the Atlantic he's gotten at least close enough to you to leave his calling card on your face."

She stopped at the chair across from him and sat. "You've done your homework, haven't you?"

He nodded but said nothing.

"They needed someone to set up a safe house here in America. I'd been working at a theater in Dublin for about two years when Billy came to me wit their offer. Free transport. A job when I got here. The way he told it there wasn't much chance they'd ever need the place. The American Irish are fond of supporting the IRA from a distance but not too interested in seeing it exported to these shores."

Dante watched her as she spoke and thought he saw something that looked like regret. "The offer was just too good to refuse, right?"

Siobhan lowered her eyes, her tone lower now, too. "Yes."

"Then Billy did the unexpected," Dante narrated for her. "He blew up that officer's club in Brussels and got fingered for it. He had to go on the run, and he showed up here on your doorstep."

She grabbed her ankles to pull them up and tuck her feet into her lap. Her shoulders slumped forward. "Yes. Six weeks ago . . . yesterday."

"Tell me what's happened since, Siobhan. He hit you at least twice that I know of. Why?"

She continued to hold her head down as she spoke. "The day they showed up Billy told me he was going to need my help in the weeks ahead. I agreed I'd do what I could. He told me I didn't understand. I'd had a free ride on the movement for two and a half years, and now I was going to have to start earning my way." She paused to push away a lock of hair that had fallen into her face. "He told me he had a long-term operation planned. It needed funding, but once that was in place he was going to use me to help him get access to certain information."

"You said *they* showed up. Billy and who else?"

"He was wit Paulie Murphy when he first appeared. Seamus Cowan was still in Ireland. He came later, once they got to work on what they had planned."

Joe felt suddenly restless. He stood and wandered to the parapet wall overlooking Chelsea, the Village, and downtown beyond.

"Billy wasn't around a lot of the time for the next month," she continued. "I heard Paulie and Seamus joking about how Billy was so expert at mixing business with pleasure. When I asked them what they meant by that they told me there was a woman involved in their raising the money they needed. A *rich bitch*, they called her. I gathered from what they were implying that Billy'd taken up wit her."

Joe wondered if Bud Costanza was right all along: that Amanda Kane had hired Mannion to kill her husband and the Tierney woman for a price. "Back to the bruises," he urged. "Billy was here for a month, and he still hadn't gotten specific about how he wanted you to help him?"

He watched her swallow hard, her eyes squeezed shut. "It was two weeks ago Monday next. When I got up from bed that morning he was waiting for me at the dining table. He asked me to sit down, and when I did he showed me a photograph of a man. The man was someone who had something Billy needed for his operation. Billy explained that the only way he knew to get it from this man was to compromise him." Siobhan shook her head and wiped at her face as tears began to roll down her cheeks. "He told me I was going to help him wit that."

"Was that man Phillip Wright?" Dante asked.

Siobhan's head came up fast, her eyes wide with surprise. Joe hurried to put her at ease. "I was in the bar Friday night, remember? I saw how you reacted to his death on the

241

news. I had the state police check the ballistics against those two Madison Avenue killings. They matched. All three people were killed with the same gun. Tell me about Phillip Wright, Siobhan.''

She sat in stunned silence, gathering herself. ''Billy and the others had been watching him. They knew he liked to drink wit his mates and chase women. Billy explained that Phillip was a family man who held a responsible position at Lloyd's insurance. He wouldn't be able to survive the scandal of a sexual compromise. My job was to lure Phillip into a situation that Billy could document. I refused.''

Dante pointed at her face. ''Judging from those bruises I'd say he hit you a lot more recently than two weeks ago.''

She shook her head. ''He didn't hit me then. He just showed me another photograph; of my sister Deirdre's children playing out front of her cottage in Ballynaskeagh. Billy and I are both from County Armagh. He knows of my sister and her family. That morning he told me I'd either help him lure Phillip Wright to a hotel room and have sex wit him or he'd have my sister's children killed.''

''Jesus,'' Dante murmured.

Siobhan nodded. ''I'd seen the change in him, and I knew he meant it. I didn't see I had much room to argue wit him. Friday before last I went to the South Street Seaport. I hooked Wright and took him to the Vista Hotel. Billy and Paulie videotaped our doin's from the room next door. I didn't know they intended to kill him. You've got to believe me when I tell you that.''

''I watched your face when you heard the news report,'' Joe reminded her. ''I believe you, Siobhan.''

She began to cry again. ''I never felt such shame in all my life. It was me I was feeling sorry for when I left that hotel the next morning, Joe. Not Phillip; *me*. He was just another drunken sod who paws and grunts at anything that'll hold still for him.''

Dante stepped away from the parapet wall and pulled a chair up next to hers. He took one of her hands in his. ''I need to know what Billy was after, Siobhan; what he needed from Wright.''

Siobhan jerked her hand from Dante's in a gesture of impatience. "Shipping lists. Not that it matters. It was all for naught. His whole grand plan depended on the money they were trying to raise. A week ago Sunday Seamus convinced Billy that his efforts were wasted. Everything had fallen through.''

Joe leaned close. "This is important, Siobhan. Believe me. Fallen through *how*?''

She heard the seriousness in his tone and frowned. "It was something to do wit Billy's woman friend; the one Seamus and Paulie kept referring to as the rich bitch. She helped Billy steal something they were supposed to be able to sell. It had something to do wit technology and some fella flying in from the Far East to buy it. That's why they brought Seamus here. He's an electrical engineer. He worked all that Friday and through the night into Saturday on it. When he told Billy there was something missing, Billy was furious. At first he refused to believe it." She stopped, her eyes getting a faraway look in them. "Saturday afternoon's the first time he hit me.''

Dante was making connections quickly now. He remembered Jumbo reporting on his conversation with Ralph Kane's daughter Elizabeth. It was her contention that her father was working on some important breakthrough; that his killer's motivation was the theft of that technology. From what Joe knew about Ralph Kane's will, Kane had been much more generous with his daughter than he was with his wife. Maybe Amanda Kane was simply attempting to get even.

"Okay, Siobhan. You said Wright was being blackmailed to provide Billy with shipping lists.'' Joe beckoned now, trying to pull it from her. "Can you be any more specific? What *kind* of shipping lists?''

She straightened, taking a deep breath. "I understand what you're asking, Joe, but I only know what I managed to overhear. It all had something to do wit insurance pools. A list wit names on it; some of them peers. And then there . . ."

"Peers?"

"Members of Parliament. Mostly of the House of Lords. There was another list wit names of ships insured by the different pools. I heard them discussing a plan to sink a ship in the Persian Gulf. They were working to tie the peers on the one list wit a ship on t'other. The peers would be responsible for covering the shipper's loss once that ship went down."

Dante could see how Mannion would need considerable financing. There had to be hundreds of ships all over the globe that were sitting ducks. Ships were huge, slow-moving targets that spent days at a time tied up to docks in remote ports. With Phillip Wright's lists in hand Mannion could pick and choose his targets, hitting only those ships whose loss would inflict heavy financial damage on British interests.

He leaned to kiss his informant lightly on the cheek and stood. "I'm sorry it had to happen the way it did, Siobhan. But I doubt you'll regret coming here or telling me what you have. Billy Mannion's already killed six people here in New York. You've probably given me the information I need to stop him."

"What's going to happen to me, Joe? Will you turn me in now?"

He smiled. "No. You ceased being a willing participant awhile ago, and I doubt the district attorney will waste time bringing accessory charges against you. I can't guarantee how the Feds will view your part in hiding Billy. Maybe it's best they never know. You're safe here. Do I have your word you'll sit tight?"

She reached her hand out for help up. As Dante pulled her to her feet, he saw her anger was gone. She was her own woman again, the same woman he'd met behind the bar at McNulty's Friday night. Instead of her earlier bitterness, her expression was determined now.

"Take care of yourself out there, Joe. You may have Billy on the run, but don't underestimate him."

NINETEEN

Amanda Kane was not waiting downstairs in the lobby of her building when Jim Quinn arrived, and Quinn wasn't the least surprised. He climbed out of his car but advanced no further than across the sidewalk. He asked the doorman to advise Mrs. Kane he was on the street awaiting her. Two could play this game.

Amanda emerged ten minutes later, casually dressed in a sweater and slacks, the concierge carrying her overnighter. The look on her face could have frozen kerosene. Jim's chauffeur took Amanda's case and placed it inside the trunk while Quinn got her settled in the seat beside him. The partition glass was already run up, and no sooner did the curbside door close than Amanda opened up.

"I can't imagine what prompted me to do it, Jimmy, but right after you hung up on me I turned on the goddamn news! Call it a hunch. Why was I so surprised by what I heard? The same two-timing shit who took me for four million dollars and probably intended to keep it for himself all along is the same shit who *found* us Billy."

"It took me as much by surprise as it did you, Mandy. I was with Bill Doyle as late as ten o'clock this morning. I just talked to him fifteen minutes ago; told him how upset we both are."

"Upset?! You're god damn right I'm upset! It's me who

245

that maniac Irishman threatened to kill, not you or your hoodlum pal.''

"Doyle wanted me to talk to you, Mandy. To assure you that you're safe and that he'll get this resolved. He knows where I'm taking you and thinks it's a good idea. Get you out of the city until this all blows over.''

Amanda, fidgeting nervously with the crease in her right pant leg, turned to peer out the window. They'd taken the 65th Street transverse and were crossing Central Park en route to the West side.

"Just where the hell *are* you taking me?'' she demanded.

"My weekend place in Pound Ridge.''

"The one you can never find the time to visit? Wonderful. You've probably got three inches of mold growing in your carpets. I'm *allergic* to molds, Jimmy.''

"I've got a housekeeper who *lives* there, Mandy. You'll like it.''

Amanda got a handle on her borderline hysteria, some of the accustomed command in her tone returning. "I want that promissory note back, Jimmy.''

Quinn slipped open the liquor cabinet door and poured himself a stiff gin. "I wish it was that easy, Mandy. A snap of my fingers and . . . *done*. You've got to understand how Bill Doyle works. The way he sees it, you paid that money to get a monkey off your back. He figures it's his business just how that's accomplished.''

She bristled all over again. "Those were the *old* rules, Jimmy. Everything has changed. Doyle decided to double-cross Billy, not me. He took a gamble that didn't pay off. Now Billy will be gunning for him, too. It isn't just in *my* interest to see Billy out of the picture now. Doyle kills Billy or Billy kills Doyle. Either way, Billy never gets my money, so I want it back.''

Quinn shrugged. "Like I said, Mandy, he might not . . .''

Amanda's hand flashed before the attorney's eyes, knocking the drink from his hand. The edge of the glass jammed his lower lip against his teeth before it tumbled to the floor.

The front of his suit jacket, shirt, and tie were drenched with gin. Quinn tasted blood.

"I said I want it back! No *ifs*, you chickenshit! You're going to pick up that phone and call him now. Tell him he either brings that note back to me tonight or else."

Quinn stared at her, his tongue gingerly probing the tear on the inside of his lip. "What's that *mean*, Mandy? You'll go to the police?"

"Not the police, Jimmy. The D.A. I co-chaired the fund-raising effort that got her elected. She and her predecessors tried five times to put Bill Doyle behind bars. You don't think she'll be eager to make a deal? Put you out of circulation at the same time and maybe even help net a man as notorious as Billy Mannion?"

There was derision mixed with disbelief in Quinn's voice. "What is it you expect she'll give you? *Immunity?* Keep dreaming, Mandy. You hired a man to murder your husband."

"And so did you, Jimmy," she reminded him. "And so did Bill Doyle. I'm not expecting immunity, and even if I plead guilty to a lesser charge I'll have my life back in what? Three or four years? It's more than I've got right now, so what have I got to lose?"

Quinn paled, realizing she might actually be serious. "You're talking crazy, Mandy. I can't believe you'd risk . . ."

"Pick up the phone, Jimmy. *Now.*"

Doyle shook his head. "Not from the car. Too easy to eavesdrop." He depressed the button on the intercom. "Find me a pay phone, Chuck. Try Tavern on the Green."

Beasley Richardson was distressed at being stuck in this surveillance backwater. Two hours ago he'd heard word of Joey's run-in with Billy Mannion, the Ray Costello homicide, and the appearance of a Westie shooter on the scene. It meant Dante was getting somewhere with this investigation while Jumbo was here staring at the front door of Amanda Kane's Fifth Avenue building. Captain Bud Costanza had refused to take any Westie connection to the Kane/Tierney homicides seriously. Costanza's announced intention to find Amanda Kane's hired shooter and "squeeze him till he squeals" involved combing through lists of two-bit pikers and pounding on a lot of doors. The entire squad was leg-, eye-, and ass-weary with Costanza's dogged but uninspired investigative technique.

The one glimmer of light at the end of this tunnel was sparked by Amanda Kane's surreptitious ride home Saturday night in the backseat of attorney James Quinn's limousine. She'd attended an event at the Sherry Netherland while Mel Busby had the detail. Earlier, Intel Division had made a direct connection between James Quinn and the Westies. At noon today, when Jumbo took over the detail, Guy Napier reported that Quinn had returned again at eight-fifteen that morning. This time he'd stayed only long enough to run upstairs and down again, briefcase in hand.

Since hearing the particulars of the construction-site shootout, Jumbo sat mentally lunging at the tether that kept him tied to this Fifth Avenue curb. He needed to talk with Joey, to tell him about these further James Quinn/Amanda Kane developments and maybe learn what Billy Mannion's war with the Westies was about.

It was 2:43, and Jumbo had just poured his second cup of coffee since lunch when James Quinn's silver stretch Mercedes pulled to the curb before Amanda Kane's awning. He watched as the man he supposed was Quinn emerged from the backseat to confer with the doorman. There was nothing physically imposing there, but his demeanor screamed confidence. His navy pinstripe suit was cut just for him. His mane of silver hair matched the paint job of his car. His walk was smooth and almost cocky. Instead of entering the building Quinn returned to the limousine and stood conversing with his chauffeur. He waited for nearly ten minutes before Mrs. Kane emerged from her building and climbed into Quinn's backseat. The detective was interested to see one of the building's uniformed personnel trail her carrying a small suitcase. It was handed to the chauffeur, who in turn placed it in the trunk of the Benz.

Jumbo cursed as he slurped too much hot coffee and burned his mouth before throwing the rest out the window. The paper cup was tossed in with the half-dozen others on the passenger-side floorboard. He started his engine and followed the limousine into Central Park.

Quinn and Mrs. Kane appeared to be headed for the West Side before the chauffeur signaled and exited into the parking area beside Tavern on the Green. It seemed a bit late for lunch, but then Jumbo figured rich people could eat whenever they wanted. He parked fifty yards behind them, grateful at least for the change of scene. There were joggers he could watch run past; some wearing skintight get-ups in eye-popping colors.

Big Bill Doyle was buried in the logistics of getting his troops out onto the streets when his nephew Tommy poked his head in the bedroom door. Before the kid could speak, Bill cut him off with a scowl and a wave of the hand.

"Not now, Tommy. Did you get hold of Shannahan and Burke?"

"Just Burke. Richie's still not answering the page. It's Quinn on the phone, Unk. Says it's an emergency."

"For the love'a *Christ*!" Doyle griped. "Again?"

To elude the police effort to find him, Doyle had quit his opulent Emerald Consolidated offices in midtown for the Norwood section of the North Bronx. He was holed up in a cramped flat above a butcher shop, and right now he was beginning to regret giving Quinn the number. He jabbed at the flashing line button on the extension and snatched at the receiver.

"What the fuck is it *now*, Jimmy? I've got a fuckin' *situation* here. I'm a very busy man."

"Amanda's having fits, Bill. She heard on the news that they've connected you to Johnny McGuire, and the way she's reading it, you never intended to pay Mannion that money. She wants her promissory note back.''

"You're joking.''

"She's friends with the D.A., Bill. *Fund-raising* friends. She's threatening to cut some sort of deal. I've got her on ice for now, but I'm not sure how long I can keep her that way.''

Doyle crushed the half-smoked Macanudo he gripped between the thumb and forefinger of his left hand. "Bullshit! She's got too much to lose!''

"That isn't the way she sees it, Bill. She sees the sky getting set to fall on her. She'd rather risk going inside for a couple years than stand around waiting for that to happen. I think she's just willful enough to do it.''

"Jesus. And you want to *marry* this cunt?''

"That's my worry, Bill. My advice to you? Give her the god damn note back. What does it cost you? We don't need Amanda Kane making waves for us right now. Not with the D.A. salivating over the idea of pinning a murder one rap on us.''

Tommy poked his head back into the room. "Richie Shannahan, Unk. Line three.''

"I'm up to my eyeballs right now, Jimmy. How long can you stall her off?''

"I can't count on being able to do that at all, Bill. She gets nasty once her heels are dug in.''

"I'll be up in the fuckin' morning. We'll talk then.''

"Bring the note, Bill. She cuts a deal, there's no way I can save us. Don't forget, she's got a copy of it, too.''

Joe Dante returned to One Police Plaza at four o'clock to meet with Gus Lieberman. Beyond the four walls of the chief's office the entire Big Building buzzed with the events of that afternoon. Within them the chief was looking at Dante with a mixture of astonishment and disbelief. Joe's return home two hours ago hadn't allowed him time to change his clothes. He sat in a chair across the desk from Gus, a can of ginger ale in one hand and his work boots up on the arm of the chair adjacent.

"You took her *where*?"

"Home. Where the hell else could I take her?"

"And you've still got her there? She's sitting in your fucking front room, right?"

Dante nodded. "Until we get Mannion that's where I want her to stay. She's been forthcoming with information in exchange for my protection. That's our deal."

Lieberman came forward in his chair, the veins in his forehead and neck bulging. "Jesus Christ, Joey! Tony Mintoff finds out you've got a cop killer's consort hidden away, he's gonna cut your fuckin' *balls* off! Not to mention *mine*! What's wrong with protective custody, for Crissake?"

"Protective custody's a glorified term for jail, Gus. For one thing, she's not Mannion's consort. And she's fed me important information. Ralph Kane's daughter Elizabeth was right about the homicide motive all along. At least part of it. That technology is what Billy was after."

"She's feeding you *bullshit*," Lieberman countered. "The two computer disks Napier and Busby found in the dead woman's briefcase? Bud Costanza took ·'em to the Magnetronics people and guess what? The data on them is all they were missing. The technology's *intact*, Joey."

Dante's attitude remained unchanged. "There's a hole in that logic, Gus. Mannion planned his theft carefully, based on reliable inside information. I hate to say it, but I think Bud Costanza is right. The 'rich bitch' Siobhan heard Seamus Cowan and Paul Murphy talking about is Amanda Kane. I still don't know her motivation, but it's not for lack of choices. Mannion had a buyer for the technology. He came away from the Overton House *believing* he'd stolen it. How could he have known that Veronica Tierney would have it in her briefcase? He expected it to be there by the computer and knew that if he didn't grab it *that weekend*, Kane was going to negotiate a production deal of his own."

Gus chewed Joe's argument over and sat digesting it. "I

guess Mrs. Kane's motivation might be something as simple as money. Considering what Costanza's investigation's turned up about her finances, it looks like she was up against a wall there."

Dante dropped his foot to the carpet and wedged himself upright. "The jury's still out on Mrs. Kane, Gus. But money was definitely Mannion's motive. He's got a new campaign planned."

Joe proceeded to detail what Siobhan had told him about the Lloyd's indemnity pools, the sinking of ships insured by Britons exposed to huge risks, and how Phillip Wright had been forced to provide Mannion with sensitive Lloyd's information.

"There's still one thing I can't figure, Gus. I don't understand what made Bill Doyle turn; send a guy like the Iceman McGuire to try and take Mannion out. The way Siobhan tells it, those two were working hand-in-hand on this."

Gus reached for his cigarettes and tapped one out. As he lit it he shook his head. "I doubt Doyle's gonna shed much light. The Organized Crime Control Bureau's got fifty detectives out combing the city for him right now. Even if they drag his ass in, he'll feed 'em the same shit he's been shoveling for years. Then Quinn'll show up and start screaming harassment. If Quinn gets a restraining order, we'll have to get enough evidence to indict before we can question him again."

Dante rose from his seat and stretched. "Maybe we'll get lucky on one of these other ends. What about my shield, Gus? You talk to Big Tony about it?"

Lieberman scowled, jerked open his top drawer, and fetched out Dante's shield case to toss it onto the blotter. "Now that Mannion's killed a cop Big Tony don't figure the mayor's got a lot of room to bellyache. There ain't no way the D.A.'ll press an investigation now."

"Thanks."

As Joe reached for the shield, Gus shook his head. "I don't know why I'm even bothering giving it back to you. Mintoff

252

finds out about you stashing the girl away like that he'll probably run us *both* outta here. You headed home?''

Joe stuffed the case into the back pocket of his dungarees. ''Yeah. It's been a long day, and I want to talk with Siobhan again. I need to know more about Mannion's habits; what drives him. You hear anything, give me a call.''

Amanda Kane had no choice but to get control of her anger once Jim Quinn contacted Bill Doyle. Doyle had promised to make the trip up to Westchester first thing the following morning. Quinn was being solicitous and trying to make a peace that Amanda was in no mood to accept. Instead of trying to explain her feelings of betrayal and distrust any further, Amanda poured herself a stiff Scotch and settled back to endure the hour-and-a-half trip upstate.

When the chauffeur turned off the road into a driveway and paused as a pair of motorized, wrought-iron gates swung inward to grant access, Amanda peered suspiciously up the pavement ahead. The driveway meandered a hundred and fifty yards up a low rise before disappearing over its top. As they proceeded slowly up that rise the roofline of a large house began to manifest itself above the hollow beyond.

Amanda knew that Jim was comfortably situated, but she had no idea he was quite this comfortable. The stretch Mercedes would run him close to two hundred thousand dollars, but that was a business expense; an attorney of his reputation had to maintain certain standards. But no prospective clients saw his Pound Ridge retreat. This was the hideaway Jim had trouble finding the time to visit. She hadn't thought it would be a dump—this was Pound Ridge after all—but neither had she expected a house and grounds of such size and elegance. Jim Quinn's weekend retreat was an eighteen-room, fieldstone-and-cedar contemporary home sprawling in three directions and surrounded by a pond, tennis court, and fifteen acres of manicured landscaping.

''You're surprised,'' Quinn murmured. ''You thought I

was dragging you off to a sordid little raised ranch buried somewhere in the boonies.''

Her scowl said as much as her words. "Is this your idea of a joke? Yesterday you couldn't come up with your half of two million dollars, but no problem. My Magnetronics stock is as good as gold. That's precious. I thought you didn't own anything a factor would accept as collateral on a million-dollar loan. This place is worth an easy five million if it's worth a nickel.''

Quinn averted his face to stare off across the lawns as he replied. "You got what you were after, Mandy. Four million is a drop in the bucket compared to what you would have lost if Ralph lived to file for divorce. I'm an accessory to his murder, same as you, but I walked away empty-handed.''

"Oh really?'' Her tone was still arctic-cool. "Last I heard you were all set to marry me and my hundred million. That's empty-handed?''

His head came back around, his own tone now cynical. "That's not a done deal.''

"And until it is, why should you risk anything else, right? You're a bastard, Jimmy.''

The limousine swung around the drive to stop beneath a covered entryway. Quinn climbed out and helped Amanda to her feet as the chauffeur retrieved their bags from the trunk. A handsome, gray-haired woman of middle years opened the front door to them on their approach.

"Mr. Quinn. So good to see you.''

The attorney smiled and stepped aside to let Amanda pass. "Thank you, Adrian. This is Mrs. Kane. She'll be staying with us for a few days. I'd appreciate it if you'd show her to the master bedroom. I'm sure she'd like to freshen up.''

Amanda was halfway across the slate-paved entry hall. She stopped and turned to confront her host. "The master bedroom. That would be *your* room, wouldn't it, Jimmy?''

Quinn shrugged and nodded. "That's right.''

Amanda turned to the housekeeper. "Then anywhere *but* the master bedroom, Adrian. I'd rather sleep on a billiard table.''

* * *

When Dante returned home late that afternoon he found Siobhan sitting alone in his loft. She was curled up with a book in the middle of his unfinished living room, her hair pulled back and the radio tuned low to a classical station. He thought she looked very much at peace, and she must have seen the relief on his face.

"You look surprised to find me here, Joe." Siobhan lifted the book from her lap and turned the cover toward him. "Coleridge? I wouldn't have figured you for it."

He grimaced, shaking his head. "A gift from my boss's wife. I lost a lot of books when my place burned. Psychology and criminology mostly. The poetry is her attempt to change my intellectual directions." He said it with amusement in his tone. "I'm afraid she hasn't had much luck."

Siobhan set the book aside and stretched. "It's been some years for me, I'm ashamed to say. We read so much of it at school and university, I suppose I felt I'd read enough. I forgot how calming it can be." Her recent mood shift, from anger to amusement and rational discourse, was as distinctive as transitions in a symphony.

"Maybe I should try some."

"You definitely should."

Dante glanced down at his filthy clothing and reached into his back pocket for his shield case. Next came the beeper, unclipped from his belt. "Right now I think I'll try a shower."

Siobhan's eyes followed his movements as he stripped out of his workshirt and stood in that sweat-stained undershirt. "A wise first step, I think. Is there any word of Billy?"

He shook his head. "Nothing yet. They located the driver of that garbage truck he and Murphy used to make their escape. The man never knew he had passengers. There was a lot of blood on top of the truck and down the side where they crawled off. Murphy looks to be hurt pretty bad." Joe started for his bedroom. "You know Billy's world better than I do, Siobhan. You know *him* better. I need to get a better

255

feel for him; for what he might do next. While I'm in there getting clean I want you to think about it.''

It was five and a half hours now since Paulie Murphy took that bullet just below his rib cage on the left side. So far he was still alive. He'd been bleeding badly when Billy left him huddled like a vagrant on West 93rd Street to double back and recover their van. Billy draped Paulie with his own clean jacket and sauntered back up Broadway to 95th Street. The scene was only just starting to swarm with cops, and Billy had no choice but to drive straight ahead through the turmoil at the intersection with Broadway. En route, at least two cops looked directly at him. Less than a minute later he stopped to hoist Paulie through the van's side door. Within the quarter hour they left the Henry Hudson Parkway for the Cross Bronx and Major Deegan expressways. It was touch and go for a moment when Monica Flynn saw her cousin lying in the back of the van bleeding like that. Then she'd responded like the seasoned health professional she was.

Billy sat at Monica's kitchen table now, his lists spread before him, while the nurse sat reading at Murphy's bedside in the room across the hall. Twenty minutes ago Monica had fixed them both frozen chicken pies in her microwave. Their plates and utensils were piled in the sink. As Billy worked, he drank his third Budweiser of the evening.

''His color's still very bad, Billy,'' Monica announced. ''Wit'out X rays there's no way to tell what damage the bullet did.''

Billy glanced up from his papers to regard the pretty, prematurely gray woman seated across the way. ''His breathing's good, i'n't it?''

''His lungs aren't what I'm worried about, Billy. His blood pressure's a better indicator, and it's still perilously low. I've got no way to tell if there's damage to the kidney or intestines. You've got to think again about me talking to one of my doctor friends.''

Billy put his pen down and stood to cross to Paulie's side.

"A doctor's out of the question, girl. We've got every copper in the whole fucking city looking for us now. You heard what they're saying on the news."

"I've seen enough bullet wounds to know this is a bad one, Billy. The chances are about even that he'd die even with proper care."

Billy shook his head, anger hardening his face now. "This wiry bastard's every bit as strong as he looks. If that bullet didn't kill him outright, he i'n't gonna die on me now. I've watched him hit flush on the jaw and knocked flat on his back only to get up and knock a man out. Paulie Murphy's a fighter."

When Dante emerged from the bathroom after his shower it was the first time Siobhan had seen him in anything but work clothes or last night's gym shorts. He was barefoot again and wearing casual gray chinos with a pullover sweater. His wet hair was combed straight back, and he looked less weary than at any time since their first meeting.

"I'm going to have a beer," he announced. "Can I get you something? A glass of wine? Something harder?"

"A beer please," she replied.

He returned from the kitchen a moment later with two bottles in one hand and a pair of glasses in the other. He pulled up a chair across from her, set both glasses on the coffee table, and poured. Siobhan accepted the glass he passed to her and raised it to her lips. It didn't hurt so much to move her mouth as it had last night.

Joe drained nearly half his glass and emptied the rest of his bottle into it before sitting back. "My boss got a little excited when I told him who's staying in my guest room. Lucky for you and me I've got a good relationship with him. He might not agree with my method, but he does think keeping you under wraps right now is our best bet."

Siobhan felt some of the weight of apprehension lift from her shoulders. "Thanks, Joe. As angry as you saw me this afternoon, I'm still appreciative of what you've done for me."

Dante nodded his understanding, and then his face turned

257

serious. "When I left here to go see the chief you told me to be careful; to not underestimate Billy Mannion. Underestimating him would be difficult after the show he's put on, but even Godzilla had a soft underbelly. I need to know more about this guy."

Siobhan sipped, started to purse her lips, and winced. "I think he'd rather you kill him than surrender, Joe. I've never seen him quit on anything. If he knows he's going to go down, he'll look for the biggest thing that's handy and take it down wit him. He's invested a lot of time and thought in this Lloyd's campaign. It'll be on his mind, eating at him, now that he's being forced to confront failure."

"The biggest thing that's handy," Dante repeated. "What kind of scale are we talking about? The stock exchange? The General Assembly chamber at the U.N.? The British mission? Something like that?"

"You came closest wit the last. Billy hates the British wit a passion. I suppose I hate them, too, but not the same way Billy does. He believes there's justification for killing innocent people in order to make a statement. Revenge today for eight hundred years of British cruelty to the Irish. He wants to see them bleed from every pore for their sins."

Dane thought about this, the fingers of one hand wrapped around his glass, his thumb tracing lines in the developing dew. "If his funding for the Lloyd's operation has fallen through, he's pretty severely limited now, isn't he? What's he got at his disposal—besides a huge pair of balls? Automatic weapons? Grenades?"

She shook her head. "When Seamus joined them he brought all manner of equipment in through Canada. Semtex and C-4 plastique. Detonators. Timing devices. A lot worse than grenades or automatic weapons when in the right hands. They say Billy and Paulie Murphy could either one of them make a bomb out of almost anything and *blow* almost anything. Wit what he's got on hand Billy could close every tunnel and bridge into New York."

"But he wouldn't," Joe mused. "Not because he *couldn't*,

but because we're not his enemy. Even if there's nothing else predictable about him, there is a method to his madness."

Siobhan watched him shift gears. His head came up and his eyes met hers with clear, straight-ahead focus.

"Where would he go when he went to ground, Siobhan? He's not only got us after him, but he's got the Westies after him, too. Where can he hide?"

She'd thought about that question all afternoon. "I truly don't know, Joe. Billy's always been terribly secretive about certain things. His training's taught him to always have two back doors to exit through before he goes in the front. At least one of those back doors he establishes independent of the movement. There is always a chance of a leak from inside."

Dante finished his beer, hoisted himself to his feet, and started for the kitchen with the empty bottle. "If Murphy's hurt as bad as I think he is, he's gonna need medical attention. Think about who you've met or heard them talk about. Doctors, nurses. I'm getting sort of hungry. You?"

Siobhan stood to follow him. "You've got any number of the ingredients for a nice soup in your fridge. Most of them are threatening to go bad if you don't use them soon."

The phone in Joe's bedroom rang. Siobhan noticed that the one in the living room and another hanging on the kitchen wall did not. Joe turned and hurried to answer.

"Damn."

"What?" she asked.

"Special dedicated line. It only rings when somebody's got bad news."

Dante disappeared into his bedroom and was gone no more than three minutes when he emerged carrying a tweed jacket, sneakers, socks, and a gun. He dropped the shoes, pushed the gun into his waistband at the small of his back, and shrugged into the jacket. Then he sat, pulling socks over bare feet.

"A couple of uniforms from the Five-Oh station house up in your neighborhood found a van abandoned in Woodlawn Cemetery. There's a lot of blood all over the inside of it. They think it might be the wheels Billy and Murphy escaped in."

TWENTY

It was dinnertime in Pound Ridge, and Amanda sat at one end of the massive walnut refectory table in the dining room while Jim sat at the other. His housekeeper had prepared a simple roast chicken Normandy style, and Jim had pulled the cork on a '66 Château Lalagune, the best Médoc in his cellar. The meal was served more than twenty minutes ago, and thus far Amanda had only toyed with her food. She'd not touched her wine at all. Her increasingly uncomfortable host looked to ease some of the tension of their current situation.

"There's something we've got to face, Mandy. You and I are both up to our eyeballs in this mess. We shouldn't be fighting; we should be circling our wagons."

A sullen Amanda looked up, unmoved. "What wagons, Jimmy? I'm standing completely exposed right now, and so are you. All day I've wondered where I'd be if you'd never told me about Ralph's visit with Joe Oliver or what you found in Josh's files. Ralph would have eventually filed for divorce, and the truth would have come out anyway. Daddy's little girl would find out she's been richer than God for twenty years. I would be humiliated and fifty million dollars poorer. I probably wouldn't have had the strength to hire *any*one to kill the son of a bitch."

"Mandy . . ."

"And what I surely wouldn't be doing is sitting here right

now contemplating the idea of the next twenty years in a cell at Bedford.''

Quinn slugged back the rest of the wine in his glass and snatched up the bottle to refill it. ''That isn't going to happen, Mandy. Even if the cops catch Mannion—which they won't— any evidence he gives against you can't be substantiated. No money changed hands. The D.A. can't tie him to you, and even if she decided to indict, there's no way she would win against me in court. You're a pillar of the community, and Billy Mannion's a Qaddafi-trained terrorist on a homicidal rampage.''

The clatter of Amanda's fork startled Quinn as she threw it onto her plate. ''And what sort of pillar of the community would I be after something like that, Jimmy? After I'd been dragged through the mud by every newspaper and magazine in the country? It doesn't matter what a jury decides. It's what people *think*. You don't see Claus von Bülow chairing any charity benefits. He had to leave the fucking country. It would destroy my life. Meanwhile Bill Doyle has that promissory note I signed. If he decided to use it against me, he could bleed me to death.''

Quinn scoffed. ''That note is as much evidence of Doyle's complicity as it is yours, Mandy. I was talking worst scenario. It's not going to happen. Bill Doyle knows the Irish community inside out. Billy Mannion can't hide from him. He'll get Billy before the cops do, and if Paul Murphy wasn't *mortally* wounded in all that craziness this afternoon, he'll get him, too. Doyle hates loose ends. He'll make sure there *are* none. Now let's make our peace, you and me. It's really nothing more than an argument over money. Considering who we are, that's absurd.''

Amanda lifted her wineglass for the first time and brought it to her lips. Quinn knew there was nothing enduring about the lighter red wines produced in Bordeaux's Médoc region, but it was the right wine for the dish. He watched Amanda's expression as she tasted it, let it linger awhile on her tongue, and swallowed. No comment. ''The money we're arguing over is my four million dollars, Jimmy. You toss off that 'considering who we are' crap like you and I coexist on the same economic level. What are we talking about here? Your net worth: fifteen, twenty million?''

He nodded. ''Closer to twenty.''

''I see. That's a nice-size nest egg for a criminal attorney, wouldn't you say? An up-by-the-bootstraps kid from the streets, even one of your proven abilities.''

''I have other interests.''

''Oh, really. And what would those interests be?''

''I'd really rather not elaborate at this juncture.''

Amanda sipped her wine again, her expression thoughtful. ''I see. But what you imply is that on a level of relative worth we're roughly equal. Certainly a hundred million is a good deal more than twenty, but if your other 'interests' continue to pay off, it won't be long before that twenty is fifty, correct? Then we'd be even *more* roughly equal.''

Quinn's expression was amused now. ''What are you saying, Mandy?''

''I'm not *saying* anything. I'm asking what you want from me. I always thought it was respectability *and* money. Is marriage to a Gregory all you're really after?''

''Don't sell yourself so short. You give fairly enthusiastic head.''

Her smile developed frost at its edges. ''Counselor, I'd get used to street whores and my right hand if I were you. Marriage is business, just like any other contract. I've always fucked who I wanted to fuck, not who I have to.''

Jumbo Richardson had to wait until Rusty Heckman relieved him in Pound Ridge before he was able to return to the city. It was seven o'clock by the time he got on the road, but tonight he was in no hurry to get home. His wife Bernice was spending a second week in Washington playing mother hen at their daughter's new apartment. As he approached the outskirts of the city on the Hutchinson River Parkway, he got a call from the Op Desk. Until he arrived at his destination he was still on the overtime payroll, and Captain Costanza was asking him to take a detour en route. There was some sort of development in the Mannion case that the Major Case whip wanted one of his people in on. Jumbo was handiest. At the intersection of the Hutch with the Boston Post Road, Richardson went west to East 233rd Street and Woodlawn Cemetery.

When Beasley arrived he found the huge cemetery crawling with NYPD personnel. He spotted two Crime Scene Unit vans as he parked, then Joey's Turbo Z. There were at least a dozen unmarked sedans like his own and an equal number of blue-and-whites. Just inside a cordon of yellow plastic crime-scene tape a battery of portable lights was set up to focus on a fifteen-year-old Dodge Tradesman van. All the doors of the vehicle were open as forensic techs crawled over it. Jumbo flashed his shield at one of the uniforms monitoring foot traffic and slipped beneath the tape. He found Joey standing with Gus Lieberman and Intelligence Division's Pete Shore.

"You don't look nearly as tired as I figure you should," he greeted Dante. "Considering the day I hear you had. Gus. Pete."

The four of them shook hands and Richardson lifted his chin toward the focus of everyone's attention. "Mannion's?"

"That's what we're trying to find out," Pete Shore replied. "Blood all over the inside of it. We're checking the type with some from the garbage truck our man jumped aboard to make his break. We got lucky. Some guy working maintenance here spotted the truck this afternoon and again when it came time to lock up at six."

"Right here between Woodlawn and Norwood," Dante murmured. "The two biggest Irish strongholds in the entire city. *Westie* strongholds. That's balls; going to ground right under their noses." Joe turned to Gus. "Siobhan told me something interesting this evening. She says it isn't in Billy's nature to quit. He'll keep going right up against it until you kill him. And if he knows he's going down, he'll look for the biggest target around; try to take it with him. When Seamus Cowan joined Mannion and Murphy here in New York, he brought some nasty playthings with him. C-4, detonators, shit like that. Enough to make this whole city remember him if he gets a chance to set it off.''

''So where's he inclined to put it?'' the chief asked. ''Could she tell you that?''

Dante stood with his hands deep in his pockets, the tip of his tongue roving back and forth over the edges of his front teeth. ''He'll try for something that will hurt Britain. That's her guess and mine, too. The question is what he knows specifically about British interests here. Probably an awful lot.''

''From those Lloyd's lists the girl told you about?'' Gus asked.

Joe shrugged. ''She says he spent a lot of time on the operation he was planning, but I don't see how he can use that stuff here. His focus was tankers in the Persian Gulf. Sinking them and trying to destroy the people liable for insuring them.''

''Why do I doubt them lists are all that specific?'' Pete Shore asked. ''I think we need to talk to Lloyd's; find out what's on them. If they cover shipping to more than just the Gulf, then it's a whole different ballgame. It's my bet that a fair amount'a foreign crude gets shipped to the big refinery Exxon's got at Perth Amboy. I know for a fact they get shipments from Venezuela, because the Feds are always searching them for dope. Lloyd's'd insure most'a that action, don't you think?''

Perth Amboy was a port city on the New Jersey coast, situated adjacent to the southern tip of Staten Island. As Shore spoke, Jumbo thought about other shipping lanes near to them.

''If you're thinking that way, who says it's gotta be just oil?'' Beasley asked. ''If our man's desperate, why wouldn't he be satisfied torpedoing a load'a Jaguars coming off the boat in Bayonne or Elizabeth? If Lloyd's can pinpoint what's included on them lists and it's bigger than just the Persian Gulf, I'll bet they bend their asses over backwards trying to cooperate.''

Lieberman agreed it was time to contact Lloyd's and then turned to Jumbo as recent activity. "I hear you took a trip upstate, Beasley. What's your read there?''

Richardson scowled, shaking his head in obvious frustration. "I can't figure *what* the fuck's going on, Gus. If Joey's right and Mannion was the shooter in the Overton House homicides, I think Quinn brought Mrs. Kane up there to keep her outta the way. The timing tells me it's definitely got something to do with this trouble between Mannion and the Westies. You mind me asking who this girl is you been talking about?''

Dante quickly brought him up to speed there, dovetailing finally into the relationship between Mannion and Amanda Kane as Siobhan described it. "She says they had a deal, and when it turned out what he'd stolen from that suite wasn't the goods he was after, Billy went wild. It's easy enough to figure why. He took all that risk going in, killed two people, and left an off-duty cop for dead. If he came away empty-handed, he'd be pretty pissed off.''

"You think he's threatened Mrs. Kane?'' Jumbo asked.

"Why not?'' Joe replied. "He plans an operation in detail, starts the wheels in motion, and when he's set to collect the money that enables him to kick it off he comes away empty. Somebody screwed something up, and I doubt Billy's blaming himself. He feels cheated, and the Billy Mannion I've observed kills people when they cross him.''

It was a few minutes after ten when Siobhan heard the elevator. For a moment a very rational fear gripped her. Then she realized a passenger needed a key to operate it and relaxed. Minutes later Dante appeared behind the mesh gate.

"Something smells good in here.''

Siobhan was curled up on the sofa once more and rose

from it to greet him. "Good enough to eat, I hope. I made more than I intended."

Joe stripped out of his jacket as he headed for his bedroom. "I'm ravenous. Everything okay here?"

"Yes. Fine. Tell me what's happened."

She headed for the kitchen as Dante disappeared. When Joe emerged from his room a minute later he was rid of his gun and beeper. He went straight to his wine cabinet and selected a bottle of red almost at random. Siobhan thought he looked tired again.

"The blood in that van was the same type as Murphy's. It'll be tomorrow morning before the lab can run enough tests on it to say it was definitely his, but I doubt we'll be disappointed. I'm switching from beer to wine. What can I get you?"

"Red wine with chicken soup?"

He glanced at the bottle on the counter, corkscrew poised over it, and shrugged. "I guess it's what I'm in the mood for. There's a bottle of Chardonnay cold. You want that instead?"

"No. Please. I'd love a glass of this."

Siobhan wasn't one for picking while she cooked, and she hadn't had a real meal since breakfast. She didn't realize how hungry she was until she placed a pair of bowls on plates and started to fill them. Once she carried them to the breakfast nook, Joe followed with the bottle and two glasses.

"I couldn't find any bread," she said as she sat.

Dante frowned and then shook his head. "I used the last of it for my sandwiches last night. Sorry." He poured, handed her glass across, and raised his own. "Salute."

They clicked glasses and Siobhan sipped. She watched as Dante dipped his spoon and had his first taste of her creation. Some of the tiredness seemed to vanish from his eyes as he swallowed.

"This is terrific."

She smiled, pleased. At no time in the past six weeks had the three louts for whom she'd been forced to cook ever complimented her. Siobhan prided herself on her skill in the kitchen and knew the soup was good. What she enjoyed right now was hearing it. "Tis nothing you didn't already have in your fridge."

Joe had a second spoonful halfway to his mouth when he paused. "I'm sorry I had to leave you alone like that tonight. I know it's been a rough day. How you making out?"

"I'm fine, Joe. Just fine. Go ahead and eat. I've not had a place where I could put two coherent thoughts together in peace for nearly two months. I've appreciated the quiet."

Dante ate that spoonful and dipped for another. "Any conclusions?"

She sipped at her wine and shrugged. "A few, I think."

"Tell me about them?" he asked.

Billy Mannion was back to his lists of Lloyd's indemnity pools when he heard Monica Flynn gasp. He turned in his chair to see her leaning over the bed across the hall, her stethoscope pressed to Paulie's chest.

"What?" he demanded. "What is it?"

She shook her head, and as he stood to approach he saw the panic in her eyes. Instead of wasting time explaining she jerked her cousin's head back and made sure his airway was clear. Then she fitted her mouth over his and blew hard. Straightening, she planted interlocked hands on his chest, palms downward, and shoved with all her might. And again. And again.

"He—just—stopped—breathing," she gasped. As she quickly repeated her mouth-to-mouth and cardiac massage procedures, Billy saw sweat develop across her brow. Rivulets of it streamed down the sides of her face and into her eyes. "No heartbeat."

Billy watched in horror as she labored for a full ten minutes, pausing only briefly to search for signs of life. Finally, with her blouse plastered to her back and ample breasts heaving, she staggered back, head shaking in surrender. "No use!" she groaned.

"What do you mean, no use?!" Billy fairly screamed. "He's *dying*, woman!"

She shook her head, her breath coming easier now that she'd ceased her exertions. "Not dying, Billy. Dead. We did everything we could for him, but like I told you, this i'n't a hospital."

Billy was on his knees now, Paulie's right hand in his own. As he squeezed fiercely he felt that slight coolness to the flesh, all that strength and vitality gone. "Aaahhngh! Nooo, Paulie lad! Nooo!" Tears filled his eyes and fell streaming down his cheeks. That fighter's visage with its broken nose and scar-thickened cheeks was calm. As Billy choked in his grief he released Paulie's hand to wrap his arms around that lifeless form. His body was wracked with quaking, uncontrollable sobs as he buried his face in his dead comrade's chest.

Amanda Kane went to bed early, but after two hours of restless tossing and turning she gave up trying to sleep. Warm milk and brandy helped sedate her when she was wrought up like this, and she rose to heat some in the kitchen. The house was quiet now. There was a nearly full carton of milk in the refrigerator and a decent Armagnac in one of the dining room decanters. Amanda set a cupful of the milk to warm.

Seven hours after arriving here she was still surprised by this place. She and Ralph had the summer house out in Easthampton, but they'd always been content to winter in Manhattan. As a girl Amanda spent weekends at the Gregory farm upstate in Millbrook. She always imagined she would purchase a country retreat one day but never had. Ralph was tight with his money, and he couldn't have been less interested in such an investment. He loathed both gardening and sitting in front of fires. He'd never learned to ride and couldn't imagine why he might want to. She realized that no matter how angry she was with Jimmy Quinn, they were two people with very similar appetites. This house was a perfect example: it was hidden away in tasteful, elegant seclusion. She could be happy coming up here on winter weekends when a Virgin Islands trip wasn't convenient.

Once the milk was heated, she poured it into a mug, laced it liberally, and left the kitchen to wander the house. While every piece of furniture was a high-quality selection, not all of them were to her taste. It felt a bit as though Jimmy had been 'decorated,' but she and her expert eye would rectify that problem with a few subtle changes here and there.

The soft piano music that caught Amanda's ear seemed to be coming from the lowest of the three wings of the house. She'd noticed on their approach that the bottom end of it was a large, glass-enclosed room. A solarium perhaps. She followed a wide hallway now to where it led down a short flight of steps to a library and game room beyond. She surveyed the dark, paneled interior of this last room with amusement. With a snooker table set dead center it had an antique barroom shuffleboard running the length of one wall. The heads of moose, wildebeest, bear, elk, antelope, and leopard were hung around the room along with game fish trophies of all varieties. There were cabinets racked full of rifles, shotguns, handguns, and fishing rods. Directly to the left of the door stood a bar, the shelves behind cluttered with liquor bottles and its surface sporting neat ranks of gleaming glasses. She located an Armagnac that may or may not have been the same as the one in the dining room and added it to her near-empty cup.

As Amanda sipped, the gentle heat of the liquor warming her, she chuckled to herself. This room declared Jim Quinn a man's man; a predator. The idea that such a notion should excite her was something of a surprise. She made up her mind at that moment that she and Jimmy were going to work something out. Toward that end she loosened the tie of her robe, pocketed the band holding her hair back, and bent forward to shake her hair loose. There was a door in the opposite wall. When she crossed and opened it the music grew louder.

The glassed-in area at that end of the house enclosed an indoor swimming pool. This was where the music was playing, the strain of a Liszt piano concerto echoing off the cavernous interior's glass to fill the room with lively melody. The flagstone expanse surrounding the pool was warm to the touch as she stepped barefoot onto it. The lights of the room were set low, obscuring visibility into the deep corners, and for a moment she was confused. The pool was empty. With the music masking most sound an unmistakable groan of pleasure barely reached her ears. It was then that she focused on an alcove just past the far end of the pool on her left.

What her eyes found was a recessed Jacuzzi. The glow of lights set below its surface illuminated bubbling water and the hot tub's two occupants. Jim Quinn sat naked on the edge of it, his right profile to her and legs dangling in its depths. His housekeeper Adrian, hair done up in a topknot and wet shoulders gleaming in the ambient light, bobbed head-bent between Jimmy's thighs. Amanda, suddenly sick to her stomach, stood exposed should either of them look her way. She'd let her robe fall from her shoulders to the crooks of her elbows, and now her scalp was suddenly afire with hot pinpricks of embarrassment.

It took the summoning of every synapse of will to resist screaming. As Amanda fought to keep her composure, she pulled the robe back around her shoulders and drifted deeper into shadow. Then she watched. This spectacle was part of the compromise she'd nearly convinced herself to accept. She would force herself to stand immersed in it; to confront it and fully realize what a fool she'd been.

Across the flagstone in that intimate little alcove the house-keeper surged suddenly from the water to kneel, straddle her employer, and fit him up inside her. Jimmy groaned again as she began to writhe above him.

"Ahhh, that's good."

"Yeah, Jim? You like that?" she crooned.

"You *know* I do, baby."

Jimmy's body went taut as Adrian laughed a wicked little laugh, the grinding motions of her pelvis quickening until Quinn's back arched and his hips jerked spasmodically. Amanda hugged herself as she watched, staying on until the bitter end of it. Then she slipped slowly through shadow to the game room door. En route to her room she paused to drain her cup and refill it from that bottle on the bar. On second thought she took the bottle with her.

Dante and Siobhan were finished with their soup but hadn't moved from their seats in the breakfast nook. Joe was on his third glass of wine and was finally starting to unwind. Across from him Siobhan had just related some of her experiences as a struggling actress in New York and was speculating now about the future.

"I've been thinking long and hard about it, Joe. About going home again. I didn't realize it until Billy threatened to kill my sister Deirdre's kids just how much I miss her. Folks would always compare us in front of our parents, us two. They'd talk about how I was sure to go far in this world because I was so bright and pretty. I couldn't miss getting myself a rich man or a good job or anything I wanted. It made me feel bad to hear them speak like that in front of Deirdre; to see how it made her feel. I've never told her that."

Dante could see the pain on her face. She'd spent the past hour telling him how she'd come to realize that not all childhood dreams are realistic adult life choices. His own images of the future, the ones he carried into adulthood, were of a hard-working family man who lived somewhere away from the city in the suburbs; who supported a loving wife and a couple of kids; who left the job at the station house at shift's end, just like his own father had never been able to do. Like Siobhan and her career as an actress in America, Dante's own dreams of childhood hadn't come true. He'd been forced to confront the reality of a life that insisted on just living itself. Like Siobhan's, his own life refused to conform.

"You don't *have* to go back," he told her. "We can make a case for you being in danger if you go home now. Immigration would have no choice but to allow you to stay."

Siobhan smiled sadly and shook her head. "I don't think

271

I'd be in much danger, Joe. Back home the folk are getting fed up. Masked men holding women at gunpoint and forcing their husbands to drive car bombs. IRA leaders raising money by trafficking drugs. Cowards 'n' criminals is what so many of them've become. It in't just the British yoke my people want to see thrown off. At the core of the IRA vision is one of an Irish Marxist state. We Irish don't want that any more'n you Americans do." She paused. "No, Joe, I think it's *time* I went home. Ireland needs me more'n Hollywood does."

Dante started to pour more wine into their glasses and discovered the bottle was nearly empty. He sighed. "Ah, well. It's midnight anyway." After collecting their plates and bowls he stood to carry them to the sink.

Siobhan followed with the empty bottle and glasses. "You rinse them and I'll load."

They did the dishes and took a minute to wipe down a few surfaces and feed the cat before heading for their rooms.

"You take the bathroom first," Joe suggested.

Siobhan had moved past as Dante reached to switch off the kitchen lights. She stopped now and stood in a pose of awkward self-consciousness. There was an uncharacteristic huskiness in her voice when she spoke. "I don't know if I've conveyed just how grateful I am for what you've done for me, Joe. I know this has been a hard time for you, too. I'm thankful you helped me like you did."

Dante smiled and started for the back of the loft with Siobhan falling in to trail alongside. "I appreciate the vote of confidence," he replied. "Can't say I expected one after putting you through what I did today." They stopped outside the bath, Joe turning to face her and bending to peck her on the forehead. "G'night, Siobhan."

In his room Dante stripped out of his clothing and slipped into shorts to stretch full length on the floor. It was a week now since he'd done anymore than borrow Diana's upstairs gym for a few half-hour workouts. His body was demanding that he get back to the dojo soon. For the moment the best he could offer it was a few basic yoga stretches as he killed time waiting for Siobhan to vacate the bathroom.

Toby the cat was waiting impatiently outside Joe's door and followed him to perch on the toilet seat as Dante brushed his teeth. The two were returning cat-in-arms to the bedroom when Joe found Siobhan sitting on the edge of his bed. She had changed into the pink flannel nightie and smiled as she digested the look of surprise on Dante's face.

"I'm probably just as shocked at myself as you are, Joe . . . and perhaps I'm assuming too much."

Dante set the cat on the floor and stood there regarding Siobhan with a gaze that was a lot steadier than his pulse rate. "Depends . . . on *what* it is you've assumed. I doubt it's too *much*."

Her relief was obvious, her smile broadening and shoulders relaxing. Joe approached to stand knee-to-knee with her and reached out to trace the contours of her face with the tips of his fingers.

"Just this afternoon I was sure you hated my guts, Siobhan. I'm not going to stand here and say I don't want this. That would be bullshit. But there's no rush. I'm not going anywhere. Are you sure this is what *you* want?"

In answer she stood, eyes locked with his, and pulled the nightgown over her head. Dante eased his hands to her waist and let them drift down over the curves of her hips. Then he pulled her to him, arms encircling and hands gliding up and down over the delicious texture of her flesh.

"How's that mouth?" he asked.

"A bit tender but dying to be kissed."

Joe took it slow, letting her own enthusiasm lead him. He loved the way her hands caressed his back and ass; the strength and eagerness of her touch. When they broke the kiss off, he stepped to pull back his bedclothes.

"Jesus, you're beautiful," he murmured.

Her smile grew broad with pleasure as she crawled into the bed and squirmed between the sheets. "So are you, mister. Something tells me this is going to be delicious fun."

TWENTY-ONE

The cops had a three-state net deployed in an effort to bring Big Bill Doyle in for questioning. In the face of it his nephew Tommy was surprised to see how calm his uncle was. As soon as he learned of Johnny McGuire's failure to hit Billy Mannion the Westie boss went matter-of-factly into his current damage control mode. The usual Cadillac limo was parked in favor of a twelve-year-old Chrysler New Yorker. The apartment above the butcher shop on Bainbridge in the North Bronx became his nerve center. Norwood, like Woodlawn to the north and Kingsbridge to the west, was an Irish stronghold. From it Big Bill could direct his search for Billy Mannion while remaining invisible to the cops. Twice yesterday afternoon and again last night he'd been able to move freely around the city, checking on the progress being made by his troops.

Tommy's uncle was an early riser, and on this crystal-clear October morning they'd hit the road at twenty past six. Their destination was the exclusive enclave of Pound Ridge up in Westchester, and Tommy was pleased his uncle didn't find it necessary to travel with any of the other boys. Big Bill considered young Tommy to be plenty muscle enough for this trip into the suburbs. At twenty-six Tommy had been in the intimidation end of the business for almost nine years.

Right now Big Bill had one of those Macanudos of his going, billows of smoke from it coming at Tommy over the seat back. The smell of it the kid could live with, but he was strictly a dope smoker himself. What was the point of spending all that good money on something that didn't get you high?

"Where's your money on the Giants-Chicago game, Tommy boy?"

As always the younger Doyle weighed his reply carefully before answering. "I've got a grand on the Bears, Unk. That six and a half points is more than I think the Jints'll cover. Look how they barely squeezed by the fucking Falcs last week."

Big Bill coughed and lowered his window to spit. "How far we got to go? I got a bladder ain't what it used to be."

Tommy was amused. How many times had he driven his uncle up here? At least a dozen. And each time Big Bill ignored scenery, signs, and everything else outside the car until they arrived. The man was a city boy to the core. "This is the exit now. Then we've got another six, seven miles up Route 137. You wanna hold it or find someplace to pull off?"

"Seven miles? No sweat. Jimmy's got bathrooms, so why pee on a tree?"

"You got a game plan here? Is this a day in the country or what?"

Big Bill grunted and coughed again. "Naw, this is strictly business. I wanna wrap it up fast."

Tommy steered them onto the exit ramp, the sharpness of the turn forcing him to slow more abruptly than he liked. "You gonna need me, or you want me to wait with the car?"

"Take a walk down to the pond and feed the ducks for all I care. Just don't wander too far off. Sorry we ain't gonna have time to take a swim and relax. Like I said, with all this craziness going on back in town I want to do this quick and get rolling."

The further north they rode on 137 the more exclusive the real estate became. Tommy had his sights set on one of these big, swanky homes they passed en route. Big Bill was getting older every day, and somebody had to fill his shoes. Of course, he'd cut down some of the trees; open up the view from the road. What was the good of having a palace if people couldn't drive by and drool?

They reached the front gate of Quinn's place at ten minutes to eight and had to wait an inordinate amount of time before being granted access.

"What gives, Unk? Ain't nobody expecting us?"

Big Bill grunted. "First thing in the morning means nine-thirty, ten o'clock in Jim Quinn's world. He probably just dragged his ass outta bed."

When they crested the low rise in the drive, Tommy shook his head the same way he always did when first glimpsing Quinn's hideaway. "Dude lives strictly *ultra*, don't he? What ya figure a crib like this'd set a man back, Unk?"

Doyle's chuckle was to himself this time. "Forget about it, Tommy boy. There's a problem with appetites like Jim Quinn's got. You indulge it once, you gotta indulge it again and again. You're never satisfied. You'd think anybody lives in a place like this has got it made in spades, wouldn't you?"

Tommy Doyle eased the Chrysler to a stop in the drive. "No question."

"Well, Jim Quinn don't. Or at least he don't *think* he does. Man with his appetites can't never get enough."

The overgrown turnout up the road from James Quinn's country hideaway made a perfect surveillance blind. Jumbo Richardson liked the cover the trees afforded and the direct sight line to Quinn's front gate. He'd just arrived to relieve Guy Napier and the two of them were relaxing in the front seat of his sedan enjoying coffee and doughnuts. Napier had surrendered the Zeiss spotting scope, and Jumbo was cradling it in his lap when a mint-green Chrysler New Yorker eased into the drive down the road.

"Hold this for me." Beasley handed Napier his paper cup. "Let's see who we've got here." The scope was already in good focus. He had to fiddle with the ring for only a second or two before he had a clear view of the car's interior. It helped that the Chrysler sat parked there awhile. Whoever had gate duty was obviously not prepared for visitors. "Hold the fucking phone," he murmured.

"What?" Napier asked. "What've you got?"

"That's Big Bill Doyle. In the backseat." Jumbo handed the scope to Napier and reached for his cellular handset. "We move on him, we blow the fucking surveillance. I'm gonna try the squad first. Then I'm calling the state police."

Guy tossed Richardson's coffee out the window and peered through the scope for only a moment before setting it on the seat between them. "That's Doyle, all right." He reached for his door release. "We can't count on having time to wait for state. If we don't, I'll take the tail."

When Quinn stepped from the house to greet Bill Doyle, his hair was still rumpled with sleep. He'd pulled on a Harvard University sweatsuit but was shod in slippers.

"Bill. Jesus. I wasn't expecting you until a little later. C'mon in. I think I smelled coffee when I passed the kitchen. Maybe we're in luck."

"Late night, Counselor?"

Quinn responded with a sly wink. "No later than usual. I guess I forgot to set the clock."

Quinn was leading the way toward the front door when it opened. Amanda Kane confronted them in her robe, her hair also disheveled.

"You brought my note, Mr. Doyle?" She asked it slowly, as if she was straining to enunciate each word. There were huge, puffy bags under her eyes, and she leaned heavily against the doorjamb with one shoulder and hip.

Doyle raised his eyebrows at Quinn. When Jim shrugged helplessly, the Westie boss flashed the socialite a patronizing smile. "That's what I've come up here to talk with you about, isn't it, Mrs. Kane? I think we'll come to an understanding once we all sit down and work this thing through."

When Amanda shook her head in disgust and straightened, the door swung wide to reveal her unseen right hand. Both Quinn and Doyle started in alarm. She had Quinn's army .45 Colt automatic, and in one expert move it was leveled at Doyle's chest.

"Like hell we'll work anything *through*, you lowlife!" she snarled. "I'm tired of being bent over by you and your prick friend here!"

The gun jumped a full two feet in her hands when she pulled the trigger. Her shot blew a bowling ball–size hole out the back side of Bill Doyle's jacket, and the Westie boss crumpled to the drive. Jim Quinn watched, stricken, as the muzzle of the Colt swung in his direction. He never heard the second discharge, the slug from it removing the top of his head and most of both ears.

Amanda spotted movement to the left of Bill Doyle's convulsing corpse. Her reaction was slowed by the entire fifth of Armagnac she'd consumed during the night. She found her target with the barrel site but never got off a third shot. Tommy Doyle prevented it by emptying the entire magazine of his 9mm Browning automatic into her chest, neck, and head.

Gunfire interrupted Richardson's call to Captain Bud Costanza. He cut the connection and bolted from the car at a dead run. Napier was a step ahead of him when he reached the gate, and the forty-six-year-old Richardson hauled himself over the top with mixed feelings about this aspect of police work. He was glad he'd lost all that weight a couple of years back; that he tried to stay in shape. What he envied were the six-foot-six-inch Napier's advantages of leverage and youth. The twenty-eight-year-old fairly flew over the obstacle. He was already sprinting full-tilt up the drive by the time Beasley dropped huffing and puffing to the other side.

The roar of an engine reached Richardson's ears as he cut onto the lawn to shorten the distance up the hill ahead. The nose of the mint-green Chrysler rocketed into view, sun glinting off its windshield and making identification of the driver impossible. Beasley watched as Napier pulled up to stand his ground in the middle of the drive, shield case held high in one hand and revolver in the other. When the car failed to slow, Guy dove for the cover of a stout tree trunk and came up shooting. He emptied his .357 magnum forward of the Chrysler's firewall. Almost instantly nasty black smoke billowed from the speeding car's tail pipe. Jumbo hurried to cover Guy as the engine rattled and died. The driver's door opened, and Jumbo rushed forward to draw bead on the car's only occupant.

"Police, asshole! On your fucking face *now*!"

The driver emerged coughing, his hands raised. When he dropped to his knees, Guy shoved him face-first to the turf. Both cops had the adrenaline pumping, and as Jumbo pulled his handcuffs from his jacket pocket his breath came in gulps.

"Doyle's driver," Beasley gasped.

Napier went down on one knee in front of the prostrate form. "What the fuck's going on up there?"

The question was met with silence. A woman's screams floated over the rise ahead, and Richardson grabbed one of the downed man's arms. "Gimme a hand. We'll cuff him to that tree."

They left the driver hugging an oak and raced ahead, screams of hysteria growing louder as they crested the low ridge. Both slowed abruptly. Two bodies were sprawled in the drive in front of the house. The screams came from a woman bent over one of the fallen men. From a distance of two hundred feet they could see copious amounts of blood splashed across the grill and hood of a silver Mercedes limousine, pooled in the drive, and covering the frenzied woman's hands.

"Holy *shit*!" Napier murmured.

Jumbo was already starting down the back side of the rise, weapon clutched before him in both hands. "Sure wish I didn't eat them doughnuts," he lamented. "God *damn*, I wish I didn't."

* * *

Christopher Newman

When Police Commissioner Tony Mintoff decreed that his old classmate Bud Costanza would continue to command Major Case until the Overton House case was closed, it left Joe Dante free to pursue Billy Mannion from inside the job. Gus Lieberman assigned him to a special task force created in concert with Intelligence Division. Early Wednesday morning Pete Shore, Dante, and Anti-Terror's Captain Harry Diaz met in Lieberman's office for the new team's first strategy session. Coffee was poured and doughnuts were circulated as Gus brought them up to speed on overnight developments. A DNA test done on the blood from the construction-site garbage truck and abandoned van found in Woodlawn Cemetery was conclusive. In both instances the blood belonged to the same man. Uniformed patrol and detective squads in the Four-Seven, Five-Oh, and Five-Two precincts in the North Bronx were putting extra people on the street in search of the fugitive terrorists.

"Operations finally tracked down the president of Lloyd's America over in Saddle River," the chief reported. "I dragged his ass outta bed around midnight. When I told him what we're up against he hit the brakes hard. Claimed he couldn't authorize access; not to information as sensitive as that without calling London. I told him he wants to save his own ass as well as mine he'd better get on the fucking line and *fast*." He paused to stub out one cigarette while simultaneously shaking another from his pack. "Soon as I hung up I called Tony at home and told him to do whatever the fuck had to be done. Call the British U.N. ambassador. Call the fucking *queen*. Light a fire under this bastard. Tony got back to me just before I left the house this morning. It looks like we're gonna get some action."

"*When?*" Shore asked. "We've got the whole Port Authority and a dozen different departments in two fuckin' states to mobilize. The sooner we get those lists the less time we spend looking up each other's assholes."

Lieberman made a calming gesture with both hands. "Their U.N. ambassador talked with Lloyd's London.

280

They've given the New York office the go-ahead. We should have something soon. Maybe within a couple hours. Meanwhile the Feds're claiming jurisdiction. The Bureau wants control of the entire op. Customs wants a piece, too.''

This last little bombshell saw Dante lose his cool. ''How the hell did *they* find out?'' he demanded.

Gus blew smoke at the ceiling and sighed. ''The British U.N. guy called the State Department. Cat's outta the bag now, Joey. By tonight it'll be all over the six o'clock news.''

As Dante sat and seethed, the outer office buzzed Gus on the intercom line. Lieberman picked up and listened a moment, his expression quickly transformed.

''Patch him through, for Crissake!'' Gus covered the mouthpiece as he waited. ''It's Beasley up in Pound Ridge. You ain't gonna fucking believe this.'' His attention returned to the phone as Jumbo came on the line. ''Yeah, Beasley. Feed it to me. What happened?''

Dante, Shore, and Diaz could only glean bits and pieces during the ensuing conversation. When the chief hung up there were still traces of astonishment in his expression.

''You wanted a Westie tie-in? Amanda Kane just blew James Quinn and Bill Doyle away with a fucking forty-five automatic. She's dead, too. Doyle's bodyguard ventilated her. They've got Quinn's housekeeper and his chauffeur detained for questioning. The Doyle bodyguard is under arrest.''

Monica Flynn had reported for her shift at Montefiore Hospital that morning and left an hour later complaining of chills and nausea. She was off running several important errands for Billy now while he was once again at work at her kitchen table. Behind him Paulie Murphy's body lay at rest behind the closed door of the bedroom across the hall. The Lloyd's lists were no longer in evidence, replaced by needle-nose pliers, diagonal cutters, a soldering iron, screwdrivers, rolls of insulated low-voltage wire in coded colors, dry-cell batteries, electronic timing devices, detonator coils, and blocks of both Semtex and C-4 explosive. His familiarity with these tools and materials was evident in the way he manipulated them, his concentration absolute and movements precise.

Billy's immersion in his task was so complete that he failed to hear the sound of movement on the flight of stairs from the garage until his visitor was halfway up them. In the next instant he was on his feet and racing for the wall behind the door. As he pressed himself flat his thumb instinctively flicked the safety of his Intratec machine pistol to the "off" position. One ear to the wall, he heard something bump up against the inside of the stairwell with a dull thud.

"Billy, could you give me some help with these. *Please*."

Mannion clicked the safety back on and pushed the Intratec into his waistband before opening the door. He found Monica about two-thirds up the flight, a leather garment bag slung over one shoulder and three more pieces of luggage at her feet. Both of the cases Billy grabbed in an effort to help were heavy.

"You made the booking?" he asked.

The nurse, still dressed in her whites, nodded. "Of course. And you were lucky. There were still several openings, even at this late hour."

"And everything's here that I asked you for?"

Monica looked slightly offended now. "The one suit was the only thing difficult. I had to go all the way into Manhattan. The clerk at the shop I found has a book to convert European to American sizes. I think it'll fit fine."

"I'll try it, and if there's anything needs doing maybe you can fix it for me. Where'd you get the other clothing?"

The nurse smiled at her own cleverness. "It's all of it used; from the Salvation Army."

Billy carried the bags into the front room and laid one on the sofa to inspect its contents. It contained a variety of shirts, sweaters, and trousers, all clean and neatly folded. "And the equipment case?"

Monica pointed to the smallest of the bags. "Inside, just like you said."

Billy opened the indicated case and extracted a moulded aluminum valise. He nodded his approval. "Perfect. So let's try on this suit." He removed the machine pistol from his waistband and began to disrobe. Monica turned her back and wandered into the kitchen to inspect progress on the bomb as he tried on the black wool trousers and jacket. He was pleased to see that the theatrical costumer's conversion tables were accurate. The garment fit well through the shoulders, chest, waist, and hips. Even the cuff and sleeve lengths were correct.

"How do I look?" he asked. He stepped into the kitchen and turned three hundred sixty degrees.

"A bit silly without your shirt. Don't you think we'd better hurry? There's not much time remaining, and it doesn't look like you're quite finished here."

"You parked your car back in the garage?" Billy asked. He stepped closer to the table and stood regarding the progress he'd made. He was close now. Very close.

"Yes. Is there anything I can carry down?"

Billy picked his .22-caliber, noise-suppressed automatic from the table and stood fondling it. "Oh, I don't think that'll be necessary. Just so long as the keys are somewhere handy."

A confused Monica became alarmed as Billy lifted the weapon, took aim at her face, and pulled the trigger. The impact with her eye at point-blank range sent her toppling backward, the noise of the shot like the muffled clapping of hands.

TWENTY-TWO

A Lloyd's executive hand-carried the requested lists to Chief Lieberman at One Police Plaza. Joe Dante, Pete Shore, and Harry Diaz immediately set about dividing those lists, grouping each vessel by port of destination. At quarter of twelve they left with Gus for an early lunch in Chinatown, taking their reorganized lists and the latest Port Authority shipping schedules with them. They settled in the chief's favorite Vietnamese dive, ordered lunch, and got down to the task at hand. Shore suggested they divide the lists into areas of concentration with him taking Perth Amboy, South Amboy, Carteret, and any other shipping in the Arthur Kill waterway between Staten Island and New Jersey. Harry Diaz was given Elizabeth, Bayonne, Jersey City, and all other traffic entering the so-called Port of Newark. That left Dante with all shipping at anchor in the Verrazano Narrows and Upper New York Bay as well as vessels docked anywhere in the Port of New York. Lieberman would meanwhile handle interagency cooperation problems and organize logistics.

"What are the chances of getting help from Major Case?" Dante asked Gus.

The chief had poured his tiny ceramic cup full of tea and was lifting it gingerly to his lips. "I wouldn't count on it," he growled. "Bud Costanza hates being wrong—or in this case only half right. As long as he's got Tony's ear he'll try to figure some way to make himself a hero. He'll have Beasley and Napier stuck up in Westchester for the rest of the day. I'll see what I can do about getting you the others."

Dante was finished scanning the list of ships and their cargoes anchored out in the bay and another list of ships tied up on the eastern shore of Staten Island. Now he was working his way through a listing of vessels tied up at the Brooklyn docks. Of the fifty-plus ships calling in his area of concentration, only a handful were registered in British Commonwealth countries. Just two were of actual British origin. According to Siobhan, British registry wasn't necessarily what Billy was after. His plan was to target British *liability*.

Joe flipped to the last page of his list and started down it when Diaz asked how Gus planned to deal with the pressure from the Feds.

"Right now?" Lieberman replied. "By stalling them as long as I can. I've got a meeting with the agent in charge of the New York Bureau office set up for two this afternoon. That's as far back as I could put him off. They know we wanted these Lloyd's lists in conjunction with our Mannion investigation, and that makes them crazy because it's *all* they know. They don't know any of what Joey's informant's revealed to us. Right now we're in the catbird seat, and they're out there sucking wind."

"Wait a minute," Dante murmured. He looked up to beckon in Pete's direction. "Hand me that shipping schedule."

Once Dante had the Port Authority schedule centered on the table before him he dragged his pencil down the list of vessel names. "Duchess . . . duchess . . . duchess . . ." Halfway down the second page his pencil stopped and started across through port location, time of arrival, and scheduled time of departure. "Here it is. The *Duchess of York*. She tied up at Pier Eighty-eight day before yesterday. Sails for Portsmouth, England at two forty-five this afternoon." He looked up, pushing the schedule across the table to Gus. "I just read an article in the Times about that ship. It's the latest and largest British long-distance luxury liner. There's no such thing as going second-class aboard it. I don't see any way Billy Mannion could resist.''

There was some serious doubt in the chief's expression as he contemplated the Port Authority schedule. ''A *passenger* ship?''

Antiterror expert Harry Diaz jumped into it here. ''The Lou might be on the right track, Chief. Mannion's proven himself more than willing to kill defenseless civilians, and that ship fits the overall target profile. It's the new pride of Britain's most visible and luxurious shipping line. Mannion's trapped here, his support from the Irish-American community cut off. If he's going down, he'll want to go down in flames. Make a statement the whole world can't ignore.'' He stopped and pursed his lips, slowly shaking his head. ''You just stop to consider the impact the crash of Pan Am Flight 103 had worldwide. This is an entire fucking luxury liner. Britain's new queen of the seas. Dante's right. Mannion *can't* resist.''

Billy Mannion didn't agree with Monica Flynn's choice of vehicles from a political standpoint, but her white 5-series BMW was perfect for the task at hand. Once the boot of the car was packed with the matched pieces of leather luggage, Billy backed the car onto Martha Avenue and started north across the Yonkers city line. At a corner two blocks up he pulled in next to a hydrant and adjusted the rearview mirror. The image of Paul Murphy lying dead flashed before Billy's mind's eye as he lifted a battery-powered transmitter from the passenger seat. Thumb on the send button he pressed lightly and watched a fireball erupt through Monica Flynn's open garage door. Upstairs the glass was blown from the living room's big picture window, shards of it raining down on the sidewalk and street. Seconds later the building's roof collapsed. Mannion slipped the car back into gear and eased away from the curb. Behind him the house was rapidly engulfed in flames.

* * *

Nineteenth Precinct

By one o'clock Chief Lieberman's special task force had received full cooperation from the New York–New Jersey Port Authority and the British shipper. The master of the *Duchess of York* granted immediate access to his ship once the police commissioner outlined NYPD fears to him by phone. On arrival at the passenger ship terminal Joe Dante and Pete Shore were led aboard and shown to the purser's office while Gus Lieberman and Anti-Terror's Captain Harry Diaz remained dockside to establish a command port.

The ship's business manager, or purser, was a gaunt, tightly wound man of maybe fifty with a clipped British accent. The prospect of having his ship blown out from under him had him shaken. Once he was apprised of the potential danger at hand he voiced his concern for the passengers and crew already aboard.

"Shouldn't we be evacuating the ship, Inspector?"

Shore moved to put him as much at ease as he could under the circumstances. "If we think it's necessary, we will, sir. Believe me. Right now what we need to do is focus on trying to figure if the *Duchess* here is really his target. Our anti-terror expert is an ex–U.S. Navy Seal. He thinks Mannion would prefer planting his explosives on board rather than attempting to attach them to the hull. Apparently there's less risk of failure in an on-board approach."

As the purser digested Shore's words he fidgeted nervously with a pencil and nodded too often. "I suppose what you're asking then is *how* this man might get aboard. Correct? That would of course depend on the time frame."

Dante eased into the conversation here, keeping any obvious anxiousness out of his tone. "We think it would be within the last twenty-four hours. Probably closer to eighteen."

"Or less," Shore grunted.

The purser frowned and bit his lower lip. "All the fresh stores coming aboard are handled by our own crew once they leave the dock. We have very tight security, which checks the credentials of anyone wishing on-board access. Of course, if your man managed to make contact with a sympathizer amongst our crew . . .''

"We doubt that," Shore interrupted. "He didn't have that kinda time, and this guy is too smooth to complicate matters like that. Too much risk of compromise."

"Might he have actually booked passage?"

Shore glanced up, frowning. "You mean bought himself a ticket?"

"Correct, Inspector."

"When would he'a had to do that?"

The purser shrugged. "We're never full this time of year. It's between the vacation seasons. We get any number of last-minute bookings. He could simply call a travel agent."

Shore glanced to Dante. "What d'ya think?"

"Worth checking out," Dante replied. "He'd need a means of getting explosives aboard. What better way than that? Pack them in his luggage."

Shore pointed to the purser's computer terminal. "You got access to those bookings?"

"Certainly. What would you like? The last twenty-four hours?" The purser seemed relieved to have something to do. He swung around in his desk chair and flicked the power switch on his terminal.

"Make it forty-eight' " Dante directed. "Let's see how many we're talking about and whittle the list from there."

The purser's fingers flew over the keyboard. After a moment's wait information began to appear on the monitor screen. "We've had seven bookings and two cancelations in that time period," he announced.

Dante and Shore stooped to peer at the screen. Joe pointed to a series of numbers after each name.

"Passport?"

"Yes, sir." The purser's finger moved from left to right across the screen. "Passenger's name, nationality, passport number, type of booking, method of payment, special considerations."

Shore straightened. "Can you print me out a list? There's

a fella at Customs out at JFK who I'm friendly with. I'll run
'em past him.''

Shortly after accompanying the luggage aboard ship Billy
Mannion took a reconnaissance stroll below decks. If any of
the ship's crew thought his progress odd, none interfered.
His garb, affable demeanor, and apparent confidence per-
suaded them to pay him no mind. Within minutes he'd discovered access to the bowels of the behemoth luxury liner.
Once he found the ship's laundry a pair of coveralls were
easy enough to steal. Billy waited until he was back in the
privacy of his stateroom to pull them over his suit. Within an
hour of stepping on board he was dressed as one of the vessel's own engine-room staff. Aluminum equipment case in
hand, he sauntered casually toward the service elevator.

Billy had only a vague idea of what he would encounter as
he rode below to the engine room. When the elevator doors
opened he was hit with a blast of air that was at least twenty
degrees warmer than other temperatures inside the ship. Here
below the waterline all amenities were swept aside in defer-
ence to efficient function. Wide catwalks stretched right and
left before him to ring the ship's operation center directly
below. The noise of machinery was near deafening. Down
in that pit at least a dozen of the ship's personnel lounged in
desk chairs before electronic consoles. None gave Billy so
much as a second glance as he started left along a row of
enclosed shops. Each area he passed was partitioned off with
steel mesh, an engraved identifying plaque on its door. Most
of those doors were padlocked: Tool Crib, Plumbing, Electrical, Welding. The door to the last shop at the end of the
row hung open, its plaque identifying it as the machine shop.

Billy slowed. Back in the recesses of the shop he could see
a figure in grease-stained coveralls hunched over a lathe, his
face shield down and sparks showering the floor at his feet.
Directly behind him a workbench paralleling the hull ran the
shop's entire width. Mannion started for the corner at the

far end, his eyes never leaving the machinist until he'd slid that case into the recesses beneath the work bench's surface.

Pete Shore found nothing remarkable about any of the names and passport numbers until he fed his friend at Customs the sixth on the list. Dante listened to Shore's end of the conversation as Pete's tone changed. One after another Shore requested a series of State Department file checks before hanging up. When he turned to face Joe and the purser, Pete had a sheet of paper in hand covered with scribbled notes.

"There ain't but one Reverend Thomas Kehoe listed with State, and his passport number's not even close. I had 'em check on the guy. He's a Jesuit priest. A social philosopher, no less. They've got his last employer listed as the Yale Theological School."

Dante turned to the purser and nodded at the terminal screen. "The method of payment listed there is American Express. Can we find out whose card that is?"

"Absolutely." Once again the purser's fingers flew over the keyboard as Joe addressed Pete.

"Let's call Yale Theological. See if they know anything about Father Kehoe taking a trip."

The purser cleared his throat. "That Amex charge was made by a party other than the passenger, Lieutenant. It was made through a travel agent in Bronxville by a Dr. Peter Canova."

"Let's check on it," Dante directed. "Meanwhile, how do we know if a passenger's boarded yet?"

The purser started out of his chair. "The chief steward should know. His office is right next door."

Dante stopped him. "You check on that credit charge." He headed for the door. "Which way? Right or left?"

The chief steward was out of his office, but his assistant placed a call to the porter's desk on the main deck at Dante's request. After making his inquiry she covered the mouthpiece.

"The Reverend Kehoe hasn't come aboard yet, sir, but his luggage was delivered about an hour ago. We sail in seventy minutes, so I assume he's expected shortly."

"You say his luggage was delivered? How?"

"Yes, sir. By another party, I assume."

Dante's pulse quickened. "How does that work? Does this other party actually come aboard?"

"They often do, sir. With one of our porters assisting them."

Joe pointed to the receiver still in the woman's hand. "This is an emergency. Let's find that porter and get him up here. I'll be next door in the purser's office."

When Dante returned to join Shore, Pete was just hanging up.

"We're definitely onto something here, Joe. Father Kehoe's out on the coast this week. In San Francisco. He's the keynote speaker at a conference on religion and homosexual rights; left Monday and won't be back till after the weekend."

"That American Express card was reported stolen only an hour ago," the purser reported. "The booking was made at nine o'clock this morning, but the cardmember didn't notice his card missing from his wallet until lunch today. He's an orthopedic surgeon and was in an operating room at Montefiore Hospital all morning. He has no idea how long the card has been gone."

It occurred to Dante that Montefiore was located just a few blocks from where Mannion's abandoned van was discovered last night. "Kehoe hasn't boarded, but his luggage has been delivered," he told them. "Let's get hold of Gus and Diaz, Pete; get this ship evacuated."

Melissa Busby was just back from lunch when she, Don Grover, and Rusty Heckman got the call from Chief Lieberman. When they arrived at Pier 88 a quarter of an hour later, Bomb Squad and Emergency Services vehicles abounded, all of them parked inside the big terminal building and out of sight of the gleaming *Duchess of York*. Melissa parked in the access area while Don and Rusty hurried ahead to report. As she approached on foot a few minutes later, Joe Dante cornered her. Melissa saw his expression and knew he'd hit pay dirt.

"You *found* the son of a bitch."

Dante glanced in the direction of the ship and nodded. "It looks like our man finally did something predictable, Mel. Beasley and the Boy Wonder still up north?"

She sighed. "What a day, huh? It looks like they're gonna miss your party. Fill me in."

Joe described what had transpired. "Once we located that porter and talked to him it clicked into place. He says a Catholic priest delivered Father Kehoe's luggage. A tall guy with dark, curly hair, memorable blue eyes, and a heavy Irish brogue. He was driving a white BMW, had a Roman collar; the whole rig. When the porter took him aboard the priest stayed behind to do some unpacking. He tipped the porter twenty bucks."

"What makes you think he's still here?" she asked.

Dante lifted his chin toward the terminal access and West Street beyond. "The white beemer is still parked out there. Billy could just as easily have walked away and left it, but no one remembers seeing him leave. Security's pretty tight, and the priest's boarding sticks out in several of the guards' recollections. Any minute now the captain's gonna order an evacuation. We've got them pulling back the conveyor that loads the bigger pieces of luggage now. Once everyone starts to leave, you and I are joining the deck-by-deck search."

Billy Mannion was stripped out of his coveralls and adjusting his collar in the mirror of one of the ship's men's rooms when the announcement came though a ceiling-mounted speaker.

"Ladies and gentleman. This is your captain. May I have your attention please." The words echoed distinctly off the tile floor and bulkheads. "I regret to report that we've had a slight spill during our fueling prior to departure. While there is no immediate danger to anyone on board, the New York Fire Department has ordered the ship evacuated as a precautionary measure. I regret any inconvenience this causes you. Please be assured that we are giving this situation our every attention and anticipate no serious delay in our departure time. If anyone is in need of personal assistance, I ask you to call . . ."

Billy lost interest in the rest of it. A fuel spill. He had no recollection of an oil barge being tied alongside. He stuffed his coveralls into one of the trash receptacles and left the restroom to peer out one of the passageway portholes. In support of the captain's evacuation request a number of fire trucks were parked out front of the terminal. Several men in fire gear were observed moving about dockside. Billy smiled to himself. For him this was no inconvenience at all. It was time to be going anyway.

As he moved toward the elevators Mannion found confused passengers beginning to emerge from their staterooms. An elderly woman spotted his clerical garb and hailed him.

"Father? I'm sorry, but could you help me?"

Billy nearly told the old bag to sod off before his survival instinct took over. "Yes, mum. What can I do for you?"

Suddenly her eyes sparkled. "Oh, I do love your accent! If I could just hold onto your arm. My footing isn't what it used to be, and I get frightened in crowds."

Mannion forced himself to be amiable, offered her his left forearm, and led her slowly down the passageway to the elevators.

"You're going back home to Ireland, Father? How nice."

God, he hated this. "No, mum. I'm just seeing a friend off. And you?"

She beamed. "My son lives in London. He's an executive with Ford over there. This trip is his birthday present to me." She looked up, a nervous girlishness in the way she regarded him. "Can you believe I'm *eighty* years old?"

"No, mum, I can't," Billy protested. "You don't look to be within ten years of that."

She twittered, blushing. "Bless you, Father."

The elevators were crowded with passengers from the upper decks, and Billy let several pass before finding one with room enough to board. Once they reached their destination they discovered a huge file already stretching from the head of the gangway back across the main deck toward where they stood. Billy had started them forward when he suddenly pulled up short.

"Something wrong?" the octogenarian asked.

Billy shook his head, apology in his tone. "I'm sorry, mum. Terribly sorry. I won't be coming back aboard, and I've just remembered my coat. How stupid of me. I left it on my friend's berth back there."

He disengaged his arm and started to turn, the reason for the backup at the head of the gangway all too evident. Across the deck the crowd was parting to make way for a team of men outfitted in heavy protective gear. It was the sort of gear worn by men in a bomb detail.

TWENTY-THREE

The Bomb Squad's Lieutenant Frank Ceccerelli briefed his team in the passageway outside the stateroom booked by the phony priest. A short man at only five foot six, Ceccerelli was built as solid as a dockside mooring bit. He'd been doing this job for seventeen years since leaving the Army Rangers as a demolitions expert, and he knew almost all the tricks. The stateroom door was left hanging partially open, and a good portion of the interior was visible. Two pieces of leather luggage sat on a rack at the foot of the berth, and a matching garment bag hung from the back of a closet door. Another smaller piece lay open atop the coverlet. Ceccerelli couldn't know whether their man had left that door open or one of the crew had. Either way, he'd taken no chances. Once his team determined that all adjacent staterooms along this passageway and those on the decks directly above and below were evacuated, he'd tied off the doorknob and given it a tug from a distance of a hundred feet. Nothing.

The lieutenant now stood face-to-face with a slender, fresh-faced kid and held him by both shoulders. The kid was dressed from head to toe in padded Kevlar. "Okay, Logan. I'm gonna send the dog in first. We'll give her just a minute, and then you go in after her. I want you on your belly and watching her every inch of the way. She starts acting like she's got something, it's up to you to decide if it's safe to check out. You got any doubts, I want you the hell outta there.''

Ceccerelli signaled the dog handler forward as Logan hit the deck to squirm into position. On the lieutenant's signal the well-fed Labrador was released. She moved cautiously into the room with Logan soon following. After making a slow tour of the room, the dog stopped at the bed and began sniffing the small suitcase sitting atop it. Logan checked behind the door for booby traps, did a visual sweep of both walls for motion sensors, and rose slowly. Only then did he advance to inspect the object of the dog's attention. When he spoke it was into the microphone mounted inside his protective hood.

''It's empty, Frank. The way she's acting, I'd say it hasn't been for long.''

Logan tried to force the dog's interest to other areas of the room. Each time he released her collar she returned to the case on the bed. Ceccerelli then entered the room followed by the dog handler and three other members of the squad.

''Looks like we've got our work cut out for us, boys,'' the lieutenant growled. ''The son of a bitch's already had a chance to *plant* the motherfucker.''

Every available member of both the Bomb Squad and Captain Harry Diaz's Anti-Terror Unit was on hand to head a deck-by-deck search. The shipboard evacuation of passengers was complete, and now the captain was evacuating his crew. Don Grover and Rusty Heckman had taken up positions at the head of the gangway to monitor traffic while Joe Dante and Melissa Busby were assigned a section of the main deck. After stepping off the elevator into a passageway lined with salons, boutiques, and a fitness center and spa, Melissa pointed thumbs in both directions.

''Which way you want, boss?''

Dante surveyed his options and pointed to their right. ''I'll take forward. We'll touch base by radio at two-minute intervals.''

Melissa surveyed the line of shops moving aft and grinned. "Must be nice, a trip on one of these. All the comforts of your local shopping mall. You ever been on a cruise?"

Joe shook his head. "Nope. The idea of playing grab-ass all over the Caribbean never appealed to me. Something like this might be different, though. A real transatlantic crossing, just like in the good old days." As he spoke his portable radio squawked. He raised it to his lips and thumbed the transmit button. "Yeah. Dante."

"Gus, Joey. What kinda progress you made?"

"Bomb Squad just gave us clearance to go in," Dante replied. "We're only getting started."

"I've got fifty more bodies I'm flying in from Brooklyn and Queens. Meanwhile you watch your ass."

Dante clicked off and looked down the passageway to where Melissa was poking into a nail parlor. "You heard the man, Mel. Go easy. Two-minute intervals."

"Ten-four, Lou." Melissa smiled to herself as she read the rate board posted above the nail-salon cash register. She never had time to do her nails with the schedule she kept. Napier claimed he didn't mind, but it made her self-conscious when she got dressed up to go out. Here a woman could do things to her nails that Melissa had never even heard of. And nail *jewelry*? She extended one hand to examine the back of it and chuckled.

"You move and I'll spatter your brain all over the front of that display case."

The voice was so close to her left ear, she could feel the man's breath. In contrast something cool touched the nape of her neck.

"You stay calm and you just might walk away from this alive, miss."

As Melissa stood frozen she saw movement out of the corner of her eye. The Billy Mannion who stepped around to confront her was dressed not as a priest but in the coveralls of a crew member. He had a Yankees cap pulled low on his brow. As he moved the barrel of his gun never broke contact with her skin. Instead it traced a path below her ear and along the edge of her jaw to a point just beneath her chin.

"You and me are going to walk off this tub together, miss. I'll take that radio."

Melissa surrendered the unit without argument. "*How* are we going to walk off, Mr. Mannion? This whole ship is swarming with cops."

"That's simple enough. I'm a last-minute straggler, and you're my escort. You're going to lead, and I'm going to follow. You so much as look crosswise, I shoot you dead where you stand."

Don Grover popped another pistachio into his mouth and flicked the shells over the rail. The exodus of shipboard personnel was slowed to a trickle now as the last of the engine-room crew emerged from the bowels of the vessel. Rusty had gone off to join the search, and most of the gangway traffic Grover monitored was coming aboard, not disembarking. The idea that he might be standing on a floating time bomb made the detective nervous, and nervousness made him hungry. The two bags of nuts he'd stuffed into his pockets that morning weren't going to last much longer. He'd already eaten his way through the first and consumed half of the second.

Down the deck a door opened, and Mel Busby emerged followed by another straggler. Don, curious to know how the search was proceeding, pushed away from the rail to inquire. He approached to within a dozen feet of Mel before he caught the look of controlled panic in her eyes.

"Hey, Donald," she greeted him. "I think this guy's the last of them."

Something was definitely wrong. Grover shot a glance at the straggler. Head down. Yankees cap pulled low. A light jacket held loosely in one hand.

"How's it going in there?" Don asked her. "What's news?"

Mel was already past him and starting down the gangway.

"Nothing yet. I'll be back in a sec, huh? I can't find my glasses. Must've left them in the car."

Grover's heart was in his mouth. He knew Melissa didn't wear glasses, and he was pretty sure that guy in the coveralls had a gun under the jacket. He stepped back out of sight of the gangway and switched his radio to Dante's frequency.

Joe Dante had proceeded to the back of the ship's health club and was confronting a door marked "Kennel Access" when he realized it was better than two minutes since he'd heard from Mel. He lifted his radio to check her progress when it squawked.

"Yeah, Mel. Anything?" As he spoke he opened the door ahead. The sudden barking of a dozen confined pets greeted him as he stepped through. It was difficult to hear and he held the radio close to his ear.

"It's Grover, Joe. Mannion's got Mel. They just walked down the gangway. Him in coveralls with a gun on her."

Dante raced to a dockside porthole and peered out. It was easy to spot Melissa's auburn hair and compact, athletic figure. She was a step away from the foot of the gangway, followed by a taller individual in coveralls and a ball cap. A rush of panic struggled to overwhelm him. He forced himself past it, trying to visualize the floor plan he'd studied earlier. There was a second compartment forward of this one, used to store the larger, trunk-size pieces of passenger luggage. When he first arrived here, a conveyor running up to it was rigged dockside, a steady stream of trunks and crates riding up it and through an open cargo door. When the evacuation was ordered the conveyor was backed away and the door closed. Joe hurried forward toward it now, his radio on transmit.

"We don't want to provoke him, Donnie. I'm gonna try to figure a way off board even if I have to go into the water. You sit tight."

"Sit *tight*? Jesus Christ, Joe!"

Dante burst into a room barely half full of passenger cargo

and found the secured cargo door. Fortunately the crew was anticipating opening that door again in the near future. Dante grabbed the wheel controling an elaborate deadbolt mechanism and twisted no more than half a turn before he was able to heave the door ajar. The brilliance of sunlight flooding the compartment was blinding. Joe was forced to squint as he peered out and found the conveyor backed no more than eight feet away.

If he noticed that it was at least thirty feet to the dock, his senses refused to register it as he set himself on the threshold of that open cargo door and launched. He lost his radio somewhere en route, grabbed the forward lip of the conveyor, and hauled himself up onto the rubberized belt. From there the angle of descent was less than thirty degrees. He negotiated the hundred-plus feet of belt in under ten seconds.

Melissa Busby's mind was racing nearly as fast as her heart. There was enough confusion inside the terminal building that no one questioned their progress through the crowd. She considered her options and was forced to conclude that she had none. She was a cop, and right now it was her duty to steer this maniac clear of innocent bystanders. If she tried anything cute, Billy Mannion would surely kill her and probably others.

Mannion got more aggressive with the gun barrel once they emerged into daylight. He prodded her ahead toward the cab rank, his voice low and murderous. "You've done us fine, bitch. Don't screw it up now. Straight ahead. Move!"

Billy selected an unattended cab, jerked open the driver-side door, and shoved Melissa in ahead of him. Before the driver could spot Mannion stealing his wheels they were already under way.

Melissa bit the inside of her mouth to keep her focus. The dangers to innocent life were greatly diminished now. All she needed was an opening. Any opening. Mannion's preoccupation with escape was to her advantage. Her only chance now was to discover a way to exploit it. She knew she'd better find it soon.

Dante raced to a side door and into the terminal building's cargo area with his shield in one hand and car keys in the other. On reaching the Customs counters he vaulted a barrier gate. His eyes searched the milling crowd of stranded passengers, and when he entered it he had no choice but to slow. Forging ahead toward the main gate, he finally picked out a navy blue ball cap. Mannion and Melissa were emerging from the crowd outside the building and walking in sunlight toward a line of idle cabs.

"Excuse me, please. Coming through. Excuse me."

People who refused to step aside got help. All the while Joe never let his eyes stray from his objective. Up ahead Mannion pushed Mel into the front seat of a cab and jumped in behind the wheel. A screaming cabbie broke away from a group of his comrades and gave chase on foot as his stolen car rocketed into traffic, tires smoking.

Dante's Turbo Z was blocked into the curb by several unmarked sedans, and he had no choice but to jump it onto the sidewalk. Pedestrians scattered from his path as he leaned on the horn and raced for an opening a hundred yards south.

"Stay cool, Mel," he prayed aloud. "Please God, don't let her do anything dumb."

Helicopter pilot Fred T. Coffey couldn't remember when he felt so good on a glorious October afternoon. For three months he'd been after the charter outfit's office manager, and last Thursday she finally relented. They'd gone dancing at Roseland on Saturday night, and Sunday afternoon he took her and her kid to the movies. Just last night his boss let him use one of the birds to go to Atlantic City for dinner and a show. They got back to the Teterboro hangar so late that she'd invited him to her place in Hackensack. Sometime around two-thirty in the morning he'd finally gotten laid. Romance was in the air.

All morning the former Marine Corps medevac pilot had flown steady on the lingering scent of Donna Kaprosian and a cool October breeze. Twice after shuttling passengers across the tri-state region he was handed cash tips. The weather was beautiful, with almost unlimited visibility. Right now Coffey sat parked on the pad at the Manhattan VIP Heliport; 30th Street on the Hudson. The river to the west sparkled, and the city to the east gleamed. His next trip was a jump out to the North Shore of Long Island, and his passengers were five minutes overdue. Coffey wasn't concerned. Short delays were typical. If they arrived within the next quarter hour, Coffey would still be home in plenty of time for his night on the town. Donna Kaprosian hadn't seen anything yet.

Right on cue a stretch Lincoln Town Car eased up alongside the heliport fence. Fred watched as a dapper, silver-haired man in his late fifties emerged from the backseat, followed by a tall, slender blonde. The blonde was all skin and bones with no top end and next to nothing bringing up the rear. Not at all Fred's type.

A burly chauffeur removed a garment bag and several other pieces of luggage from the trunk, and the couple preceded him toward the heliport access building. Fred's passengers disappeared from view, and he was reaching for his preflight checklist when a cab pulled in behind the limo, narrowly missing the luggage-laden chauffeur. The startled liveryman glared in outrage at having his path blocked. Then a man in coveralls emerged from the cab brandishing a pistol. The gunman had a redhead by the hair and dragged her with him as he hurried toward the heliport access building.

Coffey got that same surge of adrenaline he used to get when dropping into a hot L.Z. in the Vietnam jungle. Fred and his little four-seat Aerospatiale were the only pilot and bird parked on the pad. His two passengers were just emerging onto the tarmac, their chauffeur still out on the street struggling with their luggage, when the guy in coveralls burst through the door behind them. They were oblivious to what was going on, and the skinny blonde, directly in the gunman's path, was knocked sprawling.

"What the *fuck*?" Coffey exclaimed. He reached to kick his engine over while watching in astonishment as the guy in the pinstripes tried to grab the man in the jumpsuit by the upper arm. For his trouble he got himself shot point-blank in the chest.

Fred witnessed this from a distance of no more than fifty feet as his engine caught and the overhead rotors started to ever-so-slowly stir the air. He wasn't concerned with checklists or any other safety precautions now as he began to increase power. Damsels in distress or not, that guy with the redhead in tow was within twenty-five feet of him and closing fast. He had a gun, and Coffey was getting the hell out of there.

Melissa Busby was too frightened to feel most of the pain Mannion inflicted pulling her along by the hair. The world around her had disintegrated in a maelstrom of rotor wash and deafening turbine whine. She struggled mentally to get a grip on her panic, to separate it from the momentum of events. She was being forced toward a helicopter about to lift off. If Mannion was ever distracted since taking her hostage, he was distracted now. It was do-or-die time.

Mannion reached for the chopper's right-side door handle, and Melissa kicked him as hard as she could in one shin. The pain of it saw him momentarily loosen his grip on her hair. She anticipated it and dropped directly to the pavement. Billy lost her long enough for her to kick at his legs with both feet. With his gun hand on the door handle and his feet suddenly kicked out from under him, Mannion was off balance enough to fall hard.

Joe Dante arrived outside the heliport fence in time to see Melissa trip Billy Mannion. There was a man in a gray suit on the ground, a blond woman in a red dress hugging him. A burly guy in a chauffeur's cap was emerging from the access building loaded with luggage. The only helicopter was just lifting clear of the tarmac.

Dante was out of his car as Melissa bounded to her feet and began sprinting for the waters of the Hudson. Billy managed to hook his free arm and one leg over the right-side landing skid of the helicopter, and it lifted him clear of the ground as he took aim at the back of the fleeing policewoman. Dante was not going over the top of this fence. It was twelve feet of cyclone mesh crowned with a concertina of razor wire. Melissa needed his help, and the heliport access shack was twenty yards away. Joe set himself in combat stance, his Walther P-5 jumping in his hands. The bullet went high into the fuselage of the chopper but had half the desired effect. Billy gave up on Melissa.

Mannion had the redheaded bitch in his sights and was trying to steady himself against the erratic sway of liftoff when a bullet impacted with the belly overhead. He didn't hear the shot but felt the proximity of the bullet's passing. The helicopter was a good dozen feet off the deck now, affording him a good view of the terrain below. He assumed the shot came from the irate chauffeur and scanned back to where the woman knelt over her fallen escort. He found the chauffeur and saw that he was unarmed. Beyond, the gate area was empty. Billy pushed his attention past it in mounting confusion. Then he saw a lone figure standing spread-legged beyond the fence, a gun in his hands.

The impact of recognition jarred him to the core. The build, the hair, and the way the man stood were the same. Fifth Avenue. Two Fridays ago. Billy's interest in seeing the lady cop dead was abandoned. He brought his weapon around and drew bead on this other. The heat of pure hatred drove him now.

Dante saw his quarry lining up on him as he leveled his own weapon again, exhaled slowly, and pulled the trigger. A shot at seventy feet with a 9mm automatic wasn't a good bet by Vegas standards, but Joe wasn't thinking about odds. His eyes never left the target as the pistol kicked in his hands. Mannion jerked spasmodically and flailed in a desperate attempt to wrap his other arm around the landing skid. The pistol aimed at Dante tumbled harmlessly to the pavement.

Coffey was twenty feet off the pavement when he saw the redhead had somehow managed to escape. He missed seeing the black 300-ZX pull up out front, but when the man emerging from it fired a shot in his direction, Coffey's old combat experience kicked in.

"*Enough* of this bullshit," he snarled.

In two years' time Fred Coffey made over one thousand medevac landings in Southeast Asian jungle clearings. He could skim so close to treetops on the way in and back out that his door gunners and other pilots nicknamed him "Fine Line." It was a few years now since he'd dragged a skid just to see if he had the old touch. That concertina of razor wire crowning the heliport's perimeter fence was a slightly different challenge, but Fred didn't give a damn. He started the chopper forward, dropped altitude, and felt that old surge of deep satisfaction as the skids scraped wire. When he kicked in the power after the pass he could feel the weight loss on the starboard side.

"Fuck you, asshole!"

He gunned it around and out of harm's way over the river as he searched back to survey his handiwork.

When the pilot made his dive for the top of the fence Dante realized the man couldn't see what was going on directly beneath him. All the pilot knew was that a man carrying a gun had latched onto his skids. Billy didn't realize what the pilot was up to until he was just a dozen feet from the wire. He was too busy trying to hang on. The razor-wire concertina failed to catch his attention until he was just seconds from impact with it, and only then did Billy scream. A sickened feeling wrenched Dante's gut as the coverall-clad figure tried to let go, hit the wire, and became ensnared in it.

Mannion's screams changed pitch once he hit. He hung there, squirming, the knife-sharp edges of the wire sawing though his clothing and deeper into his flesh with every jerk and twist. As Dante approached he could see how profusely Billy was bleeding. Judging from the way they were pumping blood, several of the cuts appeared to be life-threatening.

Billy tried to get hold of himself, to slow his frantic thrashing in a game attempt at self-preservation. By the time Dante reached the fence directly below Mannion's position, Billy was able to focus on him.

"Get me down from here, you bloody *bastard*!" he screamed.

Dante holstered his weapon and spread his hands in a gesture of helplessness. "How, Billy?"

"Then shoot me! You can't leave me hanging here to die like a fucking dog!"

Blood ran freely down the weave of cyclone fencing, liberally splashing the ground a yard from where Joe stood. Dante stared up at Billy and saw the corpses of Ralph Kane and Veronica Tierney; Siobhan's face; Captain Ray Costello lying murdered in that stairwell, a bullet in his head.

"Wrong, Billy. There's nothing I'd like better, but duty dictates I pick up the phone in my car and call EMS." He paused to glance at his watch. "All I can do is hope. Hope they don't get to you in time." He locked eyes with Mannion, his expression impassive. "It looks like you're cut pretty bad, Billy. Losing a lot of blood fast. Average response time for calls made midtown is about twelve minutes. Think you can hang on?"

Mannion hung there staring at Dante as Joe turned and walked toward his car. As the detective made the obligatory call for an ambulance, he watched Mel Busby pause to check on the fallen man out on the heliport pad. When she broke away to hurry toward the access gate, Joe hung up and ran to meet her. He threw his arms around her as she emerged from the building, crushing her to his chest. The first blue-and-white arriving on the scene screeched to a halt behind them, and out on the heliport pad the pilot decided it was now safe enough to land.

Joe knew that this place would be swarming with cops at any minute. Many would see the tears streaming down his cheeks, and he didn't care. Right now there was nothing more important than Mel Busby hugging him as fiercely as he held her; than the feel of her heart hammering with his, beat for beat. When the chopper pilot cut his engine, Dante realized that Billy Mannion wasn't screaming anymore.

TWENTY-FOUR

Two days was all Gus Lieberman would risk letting Dante keep Siobhan in New York; the same amount of time it took the Bomb Squad to locate the explosives planted aboard the *Duchess of York*. Luckily for Siobhan, Gus saw no reason to trot her out in public. He preferred to close the file on Mannion without further muddying the waters. She and her co-operation remained his secret. Luckily for Lloyd's and the peers insuring the *Duchess of York*, Billy Mannion had set his explosives to go off when the liner docked in England.

Late Friday evening Joe drove Siobhan out to Kennedy to catch her Aer Lingus flight home. They'd spent two days of relative calm together, neither venturing outdoors for more than a quick trip to the corner deli. While the city around them buzzed in the aftermath of Billy Mannion's rampage, neither Joe nor Siobhan bothered to pick up a paper or watch the television news. They were otherwise engaged.

"I'm sorry it's got to end so abruptly," Joe apologized. He stood facing Siobhan, her hands in his. A uniformed woman at the boarding gate had just begun calling passengers by row. Judging from the number of people loitering in the gate area Dante guessed Siobhan's flight to be only half-full. With the recession taking its bite, Americans weren't traveling abroad as much as they once did. "I was getting to like having you around."

She smiled, more than a little sadness in it. "Your friend

308

Gus seemed to think there'd be trouble if I stayed. Besides, it's time, Joe. I've missed my family more in this past week than in all the time I've been away.''

Dante released her hands to wrap his arms around her, pulling her close. ''Your sister's kids are safe, you've got your life back, and all is not lost, huh?'' He hugged her hard and pulled back to look one last time at her face. He wanted to memorize it; to be able to conjure it the same way he was so adept at conjuring other, less pleasant memories.

''I don't think I'll ever be able to thank you for what you've done for me, Joe, but let me try. Come to Ireland. It's beautiful, you know.''

He grinned, his gaze holding hers. ''I just might surprise you.'' And then he kissed her one last, lingering time.

It was no more than simple curiosity that compelled Dante and Jumbo to attend Amanda Kane's funeral on Monday morning. They found Trinity Church all but empty, with only a handful of mourners scattered throughout the dimly lit interior. Neither cop stayed long. It was too nice a day outside. Now they loitered on the sidewalk enjoying the sunshine and the light breeze funneled through the building canyons of the surrounding Financial District.

''What a difference two weeks makes,'' Jumbo observed. ''This time two weeks ago everybody who's anybody in the whole fucking city was here for the husband's ceremony. There was limo-lock in the street all through here. Hard to figure it all, isn't it?''

''What?'' Joe asked. ''Greed?'' He shook his head. ''It's a disease, Beasley. A social disease. Eats its way into your brain like syphilis. Once it's got you it takes an act of God to shake it loose.''

''You surprised the daughter's in there? Mourning a mother who hated her guts and killed her father?''

Dante wasn't sure if he was surprised or not. Last week Jumbo had described the daughter as emotionless. Today Elizabeth Kane had arrived alone and was sitting alone inside the church. She wore black but looked more bewildered than grief-stricken. Joe doubted she was emotionless. Few were. In two short weeks' time she'd been rendered an adult orphan.

"I doubt she's mourning her mother, Beasley. She's mourning all the dead dreams laid to rest in that coffin; mourning for herself."

"I wish her luck. You interested in grabbing some early lunch?"

Dante shot a glance at his watch. "Can't. I've got an appointment with Gus and Lydia's travel agent."

"Yeah? What's up?"

Joe chuckled, mostly to himself. "A vacation. C of D's orders. Gus thinks I need to get away for more than the week here and there that I usually take."

A big smile spread across Jumbo's face. "Well, good for Gus. So where are you going? The islands?"

Dante stared off to the east down Wall Street. "No island you're thinking about, Beasley. This guinea's going to Ireland."

About the Author

Christopher Newman was born in San Francisco and attended the University of California at Santa Cruz and Birmingham University in England. A former merchant seaman, construction worker, and beach bum, he is author of five books in the Dante series, as well as *Mañana Man* and *Backfire*. He and his wife Susan live in New York City.

Is there no rest
for Detective Joe Dante?
Not in
Christopher Newman's
exciting police novels!

MIDTOWN SOUTH

Dante was ready for light duty, away from the
drug beat. But when your precinct borders on
Times Square, easy police work is hard to come
by. And when uncanny look-alike prostitutes
are being murdered, the case is as hard as they
come.

SIXTH PRECINCT

Newly assigned to the Sixth Precinct, Dante is
working on the bizarre murder case of art col-
lector Oscar Wembley, who was hacked to death
with a kitchen knife. Another, more grotesque
murder adds an unusual twist to the case, and
a new challenge to Detective Dante, who
thought he had seen it all.

KNOCK-OFF

A hot designer in the competitive world of high fashion is found bludgeoned to death. The stolen designs for the new fall line point to a piracy ring. The case brings Detective Joe Dante to Fashion Avenue for the toughest case of his career.

MIDTOWN NORTH

A male Caucasian has been shot dead in a Hell's Kitchen alley—that's what the report says. But once police hit the scene, the word hits the street: the dead man is a cop. A big shot from Internal Affairs. The official story says the shooter was a local lowlife. But Detective Joe Dante has other ideas—and a lot of questions.

Also by Christopher Newman...

BACKFIRE

It's 1991. At the dawn of a presidential campaign, the secret buried a generation back suddenly surfaces. To one man it means enormous profit—and incalculable risk. To a second man it means solving one lethal mystery, only to uncover another as close as his own flesh and blood. When the stakes are high, there are no loyalties and no rules—even for top-level U.S. government agents. Especially for them.

CHRISTOPHER NEWMAN